THE CONDEMNED

IRINA SHAPIRO

Cover design: Debbie Clement
Cover images: Shutterstock

Published by Storm Publishing.
For further information, visit:
www.stormpublishing.co

PROLOGUE

She came to with a hard jolt. Uncontrollable coughing wracked her body and her eyes streamed as she gulped air, but it didn't seem to fill her burning lungs. She was shaking with cold, and her clothes were wet and smelled of seawater. She tried to move, but her knees slammed into something hard and unyielding, so she held out her hands and tried to straighten her arms, but her palms met with solid wood. She was trapped in a wooden box. A coffin.

Her chest heaved with panic as the reality of her situation began to sink in. She beat her hands against the lid and screamed for help, but her voice echoed dully, the eerie silence beyond broken only by what might have been the crashing of waves or the flapping of wings. Unbearable anxiety built inside her, rushing at her like an incoming tide, each wave coming harder and faster, and reaching further inland. She couldn't breathe, couldn't see, and couldn't make any sense of what was happening. Her jumbled thoughts scurried like mice, bumping into each other and scrambling in blind panic. And then the pain came, sharp and visceral, a pain that threatened to tear her apart.

She wrapped her arms around her belly and rested her forehead against the rough wood of the coffin. She was so weak, and so tired. She knew it wouldn't be long now, and she was glad of it. She was ready. Whoever had done this had sentenced her to death, but perhaps the judgment had come down long before that. She'd gone against the teachings of the Church and the laws of man and attempted to thwart the natural order of things. She had no one to blame, for she'd condemned herself, and her child with her.

Death would be a welcome release, and as she shivered in its cold embrace, she threw her head back and let out one final cry of anguish.

A wonderful peace suddenly stole over her, taking away the pain and the unspeakable terror of those final moments. A welcoming white light enveloped her, and she felt as if she were being cradled in loving arms. They wouldn't let her fall.

"I've got you," Walker's voice said softly. "You can let go now. I've got you both." Somewhere, in the deep recesses of her mind, she heard the haunting notes of his death song—but no, this was her own death song, her final act.

She was nearly gone by the time the infant slithered from her body, its nose pressing against the back of her thighs and its hands balled into fists. Its tiny feet rested against her bottom, but she couldn't feel the connection. The child whimpered once, and again, and then grew silent as the sodden wool of her skirts smothered it as effectively as a feather pillow.

Waves crashed against the shore, and a hunter's moon rose slowly and majestically above the dusky expanse of the sea. A broken mast rose out of the water, its tattered sails hanging on by lengths of torn rigging, and chucks of broken wood floated toward the shore, along with an odd assortment of household items. A man's body lay face down in the sand, his dark hair plastered to his head. It had been the first to wash up, but it wouldn't be the last.

ONE

JANUARY 2015

St. Just, Cornwall

Quinn huddled deeper into her coat as she got out of the car. The day was overcast, the Atlantic a churning, foaming cauldron of granite-colored seawater. The waves crashed onto the beach with relentless frequency, the spray rising several feet off the sand. Several other cars were parked in the tiny car park, one of them Rhys's Land Rover. Quinn's hair whipped around her face like Medusa's snakes as she walked onto the beach and toward the barely visible cave in the craggy face of the rock. Several people milled around, chatting while they waited for her. Rhys was on the phone, as usual, and Darren the cameraman was at the mouth of the cave, positioning the portable light for the best possible exposure. A young woman in a police uniform stood next to Darren, peering into the dark recess of the cave. The police tape had been removed in readiness for Quinn's arrival.

Rhys spotted her and waved enthusiastically. He ended his call and pushed the phone into the pocket of his jacket, walking briskly toward her. "About time you got here. I thought you were coming down last night."

Quinn didn't bother to reply to the barb. She'd planned to leave yesterday around noon and arrive in St. Just in the early evening but had wound up leaving at five o'clock that morning. Alex had been fussing and crying, his little face a grimace of misery. His bellyaches were not as frequent as they had been before but still bothered him from time to time, and he had to be walked around the room for hours, until the pain subsided.

Gabe had tried to comfort the baby, but Quinn had felt awful walking out on a suffering three-month-old, so she'd remained, singing and cooing to him until he finally felt better and fell asleep in her arms. It had been too late to leave by then, so she'd resolved to go first thing in the morning after Alex's first feeding.

"Go on," Gabe had urged Quinn as he took the baby from her. "He'll be all right." Alex was pinning her with an accusing stare, as if he understood she was leaving.

"When will you be back?" Emma whined.

"Tomorrow, but I might have to spend an extra night, depending on what I find," Quinn replied.

"But you promised to take me shopping. I need stuff for school," Emma argued.

"And I will. As soon as I get back."

"Go," Gabe mouthed and blew her a kiss. "We'll be fine. Send me some photos. I wish I could go with you. This one looks interesting."

"I'll keep you posted. Bye." Quinn kissed Alex's sweet-smelling head and Gabe's unshaved cheek. Emma ducked her kiss and went off to her room in a huff to get ready for school.

"Has Darren started filming yet?" Quinn asked as she approached the mouth of the cave. Like most working mums, she had to set aside her guilt and focus on the job.

"No, we were waiting for you," Rhys replied. "Quinn, it's not pleasant."

"Rhys, at this stage, I think I've seen it all."

Quinn ducked her head and entered the cave. It was a narrow opening about five feet high. The sand beneath her boots was damp, but there was a natural ledge on which the coffin rested. The wood was warped and bleached, the nails orange with flaking rust. The lid was currently closed, but the coffin had already been opened. When Rhys had arrived in St. Just to follow up on a call to the *Echoes from the Past* hotline, he'd put in a call to the local constabulary and opened the ancient coffin in the presence of a police officer, on the off chance that the remains weren't as old as he suspected. He already knew what was inside. Quinn had only seen a photo of the skull, and it had been a disturbing image. She braced herself for what she was about to find and lifted the lid.

The skeleton lay on its side, the knees pressed against the wood of the coffin. The arms must have been crossed over the belly but now rested at an unnatural angle, no longer supported by soft tissue. The head was thrown back, the mouth grotesquely open, as if in a scream, and a hole, the size of a golf ball gaped in the top of the skull.

Quinn's hand flew to her mouth as she peered deeper into the coffin. Rhys was right, she'd never seen anything like this. Despite years of damp, she could see brown stains that discolored the wood beneath the skeleton's pelvic area. A skeleton of a baby lay between the mother's pelvic bone and the femurs of her legs. It was curled up like a shrimp, its feet pointing toward its mother's pelvis. The umbilical cord had decomposed after all this time, but it was obvious that the child had been born once the mother was already inside the coffin. Quinn bolted from the cave and grabbed onto the jagged rockface of the cliff for support as her stomach turned itself inside out. Rhys was instantly at her side, handing her a pack of tissues.

"You could have warned me," Quinn panted as she wiped her mouth and took a sip of water from a bottle one of Rhys's assistants passed her.

"I thought I had."

"Stop filming," Quinn barked at Darren, who was capturing her volatile reaction on camera.

"Are you kidding me? This is cinematic gold," Rhys argued.

Quinn gave him an accusing stare. "You're not showing that to the world."

"All right. I'll have it edited out. The viewers will see you gasp and flee and then return looking purposeful and composed, the consummate professional."

"I've never seen anything so horrible," Quinn confessed as she leaned against the rocks and took several deep breaths to calm her heaving stomach.

"What are we dealing with here?" Rhys asked, too impatient to give her a few moments to herself.

"At first glance, I'd say we're looking at a live coffin birth."

"And what's that, exactly?"

Quinn sighed. She'd come across one other coffin birth, on a dig in Rome, but it had been nothing like this. The child had been born once the mother was already dead, expelled from the body through the anus by gasses that built up once decomposition began. The baby would have died in utero, so neither mother nor child would have suffered during the birth.

"Normally, a coffin birth occurs after the death of a woman who's in the final stages of pregnancy. Both mother and child are deceased by that stage and the birth is a result of decomposition."

"And abnormally?" Rhys asked, well aware that what they were looking at was not a normal phenomenon.

"Based on the position of the skeleton, the bloodstains at the bottom of the coffin, and the position of the child, I'd say this poor woman went into labor after she'd been declared dead and laid to rest. I think both mother and child were alive at the time of the birth."

"And the hole in her head?" Rhys asked. "Do you think someone tried to murder her?"

Quinn shook her head. "The hole is not a result of blunt force trauma. That hole was deliberately made. It's too perfect to be random."

"What on earth would account for someone drilling a hole in a pregnant woman's skull?" Rhys demanded, clearly shocked by the picture Quinn was painting.

"I think the hole is evidence of trepanation."

"What the bloody hell is that?"

"It's an arcane medical procedure used to relieve pressure on the brain."

"Are you sure?" Rhys gaped at her, horrified.

"I'm fairly sure, but I won't commit to anything on film until Dr. Scott has a chance to properly analyze the remains."

"This is strictly off the record," Rhys replied. "This is you and me talking."

"I know, but I'd still like to talk to Colin first."

"Absolutely. I wouldn't have it any other way," Rhys replied. "Are you ready to go back in?"

"Yes. I will take photos in situ, then bag and label the bones. I'd like to finish up today."

"What's the rush?" Rhys asked as he followed Quinn back toward the mouth of the cave, where Darren was already adjusting the angle of the camera to film Quinn reentering the cave.

"Honestly, I just want to get it over with."

"I knew this one would get under your skin," Rhys said joyfully as he trailed her. Unlike Quinn, he had no trouble separating the professional from the personal and never allowed a case to affect him.

"Are fairies of Sunday night ratings dancing in your head?" Quinn asked, amused by Rhys's glee.

"Quinn, I know this is gruesome, and I feel the utmost pity for the poor creature in that box, but when it comes to archeological programs, this is solid ratings gold."

"Right. Let me get on with it, then."

Quinn took a deep breath and reentered the eerily illuminated cave. The low ceiling made her feel claustrophobic, and despite the glaring light directed at the inside of the coffin, she felt as if she were buried alive. Quinn pushed aside her feelings and went to work, carefully recording her findings, and removing the bones one by one and stowing them in plastic bags. She left the baby for last, reluctant to touch the tiny skull and fragile bones. She hoped the baby hadn't suffered, but there was no way to tell for certain if it had been born alive. Perhaps Colin would be able to tell her more once he spent some quality time with the remains.

Finally, having finished with the skeletons of mother and child, Quinn peered into the empty coffin. Her gaze kept straying to the bloodstains, but she forced herself to look away and keep searching. She needed to find something that had belonged to the woman. Despite the cave's cool interior, nothing was left of the woman's clothing or shoes. There were no buttons or buckles, no wedding ring or jewelry of any kind. Thankfully, a few strands of hair still clung to the skull. Colin would be able to extract DNA and run some preliminary tests before deciding whether he'd need to grind the woman's tooth to powder to extract genetic information, a costly procedure that would torpedo the budget for the program.

Quinn turned on the light on her mobile and shone the sharp beam into the corners of the coffin in the hope that a coin or a button had rolled away and settled between the slats. No glint of metal revealed itself, but a gleam of white caught her eye. She reached into the top left-hand corner and tugged. The object that had been lodged between the slats came free. It was a hair comb made of bone, a cheap trinket that would have belonged to a woman who couldn't afford ivory or tortoiseshell. The comb must have fallen out of the woman's hair while she thrashed about. The comb was narrow and long, the type used to hold hair in place rather than for brushing. Its teeth were broken, but the top remained intact, the bone carved into a flower that would be visible when the comb was inserted into the hair. It would hopefully shed some light on who the unfortunate inhabitant of the coffin had been.

Having bagged the comb, Quinn was ready to finish up for the day. She pulled off her latex gloves and laid a hand atop the woman's ruined skull, cradling it through the plastic bag. She bowed her head and whispered, "Don't worry, we will be respectful of you and your baby."

TWO

By the time Quinn emerged from the cave, the sun had come out and the sea had stilled. A glorious sunset painted the winter sky, bands of crimson and gold dramatically streaking the horizon and reflecting in the now deep-blue water of the Atlantic. The ragged cliff face that had looked dangerous and unyielding during the day was now softened by the deepening violet of the sky, giving the beach a mystical quality.

Quinn stowed the box of bones in the boot of her car and turned to Rhys, who was standing behind her. "I'll finish up tomorrow. There's no need to send the entire coffin to Colin, but I'd like to take several samples of wood for testing. Colin might be able to extract some dried blood from the boards and also tell me the approximate period of construction."

"Did you find anything of a personal nature on her?" Rhys asked, his voice low. In England, only Rhys and Gabe knew of Quinn's ability to see into the past by holding an object that had belonged to the dead. Her half-brother Brett Besson, whom she'd met in New Orleans last spring, also possessed the gift and knew of Quinn's special talent, but she preferred not to dwell on their brief but volatile relationship. He was currently serving a ten-year sentence in a Louisiana penitentiary for the attempted murder of

Quinn and her unborn baby, and although Brett had written to her in an effort to make amends, she'd not read the letter. It still rested at the bottom of her nightstand drawer, where it would remain until she packed her personal belongings for the move to the new house, and she would likely never bother to unpack that particular box. If only she could pack away the memory of what had happened along with the letter and leave it in the furthest, darkest corner of the attic, never to be opened again.

Quinn turned to face Rhys and pulled a plastic baggie out of her pocket. "I found this. It's a hair comb," she explained when she saw Rhys peering at the contents in confusion.

"What is it made of?" Rhys asked. "Is that ivory?"

"No, I don't think so. It's more likely to be animal bone."

Rhys reached for the bag and held it up. "Have you touched it with your bare hands?"

"No. And I won't be examining it tonight. I'm not ready," Quinn said.

She'd only just finished documenting her findings on her last case and turned the Fabergé necklace that had belonged to a Russian woman named Valentina Kalinina over to Rhys, who would return it to her granddaughter. Valentina had murdered a man who'd abused her and hidden his remains from the world for nearly one hundred years. Valentina's story had been a dramatic one, but at least she had survived and managed to reclaim something of her life—unlike the poor woman in the coffin, who'd met one of the most gruesome ends Quinn could imagine. She would find out what had happened to her, in time, but tonight she'd try to put the horrific images out of her mind and get some rest. It'd been a long and emotionally wrenching day.

"How about we have an early dinner?" Rhys asked. "I promise, I won't ask any more questions about our 'coffin girl.' Just two friends having a meal at the end of a workday."

Quinn would have liked nothing more than to check into the hotel, run a hot bath, and soak for a while before calling room service, but she couldn't say no to Rhys. It'd been less than a fortnight since she'd found him in his flat, unresponsive and cold to the touch, having chased a couple of sleeping tablets with Scotch after his girlfriend Haley miscarried their baby and then walked out on him, casting doubt on the paternity of the child as a parting shot. Rhys no longer mentioned the incident, but he was still fragile, and heartbroken. He would get over the loss of Haley, but the little unborn girl he'd seen sucking her thumb during the scan still gripped his heart with her tiny fingers, and he mourned her every moment of every day, regardless of whether she'd been his. Rhys had wanted a family of his own more than anything, and the loss of both partner and child had nearly killed him.

"What are you in the mood for?" Rhys asked.

"I'd kill for a curry. I've been eating bland foods for the past month, since anything I eat seems to upset Alex's tummy. I won't be nursing tonight or tomorrow morning, so I can have anything I want."

"Does that include wine?"

"Yes. I haven't had a glass of wine since I found out I was pregnant."

"I'll get several bottles, then," Rhys said, chuckling. "You can have a whole bottle to yourself."

"Let's get a takeaway and eat it in my room," Quinn suggested. "I'm not in the mood for a noisy restaurant tonight."

"Sounds good. Why don't you go check in, and I'll get the food and wine and join you in about a half hour? You look like you could use a hot shower after spending all day in that damp cave."

Quinn smiled. Rhys knew her a lot better than she imagined. "Okay, see you in a bit."

"Mm. That was really good," Quinn said as she pushed away the takeaway container and drained her wine glass.

Rhys poured her more wine and leaned back into the sofa, watching her. Something in his eyes made Quinn sit up and set down her glass.

"What is it? What are you not telling me?"

Rhys's gaze slid away from her face, toward the darkness outside the window. "Quinn, I—"

"What? What's wrong?" Quinn asked, now really worried. Rhys wasn't an overly sentimental person. When he had something to say, he said it. The fact that he seemed worried about telling her frightened her more than anything he might spring on her.

"Quinn, I had a call from Rob Malone while you were bagging the bones."

"The reporter?" she asked. She'd expected something of a personal nature, but she'd never met Rob Malone, and had only seen him on TV a handful of times. He was a handsome man in his mid-forties with thick sandy hair, blue eyes, and a ruddy complexion that was a testament to a life lived mostly outdoors. He had a trace of an Irish brogue, and a smile that lit up the screen. Quinn thought he was probably very popular with female viewers. Rob Malone reported from war zones and had a reputation for being fearless and tenacious when in pursuit of a story.

"Rob is in Afghanistan, covering the transition of power between the coalition forces led by NATO and Afghan National Security forces. The transition took place on January first."

Quinn huddled deeper into the sofa and wrapped her arms around her middle. Rob Malone was in Afghanistan. Now she understood the significance of the phone call. For the past two weeks, everyone had kept reassuring her that her twin sister, Quentin, now known as Jo, was just fine and would turn up any day after her stint in Kabul. A photojournalist, she'd traveled all over the world and taken photographs that not only touched hearts and souls, but had won several prestigious awards, which solidified her position at the top of her profession.

Jo hadn't been heard from since September, but her agent, Charles Sutcliffe, didn't seem to find it too concerning, assuring Quinn that Jo had gone without communicating with anyone for several months in the past. Jo and Quinn had yet to meet, having been separated at birth and adopted by different families, and Quinn had no idea if Jo knew of her existence or had ever received the letter Quinn had forwarded through Jo's attorney, Louis Richards, who seemed to delight in putting obstacles in Quinn's path. Her heart thundered with fear. What Rhys was about to tell her couldn't be good, or he wouldn't be wearing that expression of sorrow and concern.

"Rhys, please, just tell me," Quinn pleaded.

"Quinn, I know Rob quite well, so I asked him to make some discreet inquiries into Jo's whereabouts. I only wanted to reassure you that she's all right. To put your mind at rest," Rhys added.

"But she isn't all right. Is she?"

"Quinn, no one has seen Jo in months. Rob actually had a drink with her at the beginning of October. He said she was in good spirits and was planning an expedition into the mountains to take photos of abandoned Taliban hideouts. She was due to leave the next day."

"Are you telling me that my sister went off into the mountains of Afghanistan and hasn't been heard from since? Did she go on her own? Did no one realize that she hadn't come back? Why had no one has alerted the authorities or bothered to look for her?"

"Rob assumed Jo finished her assignment and returned home to London. As I'm sure everyone did."

"But she hadn't returned to London." Quinn blinked away tears of helplessness as a mantle of dread settled over her shoulders.

"Quinn, just because no one in Kabul has seen Jo doesn't mean anything. She could have moved on to another location that has spotty internet service. It's very common in that part of the world."

Quinn raised her eyes to meet Rhys's concerned gaze. "Rhys, I know this doesn't make any sense, but I just know something is wrong. I feel it in my bones. I've never met Jo, but I shared a womb with her. There's a connection. I always felt like something was missing, even after I had finally found my birth parents. There was just something not quite right. When I discovered I was a twin, it all fell into place. Jo is a part of me, and no matter what anyone tells me, I can't seem to shake this feeling of dread."

"I do understand. I experienced something similar once," Rhys replied.

"Tell me."

"I was about nine at the time, and school was out for the summer holidays. My brother, Owain, and his friends went out to play football, but I wasn't allowed to come because of my asthma. Mum went to work and left me at home with a ham sandwich and a library copy of *Ivanhoe*. I was content for about two hours, then something began to nag at me. I grew anxious and fearful. Thankfully, Mum had left my inhaler right on the table because the stress brought on an attack. Once I was breathing normally again, I called Mum at work. I told her something was wrong with Owain and she had to go find him. This was before mobile phones were a way of life, so Mum had no way of contacting Owain," Rhys said, smiling at the memory.

"Let me tell you, she wasn't very happy with me. She had several clients waiting for her to do their hair, and she couldn't just leave on a whim. She became so agitated that the owner of the hair salon sent his son, Sean, out to look for Owain. Sean found him lying on the ground unconscious, his friends paralyzed with indecision. Seems they got tired of playing football and started wrestling. One of the boys, who was bigger and stronger than Owain, slammed him to the ground. Owain hit his head on a jagged stone that was hidden by the grass. Sean took Owain to the hospital. He had suffered severe head trauma and remained in the hospital for nearly a week."

"So, if you hadn't called your mother..."

"His friends wouldn't have got him to the hospital in time. They just stood about, wasting precious time. So, I do understand, Quinn. I'm not dismissing what you're feeling."

"But what do I do?"

"Nothing," Rhys replied. "Sometimes waiting is the hardest

thing you can do, but you must accept that you have no control over this situation. Rob will ring me if he finds out anything more."

Quinn nodded, but cold fingers of doubt closed around her heart and made it difficult to breathe. Jo Turing wasn't okay; she knew that with unwavering certainty.

"I think I'd like to be alone now, if you don't mind," Quinn said. "I'm tired."

"All right, but I'm just across the corridor if you need me."

"Thanks, Rhys. I'll be fine. I had too much wine, and now I'm feeling maudlin and sorry for myself. I think I'll just go to bed."

"Good night, then. I'll see you tomorrow."

"Bright and early."

Quinn climbed into bed and pulled the counterpane up to her chin. The room was chilly, despite the gas fire burning in the grate, and the wind moaned outside and rattled the decorative wooden shutters. It felt strange to be alone. She hadn't realized how accustomed she'd become to sharing her bed with Gabe. She wished she could snuggle up against him and tell him about Jo. Quinn glanced at the clock on the bedside table. He was probably still awake, and she could ring him, but for some reason, she didn't want to talk about Jo just then. She'd only get more upset, no matter how many times Gabe told her not to worry and assured her that Jo would return from her assignment safe and sound.

Quinn knew her mind wouldn't be able to settle for hours, so despite what she'd said to Rhys earlier, she reached for the plastic bag lying on the bedside table. She'd seen combs like this before, and similar items could still be found today, only they'd be made of plastic rather than bone. Quinn gingerly opened the bag and reached for the comb. She hoped it had a story to tell and would show her the face of the poor woman who'd met with such an unspeakable end.

THREE
APRIL 1620

Plymouth, Devon

"Hurry up, ye lazy cow! The customers won't serve themselves," Uncle Swithin bellowed as he gave Mary a push toward a table of sailors who were calling raucously for a refill. She grabbed the jug with both hands so as not to spill the precious ale. Uncle Swithin would give her a hiding if she did, even though he was the one who caused her to stumble. Mary approached the table cautiously, making sure to keep her distance as she held out the jug and topped up the men's tankards. The sailors had been drinking since early evening and were well soused and rowdy, their lewd comments making Mary's cheeks flame with embarrassment.

A hand shot out and fastened onto her buttock, making her yelp in surprise. She wished she could slap it away, but Uncle Swithin wouldn't let her get away with offending the customers. She'd have to deal with a lot worse than a hand on her arse if she were caught in the act of defending herself. He didn't care if they offended her; he almost hoped they would. Having a fetching young woman serving the patrons was part of the appeal of the tavern, as her uncle told her time and again.

"No blowsy slatterns here. This is a fine establishment, not a brothel," he'd announced to a new customer only last night. "Why, our Mary's as pure as the Virgin. Aren't you, my dove?" Uncle Swithin cooed in her direction, clearly pleased with his own wit.

Mary had cringed at his crude words and improper insinuations. Did he really think men came to his tavern to see her? They came to drink their troubles away and spend a few hours in a place where nothing was expected of them. They could be as base as they wished, and even after her years of slaving away at her uncle's establishment, some of them still managed to shock her. Every morning found Mary on her knees, washing the floor some drunken sod had pissed on the previous evening because he was too drunk or too lazy to go out to the privy to do his business, but sometimes she had to wash away more than piss. Not a week went by that someone wasn't sick all over the tables and floor, forcing Mary to scrub up the dried vomit the following morning, the smell making her eyes water as she cringed with disgust.

Mary shook off the offending hand and retreated to the back of the tavern, where she slipped out and rushed toward the privy. She didn't really need to go, but going to relieve herself was the only way she could escape the tavern for a few minutes without being cursed at or worse, slapped by her uncle. Mary slipped behind the privy and leaned against the rough wood of the tree that grew at the bottom of the yard. She was exhausted. She'd been up since dawn, fetching water, baking bread, making porridge for breakfast, and then starting on the stew and pies that she would later serve to the customers. It was close to midnight, but the men showed no signs of leaving, and she couldn't begin to clear the tables or wipe up spilled ale until the tavern was empty.

Mary longed for her bed, but even sleep wasn't restful these days. She shared a bed with Uncle Swithin's three daughters, all under the age of ten. The girls did their bit to help during the day, or they'd get a beating from their father, but they didn't sleep quietly, especially the youngest, Beth, who kicked like a donkey and often cried out for her mother in her sleep. Uncle Swithin's wife, Agnes, had died only two months ago and the children were still coming to terms with their loss.

Mary had never really cared for Agnes, who'd been calculating and mean, but her death had meant greater responsibility and more work for Mary. Not only did she now have to look after the customers almost singlehandedly, but she had to take on the role of mother to the girls, who were still too young to fend for themselves. Her uncle, her mother's brother, had taken her in seven years ago, when she was thirteen, and although he'd made a promise to his dying sister to be kind to her only child, he worked Mary to the bone and beat her regularly, just in case she forgot to be grateful for his kindness and charity.

Mary bore the beatings, the insults, and the hard work, but what she couldn't bear was the lack of hope. She was twenty, a ripe age for marrying and having babies, but any man who so much as expressed an interest in her was driven off, told she'd been promised to another. Mary wasn't promised to anyone other than her uncle, who meant to use her as free labor until the day she died. He'd never let her go, and he made sure no man would be fool enough to marry her.

She had nothing to her name, not even a change of clothes, much less a dowry. What man would want a woman who brought nothing to the marriage? Everyone was poor, so why settle for being even poorer? Mary had been told she was pretty, but a woman who had nothing to offer was fit for nothing more than a roll in the hay, not a place in the marriage bed. She rejected all advances, especially since most of them came from drunken sailors and sweat-soaked dock laborers who tried to take liberties with her every time she came too near them.

Having spent her five minutes of freedom behind the stinking privy, Mary headed back toward the tavern, hoping the men would finally leave and let her get on with the cleaning. She froze when she saw two men heading in her direction. They were drunk, but not drunk enough to pass on the opportunity to harass a defenseless female. She shrank into the shadows in the hope they'd pass by without noticing her. She knew these men. She'd seen them at the tavern before. The older one was Captain Robeson of the *Lady Grace*, and the younger one was the quartermaster, Master Harrington. The men stopped just outside the door and looked up at the inky vastness of the nighttime sky.

"We'll be sailing on the next tide, Master Harrington," Captain Robeson said. "The cargo is loaded, the ship is provisioned, and the women are ready. We can't afford to delay any longer. Reverend Gorman wasn't able to inspire any more women of good character to join our venture."

"But we have room for three more," Master Harrington protested. "Shame to waste it."

"Indeed, it is, but even if there are women who are interested, it's not an easy decision, leaving everything you know behind. That kind of commitment takes some thinking. It would help if they were orphans, who have no family ties to hold them back. But if they are harlots or petty thieves, we're duty bound to turn them away."

Master Harrington chuckled. "That we are, Captain."

"Let's continue this conversation later. I need a piss," Captain Robeson said, his hand going to the laces of his breeches.

Captain Robeson strode toward the privy while Master Harrington stood staring up at the cloudless sky. Mary slipped into the back entrance of the tavern, glad he hadn't noticed her. Master Harrington didn't appear to be drunk, but she had no wish to take her chances.

Several hours later, Mary lay down next to Beth, making sure she didn't put any pressure on the throbbing bruise on her left cheek. Uncle Swithin had hit her hard when she tripped in her fatigue and spilled a cup of ale, and she was sure she'd still be paying for her clumsiness tomorrow. Mary wanted nothing more than to lose herself in sleep, but the conversation she'd overheard earlier echoed in her mind. At first, she'd had no idea what the two men were talking about, but then recalled a sermon preached at church a few weeks ago. The sermon itself had been unremarkable, but Reverend Gorman had made a surprising announcement at the end. It seemed the Virginia Company of London was seeking young, unmarried women of good character to venture to the New World as wives for the colonists. Those who were willing wouldn't have to pay for their passage or worry about finding themselves unwanted upon arriving in Virginia. There were hundreds of men and only a handful of women.

Any woman, no matter how homely or coarse in her manner, would be in demand as long as she was willing to work hard and procreate regularly to help populate the colony. Reverend Gorman had made it sound as if it were a patriotic duty to rescue those men from their loneliness, but Mary knew better. Everything in life revolved around profit, and the Virginia Company wouldn't be paying for a sea voyage for dozens of women if there were no gain in it for them.

Mary jerked away from Beth as an elbow struck her in the chest. What she wouldn't give for her own bed, no matter how hard and narrow. It was a luxury she could never hope to have, unless she was still there after the girls married and left her alone with Uncle Swithin.

Mary stared at the whitewashed ceiling and considered the question of profit. She didn't care a jot about the Virginia Company, but there was gain for the women, if they survived the voyage and were paired up with decent, Godfearing men. The bachelors of Virginia were men of property, according to the reverend. They farmed their own land and had the potential to expand their holdings if they were valuable to the company. *There is land aplenty in the New World, and danger as well*, Mary mused. She'd heard tales of savages who went around half-naked and were no better than the wild beasts they hunted with their spears and arrows.

She'd heard of an Englishman who married a native and brought her to England to meet the king. Mary mouthed the woman's name in the dark. *Pocahontas*. How honored she must have felt to see civilization with her own eyes and meet His

Majesty. What tales had she brought back to her people, who likely couldn't even begin to imagine the bustling cities and busy ports of England?

As she grew drowsy, Mary wondered what it was like in Virginia. Was going out to the New World a golden opportunity or a death sentence? The scariest thing of all, probably deadlier than the savages, was the sickness that had carried off so many since the land was first colonized. The Virginia Company needed women to anchor the men and bear the next generation of colonists, who'd be accustomed to the unfamiliar climate and conditions, but first the newly wedded couples had to survive.

Mary woke before dawn. Her cheek was swollen, and her head hurt from the blow she'd received last night. It was time to get up and begin her endless day, another day in which the best thing she could hope for was not to be abused. She pulled on her soiled skirt and bodice over her threadbare shift, stuck her feet into well-worn shoes, and twisted her braid into a coil before securing it with a comb. Her lovely comb was the only thing she had of any value. The thing itself was worthless, but Mary treasured it as if it were made of solid gold. Her parents had bought her that comb at a fair when she was ten, and she'd worn it every day since, using it to hold her heavy hair in place.

Mary pulled on her linen cap and reached for her cloak. It had been her mother's and the wool was worn so thin you could see through it in some places, but it was the only garment she had aside from the clothes she was wearing. The cloak wasn't nearly warm enough, but it was a barrier between her and the bitter wind that blew off the sea, tugging at her skirts and gripping her bare legs with its icy fingers.

Mary fingered the rough wool of the cloak. Would she never own anything new? Uncle Swithin had allowed her to take one of Agnes's dresses, since her own had been too short and coming apart at the seams, but the rest of Agnes's things had been passed to her daughters, who wore simple garments cut from the fabric of her gowns. Agnes had owned a few trinkets as well, but Mary hadn't been interested in those—not that they were on offer. Trinkets wouldn't keep her warm, and on days when she shivered as she went to fetch the water or buy some fish from the incoming boats, she wished for nothing more than a shawl or a pair of woolen hose.

Mary wrapped the cloak into a tight bundle and stuffed it beneath her skirt. She couldn't allow Uncle Swithin to see it or he'd know she meant to go out without permission. She grabbed the water bucket and headed out the door but left the bucket by the well and hurried toward the dock where the *Lady Grace* was gently bobbing at her wharf. The ship was a beehive of activity as the crew prepared for departure. Mary wasn't sure when the tide would go out, but Captain Robeson had said they'd be leaving today.

A burly sailor blocked Mary's path. "What ye want here, girl?"

"I wish to see Captain Robeson or Master Harrington."

"And what'd ye want with them?"

"I want to go to Virginia," she replied, raising her chin defiantly.

"What, yer husband popped ye one and now ye want to run away?" The sailor was studying her purpling bruise.

"I'm not married. Now, let me through."

"All right," the sailor grumbled. "But ye'd best not be lying."

"What's the problem, Master Rudd?" Master Harrington asked as he strode toward them. "Who's this woman?"

"Says she wants to go to Virginia, sir," the sailor replied and backed away before he could get into trouble for allowing Mary aboard.

"Is that true?" Master Harrington asked as he studied her. In the light of day, he looked less intimidating than he had in the shadowy dooryard behind the tavern, but he wasn't a handsome man. His face was craggy from years spent outdoors and his tall frame bordered on gaunt, his limbs long and thin. He reminded Mary of a grasshopper, and the image nearly made her smile.

"Yes, sir. I overheard you at the Anchor last night. You said you had room for three more women."

Master Harrington's eyes narrowed as he tried to place her. "You served us at the tavern?"

"I did, sir."

He looked at her more closely, as though assessing her as a possible bride. "How old are you?"

"Twenty, sir."

"And you're not married?"

"No, sir. My uncle wouldn't permit me to wed, on account of needing me to work at the tavern."

"Your uncle is the owner of the Anchor?"

"Yes, sir."

"A brute if I ever saw one. He give you that shiner?" Master Harrington asked sympathetically.

"Yes, sir. I spilled a cup of ale."

"What's your name, then?" he asked, his tone friendlier now. There was something in his bearing that suggested he was an honorable man, but then again, she probably wouldn't know an honorable man if she fell over one. She'd never met anyone who was worthy of the description.

"Mary. Mary Wilby."

"All right, Mistress Wilby. Follow me."

Master Harrington directed her toward narrow steps that descended below decks. It took a moment for Mary's vision to adjust to the dim passage after the bright light of the spring morning. but then her surroundings came into view. Directly opposite the steps was a good-sized cabin. Through the open door she saw a bed hung with red velvet curtains, a desk littered with maps and objects she didn't recognize, a hard-back chair, and a sturdy chest on which several books were stacked. A row of casement windows lined the back wall, but little light filtered through the thick glass. The cabin had to belong to the captain, Mary decided, since it was so luxurious. There were two other doors, one on each side of the cabin, but they were firmly closed.

Behind the stairs, a narrow opening served as a doorway. Master Harrington stopped, blocking Mary's view of what lay beyond.

"Mistress Wilby, you will address all your concerns to me, should you have any. You are not to speak directly to the captain or engage with any members of the crew. Sailors are a rough lot, as I'm sure you know from working at the Anchor. They know they'll get flogged if they so much as lay a finger on any of you, but they'll still try. They are also superstitious, and they don't hold with women aboard a ship. They'll blame you for anything that goes wrong and demand the captain throw you overboard should any trouble befall us on our voyage."

Master Harrington sighed warily and continued. "You are not to go down into the hold. Ever."

"What's down there?" Mary asked.

"The sailors are quartered in one part of the hold, and the other areas are used for storing cargo and housing the animals we bring to Virginia."

"Why would you bring animals?"

The question seemed to take Master Harrington by surprise, but he seemed amused by her curiosity. "The settlers rely on ships from England to bring them basic goods and domestic animals since neither can be purchased locally."

Mary gaped at the quartermaster, amazed that things as basic as cows or cooking pots weren't to be easily obtained if one had the coin to buy them. Try as she might, she couldn't imagine a place that was so different from England. She felt a twinge of doubt, but the thought of returning to the tavern quickly quelled her apprehension and she nodded as if the answer made perfect sense.

The quartermaster bowed his head to avoid hitting it before entering the low doorway and waited for her to follow him inside. Beyond the doorway was an open space with a wooden grille set in the ceiling, the only source of light and air. The space was small and bare, with not so much as a bench to sit on. Two slop buckets stood in a corner.

Mary looked at the women who occupied the room, hoping they'd be friendly. The women sat on the floor, their backs against the walls, their bundles of personal belongings next to them. Mary would expect anyone who was about to embark on such a momentous journey to be chattering like magpies, but the women sat in silence, their eyes filled with apprehension and doubt as they took in the newcomer.

"You will sleep here," Master Harrington said to Mary, then turned to address the rest of the women. "We will be casting off within the hour. This area will be your home for the duration of the voyage. The buckets are for your personal needs and you are responsible for emptying them. You can take turns. You may come up on deck in pairs for half an hour each day. One pair at a time. You are not to get in the way of the sailors, nor are you to speak to them or engage with them in any way. If instructed to go down below, you are to obey without question. Be warned, if you break the captain's rules, you will be punished."

"How long is the voyage, sir?" one of the women asked.

"If the weather cooperates, about two months," Master Harrington replied. "At this time of year, there could still be gales, but we're not likely to hit the doldrums. There's wind enough to carry us all the way to Virginia without slowing down."

"What about meals, sir?" another woman asked.

"You will get a biscuit and a cup of ale to break your fast and a second meal after the sailors have had their dinner at noon. I hope some of you thought to bring along some provisions." A few women nodded, but most looked shocked, as though they hadn't considered the need to bring food.

Master Harrington looked around, taking a moment to study each woman's face. "Have a pleasant voyage, ladies," he said, giving them a mocking bow before departing.

Mary walked toward the first available stretch of wall space and sat down. She didn't have a bundle of belongings or any food, just her cloak. She leaned against the wall and looked around, curious about her traveling companions. There were nine women besides herself and they ranged in age from late teens to late twenties, in her estimation, and came in all shapes and sizes. Two of the women, who looked to be about eighteen, were clearly sisters. Fair, blue-eyed, and buxom, they sat close together and held hands, their fingers clasped tightly. The rest of the women appeared to be unrelated.

The great ship heaved, and a metallic clanging filled the small space as the anchor was lifted in preparation for departure. Shouted commands and the sound of numerous feet hitting the deck came from overhead.

"We've moving," one woman whispered. She looked around, her eyes filling with panic. "I've changed my mind. I want to go home." She looked like she was about to jump to her feet and run up on deck, but her neighbor laid a restraining hand on her wrist.

"'Tis too late now, Jane. We're on our way. There's no changing yer mind now."

The woman named Jane slumped back against the wall as tears freely ran down her cheeks. Everyone looked frightened and subdued. Mary bowed her head and stared at her clasped hands, not wishing to witness the raw feelings of the other women. One woman began to pray quietly, and several others joined in.

"Perhaps it's for the best we're cooped up down here," one woman said after the prayer. "I can't bear to watch England disappear, not knowing if I'll ever see it again."

Another woman scoffed. "Of course, ye won't see England again. What'd ye think, ye'll go on out to Virginia, take a good long look at yer intended, decide he ain't up to yer standards, and come back? The Virginia Company won't pay for yer return passage. This is a one-way journey, luv. Ye've made yer bed. We all have. Whatever awaits us at the end of this voyage is our destiny." The speaker was one of the older women. She had sharp features and didn't look like she was much used to smiling.

"What if the men are brutes, and the colony is no better than a few shacks on a distant shore surrounded by flesh-eating savages?" Jane whispered.

"They're not cannibals," one of the other women replied. "They're as likely to take your scalp as eat ye."

"Take your scalp?" one of the blond sisters asked, looking horrified.

"Oh, aye, that's what they do, ain't it? They take the scalps of their enemies as trophies," the sharp-featured woman said.

"Wherever have you heard such nonsense, Gwen?" a heavyset, dark-eyed woman demanded. It seemed the women had already introduced themselves to each other while waiting.

"Why, from one of the sailors who let me aboard. I had me a little chat with him, being the first one to arrive. He said the savages are fierce and merciless. They walk about nearly naked and paint their skins black to frighten the settlers. They smear poison on the tips of their arrows, and if they don't finish off their prey with an arrow to the heart, they split their skull with a stone ax."

The women all gasped in horror and moved closer to each other for comfort.

"Oh, stop grousing," the woman next to Mary said scornfully. Wisps of carrot-red hair had escaped her linen cap, and her large brown eyes stared out of a pale, freckled face. "If the good Lord sees fit to let us reach Virginia alive, things can only get better for all of us. None of us would be here if we had something worth staying for. We'll have husbands who are strong and fit. The company don't waste good coin on sad, old weaklings. We'll have our own homes, and land, and maybe even servants."

"Servants? Well, listen to ye, Mistress High and Mighty. If there are servants to be had, it'll likely be us right here," Gwen scoffed.

"There are ships going out to Virginia, carrying indentures. Some have been sentenced by the magistrate to do seven years' penance, and others sell themselves 'cause they can't find no other way to go on. What do you think these poor wretches do once they get there?" the redhead asked. The women shook their heads, trying to understand this new concept. "They work the land if they are men, and they skivvy if they're women."

"So, why do they need us if they have women to do for them, Nell?" one of the sisters asked.

"They need us to help populate the colony. We'll be the mothers to the first generation of Englishmen born in Virginia. We'll be a part of history," Nell replied proudly. Some of the women tittered with mirth.

"You've really got a wild imagination, don't you, Nelly? I can just see us, all set up in fine houses, with servants, surrounded by acres of property and dozens of children. Will they be giving out noble titles, do you think?" the dark-eyed woman taunted the redhead. "I'd like to marry me a lordling. Always thought I had what it takes to be a fine lady." She arched her back, lifted her head, and stuck her nose in the air, making the other women laugh. "Lady Betsy. How does that sound?"

"Ye might have to call yerself Lady Elizabeth, on account of yer new title," one of the women replied with a chuckle. "Lady Betsy sounds like someone's favorite cow."

"I'll gladly be my lord's favorite cow if he milks me regularly and strokes my teats," Betsy replied. The women roared with laughter, the tension of a few minutes ago dispelled by Betsy's good humor. "We'll be all right, girls," she said, still grinning. "We've just got to believe it."

"Who decides who marries who?" Mary asked, finding her voice for the first time. "I'm Mary Wilby," she added shyly, remembering her manners.

"Oh, they have a list," Betsy replied. "I asked Master Harrington when I first came aboard. The Virginia Company paid Captain Robeson to take out a dozen women. They gave him a list of twelve men. They enter the women's names in no particular order. 'Tis all the luck of the draw. Mary, you've got the last one on the list, being the last to join this merry matrimonial expedition," Betsy mused. "Don't make him better or worse," she hurried to add when she saw Mary blanch. "Just last."

"But there are only ten of us," Jane interjected.

"Then two poor sods are out of luck," Gwen replied. "They'll have to wait for the next shipment to get their bride."

"The only poor sod is the one who gets you for a wife," Betsy retorted. She clearly didn't like Gwen, and the feeling was mutual. Gwen looked murderous but chose not to reply.

"What if they are unkind?" one of the sisters asked.

"These men haven't had a woman to hold in years, possibly decades," Nell said. "They'll be so happy to have a bit of affection, they'll treat us like royalty."

"Either that, or they won't give us a moment's peace. You don't know how men are when they have the urge come upon them. They just need to stick their swollen cock into a slippery hole. You'll be getting the *royal* treatment all hours of the day and night, my girl, and they won't be stroking your teats neither," a plump, fair-skinned woman piped in from her corner.

"Spoken like someone who knows," Gwen scoffed, dripping scorn. "What brothel have they plucked ye from, dearie?"

"I've been married twice. I know 'bout these things. Once a man has a woman of his own, he rides her day and night, whether she wants him to or not. 'Tis not all admiring glances and sweet kisses, being a wife."

"Yet here you are, going for it a third time, Alice," Betsy said, grinning lasciviously. "Being ridden must be more pleasant than it sounds."

"'Tis no great pleasure being a widow," the woman replied. "In this world, you need a man to survive." The women nodded in agreement.

"Marriage is hard work, both in bed and out, but 'tis better than being a dried-up old spinster or a widow any day," Alice said.

"Have you no children, Alice?" one of the sisters asked.

"I had two boys, aged four and six. They died this past winter," Alice replied, her voice trembling. "There's nothing left for me in England save grief and poverty. I'll gladly endure another man's needs in exchange for having a family again."

Mary leaned into the wall, wishing she were invisible. The

conversation was making her uncomfortable. She hadn't given much thought to the intimacy that'd be required of her once she was wed but was forced to acknowledge it now. She'd heard Uncle Swithin grunting on the other side of the wall night after night when Agnes was still alive, the brutal act accompanied by Agnes's pitiful cries as he hurt her. Agnes hadn't dared deny Swithin, all too aware that the beating he'd give her would be much worse than the few minutes of misery he inflicted on her when he wished to exercise his husbandly rights, but she'd washed herself with vinegar come morning, fearful of getting with child again.

What have I done? Mary thought bitterly. *I've escaped a bad situation and landed myself in a worse one, and now I have no way out. I'm trapped on this ship until I reach the shores of Virginia, and then I'll be handed over to a man I've never so much as laid eyes on. He might be cruel and violent.*

Mary was startled when a gentle hand covered her own. "Stop fretting. 'Tis human nature to fear the worst, but your future will be what you make it," Nell said.

"I'm frightened of what's to come," Mary admitted quietly.

"Well, buck up. You've an exciting voyage ahead of you, and a good man waiting at the end of it to give you a better life."

Mary gave Nell a watery smile. "You really have a nice way of looking at things."

"When you expect terrible things to befall you, they usually do."

Mary didn't bother to argue. She hadn't expected her parents to die of the fever, one after the other, or to wind up in the care of Uncle Swithin, who'd as soon beat her as care for her. She hadn't expected Agnes to die either, leaving Mary to care for the children and run the tavern with Agnes's angry, drunken husband. Mary had expected none of those things, but they had happened all the same.

She would miss the girls, she readily admitted that, but no amount of guilt over leaving them could have stopped her from going. Uncle Swithin was hard on his daughters, but he loved them in his own gruff way and would see to their well-being. They'd be all right, Mary assured herself as the ship sailed out of the harbor, especially if Swithin took a new wife. With Mary gone, he'd need a woman about the place, and if Mary knew anything of Swithin, he'd choose a young, docile lass, one who'd be good to his children. Her cousins were no longer her concern. All she had to do now was survive.

FOUR
JANUARY 2015

London, England

Alex's round blue eyes glowed with love as Quinn lifted him out of his cot and cradled him against her shoulder. His warm little body seemed to have grown a little heavier since she left two days ago. He reached up and grabbed a fistful of hair, pulling her face closer to his. He pressed his nose into her cheek and licked her, making her laugh.

"I missed you too, little man," she whispered in his shell-like ear. "I hate leaving you, even for an hour." Alex continued to flick his tongue over her cheek. "Oh, you're hungry. And I thought you were trying to give me a kiss."

Quinn settled on the bed and pulled up her top, and not a moment too soon. Alex latched on immediately, sucking as if he hadn't been fed in days. Quinn cradled his head in her palm and closed her eyes. The flat was quiet, the noises from outside muffled by the stealthy wind. Gabe and Emma had gone out to walk Rufus, a responsibility Emma took very seriously. The puppy slept at the foot of her bed, and she ran to her room to greet him the moment she returned from school.

Quinn looked around the lounge. Evidence of their impending

move was all around her. There were packing boxes in the corner, and the flat was starting to get that forlorn look places got when the things that turn a house into a home were packed away. At any other time, she'd be thrilled to be on the verge of a new adventure, but now all she could think of was Jo. When she told Gabe about Rob Malone's phone call, he'd sided with Rhys, telling her she was overreacting and winding herself up. Perhaps it was silly to panic based on such flimsy evidence, but she couldn't shake this feeling of dread. Who, in this day and age, dropped off the face of the earth for several months? Only a person who intentionally wanted to disappear or a person who had no access to civilization. She couldn't imagine Jo would want to disappear, so the only explanation that made sense was that she was someplace without access to a phone or a computer. Surely someone would know if Jo had been kidnapped by insurgents. One group or another usually claimed responsibility for an attack on the press, using the opportunity to get into the news and spread their message of terror.

Quinn had just finished nursing Alex when she heard the key in the lock and Rufus's joyful yelping as he dashed toward the kitchen, paws padding on the tile floor.

"We're back," Gabe called out.

"Mum, can we have pizza for dinner?" Emma asked as she pulled off her mittens and scarf. "I'm hungry."

"It's fine with me," Quinn replied, in no mood to cook. She was happy to be back home with her family, but still out of sorts. Between the gruesome find in the cave and Rhys's news, she felt emotionally depleted. She wasn't even hungry. She'd be happy to crawl into bed, turn out the lights, and slip into oblivion until morning.

"Are you all right?" Gabe asked as he lifted Alex out of her arms. Alex let out a squeal of protest but then seemed to change his mind. He rested his cheek against Gabe's shoulder as his eyelids drooped.

Quinn nodded. She'd already told Gabe everything. "I'll order the pizza."

After placing the call, Quinn grabbed an empty packing box and went into Emma's room. Emma was sitting on the floor, Rufus curled up on the rug next to her. They looked content together. "What do you say we start packing some of your things? We can get at least one box finished before the pizza comes," Quinn suggested. "Let's put away your books first."

"What will you read to me before I go to sleep?" Emma asked, practical as ever.

"Why don't you leave out the storybook Father Christmas brought you and pack up the rest."

"All right." Emma stood and began haphazardly placing books into the box. Quinn organized them into neat stacks to make more room. The box was only half full by the time all the books had been packed.

Emma gazed around the room. "I don't want to take those," she said, jutting her chin toward a pile of toys in her play bin.

"I thought you liked them."

"I did before, but not anymore. Maybe you can give them away. Alex won't want them. They are for girls."

"I'll donate them to charity," Quinn replied, wondering what had brought on Emma's sullen mood. She'd pack away the toys and take them to the new house, in case Emma changed her mind.

"Can I decorate my new room?" Emma asked as she tossed several stuffed animals into the box.

"Of course. Do you have some ideas?" Quinn hadn't been giving Emma enough attention these past few weeks, so maybe decorating together would help strengthen their bond.

"I don't want pink anymore."

"All right. What color would you like?"

"Something more mature."

"Mature?"

"I'm not a baby anymore, Mum. I'll be six in the summer."

Quinn tried to suppress a smile. No, Emma certainly wasn't a baby. She was changing so quickly, they could barely keep up. "Do you have a preference, or would you like to look at some decorating magazines?"

"I know what I want," Emma announced. "I want to paint the room lavender, get new bedlinens to match, and get some fairy lights to string above my bed. I also want new pictures to hang on the wall. These are babyish."

"All right, I think that sounds reasonable. What would you like a picture of?"

"Harry Styles," Emma said.

"Harry Styles?"

"From One Direction. He's so hot."

Quinn gaped at the little girl. What did a five-year-old know about being hot? But then again, this was a different generation. When Quinn was five, all she'd wanted was a pram for her doll and some new coloring books.

"Don't you think he's hot?" Emma persisted.

"Eh, well, I don't know. I haven't given him much thought."

Emma gave her a look that said everything from *you're so old* to *you wouldn't possibly understand*. She picked up Mr. Rabbit, who'd been sitting on top of her bookshelf, and looked at him thoughtfully. Until a few months ago, Mr. Rabbit had been her favorite toy, the one she reached for when she needed comfort, but he'd been displaced by her American Girl doll, a gift from Seth. The doll resembled Emma, and she had called it Emme in honor of herself.

"Would you like to take Mr. Rabbit to the new house?" Quinn asked carefully.

Emma shrugged. "I suppose I'd better take him. You know, in case Alex wants to play with him once he's old enough. When's he going to start doing things?" Emma whined as she stowed the rabbit in the box.

"What kind of things?"

"You know—walking, talking, playing games with me."

"Emma, he's only three months old. It's too soon, love. He'll start saying words and trying to walk by the time he turns one."

"That's so long from now."

"You can't rush these things."

"When, when will he start eating formula like normal babies? He's always attached to your boobs. You never do girl stuff with me. It's always, 'I have to nurse Alex,'" Emma complained, mimicking Quinn's voice.

Quinn got off the bed and sat down on the floor next to Emma. She pulled Emma into an embrace, and although Emma resisted at first, she finally melted into Quinn, ready to surrender her anger. "I'm sorry you feel neglected, Em. Daddy and I are trying our best to give you both equal time, but Alex needs me right now. I'm his only source of nourishment."

"I need you too."

"How about we have a girls' day out this Saturday? Would you like that?"

"A real day out, or a 'Hey, let's pack your books together' kind of day?"

"A real day out. We can do whatever you like."

"I'll think about it," Emma replied, but Quinn felt her relenting.

"Oh, the pizza is here. That was quick," Quinn said when the doorbell rang. She sprang to her feet, buzzed up the delivery man without checking the security screen, and went to grab her purse.

"You're not the pizza guy," Quinn observed when she opened the door and saw Rhys standing in the corridor.

"I'm sorry to come unannounced. Guess I should have brought pizza as a peace offering."

"Why would you need a peace offering?" Quinn asked as she stepped aside to let him in.

"Because I have news you are not going to like."

Quinn led Rhys into the lounge and invited him to sit down. Rhys sat, but looked self-conscious. He hadn't even removed his coat, which was a sure sign he planned to bolt as soon as he delivered his news.

"Rhys, good to see you. Will you join us for dinner?" Gabe

asked as he came into the room. "Alex is asleep," he said in answer to Quinn's unspoken question.

"Thank you, but I only came by for a few minutes. I'm sorry. This is obviously not a good time."

"Rhys, please, just tell me," Quinn pleaded. Her stomach was in knots and her head was beginning to hurt.

Rhys nodded. "I had a call from Rob Malone. After our conversation the other day, he was concerned, so he went round to the Mustafa Hotel, where Jo had been staying."

"And?" Quinn asked, her insides quivering.

"He spoke to the manager. The manager was reluctant to talk to him but finally admitted that Jo went out one morning and never returned. After a week, they collected her belongings, put them into storage, and gave away her room. He wouldn't allow Rob to see her things."

"So, a guest at the hotel went out and never returned, and the manager didn't think to alert anyone?" Quinn cried.

"Quinn, Kabul is not London. The locals don't want to get involved, especially when it comes to foreigners."

"So, now you believe me," Quinn exclaimed, looking from Gabe to Rhys. "Something is wrong. She's missing. I knew it." Quinn sank down on the sofa as tears of frustration spilled down her cheeks. "What can I do?" she wailed. "How can I help her?"

"Quinn—" Gabe began, but the doorbell interrupted him.

"That's my cue to leave," Rhys said as he stood. "I'm sorry to be the bearer of bad news, Quinn, but I thought you'd want to know. Ring me tomorrow."

Gabe grabbed money from Quinn's purse and went to pay for the pizza, leaving Quinn to sit on the sofa, staring into space. She didn't want Emma to see her crying, so she wiped her streaming eyes and plastered a phony smile on her face.

"Emma, dinner," she called out and trudged into the kitchen.

FIVE

Quinn pretended to nibble on a piece of pizza, wishing all the while she could quietly slip away to the bedroom, where she could be alone with her turbulent thoughts. Putting on an act for Emma's sake was beyond her abilities at the moment. She finally pushed away her plate. "I'm sorry. I need to lie down for a bit."

"Are you sick, Mum?" Emma asked, looking worried.

"Just a headache. It'll be all better soon."

"We'll save you some pizza," she offered, eyeing the half-full box. "Maybe you can have it for breakfast."

Emma was really suggesting that she, herself, could have it for breakfast, but Quinn was in no mood to give a lecture on healthy eating. "Yes, maybe," she mumbled and fled the brightly lit kitchen.

The bedroom was mercifully quiet and dark. Quinn kicked off her shoes and curled up on the bed without removing her clothes. Her insides felt hollow, as if someone had scooped out all her organs and left behind a useless shell. How could Jo have gone missing without anyone noticing or caring? Surely there was someone here in London who loved her, who'd worry if they hadn't heard from her. She was a thirty-one-year-old woman, she had to have someone in her life—a husband or boyfriend, or close friends. It didn't seem as if anyone was looking for her. And if they were, they wouldn't find her from London. Someone had to go to Afghanistan and look for Jo in earnest. They had to retrace her steps, talk to people she'd come in contact with, visit the British Embassy. No one vanished without a trace; someone out there knew where Jo had gone, and with whom. Someone always knew something.

Quinn closed her eyes. She was so tired, so depleted. The last year of her life had been a roller coaster, and she couldn't handle any more unexpected drops, nor could she get off this ride. Jo was her sister, her twin. Quinn couldn't go on with her life as if nothing had changed. She owed it to herself and to Jo to find out what had happened and help in any way she could.

As Quinn drifted off to sleep, her mind seemed to respond to her earlier question, her inner voice as clear as a bell. *I must go to Kabul.*

When she awoke, bright winter sunlight streamed through the net curtains. Gabe had covered her with a fleece afghan when he came to bed so as not to wake her. He was already up, and Alex's cot was empty, his yellow blanket pushed off to the side. For a moment, Quinn wished she could remain in bed and hide from the world, but she threw off the afghan and got up. She could hear Emma's voice coming from the kitchen and Gabe's measured response. He was so patient.

Quinn went to the bathroom, brushed her teeth, washed her face, combed her hair, and made her way to the kitchen, looking a little more presentable. Emma was sitting at the breakfast table eating a bowl of cereal. Gabe sat across from her, Alex in his arms. Alex was lazily sucking on a bottle, his gaze fixed on Emma, who made a face at him.

"Good morning," Gabe said. "Feeling better?"

Quinn nodded, though she didn't feel better. In fact, she felt worse, but now wasn't the time to say anything. She poured herself a cup of tea and added a splash of milk. Normally, she didn't take sugar, but today she added two spoonfuls, suddenly desperate for something sweet. "Would you like some tea?" she asked Gabe.

Gabe shook his head, watching her intently. "I'll take Emma to school and come back," he said.

"Don't you have to go to work?"

"I'll come back," Gabe repeated. "We'll talk then."

"All right."

Quinn drank her tea, then poured herself another mug and moved into the lounge, where Alex was happily playing on his activity mat. She couldn't seem to find the energy to do anything useful. On fine days she took Alex for a walk in the mornings and stopped at the shops to pick up a few things for dinner, but today she remained on the sofa, too listless to even change her clothes.

Gabe returned a short while later. He shrugged off his coat, unwound his scarf, then walked over to Quinn, who looked up to meet his gaze. His cheeks were ruddy with cold when he kissed her.

"All right?" he asked, his eyes searching her face. She knew he was worried, and she wished she could put his mind at rest, but Gabe was the one person who always understood and stood by her. He'd see things her way. Quinn waited until Gabe settled himself in a chair across from her and took the plunge.

"Gabe, I'm going to look for Jo."

She'd expected an instant response, but he just stared at her, as if he hadn't quite understood what she'd said.

"I can't just sit here and do nothing. My sister is out there somewhere, and no one seems to care. I'm going to find her."

"So, you want to go to Afghanistan to look for her?" Gabe asked, understanding finally dawning.

"I must."

"Must you?" he asked sarcastically. His eyes narrowed, and an angry flush bloomed on his cheeks.

"Gabe, come on."

"Come on what, Quinn? I can't believe we are even having this conversation. We're not talking about you going to Manchester or even Edinburgh. We are talking about Kabul. People die in Kabul. It's a war zone, in case you forgot."

"I have a responsibility to my sister."

"You have a responsibility to me," Gabe snapped, his voice brittle with suppressed fury. "You have a family, a three-month-old baby, whom you're still nursing. You have no right to put yourself in danger and go off on this wild goose chase. You don't even know if Jo is truly in danger or just taking a bit of time off. Just because she's off the grid doesn't automatically mean she's hurt."

"I won't know that for sure unless I find her," Quinn retorted.

"Quinn, I forbid it. I absolutely forbid you to go to Afghanistan."

"Are you serious? You *forbid* me? Did you really just say that? I expect you of all people to understand and not go all medieval on me."

"Is it medieval to care about the safety of your wife and the mother of your children? Does finding Jo mean more to you than your safety and the emotional well-being of your children? What would I tell them if you didn't come back?"

"Why wouldn't I?" Quinn cried.

"Because Kabul is a dangerous place, and you're obviously not thinking clearly if you even have to ask. Call the embassy, speak to Jo's agent, contact her attorney, do what you must, but you can't go to Afghanistan. I won't let you." Gabe was on his feet now, his voice rising in anger. "Quinn, if you insist on going through with this, we are finished. There will be no coming back from this, not if you completely disregard my feelings and put this misguided quest above your family. The choice is yours."

"Or what? You'll divorce me?" Quinn challenged him.

Gabe didn't immediately reply, but his cold stare was answer enough. Quinn grabbed her purse and keys and stormed out of the flat, slamming the door behind her. She was shaking with anger, her mind exploding with outrage.

"I forbid you," Gabe had said. Where did he get off? Who did he think he was to even speak to her that way? This wasn't a misguided quest; it was a rescue mission. Jo was her sister, not some mate from college or a pleasant coworker. Jo was family, she was blood, and she was in trouble. How could Gabe expect Quinn to just stand by and hope everything turned out okay? He would walk through fire to save someone he loved. Why did he expect anything less of her?

Quinn strode toward the lift and repeatedly slammed her finger into the button. She was so angry she could barely breathe. The lift finally came, and the doors opened, ready to take her down to street level, away from Gabe, and away from her children.

Quinn stared at the empty lift until the doors closed and she heard the cables shifting as the lift was called to another floor. She pressed her head to the cool metal doors and took several deep breaths. What did she think she was doing? Gabe was absolutely right. She had no right to put herself in danger. She had a family; a baby whose well-being came above anything she might feel at this moment. Gabe wasn't being medieval, he was being sensible, and very patient. She'd unwittingly put herself in danger when she confronted Robert Chatham, then she'd nearly lost their baby when Brett had locked her in that tomb in New Orleans. Given her history, her judgement wasn't as clear-eyed as she liked to believe. She was a wife and a mother, and by agreeing to take on those two roles, she'd given up the right to act on a whim and do what was best for her. She wanted to find her sister more than anything in the world, but rushing off to a war-torn country wasn't the way to do it.

Quinn slowly turned around and walked back to the flat. She let herself in and walked into the kitchen, where Gabe was warming up milk for Alex. He didn't turn around but stood facing the microwave, his shoulders rigid and his stance aggressive.

"I'm sorry. You are right," Quinn muttered. Gabe didn't reply, but some of the defensiveness went out of his posture.

"Gabe, please talk to me."

"What do you want me to say?" Gabe asked without turning around. He took the bottle out of the microwave, tested the milk on his hand to make sure it wasn't too hot, and left the kitchen, with Quinn trailing behind him.

"I want you to say you understand how I feel."

"I do understand, but that doesn't mean I will stand by and support this lunacy. I found you half-dead on the floor of that tomb in New Orleans. I died a thousand deaths while I waited for the doctors to find the fetal heartbeat to see if our baby had survived and if you were going to be all right. And then I had to explain to a four-year-old why the woman she'd come to love and trust was nearly murdered only a few months after her mother died in a car crash. I allowed your drug-addicted brother to get away with taking Emma without permission, and then I stupidly went along when you decided to hire him as entertainment for Emma's birthday party. Well, we all know how that turned out. I thank God every day Emma didn't ingest the heroin she found."

"I never meant for those things to happen," Quinn cried. It sounded horrible when put like that, as if it had all been her fault.

"No, you didn't, but they happened anyway because when it comes to your dysfunctional family, you seem unable to think clearly."

"Tell me how you really feel, why don't you!" Quinn exclaimed, using sarcasm to mask her hurt.

"I am telling you how I really feel because I'm fighting for my life here, my future. This is where I draw the line."

"What are you telling me?"

Gabe handed her the bottle. "I need some air. Please feed the baby."

Gabe turned on his heel and walked out of the room, then out of the flat, leaving Quinn quivering with guilt and shame. She wanted to be angry, to hate him for the things he'd said, but he had been right about each and every one. He could have mentioned a few other incidents, but he'd kindly abridged her catalogue of misjudgments. Quinn lifted the baby out of his crib and held him close, her tears anointing his downy black hair.

"I'm sorry," she whispered as she kissed his silky cheek. "I'm really sorry. I'll be a better mum, I promise. I'll never let you down again."

Quinn fed and changed Alex, then sat down on the sofa, her head in her hands. It was another hour before Gabe finally returned. He looked grim, and his face was covered with a sheen of perspiration. He didn't often exercise, but he must have been jogging the whole time he was gone, something he did to let off steam.

"I'm sorry," he said, his expression sheepish. "I never meant to be cruel."

"You weren't." Quinn walked into his arms and pressed her face to his chest. His heart was racing. She didn't know if it was due to the exercise or to stress, but it didn't matter. "Are we okay? You won't leave me?"

"I was never the one who was leaving."

Gabe leaned down and kissed Quinn. The kiss was soft and tender and full of emotion, and she melted into his arms, thankful that he still loved her despite everything she'd put him through.

"I know you're hurting, but running off to Afghanistan is not the answer, and you'd know that if you gave yourself time to think. I love you, Quinn, and I love our life, and I will fight with everything I've got to protect it."

"You won't have to. I'm not going anywhere," she muttered into his chest.

"Now, I'm going to take a shower and head into the office. Will you still be here when I come back?" Gabe asked. He was joking, but there was an underlying note of worry in his voice.

"Yes," Quinn replied, smiling guiltily. "I will be here, today and always. You needn't worry."

Quinn waited until Gabe left to call Rhys. Thankfully, he wasn't in a meeting and promptly took her call.

"Quinn, how are you?" His voice was filled with concern, which made her feel a little better.

She sighed. "Gabe and I had a massive row this morning," she confessed. "He threatened to leave me if I went to Afghanistan to look for Jo."

"I would tell you you're insane to even suggest such a thing, but I'm sure Gabe did a very thorough job of berating you. I certainly hope you saw sense and abandoned this crazy scheme."

"I have, but I can't stop thinking about Jo, Rhys. How can I go on with my life as if nothing has happened when she's out there somewhere, possibly hurt, or even dead?"

"Quinn, I'll go to Kabul," Rhys suddenly announced.

"What? Are you mad?" Quinn demanded.

"I have a press pass. I can go just about anywhere, and people will answer my questions because I'm employed by a legitimate news outlet. I can find out what happened to Jo and hopefully bring her back."

"Rhys, that's an absolutely terrible idea. Why would you do that? Why would you put your life on hold and rush off to a country at war to look for a woman you barely know?"

"First of all, I have no life just now, so there isn't much to put on hold. I look for things to keep me from going home. I can't bear the silence, or the emptiness I feel when I walk through the door. My daughter would have been born two months from now, but instead, all I can do is stare at the picture of the scan on the fridge, because that's all I have left of her. The bottom dropped out of my world, so perhaps I need to focus on someone else for a while."

"And second?"

"And second, I don't have to know Jo; I know you."

"And that's enough of a reason for you to fly off to Afghanistan?" Quinn smiled through her tears as she tried to understand Rhys's sudden eagerness.

"Yes, that's enough of a reason. I can't stand to see you suffer. I'd go mad with grief if Owain went missing, so I can understand your pain. Gabe is an only child; he's never experienced that bond between siblings. Look, Quinn, I'll make you a deal. You work on this new case and give it your full attention. I will go to Kabul and leave no stone unturned to find Jo. What do you say?"

"Rhys, I won't knowingly send you into danger."

"You're not sending me. I'm volunteering. Will you take up the reins of the program while I'm gone?"

"On one condition. If you don't find Jo within a fortnight, you will return and give up this mad scheme."

Rhys thought about that for a moment. "All right. I agree."

"When will you go?"

"As soon as I can make the arrangements."

"Thank you, Rhys," Quinn said softly.

"You're welcome."

SIX

MAY 1620

Somewhere in the Atlantic

Mary stretched out on the hard wooden floor and wrapped herself in her cloak. Thankfully, with the approach of summer, the weather had warmed up considerably, the howling, bitter wind replaced by a gentler spring breeze. Still, at night it grew cold, and Mary and Nell often snuggled together for warmth.

Mary had become friendly with all the other women, given that there was nothing much to do but talk. After years of hard work and little rest, Mary found herself spending hours each day just being idle, a pastime she found nearly as difficult. There was nothing to do, and nowhere to go. The brief strolls on deck were usually accompanied by baleful stares from the sailors and lewd comments, whispered behind hands and coupled with insolent smirks and rude gestures. It was safer down below, but the lack of even the most basic comforts was difficult to bear.

The buckets reeked of human waste and often tipped over when the ship tilted and rocked on the roiling waters of the Atlantic, leaving the small space virtually uninhabitable until it was thoroughly washed with sea water. The women stank of unwashed bodies, menstrual blood, and simmering discontent. The further they traveled from England, the more unsettled they felt, having left a life they knew, but not having yet had a glimpse of the life that awaited them on the distant shores of the American continent.

Mary spent most of her days talking to Nell and Betsy, with whom she felt most comfortable. The sisters, Faith and Prudence, kept mostly to themselves, and the rest of the women were younger and more idealistic, except for Alice, who'd been widowed twice, and Gwen, who was sour and quarrelsome by nature. Being forced to spend so much time in each other's company led to arguments, and there had even been a near fist fight when Gwen called Rose's intended, who'd died several months before Rose made the fateful decision to sail to Virginia, a "hapless milksop." Mary avoided Gwen as much as possible. The woman's bitterness filled every crack and spread like a noxious odor, poisoning what was already a difficult journey.

"I feel sorry for the poor sod who winds up with her for a wife," Nell whispered to Mary one night. "Imagine having to wake to that sour mug every morning."

"I'm more worried 'bout what I'll have to wake up to," Mary replied. "Surely, not all the bachelors are young and well-formed."

"Be easy in your mind, Mary. No point fretting about something as hasn't happened yet. You might get the best one of them all."

"Thanks, Nell, but I find it hard to share your shining dream of the future. I've spent the past seven years living above a tavern. If you want to see a man at his worst, just wait till he's had a few pint pots."

Nell sighed. "I won't argue with you there. I only hope there aren't too many taverns in Jamestown."

"If what I've seen so far is anything to go on, the first two permanent buildings erected in Virginia must have been a tavern and a church."

Nell giggled. "Well, then let's hope the third wasn't a whorehouse."

Nell was often the first to fall asleep, while Mary lay awake for a long time, thinking and wondering. She was too shy to ask for information, which made her doubly grateful for Betsy, who had all the reserve of a hunting dog on a fox hunt.

"So, how does it work, Master Harrington?" she badgered the quartermaster, who, despite his stern looks and curt answers, seemed to find her amusing. "How will we know our intended, and what will happen once they take us to their homes? Will we be living in sin?" Betsy asked, batting her eyelashes as if living in sin with Master Harrington was her fondest dream.

The quartermaster sighed and gazed heavenward, likely asking the Lord for patience. "You will come ashore with me, and I will make the introductions."

"Have you met our future husbands, then?" Betsy persisted.

"No, Mistress Smyth, I haven't, but I'm one of two people on this ship who have the authority to take charge of you once we dock, the other being the captain, and he can't be bothered with you lot. He's got more important business to attend to. After we dock, I will escort you to church, where you will meet your intended and be wed."

"What? Right away, like?" Betsy gasped.

"Right away. Revered Edison will not permit any of the men to take their women home until their union has been sanctioned by the Church."

"Master Harrington, can we trouble you for some water and soap before we reach Jamestown?" Mary asked shyly. "I'd like to wash and launder my clothes."

Master Harrington wrinkled his nose and looked at the assembled women. "That's a fine idea, Mistress Wilby. You won't be winning any hearts smelling as you do now."

"You piss-drinking son of a poxed whore," Gwen hissed at Master Harrington's retreating back. "I'd like to see how fine you'd look after being caged for weeks on end and eating nothing but hard tack and salted pork."

"Come now, Gwen, he's not so bad," Betsy said, giving Gwen a sharp look. "At least he answers our questions and treats us with respect."

"Respect?" Gwen spit the word out as if it were poison.

"If Master Harrington felt inclined to abuse his position, things could have gone a lot harder for us. He is a man, after all, one who's denied the comforts of a woman for months on end. He wouldn't be the first to help himself to what's right under his nose."

"You are right there, Betsy," Alice agreed. "He's a true gentleman, no doubt about that. And he keeps the sailors in line. For all their crude comments, not one of them has laid so much as a finger on any of us."

"I can't wait to get off this ship, Nell," Mary said quietly. "Whatever awaits us on shore has to be better than being trapped in this wooden box for two months."

The following morning, when Mary and Nell were allowed up on deck, she decided to ask Nell the question that had been plaguing her for weeks. All the other women spoke of their lives back home, and Mary knew more than she ever wished to about the circumstances that had led them to the *Lady Grace*. Nell, on the other hand, was always evasive when asked about her past, and adept at redirecting the conversation toward someone like Alice, who liked nothing more than to talk about herself. Except for Faith and Prudence, who had each other, all the women were either orphaned or widowed and had no one to rely on but themselves.

"Nell, did you leave anyone behind in England?" Mary asked when they leaned against the ship's railing. It was a glorious spring morning. The ocean was as placid as a puddle after a heavy rain and the sky a deep blue, its perfection unmarred by even a single cloud. Even the sailors seemed to be in better spirits and called out a greeting to the two young women as they came up from the bowels of the ship. Master Harrington had tipped his hat to them and smiled, wishing them a pleasant stroll.

Nell turned to look at Mary, her expression thoughtful. Mary thought she might not answer, but she did, her voice surprisingly quiet. "I have parents and two younger brothers."

Mary tried to hide her astonishment by fixing her gaze on a seagull that swooped down to the water and came back out with the hapless fish flapping in its beak. "If my parents were still alive, I'd never leave," Mary finally replied, hoping the sentiment wouldn't upset Nell. "What decided you to go, then?"

"An offer of marriage."

"Was the man so awful?" Mary asked, wondering why Nell would need to cross an ocean to get away from someone who wished to marry her.

"No, he was wonderful, handsome, and kind. I'd known him all my life and always thought I'd marry him when the time came."

"I don't understand," Mary said, searching Nell's closed expression.

Nell sighed and turned away from Mary, staring out over the tranquil sea. "My ma was sixteen when she wed. Da said she were all rosy cheeks, riotous curls, and a smile as could coax out the sun on a gloomy day. He'd never seen anything so beautiful as her when he stood up next to her in church."

Mary remained silent, waiting for Nell to continue.

"My ma is thirty-four now. Her hair, what's left of it, is all gray. She's lost half her teeth and her hands are so raw from doing chores and cleaning fish from morning till night, they look like bloody meat. She birthed nine children and buried six, three of them still-born. She's lived a life of unrelenting hardship and crippling poverty and will likely not live to see her fortieth birthday." Nell sighed and brushed away a tear that slid down her pale cheek.

"Had I married Toby, a fisherman like my da, I'd have lived my ma's life. I'd work my hands raw from the time I awoke to the time I fell exhausted into bed. I'd bear children who'd have less chance of surviving than a pup born to a stray dog, and I'd get old before my time, turning into a toothless hag who barely has enough energy to speak to her children at the end of the day for being so careworn. I don't want that for myself, Mary. I want a chance at a better life."

"How can you be so sure you'll have a better life in Virginia?" Mary asked.

"There are opportunities in Virginia, Mary. A man can work to better his lot. He can buy land, expand his holdings. What can a poor fisherman do other than pull fish out of the sea and hope he doesn't drown for his pains? With Toby, I wouldn't so much as have a bed of my own, much less a home. I'd have to move into his parents' dwelling, a shack that's already home to seven people. Toby might love me now, but will he still love me once my looks are gone and my spirit is broken? Will I still love him when he becomes a broken old man who'd rather sleep on a floor smeared with fish guts than lie down next to his wife?"

"You're a brave lass, Nell. I'd not have the courage to do what you did."

Nell nodded, still staring at the ocean. "Don't tell the others. They wouldn't understand."

"I think they would, but I'll not breathe a word. I hope you find what you're looking for."

"I will, and so will you if you stop looking back and face forward. That life is behind us now. All we can do is make the best of the one that's to come. I think I'd like a moment alone now, if you don't mind."

Mary left Nell by the railing and took a turn about the deck. Master Harrington had forbidden them to walk around on their own, but she needed to stretch her legs and think on what Nell had told her. She admired Nell's courage and practicality, but she also pitied her. She'd never see her family again. It was as if they had all died the day Nell left England. As she ambled along, oblivious to the lewd stares of the sailors, Mary wondered if a prosperous life was worth such a sacrifice. Would she have been able to walk away from a man who'd loved her all her life? Probably not. She wasn't as strong as Nell, or as pragmatic. Nell was three years her junior, but she was years ahead of Mary in her thinking.

Perhaps it's time I started acting more like a woman and less like a child, and tried to forge my own future, like Nell, instead of meekly going along with what life has in store for me, Mary thought defiantly. She'd taken the first step by taking her leave of Uncle Swithin. She'd taken charge, and it felt good. Nell was right; it was time to start looking forward and make the most of what life in Virginia had to offer.

SEVEN

JUNE 1620

Off the Coast of Virginia

A ripple of excitement ran through the women when they heard the joyful shout, "Land, ho!" coming from above. It wouldn't be long now until the ship came into port and they would finally disembark and come face-to-face with their future.

When Betsy and Mary came up on deck later that day, Mary stared into the distance until her eyes watered but couldn't make out anything resembling a port, but it didn't matter. She could clearly see the shore now, and it was a welcome sight. After nearly eight weeks aboard the *Lady Grace,* she was desperate for solid ground beneath her feet and a decent meal. Mary's bowels felt leaden after nothing but tack and thin slices of salt pork for nearly two months, her shift was crusted with dried sweat, and her hair felt as if it were moving of its own accord, the thick tresses home to countless lice.

"I have butterflies in my stomach," Mary said, using an expression she'd heard from someone once. It had caught her fancy, but she hadn't had an opportunity to put it to good use until today.

"That ain't what I would call it," Betsy replied with a giggle. "If I don't move my bowels soon, I think I'll explode. I just hope my handsome new husband isn't standing too close to me when it happens. Lord, what I wouldn't give for a slice of freshly baked bread smeared with butter and a thick cut of roast beef with buttered peas and parsnips, followed by a dish of syllabub all to myself."

"Is that what you normally ate at home?" Mary asked, stunned. She'd never known the delights of roast beef or the exquisite sweetness of syllabub on her tongue. The most luxurious meal she'd ever had was a stew flavored with bits of meat and a slice of stale spice cake.

Betsy rolled her eyes. "Of course not, you silly goose, but a girl can dream, can't she? Mayhap I'll marry a rich planter and get to eat succulent meat and pudding every day of my life." Betsy grinned hugely, making Mary laugh. "But at this moment, I'd settle for a cup of broth and a bowl of hot porridge. My teeth are aching from grinding those rock-hard biscuits, and my belly is desperate for anything that ain't cold and stale."

"You think they're expecting us?" Mary asked, squinting at the wild-looking shoreline in the hope of seeing anything resembling a town. All she could make out was thick foliage.

"They must be. Surely a ship on the horizon is not an everyday occurrence in these parts."

"I don't see anything," Mary complained.

"Me neither," Betsy replied. "Come, our time's up."

Mary and Betsy returned to their cramped space to allow the next pair of women to come up for some air. Mary sat down and leaned against the wall. Now that they were close to the end of the voyage, she felt like she couldn't wait another day to set foot on land, and all the other women seemed to share her impatience. Everyone was restless and sharp with each other, desperate to finally discover what lay at the end of their journey. Only Nell seemed calm. She was curled into a ball, sleeping peacefully on her cloak, as if the next few days were of no consequence to her.

True to his word, Master Harrington had provided the women with buckets of rainwater, bits of lye soap, and a copper tub for washing their clothes. They had to be economical and take turns, but it was better than nothing. Since Mary had been the last to board, it had been decided she'd be last to wash. Mary didn't think this logic particularly fair but decided not to argue. If she washed last, she'd be the freshest by the time they disembarked. She watched Jane wring out her clothes and hand them to Alice and Rose, who were about to go up on deck. Master Harrington had allocated a spot where the women could hang their clothes to dry, and since Jane could hardly go up in her shift, she had to ask others to do it for her.

"'Tis your turn, Mary," Jane said, pushing the tub toward Mary. "There's no more water left, but Master Harrington said you may draw some from the barrel on deck."

Mary poured the dirty water from the tub into a bucket and went up on deck. She tossed the water overboard and filled the bucket with clean water. She was practically tingling with anticipation as she came back down and began to remove her outer garments. She was going to keep her shift on and wash beneath it, but Nell, who'd woken up, offered to use her cloak to screen Mary from prying eyes.

Mary used a wet rag to cleanse her body, then washed her hair, careful to allow the water to run off into the copper tub. She then used the soapy water to launder her shift and stockings. There wasn't enough water to wash the rest. Her shift went in first, followed by stockings. Mary soaked the shift for as long as she could, then carefully scrubbed at the fabric, fearful the threadbare linen would come apart in her hands. She washed her cap as well, then asked Faith and Prudence to hang up her things on deck while she sat wrapped in her cloak to cover her nakedness. She used the comb to brush out her hair. It took a long time, since the comb only had five teeth, but time was something she had plenty of. Master Harrington said they wouldn't be coming ashore for at least another day. Mary plaited her hair, wrapped the cloak tighter around her body, and sat back down.

Thoughts of her future home occupied her mind, but she had

no wish to voice them for fear that others would make snide comments or disabuse her of the idea that she might have a real home. What would it be like, her husband's house? The prospect of having something to call her own was almost more exciting than the promise of marriage. In her experience, husbands didn't spend much time at home. It was the domain of the wives, and she hoped she'd be able to make their house pleasant and comfortable, if it wasn't already.

Mary wrapped her arms around her legs and rested her chin on her knees. Eager as she was to get off this ship and begin her new life, she would miss Nell and Betsy. She'd never had an opportunity to forge close friendships, so having the support and endless good humor of the two women had made the voyage not only bearable, but almost pleasant. She hoped they'd be able to see each other once they were settled, but since she had no real notion of how large the colony was, she dared not hope they'd be close enough to each other to visit.

It took another full day for the ship to finally dock, and several more hours until Master Harrington came down to fetch the women. Dressed in a clean shift and stockings, her hair brushed, neatly plated, and pinned up beneath her cap, Mary felt as ready as she'd ever be to meet her future husband.

"I'll miss you, Master Harrington." Betsy's tone was playful, but there was a tremor in her voice. She was clearly scared witless of what awaited her on shore.

"Unfortunately, I can't say the same," the quartermaster replied. "I'm more than ready to discharge my duty and see the back of you."

"Come, Master Harrington, it wasn't that bad of a voyage, was it? At least ye had something pretty to look at," Alice purred, fishing for a compliment. She rested her hand on her hip and drew herself up, making her breasts appear fuller. Master Harrington fixed her with a look that seemed to convey that he'd rather look at something he'd scraped off his shoe.

"It wasn't bad, as far as sea voyages go. We didn't encounter any terrible storms, and no one died, which is always a blessing. Now, if you'll be so kind." Master Harrington gestured toward the door, inviting them to leave their shipboard home.

The women followed him like chicks padding after a mother hen. Master Harrington had been their champion, their protector on this voyage, and they were afraid to part from him and go off into the unknown. They lowered their eyes as the sailors ogled them and made colorful comments about what awaited them that night. No one had really spoken of it, but they surely all knew how this day would end, unless some of them weren't wanted.

Mary took in her surroundings as soon as she came up on deck. She still held out hope of arriving in a bustling town, but the *Lady Grace* was the only ship moored at the single narrow dock that passed for the port of Jamestown. There were no houses, no taverns, and no other vessels in sight. There weren't even dock workers, ready to unload cargo from the newly arrived ship. Everything was green: the water that lapped at the shore, the grass that blanketed every open space, and the trees that grew so close together they offered no glimpse of anything beyond. The air was filled with birdsong rather than the shouts of men and the sounds of a working port.

The women looked around, their faces a testament to their shock. Where was everyone? And everything? Where was the settlement they'd heard so much about?

"Follow me," Master Harrington said and began to walk, following a gently sloping track into the woods. Mary's legs wobbled like jelly after two months aboard a ship. As the track grew steeper, she quickly tired and found herself out of breath. Betsy panted with exertion as she came alongside her.

"Where's Jamestown, Master Harrington?" Betsy cried in dismay.

"It's just there," the quartermaster replied, pointing straight ahead.

Along with the rest of the women, Mary strained to see something, but all she could make out were more trees. They walked for about a quarter of a mile before emerging into an open space resembling a dry moat; it surrounded a tall wall constructed of thick logs that were whittled to sharp points at the top, like teeth piercing the sky. The only opening in the wall was a wide gate that stood open to welcome them.

Master Harrington herded his charges through the gate, where a small crowd of onlookers had gathered to stare at the newcomers and call out words of greeting. Mary's head swiveled, her mouth open in shock. She'd expected the settlement to resemble an English town, but what she saw was a cluster of daub and wattle houses grouped around a central space. Two buildings were readily identifiable: the smithy, standing silent, and the church, which was no more than a large hut with a wooden cross at the top.

"Welcome, lovely ladies," someone called out from the crowd. "You're a sight for sore eyes. I wish one of you was meant for me." A few people laughed, and someone playfully cuffed the young man who'd shouted at them.

The group of well-wishers consisted mostly of men, their faces hungry and eager as they looked at the newly arrived women. There were two women at the back of the group, but they looked grim and unwelcoming, their gazes narrowed as they appraised the arrivals. A richly dressed man emerged from the biggest house and strode toward the church, pausing briefly to give the women a stiff bow before continuing. A middle-aged woman, who had to be his wife, smiled warmly at the women before shutting the door.

"Who's that, then, Master Harrington?" Gwen called out. "Is he my future lord and husband?"

The women sniggered, but Master Harrington held up his hand. "That's Governor Yeardley—and his lady," he added.

He then shepherded them into the dim confines of the church. Sharp beams of sunlight filtered through the slats in the walls and striped the dirt floor and rows of narrow benches. The two front pews were occupied by men of various ages, their heads turned toward the door, their gazes fixed on the women. The men looked anxious but eager, and some of them made to rise as the women filed in. A clergyman stood at the front, his head tilted to the side as he surveyed the women. The governor stood next to the minister, his plumed hat in the crook of his arm. He was smiling, but the smile didn't quite reach his eyes.

"Master Harrington, good to see you back," he called out. The quartermaster offered a sweeping bow by way of greeting. "And this time you bring us a precious gift. Please come in. Come in," he said, speaking to the women for the first time.

He exchanged a brief look with another man, who stood silently next to the minister. He wasn't tall and had blunt features and a piercing dark gaze that seemed out of place in a pale face framed by fair hair. A fat pearl earring dangled from his left earlobe, and he wore a pristine white ruff and a richly embroidered velvet coat with matching breeches, unlike the governor, whose attire was very fine but more casual. He frowned and turned to Governor Yeardley once it became evident that all the women were inside the church.

"There are only ten," he complained. "Captain Robeson was authorized to deliver twelve brides."

"I'm sorry, Secretary Hunt, but we were unable to procure two more suitable women without delaying our voyage by several weeks." The secretary nodded but looked sour as he gazed over the now-nervous men.

Master Harrington extracted a folded sheet of paper from the pocket of his doublet and handed it to the minister, who unfolded it and scanned the contents, his lips moving as he silently read the names. He looked at the assorted men and called out two names. The two men reluctantly stood, their faces drooping with disappointment.

"Better luck next time, gentlemen," Governor Yeardley said. He patted the man closest to him on the back in a gesture of support, and the man gave him a watery smile before walking down the nave toward the door.

"Very good. Shall we proceed?" the minister asked, deferring to Governor Yeardley.

"By all means, Reverend."

The reverend nodded and looked over the assembled company. He was younger than any clergyman Mary had ever seen and had the physique of someone who spent his days toiling in the fields rather than spreading the word of God. In fact, Governor Yeardley appeared to be the oldest person in the church, being close to forty, in her estimation.

"Good afternoon. My name is Reverend Edison," the minister announced. "Welcome to Virginia. Let us take a moment to praise the Good Lord for delivering you all safely to our shores before we proceed." The reverend bowed his head and waited for everyone else to do the same, then began to pray. The men bristled with impatience, but Reverend Edison wouldn't be rushed. He seemed to be enjoying himself.

"Shall we get on with it, Reverend?" Governor Yeardley prompted him as soon as he finished with a heartfelt "Amen."

"Certainly. I will read out the name of the man, followed by the name of his intended. When your name is called, come and stand in front of the pulpit, side by side."

Reverend Edison finally began, and the women took their places next to their future husbands. The couples were silent, studying each other and smiling shyly as they tried to reconcile what they'd imagined these past months to reality. None of the men were very handsome. They were a rough lot, hardened by backbreaking work and toughened by lack of affection. Two of the men were probably the smiths, judging by their soot-covered hands, and they stood stiff-backed and proud next to Faith and Prudence, whose hands were clasped. *At least the sisters won't be separated*, Mary thought as she waited her turn.

Her head snapped up when she heard Nell's name. Nell squeezed her hand and went to join a heavyset, bushy-haired man with a beard so thick it resembled a bird's nest. Nell smiled at him, and he lit up, strong white teeth flashing within the beard.

Several more names were called, including those of Betsy and her intended. He looked at her with open admiration and smiled happily, making Betsy blush. Her future husband was tall and broad with clear blue eyes and a mane of dark hair tied back with a leather thong. His nose was a bit crooked, as if it'd been broken in a fight and hadn't healed properly, but otherwise, he was one of the more attractive men in the church. Betsy stole a peek at Mary and smiled broadly. She could have done worse, her gaze was saying.

Gwen had been paired with the oldest looking of the men. He had to be around thirty-five and had a pinched look on his gaunt face. His nostrils flared with distaste when he beheld his bride, and he had the air of a man about to be led to the scaffold. Mary thought they were perfectly matched.

"John Forrester, Mary Wilby."

Mary's gaze flew to the man who stood and came toward her. He smiled, revealing surprisingly straight white teeth. He wasn't obviously handsome, possibly because he was whippet-thin and had a narrow, suntanned face, but he had kind brown eyes and sandy hair that was neatly brushed from his brow and tied back with a black ribbon. His clothes weren't fashionable, but he looked clean and tidy, which was more than she could say for some of the others, who looked as if they'd come into Jamestown directly from laboring in a field. She suddenly realized that it was very likely they had. They'd had no way of knowing when the ship would arrive or when it would be time to claim their brides, and their farms couldn't be neglected.

Once all ten couples stood facing the pulpit, the reverend gazed at them solemnly and opened his Bible to a page he had marked with a red ribbon. He seemed ready to begin when Governor Yeardley held up his hand and smiled apologetically.

"I'd like to say a few words before the ceremony, if I may," the governor said. "Once you're wed, you'll be too eager to go home to spare me even a few moments," he joked. "And I certainly don't blame you, given the obvious charms of our long-awaited brides."

He beamed at the assembled couples. "Dear ladies, I welcome you to Jamestown and wish you much joy in your new life. Until you began to arrive, our little colony was nothing more than a primitive outpost, but now it's a thriving community that will continue to grow through the new families we will create today." He raised his eyes to the rafters and intoned, "'And God blessed them, and God said unto them, Be fruitful, and multiply, and replenish the earth, and subdue it: and have dominion over the fish of the sea, and over the fowl of the air, and over every living thing that moveth upon the earth.' Reverend Edison, whenever you're ready."

Reverend Edison nodded and began.

Mary could barely concentrate on the words of the service. She hadn't permitted herself to dream of her wedding often, but when she had, nine other couples had never figured into her fantasy. She'd imagined walking down the nave toward her beloved, feeling nervous and shy, but also happy and excited. She likely wouldn't have a new gown to wear, but she'd have a bunch of posies in her hands, and maybe some wildflowers in her hair. She couldn't fill her imaginary congregation with faces of family and friends, but in her dream, she felt their benevolence and knew they were full of good wishes for the happy couple. Except for the other couples, the governor, and Master Harrington, who looked as if he couldn't escape quickly enough, there was no one present. The couples looked nervous and somber as they made their vows to each other, and there wasn't a flower in sight.

"I now pronounce you husband and wife," Reverend Edison said to each couple in turn. "May God bless your union."

Mary stared at the tips of her shoes, suddenly terrified. She'd anticipated the wedding, but what was to come after was completely unknown. What would happen now? What would her new husband say to her? What was she to say to him? Mary glanced at Master Forrester to find him looking down at her. He looked as confused and uncertain as she felt, and his obvious lack of courage endeared him to her. He was nervous too, and possibly a little scared.

"Shall we?" he asked, giving her his arm. His voice was softer than she'd expected, and his turn of phrase educated. "The plantation is four miles south of the settlement. It will take us no more than an hour to get home. I expect you're tired from your journey."

"I am," Mary replied.

"As soon as I heard you'd be coming ashore today, I bid Travesty to prepare a fine meal in your honor. I'm very happy you're here, Mary." He looked into her eyes as he handed her onto the bench of his wagon.

"I'm glad to be here, Master Forrester."

"John. Call me John."

"John." The name felt strange on her tongue, but she'd get used to it. *I'm to share my life with this man from this day forward*, Mary thought, still bemused. Nothing seemed quite real, not the tiny settlement that was the heart of the colony nor the man who took his seat on the bench next to her. "Who's Travesty?" she asked. Sometimes focusing on practicalities helped settle the mind.

"Travesty is my indentured servant. She looks after the house and animals, while Simon and I work the plantation. We have a field of maize and a field of tobacco."

"And who is Simon?"

"Simon is also an indenture."

John fell silent. He held the reins loosely in his hands as the horse trotted down a narrow, dusty lane. Mary gazed dispassionately at the fields and dense woods that lined the road. She peered into the distance, hoping to catch a glimpse of anything manmade, but saw nothing on the horizon save a sea of green. Where were all the houses? And the people? Surely there were homesteads at the edge of those fields, and colonists who inhabited them. Master Harrington had mentioned that to date there were nearly one thousand settlers residing in Virginia. Where were they?

"How long have you been here?" Mary asked, desperate to engage John in conversation to distract her mind from her unhappy thoughts.

"Jacob and I came out eight years ago. Jacob was my older brother. He died three years ago of a snake bite," John explained. He looked unbearably sad at the mention of his brother.

"I'm sorry," Mary said. "That must have been very difficult for you."

"It was. After Jacob died, I tried to manage on my own for about a year but soon realized I'd have to get help. It took nearly all my resources to purchase Simon's indenture contract, but Travesty came cheap. I acquired her a year later," he added.

"Have you ever seen any savages?" Mary asked, her voice catching. The women had spent much of their voyage discussing the natives. They had little information to go on, but what they thought they knew had left them trembling with fear.

"I have."

"Are they as fierce and merciless as people claim?"

"They are like nothing and no one I've ever encountered. I've never conversed with one, but they come into Jamestown on occasion, so I've seen them up close."

"They're allowed to just walk in?" Mary gasped, alarmed.

"The colonists wouldn't have survived without trading with the Indians. The natives offered some helpful practical knowledge as well. They might be primitive, but they understand this land in a way we never will. They've lived on it for centuries."

"And Governor Yeardley trusts them?"

John shrugged. "Yeardley is a shrewd fellow. He trusts them as long as they are useful to him, but he'll turn the muskets on them the second they pose a threat."

Mary sighed with relief but then recalled that she would be living on a plantation in the middle of nowhere, vulnerable to attack. "Have they ever come near your plantation?"

"I haven't come face-to-face with any, but I'm sure they have. They consider this their land, and they go where they please," John replied matter-of-factly. He didn't seem particularly worried, or maybe he was feigning indifference for her benefit, so as not to frighten her.

"Do you have a musket?" Mary asked, her voice trembling.

"Of course. Simon has one too. Don't worry, Mary. They've no interest in us. You'll be safe, I promise." John laid a hand over

Mary's and patted it awkwardly. "It will be all right. We will be all right."

Mary nodded. She'd have liked to thank John for reassuring her, but the lump in her throat made it difficult to speak. She was frightened, not only by the prospect of living in such close proximity to Indians, but by the utter lack of civilization that came as a shock despite her best efforts to prepare herself for the primitive conditions of the colony.

EIGHT

Mary's breath caught in her throat as they approached John's plantation. She leaned forward, straining to see her new home. At last, it came into view. The house, or more accurately cabin, was built entirely of wood. It wasn't very large but looked sturdy and well proportioned. There were two outbuildings and a well in the middle of the yard, which was surrounded by a wooden fence.

"That's to keep the larger animals out," John explained as he helped her down from the wagon.

"Larger animals?"

"Like deer. They'll decimate the kitchen garden given the chance."

John led Mary toward the house. The door opened and a woman stepped out onto the narrow porch. She appeared to be a few years older than Mary and was attractive in a lush, overblown sort of way. Whereas Mary was short and thin, the woman was of a goodly height, and had the full breasts and rounded hips men found so appealing. Her hair, which peeked from beneath her linen cap, was very fair, and her eyes large and blue. Despite her smile of welcome, she wore the care-worn expression of someone who'd had much sorrow to contend with.

"Welcome, mistress," she said and bowed her head.

"Thank you. I'm Mary."

"Travesty Brown, ma'am."

Travesty stepped aside and Mary entered the cabin, followed by John. The interior smelled of pine and stewing meat, and Mary's mouth watered with hunger. She hadn't had a home-cooked meal in two months and hadn't eaten anything since a meager breakfast of gruel and ale that morning. Her stomach growled but thankfully not loudly enough for John and Travesty to hear.

Mary looked around. The cabin was divided into two distinct parts. On one side was a quilt-covered bed and a wooden trunk that also served as a nightstand. A pewter candlestick and some personal items rested on the lid. On the opposite side was the hearth, a table and two benches, and a shelf that held cooking utensils and jars. In the center, effectively dividing the cabin in two, was a ladder that provided access to a loft.

There were two windows, both facing the front of the cabin, that were outfitted with a length of rolled-up leather that could be lowered to cover the window. There were also wooden shutters that could be inserted during cold and inclement weather, but at the moment, they rested against the wall. The cabin was clean and tidy, and very cozy.

"John, it's wonderful," Mary said and meant it.

"I'm glad you like it. Mary, I must go out for a time. Simon's been in the fields on his own since morning, and he'll be needing my help. Travesty will help you settle in, and once Simon and I return, we'll all sup together to celebrate your arrival."

Mary's face heated with embarrassment and she stared at the tips of her shoes. "I don't have anything but the clothes I stand up in. Not much settling in required."

John smiled and walked over to the chest. He removed the items from the lid and opened it, taking out a length of russet-colored cloth. "When I learned I was to finally have a wife, I purchased this in anticipation. Please accept it as a wedding gift.

There should be enough here for a new gown, and there's some linen as well, for a new undergarment."

"Oh, John, thank you," Mary cried. "I'm afraid I don't have a wedding gift for you."

"You being here is gift enough."

John handed her the cloth, kissed her chastely on the forehead, and left. Mary fingered the cloth. It was finely woven and thick, the type of cloth that would wear well and stand up to repeated washing. And the russet would go well with her own coloring. Her chestnut hair and blue eyes weren't enhanced by drab colors—not that she'd ever been given a choice in the past. Her faded blue skirt and brown bodice were hand-me-downs from Agnes, and much worn.

"You must be hungry," Travesty said. "I'm making stew for supper, but there's bread, butter, and fresh milk to tide you over."

"Yes, thank you. I am hungry. I haven't had a proper meal since I left England."

Travesty nodded, possibly recalling her own voyage across the Atlantic. "Come and sit down, then."

"Won't you join me?" Mary asked. She wasn't at all sure how one was supposed to treat an indentured servant, but she was grateful Travesty was there. To have another woman to talk to was more than she could have hoped for. With John and Simon out in the fields all day, the cabin would get lonely, and she expected the only time she'd see other settlers would be when they went to church on Sunday. Mary hoped she'd have a chance to see the women she'd arrived with, particularly Nell and Betsy, and hear about their homecoming.

"Thank you, ma'am," Travesty said. She poured two cups of milk, put out a dish of butter, and set a pan filled with something round and yellow on the table. The contents smelled unfamiliar, and a little sweet. Travesty cut two thick slices and put one on a plate for Mary.

"Thank you, but what is that?"

"It's bread made of maize. Or cornbread, as some like to call it. It's very tasty once you get used to it."

Mary broke off a piece and put in into her mouth. The bread was grainy and crumbled on her tongue, but it had a pleasant, if unfamiliar, flavor.

"Do you like it? It tastes better with butter."

Mary buttered her slice and took a good bite. "Yes, I like it," she declared. "I do believe this is the first time I've tasted something new."

"Enjoy it, then. I daresay you'll be experiencing many new things in this foreign land."

Mary longed to ask Travesty all kinds of questions but didn't wish to put the woman off with her prying. They'd talk more in time, but for now, she had other concerns.

"Travesty, I'd like to wash my clothes. The quartermaster allowed us some water for washing, but there wasn't enough left to wash my gown and it's terribly soiled."

"Well, there's an easy enough way to fix that. There's a creek 'bout a quarter mile from here. We go there to bathe, and to wash our things when weather permits. You can see to your needs, and I will wash out your gown. It'll dry by the time the master returns."

"Will it really?" At home, it took days to dry anything. Clothes either steamed dry in front of the fire or were hung outside, but were still damp by the time Mary brought them in.

"Oh, yes," Travesty replied. "The sun is that much hotter here than it was back home," she said wistfully. "'Tis my second summer here, and I still can't get accustomed to the infernal heat."

Mary finished her meal and got up from the table, ready to follow Travesty to the creek, but Travesty wasn't ready to go. She covered the butter dish, stowed away the jug of milk on a shelf, then brushed the crumbs off the table and wiped the plates with a rag, setting them on the shelf next to the milk. Mary liked Travesty's diligence and wondered if she should have offered to help her tidy up. Travesty didn't seem to expect it, so Mary waited patiently until Travesty finished what she was doing. Travesty was about to follow Mary out the door when she remembered something and turned back to grab a cake of soap and slip it into the pocket of her apron.

They walked down a narrow footpath that led toward dense woods. Mary hung back, suddenly frightened, but Travesty's step was confident and brisk. They walked in single file until the woods gave way to a clearing, where a creek flowed merrily between grass-covered banks dappled by golden sunlight.

"Shall I wash your shift?" Travesty asked as she knelt by the water's edge. "I always wash mine while I bathe."

Mary's shift was damp with sweat after the hot ride to the plantation, but she couldn't remove it in front of Travesty and allow the other woman to see her nakedness. It wouldn't be proper, so Mary shook her head. "I'll keep it on."

"All right. Suit yourself," Travesty replied. Mary peered at her. Did Travesty regularly bathe in the creek naked? Surely, she wouldn't risk it with two single men nearby. Mary couldn't help but wonder how she'd managed all this time. She was a beautiful woman, and still young. Surely the men were well aware of her charms. How had they resisted falling into sin? Or had they?

Mary stepped into the water. At first, it seemed too cold, but after a few moments, it became deliciously refreshing. Mary dipped down and wet her hair. It wasn't as greasy and lank as it had been after months on board, but it could use a proper wash now that she had an unlimited supply of clean water. Mary lathered it with the coarse soap Travesty had given her and rinsed it out twice.

Having finished bathing, she came out and sat down on the grassy bank. A gentle breeze caressed her face and she felt pleasantly cool in her wet shift. She took a deep breath. This place even smelled different from England. There was an underlying hint of rich earth beneath the fecund smell of sun-warmed vegetation. The air was heavier too somehow, moister, and the sun hotter, even in the shade.

"Does it get much hotter than this?" she asked Travesty, who'd finished washing out the skirt and bodice and hung them on a low branch to dry.

"Oh yes. July and August can be brutal. There are days when there isn't a breath of air, just relentless heat."

"Do you miss home, Travesty?"

Travesty's gaze slid away from Mary, her eyes fixed on the opposite bank. "At times."

"Where are you from?"

"London."

Mary remained silent, hoping Travesty would reveal more details of her previous life, but the older woman grew quiet and pensive. *All in good time*, Mary told herself.

"Thank you for washing my things," Mary said. "I was afraid John would take one look at me and send me packing."

"Any woman who comes to these shores is welcomed and valued, even the likes of me."

Mary nodded in acknowledgment, unsure what to say. Travesty was comely, but the wariness in her narrowed gaze and the stern line of her mouth were impossible to hide. Mary wondered if there was a story behind her unflattering name but didn't ask for fear of being impertinent.

After sitting in companionable silence until Mary's clothes were dry enough to wear, they made their way back to the cabin.

"Perhaps you'd like to rest for a bit," Travesty suggested once they were indoors.

"Is there nothing I can help you with?"

"You'll have your hands full soon enough, mistress. Lay down your head. Today is your wedding day."

The words startled Mary. She'd quite forgotten she had been wed only hours ago. Nothing felt quite real in this green world where there were no signs of human habitation as far as the eye could see. Mary lay down on John's bed and slipped into a fitful sleep, dreaming of churning waves, strange men, and leafy tunnels that led nowhere.

NINE

By the time John and Simon returned from the fields, the glaring light of day had been replaced by the golden haze of early evening, and the heat had subsided somewhat, making the inside of the cabin more comfortable. Outside, the night was alive with the trilling of birds and the chirping of insects.

Mary had modestly pinned up her hair, not wishing to look wanton in front of her new husband, but left the cap off. It was her wedding day, after all, so she'd allow herself this one vanity. Travesty, who looked downright sullen, had supper ready and the appetizing aroma of meat made Mary's mouth water with anticipation. She was surprised to see another pan of cornbread appear on the table.

"Is there no regular bread?" she asked Travesty, wondering if John was partial to maize.

"There's not much wheat grown here in the colony," Travesty replied. "We must make do with what we have, and what we have is corn. We're lucky to have a cow," she added as she set the table with wooden bowls and spoons. "There's some as don't have a cow or a goat, so can't make butter or cheese."

"Is there a market?" Mary asked.

Travesty scoffed at Mary's naïveté but schooled her face in an expression of patience before replying. "'Tis not like home here, mistress. There's no market day, as such. Most goods come to us by ship. Those who can afford it buy what they require; others do without." It was clear from Travesty's aggrieved tone that she was one of those used to doing without.

"What do the ships bring?"

"Cloth, tools, items of furniture, foodstuffs, and livestock."

"Are there any dogs in the colony?"

At that, Travesty laughed out loud. "What a question!" She shook her head, still chuckling. "No, there are no dogs. The closest thing to dogs out here is wolves."

Mary was about to ask more questions when the door opened, and John walked in. His hair was dripping wet and his shirt was damp, so he must have washed his hands and face before coming into the house. His boots were covered with mud, and he trailed dirt onto the scrubbed wooden floor.

Mary glanced at Travesty, who stood by the hearth, hands on hips, scowling in John's direction. John had the decency to look shamefaced but didn't apologize to Travesty for mucking up her clean floor. Instead, he smiled at Mary and bowed from the neck, acknowledging her as the mistress of the house.

Mary glanced over his shoulder, her attention directed to the man walking behind him, who could only be Simon. He stood about a head taller than John and looked to be in his mid-twenties. He was a well-made man whose mane of tawny hair fell in gentle waves around his face. His thickly lashed eyes were the color of the sky on a clear summer's day, and his fair skin glowed as if kissed by the sun. He wore no beard, so Mary got a good look at his full lips and strong jaw. Her breath caught in her throat. Simon was the handsomest man she'd ever seen, and judging by the glint of amusement in his eyes, he was well aware of his effect on her.

"Welcome, Mistress Forrester," Simon said as he bowed formally to her. "I wish you and the master much joy in your life together."

"Thank you, Master, eh..."

"Faraday. Simon Faraday."

"Master Faraday," Mary repeated. She knew she should look away, but her gaze remained glued to the beautiful man who towered over her. Heat flooded her cheeks, and a smug smile tugged at the corners of his mouth, but he instantly looked away, focusing on Travesty instead.

"That smells divine, Travesty. I hope there's enough for second helpings."

"There's plenty. I'd never let you go hungry," Travesty rebuked him. She didn't seem at all impressed by Simon's good looks. If anything, she seemed annoyed. She sucked in her breath loudly, as if barely managing to suppress her irritation. Perhaps she was still angry about the floor.

The men took their seats at the table, leaving Mary standing awkwardly by, unsure what she should do as the mistress of the house. Travesty preempted her offer of help by asking, "Shall I serve now, mistress?"

"Eh... of course," Mary replied.

"You'd best sit down, then," Travesty said as she ladled stew into bowls and set them on the table, serving John first. She pushed a bowl in front of Mary, then served herself. Travesty took a seat next to Simon but left enough room between them to make sure their elbows never touched, even by accident. Her lip was curled with distaste, which seemed to amuse Simon.

John waited for her to settle down before saying, "Travesty, in the future, you'll serve Mistress Forrester before serving Simon."

"Of course. Sorry, sir. I meant no offense," Travesty muttered.

"None was taken," John replied smoothly. He clasped his hands in front of him and bowed his head, waiting to speak until the rest of them followed suit.

After a brief grace, Travesty poured everyone a cup of ale, making sure to fill Mary's cup before Simon's, while John divided the cornbread into four shares and handed everyone their piece. Mary watched with interest as the men crumbled their bread into the stew and did the same. The sweetness of the cornbread offset the savory richness of the meat, creating a flavor unlike any she'd experienced before.

"Not bad, eh?" Simon asked her. He grinned at her in a way that was entirely too familiar, but John didn't seem to mind, or notice. He ate heartily, enjoying the food and the company. They talked of the farm, the happenings in Jamestown, and the newly arrived ship.

"I'll go into Jamestown on Friday," John said.

"Wait a few days, John," Simon replied. He took a deep pull of ale, his gaze settling on Mary for just a moment before sliding toward John. "Give them time to unload. You know they always take off the foodstuffs first."

"By the time they fully unload, all the tools will be gone. We need a new scythe."

"Can't Will Garrity fix the one that's broken?"

"I don't believe so. The blade's rusted through." John set down his spoon and looked at Mary, his gaze thoughtful. "Would you like to come into town with me, Mary?"

"Oh yes. Thank you, John, I'd love to. Perhaps I'll see some of the women from the ship."

"I saw you talking to the redheaded lass. She wed Thomas Kirby. His plantation is adjacent to mine. Ours," John amended with a shy smile.

"Is it really? But I haven't seen any other houses."

"It's about two miles south of here." John made a gesture with his hand, pointing toward the Kirby property.

"That's not very far," Mary said, wondering if John would object to her visiting Nell.

"Travesty, do we have any strawberry jam left?" John asked.

"You make strawberry jam?" Mary gaped. She'd never tried it but imagined it to be a decadent treat.

"There are wild strawberries in the woods," Travesty replied. "I pick them when they're in season and make jam. 'Tis a lovely thing in the dead of winter to have a taste of summer on your tongue. I have one jar left."

"Well, why don't you accompany the mistress to the Kirby plantation one of these days and bring them the jam as a wedding gift? No harm in being neighborly, is there?" John asked, giving Mary an indulgent smile. "Would you like that, Mary?"

"Yes. Thank you, John. I would love to see Nell."

"It's settled, then. And, Travesty, maybe you can show Mary where to pick the berries. Sounds like she likes jam."

Mary felt a pleasant warmth spread through her belly. John wasn't nearly as handsome as Simon, but he was kind and considerate, a rare quality in a husband, by all accounts. And the promise of seeing Nell made her feel less alone in a place where she was still a stranger. They'd have much to talk about, but the visit would be made uncomfortable by Travesty's presence. She'd have to find a way to discourage her from coming along. She didn't expect it would be too hard. Travesty didn't strike her as the visiting type.

After supper, Travesty quickly cleared up and climbed up to the loft after wishing them a good night, and Simon retreated to the barn, where he slept, leaving the newlyweds alone. Mary stood awkwardly in the middle of the room, her gaze glued to the floor, unsure what to do.

"Shall we go to bed?" John asked.

Mary nodded. Now that the moment was upon her, she felt nervous and self-conscious. Did he expect her to disrobe in front of him? John noticed her discomfort and turned his back, giving her a little privacy. Mary quickly undressed and climbed into bed, taking the side closest to the wall.

John removed his breeches and hose but left his now-dry shirt on, and climbed in next to her. He blew out the candle, but left the leather blind open, allowing a fresh breeze and a beam of silver moonlight to stream into the room.

The night was full of unfamiliar sounds and scents. In Plymouth, the smell of the sea laced with the stink of rotting fish and spilled ale wafting up from the taproom was a constant companion. The mattress she'd shared with her cousins stank of dried urine, stale sweat, and unwashed hair.

Mary closed her eyes and inhaled deeply. The night air smelled of something sweet and fragrant, like honeysuckle, and the linen on John's bed must have been freshly laundered and aired. The man next to her smelled of musk, hot sun, and tobacco smoke, not an entirely unpleasant combination.

When John's hand slid beneath the coverlet, Mary braced herself for his touch, but he reached for himself instead. She lay still, staring at the ceiling as John stroked himself, his breath growing more ragged by the minute. His eyes were closed, but his face was tense with concentration, and he grimaced as if in pain. Mary peered at him from beneath her lashes. What was she to do, pretend to go to sleep, offer to assist him, or just lie there quietly until he finished whatever he was doing?

Just when she thought he wasn't going to touch her at all, John rolled on top of her, pushed up her shift and positioned himself between her legs. She tried not to squirm as he attempted to penetrate her. It took a few tries, but eventually she felt the length of him inside her. It was intrusive and uncomfortable, especially once he began moving in a sort of rhythm, but the act was over before she had time to reconcile herself to what was happening. She felt an unfamiliar wetness between her legs once John finished and withdrew. He looked like he was about to say something but seemed to change his mind. He gave her a chaste peck on the lips instead, then rolled onto his back, closed his eyes, and was asleep in moments, his breathing even and his face relaxed.

Mary stared at her new husband, her eyes filling with tears of disappointment. She had no experience of men, had never even been properly kissed, but although John hadn't hurt her, their coupling seemed entirely devoid of any feeling. John hadn't kissed her or even looked at her. The men at the tavern always made lewd comments when she served them, their suggestions growing bawdier as drink loosened their tongues. The things they'd said had made her blush, but she knew the sentiments were based on experience. There was one man in particular who came in nearly every night. He'd followed Mary outside one night, pinning her against the wall of the tavern, his hot breath on her neck.

"I'd like to suckle those lovely breasts," he'd panted as he ground his swollen cock against her belly. "And then I'd like to stick my tongue inside your wet cunny and taste just how much you want me."

Mary had kneed him in the groin and fled, but the images he'd planted in her mind had stayed with her for a long time afterward. Did men really do such things? She thought not. Lust was a sin, and married couples were supposed to lie together only for the procreation of children, but those drunken words had stirred something inside Mary. Not until tonight, when she'd felt Simon's warm gaze upon her, had she thought she'd enjoy any man touching her in such a familiar fashion.

She closed her eyes and imagined Simon lying next to her, his body long and hard, his hands warm and unchecked as he explored her body. Mary felt an odd tingling in her private parts as she imagined Simon's head bent to her breast, his soft lips sucking her nipple. She slid further away from John and pressed herself against the wall. Her momentary arousal was quickly replaced with shame, her mind furiously chastising her for her ungodly thoughts. John was her husband, for better or worse, and she'd think of no other.

Mary looked at John, whose face was silvered by moonlight. The hollows of his cheeks were lost in shadow, and his lashes fanned out against his pale skin, making him look vulnerable. Mary had to assume that he hadn't been with a woman since coming to Virginia, and possibly not even before then. He was unused to female company and ignorant of the desires of a female body. They were strangers to each other. What affection could there be between them? They had a lifetime to nurture their bond and learn about physical love. Tomorrow would be a new day, a day in which she'd begin learning how to be a dutiful wife to John Forrester.

TEN

JANUARY 2015

London, England

Quinn set aside the comb with a sigh of frustration. She was eager to discover what had happened to Mary, but the vision became blurred around the edges, a sure sign that Quinn's mind wasn't truly in the past. This happened rarely but was a clear indication that she should wait to return to Mary's story until she was ready to give it her full attention.

At present, her thoughts were firmly rooted in the here and now. She glanced at her watch. Rhys had left for Afghanistan only that morning. It had taken over a week to get his press pass in order, obtain a visa and a yellow fever certificate from the National Travel Health Network, and find an available flight. Rhys had upgraded his mobile plan, so his phone would work in Afghanistan and he could keep in touch with Quinn and his office, but had warned Quinn that he wouldn't be checking in daily.

"I'll ring you when I've got something to tell you," Rhys had said. "So, don't fret if you don't hear from me right away. Just concentrate on doing your job. I expect to be presented with a riveting story when I get back." He'd smiled, his eyes warm with affection. "Quinn, I'll do everything in my power to find Jo. I promise."

Quinn had nodded, unable to reply due to the lump in her throat. She still couldn't quite believe Rhys was doing this for her, and felt a mixture of gratitude, guilt, and impatience. She knew it would take time to locate Jo, just as she knew that every day would be an agony of frustrated anticipation until she finally heard something definitive from Rhys.

"Don't do anything foolish," she'd said once she was sure she could speak without bursting into tears.

"I never do anything foolish," Rhys had replied, grinning.

"You just keep telling yourself that."

"I do. Every day." Rhys had kissed her on the forehead in a fatherly fashion and promised to stay in touch.

Rhys must have landed by now, Quinn thought as she headed into the kitchen to start on dinner. Emma and Gabe would be home soon. Emma had requested shepherd's pie, one of her all-time favorites, and Quinn would serve it with a side of broccoli, a vegetable Emma didn't completely despise. Quinn had prepared the ingredients for the pie earlier in the day while Alex napped, and took them out of the refrigerator now that she was ready to prepare the dish. She layered the sautéed ground beef, vegetables, and mashed potatoes in a pan, sprinkled the finished product with shredded cheese, and pushed the pan into the oven. By the time they were ready to eat, the pie would be done, its crusty top smothered with a golden layer of melted cheese. Delicious, and so easy. Quinn smiled to herself. She was really getting a handle on this mothering thing, she decided.

She had just started setting the table when she heard Gabe's key in the lock, followed by Emma's angry voice and the slam of her bedroom door. Quinn abandoned her task and stepped out into the corridor, ready to play the role of peacemaker. Gabe shrugged off his coat and rolled his eyes in exasperation before drawing Quinn into a hug and resting his chin atop her head. She could feel the frustration coursing through him and held him silently for a moment before her curiosity got the better of her.

"What happened?"

"Emma refused to wear her coat. I told her we wouldn't be going home until she put it on. She held out for about ten minutes, then complied when she realized I'd meant what I said. She wouldn't speak to me the whole way home and tore off the coat as soon as we walked in."

Emma's pink coat lay on the floor by the door, where she'd thrown it in a fit of anger. Quinn shook her head in dismay. "Let me talk to her."

"I think you had better, while I say hello to the child who still likes me."

Quinn knocked on Emma's door and entered without waiting to be invited. Emma was too young to be allowed to refuse her entry. She sat on the bed, looking mutinous. Her arms were crossed in front of her belly and her feet drummed against the wooden bedframe.

"Hi, Emma," Quinn said. "May I sit down?"

"If you want."

"What happened?"

"Dad made me wear that stupid coat," Emma mumbled angrily.

"It's cold outside. He didn't want you to get ill." Emma didn't answer, so Quinn tried another tack. "Do you feel uncomfortable in the coat?"

"You could say that," Emma snapped.

"Is it too small?" The coat was from two years ago and had been purchased by Emma's mother Jenna, before she died. Quinn had thought Emma might want to hold on to it as long as possible, particularly since it still fit, but Emma seemed to have other ideas.

"No, it fits fine."

"What's bothering you, then?" Quinn asked gently.

"Maya said I look like a silly baby in it. It's pink," Emma spat out.

"You used to like pink. And who is Maya?"

"I don't like pink anymore. Pink is for babies. I told you that already. I want a new coat, and Maya is my best friend," Emma added matter-of-factly.

"If she's your friend, she should be nice to you."

"She is. She's trying to help me. Maya knows about clothes. Her mum works for a fashion magazine." Emma gave Quinn's comfortable outfit a pointed stare, clearly implying that knowledge of fashion was not something Quinn would ever be accused of.

Quinn tried to suppress a smile. "And what color coat would you like?"

"Black."

"That's awfully morbid, isn't it?" Quinn asked, belatedly realizing that Emma would have no idea what the word meant.

"You have a black coat," Emma challenged her.

"I'm a grown-up; you're five."

"So, it's all right for me to be laughed at?" Emma demanded.

"Would you like me to call the school and speak to your teacher? Maya has no right to laugh at you."

"Yes, she does. She's right, and don't you dare call my teacher. Everyone will know I told on Maya, and they'll never speak to me again," Emma bristled.

"I see. All right. I won't call the school if you don't want me to. How about we go shopping this weekend and find you a more appropriate coat? Maybe a blue one to match your pretty eyes?"

Emma thought about this for a moment. "I won't wear the pink one ever again."

"You'll have to wear it until we buy a new one. It's too cold to go without."

"No! I'd rather freeze."

Quinn tried to rein in her frustration. "All right, how about we find a coat online? We can have it delivered by tomorrow. What do you say?"

"Really?"

"Really. You'll have to wear the pink coat for only one more day."

Emma considered this for a moment. "Fine, but I will take off the coat before we walk into the school and put it on again after we leave the building. I don't want anyone to see me."

"You'll be cold without a coat during recess."

"I'll ask to stay inside," Emma retorted.

"All right. I'll tell Daddy, and he will allow you to take the coat off just before you walk in."

Emma nodded, mollified. "Dinner smells good," she said.

"Why don't you change into something more comfortable and wash your hands," Quinn suggested.

"Can we look for a new coat after we eat?" Emma asked as she slid off the bed.

"Yes."

"What's got into her?" Gabe asked when Quinn returned to the kitchen. He was sitting at the table, holding Alex, who was eyeing the cutlery with interest.

"Maya, who happens to be Emma's new best friend, thinks pink is not an acceptable color choice."

"Do you think Emma's being bullied?" Gabe asked.

"I don't think it's bullying, per se, but I do think there will always be children who'll make others feel insecure. Have you seen some of the girls in her class? They look like they're five going on fifteen. Last time I dropped Emma off, one girl was wearing lip gloss and nail varnish, the same shade as her mother's."

"Yes, I've noticed that. Why would parents allow that?" Gabe asked, looking perplexed.

"Parenting has changed dramatically over the years. People are a lot more permissive these days. They don't like to upset their kids."

Gabe looked up at her, his gaze clouded with confusion. "Isn't parenting by definition upsetting kids and getting them to do things they don't want to do?"

"Not anymore, it seems. It might be a good idea to invest in some parenting manuals and maybe find a parenting group for me to join. Emma loves me, I think, but the fact that I'm not her biological mother will come up in every argument, especially once she gets older."

"I hope not. You are her mother now, biological or not. You love her."

"I do, but she'll forget that the moment I do something to displease her," Quinn argued.

"She was very angry with me, and I *am* her biological father," Gabe replied. He smiled wistfully. "My father would have made me apologize, then send me to my room without dinner. He was a great disciplinarian. Of course, my mother would then sneak up to my room and bring me a sandwich," Gabe said. His eyes misted with tears. "I miss my dad."

"I know you do. I miss him too."

"Who do you miss?" Emma asked as she sauntered into the kitchen, her anger forgotten. She'd got her way, and her glee was evident.

"Grandpa Graeme," Gabe replied. "He was hard on me at times, but I loved him, and I miss him very much."

"He would have liked Rufus," Emma said as she took her seat at the table.

"Yes, he would have," Quinn said. She reached for Alex and lifted him off Gabe's lap. "It's off to the playpen with you, young sir."

Alex grinned happily, unaware that he was being banished to the other room for the duration of the meal.

"Anything from Rhys?" Gabe asked as he served Emma a piece of steaming pie.

"Not yet. I should have never allowed him to go," Quinn replied.

"He doesn't need your permission," Gabe reminded her gently. "He's a grown man, Quinn, and I think he was looking for a reason to take a break from his life for a short while. This might be just what he needs to recover from his loss."

"I hope you're right." Quinn swallowed a forkful of shepherd's pie but barely tasted it. Rhys had been gone for less than a day, and already she felt a knot of anxiety tightening in her belly. She hoped she'd hear from him soon.

Gabe laid a hand over hers, smiling into her eyes. "Prudence, Quinn," he said gently.

Quinn rolled her eyes in response, making him laugh. They had both been doing a lot of that lately.

ELEVEN

JANUARY 2015

Kabul, Afghanistan

Rhys had expected dry, dusty heat to envelop him as soon as he walked out of the airport, but instead he was met with a chill worthy of England. The sun shone brightly—not something he was used to in January—but gave no warmth. The nearby snow-capped mountains were dun-colored with an occasional smudge of green where vegetation had managed to force its way through the cracks and take root.

Rhys looked around, suddenly overwhelmed by the task at hand. He was a storyteller, a producer, not an investigative reporter. He hated the idea of letting Quinn down, but maybe his offer to come in search of Jo Turing had been too impulsive, made by a man who'd recently suffered a trauma and wasn't thinking rationally.

"Rhys! Over here, mate!" Rob Malone called out to him as he pulled up in a dirt-splattered Jeep. "Sorry I'm late. There was a roadblock."

Rhys tossed his case into the back seat and climbed in next to Rob.

"Where to?" Rob asked as he joined a queue of cars waiting to exit the car park.

"The Mustafa Hotel," Rhys replied.

"Okay," Rob replied, grinning. "It's good to see you, Rhys. It's been—what—five years or more?"

"About that," Rhys replied as he looked around, eager for his first glimpse of Kabul.

"I heard you're getting married," Rob said as he turned onto a central road congested with traffic. He pressed on his horn, and its blare startled Rhys out of his reverie.

"Not anymore." Rob looked like he was about to ask more questions, but Rhys cut him off, desperate to change the subject. "How's the family?"

"My brood is fine. My oldest is graduating uni come June, and my little one just started primary school. She's not best pleased she has to go to a school where her mum's a teacher."

"When are you going home?"

"Soon. Colleen will divorce me if I don't show my face at home once every few months."

"I thought divorce wasn't an option," Rhys joked, referring to Rob's staunch Catholic beliefs, of which he made no secret.

"She'll get a papal dispensation," Rob said. "She's like that, my Colleen," he added with an affectionate grin.

"Can't say I blame her."

"She can see my ugly mug on the news if she misses me," Rob joked. "All she does is berate me when I'm at home anyway. I'm nothing but an inconsiderate eejit, by all accounts, and a useless da. I tell you, Rhys, being a father to four lasses is no walk in the park. Every time I come home, I have to get to know those girls all over again. I love them to bits, but I don't get them, especially the older two. The younger ones just want a cuddle and a present, but Bethan and Aislinn are a mystery to me. Now, it's all makeup, and parties, and lads. They listen to music I can't relate to and talk in slang that sounds like a foreign tongue to an old paddy like me. At least with a son, I'd be able to talk football and rugby."

"It's not too late," Rhys replied, chuckling.

"I'm too old for babies. Besides, I'm sure an old pro like you has heard of the luck of the Irish. I'd have another girl for sure, maybe even twin girls just to hammer that nail deeper into the coffin. No, I'm done. Maybe, in time, I'll have a grandson. That'll be fun."

"I wouldn't mind twin girls," Rhys said, his voice too soft for Rob to hear. He had no desire to share his pain with anyone, least of all someone like Rob Malone, who took his beautiful family for granted and spent at least six months out of the year away from them.

"You know, Rhys, if I was a more curious type of bloke, I would ask you why you've come into a war zone to search for a woman you barely know."

"Good thing you're not, then," Rhys snapped. He was annoyed with Rob for prying, but more so for asking the question he'd been asking himself since he left Quinn's flat the night he volunteered to come on this lunatic mission. Why was he really here? Was it to redeem himself in some way or to get out of his comfort zone and remind himself that his problems were nothing compared to those of people who lived with oppression, death, and destruction every single day?

Rhys looked around with interest as they drove into Kabul. The traffic moved very slowly, the street congested with all sorts of vehicles, many of them military. The streets were thronged with people, mostly men, Rhys noted, who wore their traditional clothing and seemed to just be milling about rather than going somewhere. Given the hour, he'd expected most people to be engaged in some sort of work, but these men seemed to have nothing to do other than watch the passing cars and talk amongst themselves.

Several women walked by, wearing colorful dresses and headscarves, and children of various ages darted from place to place, their eyes too knowing for such young faces. Stands lined the road, where young men sold fruit and other types of food, and Rhys watched as two women dressed in burkas approached a stand and made a purchase after several minutes of haggling with the seller.

"I hadn't expected it to be so crowded," Rhys remarked as they inched forward.

"It's a city of six million," Rob replied. He looked tense and his eyes kept darting around the perimeter.

"Why the holdup?" Rhys asked. "Was there a road accident?"

"We're approaching a checkpoint," Rob explained. "There are many set up on roads leading into the city."

"What are they checking for?" Rhys asked, feeling awfully naïve. He was known for his meticulous preparation when working on a program, but he hadn't spent nearly enough time reading up on Kabul.

"Explosives. The checkpoints are a way to minimize suicide bombings within the city. Problem is, if they stop someone who's actually a bomber, he'll blow himself up right at the checkpoint rather than allow himself to be taken into custody."

"You mean we're sitting ducks?" Rhys asked, the magnitude of what he'd done finally beginning to sink in.

"In a sense."

"But what of all these people?" Rhys asked, meaning the Afghans who walked around as if they were taking a stroll through a park.

"They're used to it, and know it can happen anywhere at any time."

"What a way to live," Rhys muttered. "It's little wonder Colleen is threatening to divorce you if you don't come home."

"I'll be all right as long as I leave before the fighting season starts," Rob said as the Jeep finally began to move toward the checkpoint.

"The fighting season?"

"The annual spring offensive launched by the Taliban. It's a prolonged period of mind-blowing violence. If you know what's good for you, you'll be gone by the beginning of March."

Rhys breathed a little easier once they passed the checkpoint and headed into the sprawling center of Kabul. "A shimmering ribbon of progress," Rhys said quietly.

"What's that?"

"It's a line from a program I worked on about the Silk Road," Rhys replied. "It stretched from China to Rome and passed through Afghanistan. All the countries along the road reaped tremendous benefits. The trade brought riches, progress, and cultural diversity."

"Where is it, this road?" Rob asked as he maneuvered the Jeep down a narrow street.

"It wasn't an actual road, it was a series of trade routes used thousands of years ago, before the birth of Christ. In those days, Afghanistan was a rare jewel on a string of gems that was the Silk Road. It was such a desirable location that it drew the attention of the Persians and then Alexander the Great, who conquered it and added it to his empire. He built several cities, all named Alexandria after himself."

"Hmm, I didn't know that," Rob said. "I just assumed this place was always Satan's asshole."

"It was quite beautiful once. There are over one thousand archeological sites in Afghanistan," Rhys added. He wasn't sure why he felt the need to defend this war-torn land and its people's culture, but he suspected it was because he saw with his own eyes how low it had been brought since its days of glory. "This is the only place on earth where you can find lapis lazuli."

"What's that, then?"

"It's a beautiful blue stone that's been highly valued since antiquity. It's very rare."

"There's something else here that's been highly valued since antiquity," Rob replied. "Poppies."

He didn't get a chance to elaborate because they pulled up to the sprawling, outdated edifice of the Mustafa Hotel.

"It's not exactly the Ritz, but it's habitable," Rob said as he parked the Jeep and began walking toward the entrance.

"I'm not here for the amenities."

Rhys checked in and made his way to his room on the second floor. The room was even shabbier than the foyer, with a narrow, lumpy bed and faded curtains the color of rotten apricots. The décor looked as if it hadn't been updated since the 1970s, if the hotel had been around then. Rhys took out his mobile and tapped on his inbox. Nothing happened.

"There's no Wi-Fi in the rooms, but there is an internet café downstairs," Rob said, watching Rhys with a smile of amusement. "I hope you brought a converter to charge your phone."

"Yes, I have one, although I'm not sure my mobile will do me much good."

"You're better off using the landline if you want to call home. The signal is spotty here, because of the mountains."

"Right."

"Well, you must be tired. Shall we have dinner later? This place doesn't look like much, but the food is not half bad."

"Sure. Thanks, Rob."

"Look, Rhys, go easy. All right?" Rob said, his voice low and serious.

"How do you mean?"

"People here don't respond to demands or bullying."

"I wasn't planning on bullying anyone," Rhys replied, surprised Rob would suggest such a thing.

"What I mean is, these are poor folk who don't have much left to lose. If you want something from them, make it worth their while."

"You mean bribe them for information?" Rhys asked, not entirely surprised by Rob's sage advice.

"Not bribe—pay. Think of it as an exchange. You would pay for goods. The information you seek is their only asset. You can't blame them for trying to sell it for the highest price."

"Thanks, Rob. I understand."

"Good man," Rob said and clapped Rhys on the shoulder. "See you at seven?"

TWELVE

Rhys glanced at his watch. He had several hours before he was due to meet Rob, but the first thing he had to do was take a shower. Even his eyeballs felt gritty after the drive in the open Jeep. He grabbed a towel and a change of clothes and walked down the hall to the communal facilities. The bathroom was relatively clean, but he'd seen more luxurious bathrooms in a caravan. He stripped off his clothes, then turned on the water and watched it trickle down, the water pressure barely stronger than that of a melting icicle. *Oh well, when in Rome...*

After his less-than-satisfying shower, Rhys headed down to reception. It was the most natural place to start his inquiries and there was no time like the present. He asked the young man behind the desk for the hotel manager and was met with an expression of pure trepidation.

"It's all right, I'm not here to complain," Rhys reassured the young man. "I need to speak to him regarding a personal matter."

Looking somewhat mollified, the young man picked up the phone and made the call. A few minutes later, a middle-aged man with a luxurious moustache came out of a door behind the reception desk. He wore a black suit, a tie, and a phony smile.

"Good afternoon, sir. I'm Aasif Zahir, manager of this hotel.

How may I be of help?" Rhys saw tension in the man's face despite the smile. Mr. Zahir probably had his hands full with Westerners whose expectations couldn't possibly be met in an establishment like this one.

"Mr. Zahir, my name is Rhys Morgan, and I'm looking for a friend." Rhys extracted a photograph of Jo from his shirt pocket. "She stayed at this hotel until sometime in December, I believe. Then all communication ceased."

Mr. Zahir tried to keep his expression bland as he looked at the photograph, but Rhys saw a spark of recognition in his dark eyes. The man raised his gaze to Rhys's face and studied him for a moment, as if deciding whether to tell him the truth, before answering.

"Yes, Miss Turing stayed here for some time. She went out one day in December and did not return."

"Do you still have her possessions?" Rhys asked.

"I can't show you her things, Mr. Morgan. They're private."

"Mr. Zahir, I'm not here to steal her laptop or riffle through her knickers. I'm simply searching for clues as to where she might have gone so I can try to find her. Please, let me see her belongings. You can stay and observe me to make sure I don't take anything," Rhys added, hoping this made him sound transparent. He didn't bother to berate the man for not calling the authorities. Mr. Zahir didn't seem to want to involve himself in Jo's disappearance and clearly didn't see the whereabouts or well-being of the guests as his responsibility once they left the hotel.

"All right," the manager said with a sigh. "Follow me."

Rhys followed Mr. Zahir into a windowless room at the back of the hotel. Rows of metal shelves filled the space. Some were empty, but most held suitcases, items of clothing, books, tablets, and even laptops. There were cardboard boxes filled with mobile phones, sunglasses, and coins. Mr. Zahir led Rhys down a long row toward a shelf where he pointed to a nondescript case. The tag read Jo TURING.

Rhys took down the case, set it on the floor, and opened it.

Inside were Jo's clothes, haphazardly packed by some maid who'd been ordered to clear the room, a paperback copy of *A Tale of Two Cities*, toiletries, and shoes. In one of the zippered compartments, Rhys found her passport and a small notepad. He took out the notepad and flipped through the pages, which were covered with scribbled words, fragments of sentences, and numbers. One of the pages read, "See Ahmad Khan." The name was doubly underlined.

"Do you know who this Ahmad Khan might be?" Rhys asked the manager, who looked as if he'd just swallowed a spoonful of acid.

"He's one of the waiters. I don't know what she wanted with him. He's a good boy."

"Is he here now?"

Mr. Zahir shook his head. "He'll come at six for the dinner shift. He won't be able to help you."

"I only want to ask him some questions. I'm not here to lay blame, Mr. Zahir. I only want to find my friend," Rhys reiterated. He couldn't blame Mr. Zahir for being fearful. This wasn't London or New York; this was Kabul, a city that had been torn apart by conflict, invaded, and plundered by various foreign armies for longer than a millennium. Mr. Zahir had to tread carefully if he wished to keep his job and support his family. Rhys briefly wondered if Mr. Zahir was in any way related to General Zahir, who'd been the chief of police until his recent resignation. Most likely not. Zahir was a name common to the region.

"Will you be in your room at six?" the manager asked. "I'll send Ahmad to see you. Mr. Morgan, Ahmad's family relies on his job to survive," he added, his tone sharp.

"I understand, Mr. Zahir."

Rhys followed the manager out of the claustrophobic room and returned to his own. He sat on the bed and stared out the window. The golden glow of a winter afternoon had turned to the gentle lavender of twilight that made the previously dull-looking mountains suddenly appear picturesque. Calls to evening prayer blended with the cacophony of traffic. The room was too stuffy, and the bed too hard, but Rhys wasn't in Kabul for a holiday. He reclined on the bed and folded his arms, lacing his fingers behind his head. He had about an hour before the waiter arrived, so he allowed his eyes to close, overcome by jet lag and a feeling of hopelessness.

THIRTEEN
JANUARY 2015

London, England

Quinn pushed open the door to the mortuary and the familiar smells of carbolic, formaldehyde, and death assaulted her. Through the Plexiglas window on her right, she saw a body covered with a green hospital sheet lying on the slab, awaiting its appointment with Dr. Scott's scalpel. Neither Colin nor his assistant, Dr. Dhawan, were in the lab.

Quinn walked down the corridor until she reached Colin's office. He was at his desk, his gaze fixed on the computer screen as he typed rapidly. His hair was gathered into a messy man-bun and a surgical mask hung around his neck, like a droopy necklace.

He glanced up and smiled. "Quinn, come in. Lovely to see you. How's the family?"

"They're well, thank you. It's been some time since we've seen you and Logan."

"Logan's been taking extra shifts at the hospital," Colin replied as he finished what he was doing and turned to face Quinn.

"Why?"

"He wants to keep an eye on Jude."

"Is Jude not doing a satisfactory job?" Quinn asked. It didn't require much skill or effort to do the job of a hospital porter, but Jude was a musician and the dull, often-unpleasant job wasn't one he aspired to keep, despite his brother's best efforts at keeping him in line. Jude missed his music and his vagabond lifestyle, two things that inevitably got him into trouble.

"Once an addict, always an addict," Colin replied matter-of-factly. "Jude has been on the straight and narrow for several months now. He's attending his methadone program and keeping clear of his friends, who are enablers one and all, but Logan's afraid he'll slip up if left on his own for too long."

"Do you think he will?" Quinn asked.

"I very much hope he doesn't, but the stats are not in his favor. Most users relapse; it's a sad fact. Jude is too talented, too artistic. He won't last long emptying bedpans and taking out the rubbish. He longs for the adrenaline-fueled high of performing, and he misses his girlfriend. Bridget is not making things easy for him."

"No, I didn't think she would. She does love him, I think," Quinn said. She felt sad for the young couple. They were so attractive, so bright, but neither had been strong enough to turn their back on the seductive embrace of heroine for long.

"She does, but she's not good for him."

Quinn nodded. She wished she could help Jude in some way, but he didn't want her help. Their complicated relationship was made more fragile by the fact that they hadn't shared a childhood as Logan and Jude had done. Jude still saw Quinn as an interloper, someone who didn't quite belong in his family, but he seemed to be coming around to the idea of having a sister.

"Have you seen Sylvia recently? How is she?" Quinn asked. She hadn't seen her birth mother in several weeks, but they'd exchanged a few text messages and phone calls, their conversations centering on safe subjects, such as Alex and Emma, and Quinn's decorating ideas for the new house.

"As well as can be expected," Colin replied. "She's glad Jude is back, and she has him to fuss over. She's driving him mad, of course, but I think he secretly likes it."

Colin reached for the box of latex gloves on his desk and handed Quinn a pair before pulling on his own. "Shall we?" he said as he rose to his feet and led her toward the lab at the end of the corridor. "I must admit, this case has absolutely fascinated me, Quinn. I don't often get emotional over people who died hundreds of year ago, but this poor lass has managed to break through my shield of indifference."

"Yes, I feel the same way."

The two skeletons were laid out on a metal slab, the tiny baby next to its mother. Colin flipped on a switch, and fluorescent light flooded the slab, turning the bones from gray to gleaming white.

"Good morning, Dr. Allenby," Dr. Sarita Dhawan called out as she walked into the lab, a file folder in her hands. Despite her cheerful greeting, she looked upset and tossed down the folder with some force. "I'm afraid I have some bad news, Dr. Scott. The Hawthorne lab's been closed down due to cross-contamination. It might take more than a week for it to reopen," she said with obvious disgust. "I'm sorry, Dr. Allenby, but I don't have the results for you. We'll have to send new samples once the lab reopens, since the ones we sent already are no longer viable."

"It's all right. I can wait," Quinn replied, trying to hide her disappointment. She'd hoped to learn more about Mary and her child, since scientific information went a long way to fleshing out the narrative about the lives of the subjects of *Echoes from the Past*. Quinn could hardly reveal to the world that she saw Mary in her visions. She needed cold, hard facts to validate her story.

"No matter," Colin said as he approached the skeleton. "I can still give you something to go on."

Quinn looked down at the female skeleton. Dr. Dhawan had reconstructed it on the slab, so it was no longer in the position Quinn had found it in upon entering the cave. Looking at it now, she couldn't see any trace of agony in the skeleton's posture or skull. The bones had been cleaned, the blood washed away, and the jaw, which had been opened as if in a scream, had been closed.

The skeleton of the baby now rested next to its mother's arm rather than just below her pelvis, behind her legs.

"So, what can you tell me about her, Colin?" Quinn asked as she reached out and gingerly touched the skeleton's hand.

"We performed all the usual tests, except for DNA sequencing. Since we have viable hair follicles, there's no sense incurring additional expense unless we require more in-depth information. We've also been able to obtain a blood sample from the wood, which should tell us more. I'll have those results for you once the lab is fully operational again," Colin said, smiling apologetically. "In the meantime, I can share my own findings with you, which I stand by one hundred percent."

"I've never questioned your expertise, Colin," Quinn said. "You're the best in your field."

Colin colored with pleasure at the compliment. "Maybe not the best, but I do know my skellies, and this one has lots to tell. Carbon-14 dating shows that she lived in the sixteen hundreds. Early to mid-sixteen hundreds, I think. If you look at the skull, you'll see that the sagittal suture is not fully fused, so she was definitely under the age of thirty-five, and judging by where the ribs join the sternum, I'd put her in her early twenties."

"How can you tell from the sternum?" Quinn asked.

"The sternum is not a weight-bearing bone and is unaffected by childbearing, so it's a fairly accurate marker for age. My estimation is supported by the state of the pelvis. The pubic symphysis is not severely pitted or craggy, confirming that she was fairly young, but there are soft marks on the cartilage that suggest she had given birth. Now, whether she gave birth only to this baby or had experienced birth before is impossible to tell. Given her approximate age and the time she lived in, it's very possible she'd had other children before this one."

Quinn tore her gaze away from the tiny skeleton of the baby. Every time she looked at it, she thought of Alex and how lucky she was to have a healthy baby. Had she lived in an earlier era, Alex surviving the birth or the first year of his life would not be a given.

Even during the reign of Queen Victoria, which wasn't all that long ago, only half the babies born made it to their first birthday, but that didn't guarantee they'd survive into adulthood or even reach the tender age of five.

Oblivious to Quinn's melancholy, Colin went on. "Since there was no cloth to sample or any other material objects, we have to rely on other clues to tell us something of her social background," he said, moving his hand to the skull. He ran his latex-covered finger along the skeleton's teeth.

"Her teeth are somewhat worn, but not enough to suggest she suffered long periods of hunger. I do believe her diet wasn't extremely varied, which suggests that she didn't come from the upper classes. That theory is supported by the ridges on her wrists. This woman worked with her hands. These types of ridges can be found in most women of that historical period, since everything was done by hand, from kneading dough to sewing to milking cows. Even fetching water from the well would leave its mark."

"So, she fell somewhere between a beggar and a lady," Quinn concluded.

"Exactly so. Now for the baby." Colin sighed, betraying his own sadness. "I can't say with any certainty if the child was alive at the time of the birth, but the mother definitely was. Given the amount of blood and her position in the coffin, I'd say this poor woman went into labor after being interred. I've seen coffin births where the mother died while heavily pregnant and the gasses that built up during decomposition forced out the lifeless child, but this is not one of those cases. She definitely lived through all or part of the labor. Poor soul," Colin said. He patted her skull affectionately, as if the gesture could somehow soothe her.

"Is there anything you can tell me about the baby?" Quinn asked.

"I've compared the length of the bones to markers for the sixteen hundreds, and I believe the child was full term. I can't determine its gender just by examining the skeleton, but I think we'll get more information from the DNA results. Believe it or not,

I was able to collect a few hairs that must have belonged to the baby. Had the coffin been buried in earth, the fine baby hair wouldn't have survived, but because the coffin was in the cave, which had its own microclimate, some DNA information survived. It's fascinating, really," Colin exclaimed as he looked down at mother and child. "I wonder why her coffin was left in that cave. Doesn't make any sense."

"No, it doesn't," Quinn agreed. "If someone laid her in a coffin, it stands to reason they meant to bury her. If she'd been marked as a suicide or a heretic, she would have been buried at the crossroads with a stake through her heart. It's almost as if someone wished to hide the fact that she died."

"I think that might have something to do with the gaping hole in her head," Colin said. "There are some who would view what was done to this woman as murder. Not only had someone trepanned her, but they sealed her in a coffin while she still lived, condemning mother and child to death."

"It's savage," Quinn said. She couldn't tear her eyes away from the hole in the top of the skull. "Are you sure this was done intentionally?"

"Oh yes. The edges are too smooth to be the result of an accident or an attack. Had she been bashed over the head, her skull would be cracked, the opening jagged. This is a perfect circle, the result of using a medical tool," Colin said, running his fingers along the edges of the hole. "This was very much intentional."

"Thank you, Colin. Please let me know when you have the DNA results."

"I'll ring you. Quinn, would you and Gabe like to come for dinner one night?" Colin asked. He blushed prettily. "I've been taking French cookery lessons. To relieve stress," he explained. "Dealing with dead people can be murder."

Quinn laughed. "Will you spoil us with escargot and foie gras?"

"I'm not that advanced, but I can offer you onion soup and duck breast in a cherry glaze with rosemary roasted potatoes."

"I'm salivating already," Quinn confessed.

"Good. I'll check with Logan to see when he has a free evening and we'll put something on the calendar."

"I'll look forward to it."

Quinn accepted a file folder with a copy of Colin's findings from Sarita and made for the door. She was grateful Colin hadn't asked about Jo. She hadn't heard from Rhys, and although she knew it was too soon to expect any answers, her heart did a flip every time her mobile rang. The best way to distract herself from worrying about Rhys would be to spend an hour in the seventeenth century, and if she managed to get Alex down for a nap when she got home, that was exactly what she'd do.

FOURTEEN
JUNE 1620

Virginia Colony

Mary sat next to her friend, her back against the rough wooden planks of Nell's new home. The walk had taken close to an hour, but Mary hadn't minded. It was nice to be on her own for a bit and have time to sort through her jumbled thoughts as she followed the narrow dirt road that wound through the woods. At first, she'd been afraid and peered into the dense forest until her head ached, half expecting to see a band of naked savages come swooping down on her, but John had been correct in assuring her she had nothing to fear and no one would harass her. Once again, he'd suggested taking Travesty along, but Mary had explained to him why she preferred to go on her own. She had no wish to have her visit with Nell spoiled by Travesty's sullen demeanor and obvious impatience.

John's irritation with her had been fleeting but evident enough to prevent Mary from pressing her point. She had no experience of John's anger and had no way of knowing if he might forbid her to go altogether or even strike her for defying him. He would be well within his rights, a fact that had registered with Mary only after she'd left the cabin. However, rather than insisting, John had shrugged and said, "Do as you will," and left the cabin without a backward glance. Travesty, who'd come in at that moment carrying a pail of milk, was only too relieved not to have to accompany her mistress and said so.

"I've enough to be getting on with without playing nursemaid," she muttered under her breath.

"Good thing I'm not asking you to, then," Mary retorted, annoyed with Travesty's insolence. She could at least make a pretense of treating Mary as her mistress, and not her equal. "If you'll give me the jar of jam, I'll be on my way."

Travesty silently handed Mary the stone jar, which was heavier than it looked, and went back to the milk, which she was about to pour into the butter churn. Mary stowed the jar in her basket and set off.

Once she got over her initial fear, Mary began to enjoy the walk. It was warmer than she was used to, and she was perspiring freely, but the sun shone brightly out of a cloudless blue sky and the birds sang merrily, making her feel like she wasn't quite alone. There wasn't much to see, save never-ending woods and green fields, but it was still a new experience and Mary relished it. She'd been in Virginia for nearly a week, but her impressions were limited to her first sighting of Jamestown and John's plantation. She hadn't met anyone besides Simon and Travesty, who were still strangers to her, as was her husband, who seemed to hardly notice her now that she was a permanent fixture in his house. Yet, despite the newness of it all, Mary's life in England seemed like a distant dream from a long time ago, so her memory of it was blurred and fragmented.

As Mary walked along, she pondered how it was possible to feel so far removed from something you'd known all your life. How long did it take to adjust to something this foreign and unexpected and come to accept it as one's new home? She supposed she'd find out soon enough. Whether she liked Virginia or not, there was no going back, especially now that she was a married woman. Mary still grappled with that notion, but she reckoned she'd become accustomed to it soon enough. She had no choice. She did look forward to hearing Nell's thoughts on her new life. Nell's comments were always brutally honest but also surprisingly uplifting. She hoped an hour with her friend would help her see her situation in a new light.

"So, how do you find your husband?" Mary asked Nell as she took a sip of cool ale.

"I didn't find him very pleasing at first," Nell replied, wrinkling her nose eloquently. "He'd been on his own too long, poor man. No woman to remind him to bathe or wash his clothes. Or clean his pigsty of a dwelling."

"But you took care of that right quick," Mary replied, smiling at her friend. Nell wasn't one to waste time on diplomacy.

"Oh yes. No one will ever accuse Thomas of being handsome, but he'll be well turned out, or my name isn't Nell Kirby. Lord, it does sound strange when I say it, doesn't it?" Nell asked, referring to her new surname.

"I'm not much used to Forrester yet either," Mary confessed. "Although it's a fine name, to be sure."

"Mistress Forrester does have a nice ring to it. Kirby sounds like a pickle," Nell complained.

Mary giggled. "Mistress Kirby sounds just fine."

"Where was I? Oh yes, I ordered Thomas to take a bath, lopped off half his hair—it was halfway down his back, would you believe it? He likely hadn't bothered to cut it since getting to Virginia—shaved his face, so I could get a proper look at it, and washed and mended his clothes. He's a different man from the one I stood up with in church."

"And do you find him good company?" Mary asked.

Nell shrugged. "I didn't sign on for stimulating company when I agreed to marry a man I'd never so much as set my eyes on. He's not much used to talking, having been on his own for so long, but he's coming 'round. What about your husband?"

"He's very reticent," Mary complained. "At first, I thought it might be just nervousness and the strangeness of it all, but he seems content with the way things are."

"And how are things, exactly?" Nell asked.

"The only time John and I are on our own is when we go to bed, and he's asleep before I so much as wish him good night. At all other times, the two servants are about, and although John likes for them to treat me with the respect due to the mistress of the house, he barely takes notice of me himself."

"Give him time, Mary. He's not much used to having a wife. Try to draw him out," Nell suggested.

"And how do I do that?"

"Get him on his own for a bit. Ask about his life before he came to Virginia, his family. Surely he must miss the people he left behind. Once he gets talking, tell him something of yourself, of who you are. Every relationship needs to start somewhere."

"That's sound advice, Nell. Thank you. And how are the other aspects of married life?" Mary asked, her cheeks flushing with embarrassment.

Nell shrugged. "I wasn't expecting much, so can't say I was disappointed."

"Have you and Toby ever, you know...? Did you know what to expect?"

"Enough to know that big lug wasn't going to know his way around a woman's body," Nell answered, deftly avoiding Mary's question about Toby.

"How could you tell?"

Nell looked at Mary for a long moment, her gaze searching. "You really are an innocent, aren't you? With some men you can just tell. It's the way they look at you, the way they touch you. They know what they're about, and once they have their way with you, you can't wait for them to do it again. Given that I'm explaining this to you, I take it your wedding night wasn't one of those occasions."

Mary's cheeks flamed. She hadn't intended to discuss this with Nell, but she had no one else to ask. She had no mother or sister to guide her when it came to her wifely duty, and she could hardly confide in Travesty. "It was all right," she answered in a small voice.

Nell's laugh rang out over the stillness of the sun-drenched yard. "Well, I reckon that's a start."

"You think so?"

"Mary, your husband was the pick of the litter in this flea-infested colony, if the other louts waiting for us in that church are anything to go by. He's handsome, clean, and mannerly. He might not be an experienced lover, but he's been on his own these many years, with not a woman in sight, if you don't count Mistress Calamity, or whatever her name is. He's probably forgotten what goes where, if he ever knew to start with. Unless they had coin to spare to visit a brothel before they left, these men are as innocent as babes in arms. They've learned how to carve a settlement from the wilderness. They've mastered growing new crops. They'll figure out where to stick their cocks," Nell said matter-of-factly.

"He's kind to me," Mary supplied, suddenly feeling disloyal to John. After all, he had given her a wedding present and allowed her to visit Nell, when another husband might have forbidden her to take time away from her domestic duties.

"Ain't that the truth of it? I asked my Tom if I can go visiting, and he said, 'There's too much to be getting on with, me girl. Ye've had yer way with me person, now turn yer eye to the 'ouse and beasts. I ain't had me a proper meal since coming to this 'ere god-forsaken place. Ye need to feed me up.'" Nell's gruff tone and facial expressions meant to mimic her husband made Mary laugh.

"He doesn't look like he's been starving to me," Mary replied, recalling Tom's round belly straining against the buttons of his ill-fitting doublet.

"That's because he's been subsisting on corn mush and jugs of ale." A happy smile tugged at the corners of Nell's generous mouth. "I'm glad you came, Mary. It's so nice to talk to a friend. I mean to make the best of my situation here, but I can see it won't be easy. I'll be most grateful for a bit of company now and again."

"I'll come as often as I can," Mary promised as she rose to take her leave. "I best be getting back though. There are chores to be seen to."

"If I had me a servant, I'd put my feet up and pretend I'm a great lady," Nell said, lifting her nose in the air in imitation of a lady of leisure.

"In John's house, I think it's Travesty who's the great lady. She's got the airs of one."

"Is that her real name?" Nell asked.

"Must be. Why else would anyone call herself something that brings misfortune to mind?"

"Funny, that," Nell said. "Well, I'm glad my mother didn't call me something peculiar like that."

FIFTEEN

Mary took Nell's advice to heart and decided to try it out that very evening. She waited until John stepped outside after supper to smoke his pipe, as was his custom. Simon often joined him, but tonight Simon went directly to his loft to get some rest after a long day. Mary left Travesty to clear up after supper and followed John outside, taking a seat next to him. The scent of tobacco enveloped her, but she made no move to rise; she was used to it from years spent working in the tavern. John's gaze was fixed on the sky, which was a violent shade of pink streaked with slashes of gold. The sun had just slipped below the tree line and it'd be fully dark within the hour, another day gone.

"Tell me something of your family, John," Mary invited. She didn't dare touch him without being invited to or sit too close for fear of overstepping some unspoken boundary, but conversation was something she could initiate.

John looked surprised by the question. "There isn't much to tell. I'm one of four children. My mother died when I was seven," he said without much feeling. Mary supposed he could barely remember his mother, much less miss her. "An ague took my father when I was nearly eighteen. My oldest brother, Peter, inherited the mill and the house. While Jacob and I would always have work and food enough to feed our families, we'd never have anything of our own, so we decided to try our luck in Virginia."

"You must miss him terribly."

"I do."

"You said there were four of you," Mary prompted.

"I have a sister."

"Older or younger?"

"Older."

"What's her name?"

"Marge. Her name is Marge," John barked. Mary drew back with a start. "Why are you asking me all these questions?"

"I-I'm sorry," Mary stammered. "I didn't mean to offend. I only wanted to get to know you a little better."

John looked instantly contrite. "It is I who am sorry. I'm just tired, Mary. After hours spent in the field, baking in the hot sun, all I want to do is enjoy a few moments of peace. I've no wish to talk about the past."

"I'll leave you to it, then." Mary got to her feet and returned to the cabin. John had apologized, but his rejection stung her. Surely a few moments of conversation wasn't too much to ask for. He gladly conversed with Simon most nights when they sat outside, side by side, sucking on their pipes. Of course, the men could always talk about the crops and what needed doing the next day, but she was still hurt. How was she to establish any sort of relationship with her husband when he had no interest in talking to her?

Mary sat down on the bed, removed her cap, and used her comb to brush out her tangled chestnut tresses. It took a long time, since the comb was so small and narrow, but it was the only thing she had to hand, and the repetitive motion soothed her.

John finally came in and put his pipe in its place on the mantel. He watched Mary for a few moments.

"You have lovely hair, Mary," he said in a conciliatory tone. "Have you no proper comb?"

"'Tis the only thing I own," Mary replied. It didn't surprise her that John hadn't noticed her lack of personal possessions, given that he barely looked at her at all, but she was still hurt by the implication that he'd married a woman with nothing to her name.

John nodded but said nothing further about the comb. "I'm going into Jamestown tomorrow. Do you still wish to come?"

"Yes, I do," Mary replied, somewhat mollified. She finished brushing her hair, braided it, and prepared for bed. She thought John might lie with her tonight, since he'd complimented her on her hair, but he quickly undressed and went to sleep, his back turned to her in a silent rebuke. He hadn't touched her since their wedding night and Mary wondered if he was still cross with her despite his promise to take her into town.

The following morning, Mary ignored her sagging spirits and joined John on the bench of the wagon directly after breakfast. He seemed to be in a fine mood, and she tried once again to draw him into conversation. John didn't get angry with her, but although he answered her questions patiently, he asked her nothing about her own life before coming out to Virginia. She wouldn't have had much to tell him if he had, but she wished he'd show more interest in her than he did in his only cow. John asked after the cow's health every morning, nodding his head in approval when Travesty assured him the beast was well. Mary supposed the cow was worth its weight in gold, but given the state of the colony, so was a wife. There were hundreds of unmarried men and only a handful of women. More were coming, to be sure, but a wife was to be prized and appreciated, Mary concluded defiantly, as the wagon rolled toward the settlement.

"If you had to do it all over again, would you still come to Virginia?" Mary asked to break the silence that had settled over them after John replied to her last question.

"Aye, I would."

"Even if you knew you'd lose your brother?"

"It was Jacob's idea to come. He wanted land of his own, and he wasn't about to get a parcel with his name on it back in England. I'd still be milling grain from morning till night if I'd stayed."

"What was it like when you arrived?" Mary asked.

"Much the same."

John's curt reply put an end to Mary's questions. She held on to the bench as the wagon rattled over the narrow, rutted road, and looked around with interest. Now that she wasn't as tired or overwhelmed as she had been that first afternoon, she was curious to see the town and discover for herself what to expect from her new surroundings. She could see the tall masts of the *Lady Grace* rising above the tree line, the canvas sails furled, the flag proudly flying in the breeze. She wondered when the ship would set sail for England and if anyone would be returning home, having found colonial life not to their liking.

Overcome with curiosity, Mary ignored John's reticence and peppered him with questions, hoping to draw him into telling her about the inhabitants of the colony. She wanted to know what people did in their spare time, if they had any. Were there ever celebrations or dances? Did folks help each other, or did people tend to keep to themselves, protective of their privacy and possessions? Mary also wished to know what happened to those who sinned or broke the law but was too afraid to ask. She'd noticed the wooden stocks mounted on a platform in the center of the settlement, but she hadn't seen anything more sinister, like a gibbet or a gallows.

Mary leaned forward and peered toward the wide-open gate. Three individuals emerged from the settlement and walked toward the oncoming wagon. At first, Mary assumed they were women, on account of their long, flowing hair, but as they drew nearer, she saw they were, in fact, men. Mary's eyes flew to John's face as her heart hammered with fear, but John didn't seem alarmed by the sight of the Indians. They strolled along at a leisurely pace, talking amongst themselves. Mary stared at the men, shocked. They were naked from the waist up, the skin of their chests and arms brown and smooth where it wasn't painted a garish red. It was the paint that originally made her think they were clothed in homespun of madder-dyed red and brown. Narrow breeches covered their legs, but they wore some sort of clout around their hips. Vicious-looking knives hung at their sides, and there were feathers and shells woven into their long hair, but only on the left side. The Indian in the middle wore a cloak trimmed with fur and feathers over his bare torso. The other two carried bulging leather satchels slung over their shoulders.

As the distance between the wagon and the Indians narrowed, Mary could now see their faces, which were also painted red in places. Two of the men had raven-black hair and eyes, but the third, the one who was staring straight at her as if she were a curious specimen he'd never seen, had rich brown hair and eyes the color of a stormy sea. The men acknowledged John by nodding and raising a hand in greeting, and John responded by offering a half-hearted wave. The Indian who'd been staring at her averted his gaze when his companion said something to claim his attention. Mary scooted closer to John as the Indians came abreast of the wagon, but they paid her no mind and continued on their way, conversing in their strange tongue.

"What are they doing here?" Mary whispered as soon as the wagon passed the men.

"They come to discuss business with the governor."

"What business could they possibly have?" Mary exclaimed.

"Trade. They likely heard a ship had come in and came to barter."

"Barter for what?"

John shrugged, uninterested in the conversation. "They trade animal skins for goods that come in from England."

"What type of goods?"

"Steel, for example. Their weapons are made of sharpened stone, but now they know that steel is more effective. They need blades for their daggers, and they want muskets."

"Does the governor welcome them into Jamestown?" Mary asked. She was shocked by what she'd just learned but tried not to show it since John didn't seem the least bit put out.

"The governor would welcome the devil himself if there was profit to be had," John replied bitterly.

"Is he not an honorable man?"

"Mary, being honorable doesn't preclude powerful men from growing rich off trade and acquisition. Governor Yeardley is a shrewd businessman and politician. It's better for everyone to keep peace with the natives and engage them in trade."

"Is that all it takes to keep the peace?"

"The governor says that they are like children. They're not capable of sophisticated thought or analysis of a situation. As long as they are placated and indulged, they're happy."

"You wouldn't give children muskets and blades," Mary argued, mystified by this view of people who were described as savage.

"No, but you wouldn't engage them in intellectual discourse either. Governor Yeardley knows what he's about." John snorted with derision. He didn't seem to think much of the governor or his methods.

"I suppose," Mary muttered, shocked to the core that a nobleman would consort with half-naked savages and freely give them weapons that could be turned on the colonists.

John tethered the horse by the curtain wall and helped Mary down from the bench. "We'll continue on foot from here."

Mary followed obediently, her head swiveling from side to side as she took in the settlement with fresh eyes. Several men stood in the street, conversing. Some were well-dressed, while others wore the universal uniform of the poor: filthy shirts, patched breeches, and threadbare doublets.

"Who are those men?" Mary asked when she saw two fine gentlemen coming out of what she presumed was the governor's house. The men were dressed in suits of rich velvet, their swords slapping against their hips as they walked. One man had a large pearl drop earring hanging from his ear, and she recognized him as the man she'd seen at the church when she arrived, while the other wore a gold chain around his neck, adorned with a large medallion.

"The one with the earring is the secretary of the Virginia Company. The one with the medallion is the marshal. Look, Mary,

I need to go into the tavern. Will you be all right on your own for a bit?"

"Why can't I come with you?"

"Because women are not allowed in the tavern. Go to the smithy and see your fellow travelers. I shan't be long."

Mary watched as John disappeared into the tavern, then she walked over to the forge, following the loud banging of a hammer on metal. The men who had married Faith and Prudence were hard at work, each one focused on his own task.

"Pardon me," Mary called out self-consciously.

The men looked up at her. Their faces were covered with soot and they looked none too pleased to be disturbed while working. "What is it, mistress?"

"I was wondering if I might have a word with Faith or Prudence. We arrived on the *Lady Grace* together," Mary explained.

"Right. I remember you," one of the brothers said, an appreciative grin tugging at his lips. "Go round the back. They're in the house."

Mary followed the instructions and knocked on the door. Faith yanked it open as if she were angry, but her expression softened when she saw Mary.

"Mary, come in. It's good to see you." She stepped aside and invited Mary into the smiths' house. Prudence was by the hearth, stirring something in the pot, but she set down her spoon and came forward to give Mary an affectionate hug.

"How is it with you, Mary?" she asked as she reached for a jug and poured Mary a cup of beer. "Come, have a seat."

Mary sat down and looked around. The place was small and dim, and banging from the smithy reverberated through the room. Two curtained bedsteads occupied the space by the walls, with the table and two benches in the center. Mary had thought being a blacksmith guaranteed a good living, but judging by these humble quarters, it was more profitable to own land. John's cabin was light and airy, and much more pleasant than this hovel the two couples were forced to share.

"I'm well. John has been very kind," Mary replied. "How about you? How do you find your husbands?"

"We'd have to spend time with them to find out," Faith scoffed. "They're always either at the smithy or the tavern, but I can't say as I really mind. From what I've seen so far, they can stay there."

"Faith!" Prudence exclaimed.

"'Tis the truth, and I'm not ashamed to admit it," Faith replied, her hands resting defensively on her ample hips. "We've come halfway around the world to find men no better than ones we could have had in England."

"Men are men," Prudence snapped. "Didn't realize you were expecting to marry a princeling."

"I never held out for a princeling, but a man sober enough to consummate a marriage would do me very well," Faith retorted.

Prudence's face turned beet red. "At least yours managed to stay awake long enough to finish what he started."

Faith turned to Mary, her mouth twisted in a mirthless grin. "Did your man manage to seal the deal?"

Mary nodded. She hadn't minded discussing things with Nell, but she'd never grown close to the sisters and was mortified to be put on the spot in this manner. "He did."

"And was it bearable?" Faith asked.

Mary nodded again. She wanted nothing more than to leave this suffocating hovel and get back outside. Whether John had completed his business at the tavern or not, she had no wish to spend any more time with Faith and Prudence. "Thank you for the beer," she said and sprang to her feet. "John will be wondering where I've got to."

"Must be nice to have a husband who knows you exist," Faith replied. "Come again soon, Mary. It was good to see you."

"I'll see you in church," Mary said as she backed out.

She took a turn around the settlement, walking slowly and taking in everything she saw. There wasn't much, but it was better than soaking up the bitterness that had permeated the smiths' cottage. *I'm so blessed*, Mary thought as she stopped in front of the church. *I have a husband who is kind and considerate and doesn't seem to overindulge in drink. This time, good fortune is on my side.*

Mary smiled brightly when she saw John emerging from the tavern. He held something long and thin wrapped in sacking and his leather bag seemed fuller than when they'd arrived.

John returned her eager smile and beckoned to her. "Are you ready to leave? Did you see your friends?"

"Yes. I'm ready to go."

They walked back to the wagon and climbed in. John carefully laid the scythe blade he'd bought in the back of the wagon but didn't immediately take up the reins. He reached into the bag and withdrew something wrapped in muslin. He turned to her and took her hand. "I got you something."

"John, you've already given me a wedding gift," Mary protested.

"Then don't think of it as a wedding gift."

John handed her the muslin-wrapped package. Mary unfolded the fabric carefully, unsure what to expect. Whatever John had purchased was hard and oddly shaped. Mary gasped with delight when she took out a hand mirror and a hairbrush. The frame of the mirror and the brush handle were made of polished wood and carved with a pattern of vines.

"Oh, John," she breathed. "They're beautiful."

John blushed with pleasure. "You were in need of a brush."

Mary blinked away tears. No one had been this kind to her in a long time, not since her parents were alive. She'd forgotten what it was like to receive an unexpected gift or to trust the sentiment behind it. Mary glanced around to make sure no one was around, then leaned forward and kissed John's cheek. John had explained to her that public displays of affection were forbidden in the colony, even between husband and wife, but she couldn't let his gesture pass without acknowledging it in the only way she could think of.

John grinned and took up the reins. "Shall we go home, Mistress Forrester?"

"I think we shall," Mary replied, grinning from ear to ear. She folded the piece of muslin carefully. It'd make for a good handkerchief, something she could make for John to repay him for his kindness.

SIXTEEN

JANUARY 2015

Kabul, Afghanistan

At first, Rhys thought the knocking was part of his dream, but it grew louder, forcing him to claw his way back from deep slumber to consciousness.

He looked at his watch. It was almost six o'clock. Rhys bolted out of bed and went to open the door. A young man of about seventeen stood in the corridor. He was very thin, and his upper lip was covered with a soft fuzz meant to represent a moustache. A sparse beard shadowed the lower half of his face but failed to disguise the acne spots on his skin. His expression was one of a deer caught in the headlights, surprised and frightened at the same time.

"Hello," Rhys said, smiling in welcome. "Are you Ahmad Khan?" The young man nodded. "Won't you come in?"

Rhys stepped aside to let Ahmad into the room. He came in but stood as close to the door as possible, as if he were going to bolt at any moment.

"Ahmad, I just want to ask you a few questions. Is that all right?" Another nod. Rhys took out a photo of Jo and showed it to the young man. "Do you remember this woman?" A nod. "Ahmad, Jo Turing has been missing for several weeks, possibly more. I found your name written on her notepad. Why would she have made a note of your name?"

Looking at the young man, Rhys couldn't begin to imagine what Jo would want with him. He seemed to be afraid of his own shadow, or more likely, losing his job. There had to be countless other young men who'd be only too happy to take his place, eager to earn steady wages and pocket generous gratuities from the Westerners.

"Miss Jo need guide," Ahmad mumbled. He stared at the tips of his scuffed shoes.

"Are you a guide?"

Ahmad shook his head. "My brother is. He do it for extra money."

"Did your brother take Miss Jo into the mountains?"

He nodded miserably but still hadn't looked up.

"Ahmad, I need to speak to your brother. Where can I find him?"

Ahmad finally lifted his face. His dark eyes were brimming with pain. "Ali hurt," he said.

"Is he in a hospital?"

"He at home."

"Can I see him for just a few minutes? I won't tire him out."

"Ali hurt bad."

"Is he conscious?" Rhys asked carefully, not wanting to cause Ahmad further distress.

"I don't know what that means."

"Is he awake?"

"Sometimes. He in pain."

"Ahmad, is there anything I can do to help?"

Ahmad didn't reply right away, but Rhys suddenly recalled Rob's advice. He reached into his pocket and extracted several bills. He quickly did the math in his head and peeled off a thousand Afs, which would be equivalent to approximately ten quid. He held out the bills to the young man. Ahmad looked uncertain but finally took the money and pocketed it. He walked over to the nightstand and scribbled something on a notepad, then ripped off the page and handed it to Rhys.

"Go there tomorrow after ten."

"Thank you," Rhys said, but Ahmad was already rushing toward the door.

Rhys studied the address Ahmad had written down. He could barely make it out, but Rob or Mr. Zahir would be able to help. At least it was a lead.

Rhys changed into a clean shirt and headed downstairs. He was early, but he'd sit at the bar and have a drink while he waited. According to Rob, the Mustafa Hotel was one of the few places in Kabul that served alcohol, and although the prices were exorbitant, Rhys was ready to pay whatever it took to get a glass of red wine.

SEVENTEEN

JANUARY 2015

London, England

Quinn had just finished folding the laundry when she heard the doorbell. She had invited Sylvia over, knowing she desperately wanted to visit with her and the baby. Quinn had offered to make lunch, but Sylvia had told her not to bother. She was bringing something.

Quinn buzzed her up and set the basket of laundry out of sight. The flat was chaotic enough with all the packing boxes and bags intended for charity. Quinn opened the door to find Sylvia bearing a large tray covered with foil.

"Steak and ale pies," Sylvia said as she handed the tray to Quinn and began to divest herself of her coat and scarf. "I keep making Jude's favorite dishes. I think if I make the right thing, he'll be tempted to eat, but he doesn't have much of an appetite these days," Sylvia explained. "He nibbles on toast in the morning and buys chips for lunch when he's at the hospital."

"He'll turn a corner, Sylvia. You'll see," Quinn said. "These things take time." She felt guilty for feeding Sylvia platitudes, but she had no idea what to say, or what would help. Jude was on a journey of recovery. It might take weeks, months, or years for him to beat his addiction. She didn't dare think, even to herself that he might relapse.

"Shall I make us a salad to go with the pies?" Quinn asked as she turned toward the kitchen.

"Sure, why not? May I?" Sylvia asked as she approached Alex, who was lying on his activity mat.

"Of course."

Sylvia carefully lifted Alex off the floor and cuddled him against her soft jumper. Alex, who normally broke into a smile when picked up, stared at her with deep suspicion. His expression seemed to be saying, *One wrong move, lady, and I'm calling for Mum.*

"He's grown," Sylvia said wistfully. "He's starting to look more like you."

Quinn poked her head out of the kitchen. "You really think so?"

"I do. I know everyone says he's the spitting image of Gabe, but there's something in his gaze that's all you. He will change all the time, you know. Logan looked just like his father when he was little, but then he began to resemble me by the time he started school. He still looks like me," Sylvia said proudly. "Jude still looks like his dad. Always has."

"I never knew Jenna personally, but I do see something of her in Emma from time to time. She must have something of her personality as well. She takes us by surprise sometimes," Quinn said, recalling the request for a Harry Styles poster.

"Girls are more difficult than boys. Everyone always says so. I wouldn't know," Sylvia muttered. Having given birth to two girls and abandoned them, she had no inkling of what it was like to raise daughters. "Have you had any word?" Sylvia asked as she walked into the kitchen.

Alex instantly brightened when he saw his mother. Though he didn't reach out his arms, he leaned toward Quinn with his whole body, demanding to be taken from this strange lady.

"He wants you," Sylvia said. "I'll make the salad."

Quinn took Alex and kissed his downy head. He pressed his cheek against her breast and sighed as if he'd come home. "I haven't heard anything yet," Quinn said, replying to Sylvia's earlier question. "I wish Rhys would call, but it's early days yet. I keep looking at Jo's photos. There are so many online. She looks like Seth."

"Yes, I think so too. I wonder what she's like," Sylvia mused as she sliced several tomatoes. "Do you think she'll agree to see me?"

"I really can't say, Sylvia. At this stage, I just hope she's all right."

"Me too." Sylvia stopped cutting and stared toward the window, obviously needing a moment to compose herself. "I'd give anything to do everything over again," she said softly. "I've made such a mess of my life."

Quinn opened her mouth to offer another platitude but promptly closed it. Sylvia had made mistakes, serious ones. No one, least of all Quinn, could tell her she'd done the right thing. She hadn't needed to keep her children, but the least she could have done was go through the proper channels rather than abandon her twins the way she had. Even if she'd left them together, things might have turned out differently for the girls. Now, thirty-one years later, Quinn and Jo had yet to meet, and Sylvia might have another chance at establishing a relationship with a daughter she'd walked away from, if Jo was forgiving enough to allow it.

"Let's take it day by day, shall we?" Quinn said instead. "I will let you know as soon as I hear from Rhys."

"It's not like he'll ring me himself," Sylvia said bitterly.

Quinn didn't reply. Rhys's relationship with Sylvia was a complicated one, and she had no desire to get in the middle. Nor did she often mention Seth in front of her birth mother. Sylvia and Seth had yet to meet again after all these years. Neither one had any desire to see the other, despite sharing two children and a grandchild.

"How is he? Rhys, I mean," Sylvia asked. "I heard what happened from Logan."

"As good as can be expected. He's sad."

"He never loved her, you know," Sylvia said as she popped the two pies into the oven and began to set the table. "It's the baby he wanted. Had I been ten years younger—"

"I'll just nurse Alex while the pies are heating," Quinn interjected, having no desire to rehash Sylvia's relationship with Rhys. She secretly agreed that Rhys hadn't really loved Haley but had no wish to betray his confidence and feed Sylvia's curiosity. Quinn left the kitchen and settled on the sofa. Alex was already smacking his lips, ready for lunch. She'd fed him only two hours ago, but he seemed ravenous as he latched on, sucking furiously.

"You should talk to your pediatrician about starting him on solids," Sylvia said as she emerged from the kitchen and sat across from Quinn. "He'll stay full longer and sleep through the night."

"He sleeps through the night now, but you're right, I think he's ready for something a little more satisfying."

Sylvia chuckled. "I wouldn't call baby food satisfying, but it will make him happier."

"I think a steak and ale pie would make him happier," Quinn joked. The pies really did smell divine, and Alex wasn't immune to the appetizing aroma. Quinn saw him sniffing curiously at the air once he finished nursing. She buttoned her top and carried him to the bedroom, where she put him down in his cot and turned on the baby monitor.

"See you later, little man," she said, smiling down at him. "I expect you to be sound asleep by the time I come back." *And hopefully you'll sleep long enough for me to visit with Mary*, Quinn added silently. She didn't think Sylvia would stay too long, which was just fine. Their visits were still awkward, and without the adorable distraction of Alex, they had little to talk about.

EIGHTEEN
JULY 1620

Virginia Colony

Mary eased her back and held up her hand to shield her eyes. The sun was blazing in a cloudless sky, the air so thick with moisture she could hardly draw breath, and it was only mid-morning. She leaned on the wooden handle of the hoe and allowed herself a moment to rest. Her linen chemise clung to her body, and her scalp was uncomfortably damp. She'd never experienced anything like this in England, and, according to Simon, the worst was yet to come.

Mary cast a critical eye over the kitchen garden. She'd weeded and watered it. Now it was time to go inside and begin the daily chore of grinding dried corn into flour to make bread. Well, the corn could wait, Mary decided. She needed to cool off before Travesty found her insensible in the vegetable patch.

Mary cleaned the hoe and returned it to its proper place. Tools were precious and not easily replaced. She then turned her footsteps toward the creek. She should have told Travesty she was leaving but was afraid the woman would offer to come along. Mary was grateful for the company, given that she would have spent her days entirely on her own if it weren't for Travesty's presence, but at times, Mary thought solitude might have been preferable. Travesty was a hard worker and still shouldered most of the household chores, but there was something in her veiled gaze and the sharp angle of her shoulders that spoke of bone-deep anger.

And then there was the silence. Mary wasn't someone who needed to indulge in a constant stream of chatter, but Travesty went for hours without saying a word, fueling Mary's reluctance to initiate conversation. They each had their routine and followed it. The only thing that seemed to paint a smile on Travesty's disenchanted countenance was the sight of Simon coming through the door in the evening. It was like the sun coming out after days of rain and lighting up the now-clear sky, except that it didn't last. Travesty seemed ashamed of her regard and worked hard to hide it, not only from Simon, but from John and Mary as well.

Mary stopped when she entered the cooling shade of the trees and took a deep breath. Here, in the woods, the air was cleaner and fresher, the harsh glare of the sun blocked by the nearly impenetrable lushness of summer leaves. The wood was filled with the trilling of birds and the stealthy sounds of small animals moving through the underbrush. The creek gurgled invitingly, its sun-dappled surface sparkling like a band of liquid gold.

Mary stepped out of her shoes, rolled down her hose, and pulled off her cap, releasing her damp hair. The soft grass beneath her toes felt cool and refreshing, and suddenly she knew she wouldn't be bathing in her chemise. This was John's land. They had no close neighbors, and Travesty was busy preparing dinner for the men. Who'd know that Mary had taken a dip without the protective cover of a layer of fabric?

She untied her skirt and petticoat, unlaced her bodice, and pulled the sweat-soaked chemise over her head. Mary dashed toward the creek before she had a chance to change her mind and feel embarrassed by her brazenness. The cool water embraced her, forcing a sigh of pleasure from her parched lips. She took a deep breath and sank beneath the surface, allowing the creek to flow over her as her hair floated around her head, spreading above her like a lily pad.

She finally came back up and pushed the wet ropes of hair out of her eyes, but the rest of her remained below the surface, enjoying the cool water flowing over her skin. She looked up at the shafts of light piercing the canopy of leaves and closed her eyes, inhaling the piney scent of the forest.

This is a perfect moment. The unbidden thought came into Mary's head. *A perfect, unspoiled moment.*

She didn't have any soap but washed as best she could and rinsed out her hair. It hung nearly to her waist when she finally emerged from the creek and reached for her clothes.

She hadn't noticed him at first. He was so still as to appear to be a stout limb of the tree he stood beneath. His gaze was fixed on her, his lips slightly parted, his arms at his sides. Mary froze with terror. Her mouth went dry, and her extremities turned ice-cold as she backed toward the creek but then recalled that she was naked. She snatched up her chemise and held it in front of her, her eyes never leaving the man's face. He hadn't moved, but she felt the threat as keenly as if he were wielding a knife.

When the man finally shifted, Mary's breath caught in her throat and a low scream escaped her lips. She sounded like a frightened animal, sure it was about to die. He held up both hands, palms outward, to show her he was unarmed. It was only once he left the sanctuary of the tree that she realized she'd seen him before. He was the Indian she'd seen on the way to Jamestown, the one with the gray eyes. As he moved toward her, Mary squeezed her legs, afraid her bladder would let go in her terror.

"I won't hurt you," the man said. "You need not be afraid."

Mary took another involuntary step back. Her mind had to be playing tricks on her. The man spoke perfect English.

"I will turn around and allow you to dress," he offered, and turned his back. When she'd seen him on the road to the settlement, he'd worn buckskin breeches, but today he wore only a clout that left his long, muscular legs bare. His hair hung down his back and was almost as long as her own, and his face was devoid of any paint. He'd been carrying a spear, but he'd left it propped against the tree, so he was nearly as naked and defenseless as she was, except that he was a muscular man who could overpower her easily if he chose to.

Mary hastily pulled on her chemise and petticoat. She fumbled with the laces of her bodice, her fingers clumsy and shaking as she tried to fasten it. She wondered if he'd pursue her if she ran, but she'd have to go right past him to get back to the cabin, so it wasn't worth the risk.

He finally turned around slowly. He took in her garments and watched with some amusement as she pulled on her cap.

"You have beautiful hair," he said. "Why do you cover it?"

"You are on my husband's land," Mary snapped, striving to regain some control over the situation.

"How can land and sky belong to anyone?"

Mary wasn't sure what to say to that, so she tried a different tack, since he seemed in no hurry to be on his way. "You speak English."

"Yes."

"What is your name?"

The man said something quite unpronounceable to her English ears, then chuckled at her stupefied expression. "My name means 'Walks Between Worlds.'" He hadn't come any closer or looked like he meant her any harm, so Mary decided to give in to her natural curiosity.

"What an odd name. Why do they call you that?"

The Indian was about to explain when Travesty's shrill cry filled the peaceful forest. "Mistress! Mary! Where are you?"

Mary turned in the direction of Travesty's voice, partially glad she was no longer alone with this strange man and partially annoyed at the interruption. She really did want to know about his name. She turned her gaze back to him, but the man was gone. He'd melted into the woods as quietly as he'd appeared.

"Praise the Lord you're safe," Travesty exclaimed as she burst through the trees. "I didn't know what to think when I found you gone. I thought you'd been carried off by the savages."

"Has that happened before?" Mary asked, suddenly realizing how close she'd come to this unspeakable fate.

Travesty shrugged. "Not that I know off, but one must always expect the worst from those heathen devils."

"I needed to cool off," Mary explained as she picked up her hose and stuck her feet into her shoes. "Does one ever get accustomed to this infernal heat?"

"I couldn't say. I've yet to find out."

Mary followed Travesty back to the cabin. Having nearly lost her mistress, Travesty was unusually forthcoming. "I don't know what I'd tell the master if I couldn't find you. He relies on me to keep you safe."

"I can look after myself, Travesty."

"I know you can, but I've been looking after him for so long, I suppose I think of it as my duty to look after his wife."

"So, John has been a good master to you?" Mary asked. She had no reason to think he hadn't been, but wanted reassurance that she wasn't wrong in her estimation of the man. Many a master beat his servants. She knew that only too well after spending several years under Uncle Swithin's roof and feeling the back of his hand against her face or the sting of his belt against her back. She hadn't seen John raise his voice or hand to Travesty, but he might have been unkind to her before Mary came.

"He saved me," Travesty said, her voice soft with reverence.

"From what?"

"From certain death." Travesty wiped her damp forehead with her sleeve and turned to face Mary. "I was one of the first indentures to come out to Virginia. I'd never been out on the water before, much less in a great ship in the middle of a vast ocean. They said I'd get my sea legs after a few days, but I fell ill and stayed ill for the whole of the crossing. I could hardly keep anything down. After a fortnight, I was so weak I could barely raise my head to puke into the bucket."

"That must have been awful," Mary said, knowing only too well how long and difficult the crossing had been.

"I wasted away day by day. The only thing that kept me tethered to this world was the fear of my body being thrown overboard, my remains devoured by sea creatures. The sailors carried me ashore on a wooden plank when we arrived and laid me down in the church, certain I would die before the week was out. No one wanted to bother with me. They'd have left me to die, had the master not taken pity on me and purchased my indenture contract. Had I died, he'd have lost his money, but he brought me back to the cabin and nursed me back to health. It took weeks for me to leave my bed, but once I did, I swore I'd devote my life to repaying his kindness."

"Travesty, how did you come to be here?" Mary asked.

"I'm not a criminal, if that's what you're suggesting," Travesty snapped.

Mary swallowed back a retort. Innocent people didn't get sent down to Virginia. Most indentured servants were criminals who'd been lucky enough to escape the noose, so Mary had valid reason to assume Travesty was one such case.

"I came here of my own volition."

"You sold yourself into indenture?" Mary asked, incredulous that anyone would do such a thing.

"Desperate people do desperate things," Travesty retorted.

Mary sighed. That was something she could understand only too well. She'd been desperate to escape, and coming across the world to marry a man she'd never set eyes on, who now held her fate in his hands, was nearly as desperate as selling yourself into servitude. Marriage was servitude, except the contract didn't expire unless one of the parties died.

"I was destitute and alone. I had nothing left to lose," Travesty said with a deep sigh.

"I felt much the same when I decided to come out," Mary said, thinking she might finally establish a bond with the other woman, but Travesty's head shot up and her eyes bore into Mary. Spots of color appeared on her cheeks.

"Don't compare yourself to me. You came here knowing you'd be looked after, married to a man who'd consider himself lucky to have you. What have you sacrificed? What have you lost?" Travesty cried angrily.

"What have *you* sacrificed?" Mary retorted, infuriated by Travesty's tone and erroneous assumptions. She knew nothing of Mary's life or the circumstances that had led her to the *Lady Grace*.

"Nothing. It was all done for me. One day I had a home and a family. I had three children and a loving husband who provided for us. We weren't wealthy, but we were comfortable, and secure." Travesty blinked away tears. "And then the summer of 1618 came. We were happy for the fine weather. It'd been a cold and bitter winter. The sun shone every day, it seemed—warm, life-giving, beautiful. But life-giving things can turn ugly," Travesty said sharply. "The days grew warmer, and the golden sun warmed the refuse heaps and brought the flies. There'd been no rain for weeks to cleanse the streets. And then it came, the Black Death. First one case, then another. The city officials sent searchers. Do you know what searchers are?" Travesty demanded, hands on hips.

"No, I don't believe we had them in Plymouth."

"No, you likely wouldn't. The searchers went to houses where there'd been a death to assess the cause. Some were savvy enough to pay off the searchers, to turn them from their door with the verdict of consumption or fever. But my Stephen was too honest, too naïve. When my brother, who lived with us, took sick and died, Stephen allowed the searcher to do his job. By the end of that day we were locked in, quarantined for forty days, all of us together in one room. They put a watcher outside our house to make sure we didn't escape."

"I'm sorry, Travesty," Mary said, only now understanding the horror of what Travesty must have endured.

"My youngest, my only boy, was the first to go, followed by

Stephen, then my two girls. I can't even bring myself to utter their names for fear I won't be able to recover. They all died within the first ten days, and I was left to watch them rot. Oh, the carts came to take away the dead, but I couldn't bear to part with them. I couldn't bear to be left alone. They were taken eventually, to be dumped into a pit and swallowed by the earth, without so much as a word from a minister or a wooden cross to mark their graves. I spent the rest of the time alone in a house that had been full of life only a fortnight before. And then I was put out in the street. I had no money to pay for rent or food. My husband was gone, and I had no way to earn a living, other than to whore."

"So, you sold yourself into indenture?"

"It was better than selling myself to countless nameless men. I thought I'd have a chance here."

In a colony full of unmarried men who'd give anything for the love of a woman, Mary thought. *And of all the plantations, you had to end up at one where the master couldn't be seduced.*

"I thought he'd marry me," Travesty said, smiling bitterly. "I thought he'd elevate me from the pit of hell my life had become, but no, he had no interest in me, despite everything I did to make him happy. Instead, he married you."

Mary bowed her head and stared at her folded hands. Why had John married her? He could have just as easily wed Travesty. She was still young enough to bear children and warm his bed, if that was what he wanted, although she had her doubts on that score. Mary raised her eyes to Travesty's still-beautiful face. No, he wouldn't have married Travesty. She was a sensual woman, even Mary could see that. Travesty had been married, had known the love of a man. She'd have expectations of a husband, she'd make comparisons. John needed a blank page, a woman who hadn't been touched, a woman who wouldn't know the difference between an ardent lover and a man who braced himself for the act that was supposed to come naturally to him. They'd been wed for over a month, but he'd only touched her twice during that time, and both times had been swift and impersonal, just another task to be performed before finally going to sleep.

"You will be free to marry once your contract is up," Mary said. She knew that was inadequate consolation, but it was better than nothing.

"Oh yes, won't I just? That's five years from now, and I will be thirty by then—old, used up, and barren. It'll be too late for me, and I'll be lucky if anyone wants me since I'll be starting anew with nothing but the clothes on my back."

"I'll help you, Travesty. I won't let John send you away with nothing."

Travesty's eyes narrowed in scorn. "If anyone can help me, it's Simon, not you. You have no say in anything, you foolish girl. No say at all."

With that, Travesty turned on her heel and stomped toward the cabin, her back ramrod straight, her head held high. Mary followed on her heels like a dejected puppy. Travesty was right. Mary had no say in anything and likely never would. She wasn't sure what Travesty thought Simon could do for her, but he certainly had more influence with John than the two women ever would, so perhaps he would put in a kind word for his fellow indenture.

NINETEEN
JANUARY 2015

Kabul, Afghanistan

Rhys held on for dear life as the Jeep bounced over the rutted road. He wasn't sure if the craters were the result of nonexistent maintenance or past explosions that had gouged out chunks of asphalt as they tore off entire sections of walls from the grim-looking buildings that lined the street. Despite the damage, the buildings were still inhabited, and people carried on with everyday life in the sections that had been left undamaged.

Having left the central part of Kabul, they were now in a poorer section of town, one that looked like a film set for a war film. Except this was reality. Exposed metal beams, broken windows, and piles of rubble covered nearly every block, making walking down the street a perilous business. Ragged children played among the wreckage, calling out to each other and pretending to shoot their playmates with sticks. Several women passed by, their attire ranging from burkas to traditional Pashtun dresses. The colorful embroidered caftans looked incongruous amid the dusty ruins of what had once been apartment buildings.

Rob finally stopped the Jeep in front of a gray building. The walls were pockmarked with bullet holes and the windows—those that were still intact—were small and grimy.

"Is this it?" Rhys asked.

"I'm afraid so. Come."

They got out of the Jeep and walked toward the door. The flat was on the ground floor. Rhys knocked, hoping they wouldn't be turned away before they had a chance to state their business. A woman dressed in a faded red kaftan over narrow leggings opened the door. Over her graying hair, she wore a loose scarf that she instantly adjusted for modesty's sake.

"I'm sorry to bother you, Mrs. Khan. My name is Rhys Morgan, and that's Rob Malone. We are from the BBC, but we are not here in our professional capacity. We are simply looking for a friend. Your son Ahmad said we could come speak to Ali," Rhys said.

He hoped the woman understood some part of what he'd said. Mrs. Khan must have been forewarned by Ahmad because she nodded and gestured for them to follow her. An older man, presumably the boys' father, came out of a back room. He was dressed in the traditional loose cotton shirt and trousers, and his feet were bare.

Mr. Khan directed an angry look toward the Westerners and shepherded his three daughters, who'd appeared from what must be the kitchen, to see who'd come to see them, out of the way. The girls, all younger than Ahmad and dressed like their mother, stared at the strangers, their dark eyes wide with curiosity. A torrent of harsh words from their father sent them back to the kitchen.

Mr. Khan gestured toward the back room. It was unbearably shabby, with peeling blue paint and a narrow window covered with a length of bright patterned fabric tacked onto the top window frame. A threadbare rug covered the floor between the two low beds that were positioned along the walls, across from one another. A young man, possibly a year or two older than Ahmad, lay on the bed furthest from the window. His head was wrapped in white gauze marred with dried blood. His right hand

and shoulder were bandaged as well, and one of his legs ended at the knee. The stump was thickly wrapped, but the wound still oozed blood, soaking the bandage. His eyes looked glazed as he stared up at the low ceiling, transfixed by the flies that circled overhead.

"Hello, Ali," Rhys said softly.

The young man didn't move, but his gaze slid toward the visitors.

"My name is Rhys Morgan. I've come from England. I'm searching for Jo Turing. She's my friend. I believe you know her."

Ali paled at the mention of Jo, and his uninjured hand grabbed for the blanket, scrunching the fabric between his fingers.

"Ali, did you take Jo into the mountains?" Rhys asked softy. He didn't want to sound accusing and frighten Ali into keeping his silence.

Ali nodded.

"Was that when you got hurt?"

Another nod.

Rhys was just about to ask another question when Mrs. Khan came into the room bearing a tray with tea glasses, a tall pot, and a plate of biscuits. She looked from Rhys to Rob, then poured the tea. "Please," she said, gesturing toward the glasses.

"Thank you," the men said in unison and reached for the glasses. These people didn't look like they had anything to spare; to refuse their generous offer of tea would have been rude.

Rhys took a sip of the strong, hot tea. Mrs. Khan had sweetened it generously, probably using sugar she could ill afford to share with strangers. The taste of the tea made him suddenly homesick for London. His loss was still fresh in his mind, but it was nothing compared to the misery he saw all around him, particularly in the mangled young man lying on the bed. There was a small nightstand next to the bed, but there was nothing on it save a glass of water. There were no painkillers to help him manage his pain, or even sleeping tablets to help him find oblivion from his predicament even for a few hours.

"Ali, please, what happened to Jo?" Rhys asked, fearing he wasn't going to get an answer.

Ali struggled to raise himself on one elbow and looked at Rhys. He resembled his brother, except for the lines of pain etched around his mouth. "I take Miz Jo to mountains."

"Why would you take her to such a dangerous place?" Rhys asked, unable to stop himself. Jo must have paid him well enough to overcome his objections, if he had any.

"She ask to go. She pay good. We go before too much snow. I drive in friend's truck. Miz Jo, she take pictures but want to get closer. I turn off road and drive on track. There's IED. Big explosion. Then shots. They shoot me in shoulder."

"And Jo?" Rhys pleaded. "What happened to Jo?"

"Miz Jo dead," Ali whispered. Tears slid down his hollow cheeks. "My fault."

"Did you see her die?" Rhys asked. He barely recognized his own reedy and tearful voice.

Ali nodded. "She dead."

"Who helped you?" Rhys asked. Someone must have come along and taken Ali to a medical facility. He would have died otherwise.

Ali shrugged. "I wake up in Cure Hospital."

"Is that when you lost your leg?" Rhys asked gently.

Ali nodded again. "Bone shattered. Need to come off."

"Ali, I need to find Miss Jo's body. Where did this happen?"

Ali called out in his own language and his father came into the room. Ali explained something, and the man left and returned with paper and a pencil, which he handed to Ali. His father looked angry, and a rapid stream of words flew from his mouth.

Ali nodded and replied curtly. He then drew a crude map and marked the spot with an X. "Here. But don't go. Don't go," he said again more vehemently.

"Thank you, Ali. And it wasn't your fault," Rhys added. Ali turned his face to the wall.

Mrs. Khan stood just outside the room, ready to show them

out. "Thank you, Mrs. Khan," Rhys said. He took out all his cash and pressed the bills into the woman's hand. "For Ali," he said.

The woman's eyes filled with tears of gratitude and she squeezed Rhys's hand. She clearly didn't speak English, but her eyes said it all. Rhys's money wouldn't make much difference in the long run, but perhaps it would buy her son some immediate relief.

"I'm sorry, Rhys," Rob said as soon as they climbed back into the Jeep. "I suspected Jo wouldn't be coming back but didn't want to say anything. You were so hopeful. Kabul is bad enough, what with several bombings per week, but going into Taliban territory is suicide."

"Ali said she was taking photos," Rhys said. "What would she have been photographing out there?" He was still trying to wrap his mind around what Ali had said, hoping against hope that there was some way Jo might have survived the ambush.

"Rhys, the mountains are riddled with caves. They are perfect hiding places, and not only for the Taliban. Most of the heroin that finds its way to Europe is produced right here in Afghanistan. They have ninety percent of global market share on illegal opiates. Opium is their biggest export. There are insurgents in these mountains, but also warlords and drug traffickers. Jo came too close to something she wasn't meant to see. If the explosion didn't kill her, then a bullet did."

"But Ali survived."

"Ali is not important. He's a nobody. He's not worth killing, but Jo Turing is a world-renowned photojournalist. She can do serious damage. She's gone, Rhys. I'm sorry."

Rhys buried his face in his hands. He felt hollow and numb with grief. Jo had been young and vibrant, and so full of life. To die so randomly was pointless and unfair. Why did she have to go trekking into the mountains that were riddled with explosive devices planted by the insurgents and landmines left over from the Russian occupation? Surely no photo was worth such risk. Ali should have known better than to take her, but having seen the poverty of the Khan family, Rhys could hardly blame the young man. Jo must have paid him handsomely to take such a risk, and now his life was ruined. Surviving in Afghanistan was hard enough when you were whole, but to lose a limb was as good as a death sentence. Ali would end up begging in the street if his family couldn't afford to care for him.

"What now?" Rob asked. "Will you tell her sister?"

"No. Not yet. I must find Jo's remains. If I can't bring Jo back alive, I'll at least bring her home to bury. I won't leave her here."

"Rhys, how in the bloody hell will you find her remains?"

"Someone brought Ali to the hospital. Someone found them out there in the mountains. Surely they didn't leave Jo there to be devoured by animals and roasted by the sun."

"I wouldn't be so sure. Ali was still alive. Jo wasn't."

"Ali got hurt in that explosion," Rhys protested. "He lost a leg. He was in agony, and in shock. He says Jo died. Maybe she did, but I won't give up until I know for certain."

"All right, then. Where to now?"

"To the hospital where Ali was taken. After that, to every other hospital in Kabul."

Rob nodded. "You missed your true calling sitting behind your posh desk, mate. You should have been an investigative reporter."

"There's more than one way to make a difference, Rob."

TWENTY

Rob parked the Jeep in front of Cure International Kabul Hospital. The single-story stone building looked more like a penitentiary, but it was one of the best hospitals in Kabul, offering not only medical care to poor Afghan families but also training programs for local doctors and nurses, who were in short supply.

Rhys followed Rob inside. The interior was warmer than the outside, but not by much. Numerous people were waiting patiently to be seen, their faces masks of resignation as they stared into space or followed the goings on with some interest. Two young mothers tried to soothe crying children, and several injured men sat together in stony silence, blood seeping through make-do bandages as they waited to be attended to.

"Excuse me," Rhys said to a middle-aged woman behind the desk. "I'd like to see the hospital director, please."

The woman stared at him as if he'd said something grossly inappropriate. But she quickly recovered from her shock and returned her attention to whatever she'd been doing.

"The director is a very busy man," she said, without looking up.

"I realize that, but I really need to speak to him. It's rather urgent."

"You can sit down and wait, but I guarantee nothing," the

woman said, dismissing him by turning her back to look for something in a filing cabinet behind her.

But Rhys wouldn't be deterred. When she turned back to her desk, he took out his press pass from his pocket and showed it to the woman, giving her a moment to study it. "I'm from the BBC. I'm here to write an article about your hospital and the important work you're doing. That sort of coverage can help increase donations and funding."

The woman's eyes narrowed as she studied him more carefully. "A reporter," she said, her voice dripping with disgust.

"Yes, a reporter."

"Sit," she barked.

"I think you'd better do as you're told." Rob chuckled as Rhys lowered himself into a hard plastic chair next to him. "She likes you," he added with a smirk.

"Do you think we have a chance of seeing someone today?" Rhys asked.

"Probably not, but it's not as if you have somewhere to be. This is not a place where things happen quickly."

"Right," Rhys said. He wished he had something to read. "What are you doing?" he asked as Rob settled more comfortably in his chair and fixed his gaze on the screen of his mobile.

"Playing Candy Crush. It doesn't require Wi-Fi."

"Seriously?"

"It's very relaxing. Give it a go."

"No, thanks."

"Suit yourself. This might take all day."

And it did. By mid-afternoon, Rhys was hungry, thirsty, and frustrated. People came and went, new casualties arrived, and patients who'd been released left, but still he and Rob sat in the plastic chairs, waiting to be seen. Rob managed to procure some tea, which only made Rhys hungrier. He should have had a heartier breakfast, but he hadn't been very hungry that morning and settled for tea and toast. His stomach growled, and he gave Rob a lopsided smile.

"I can step out and find us something to eat," Rob offered.

"There's no food allowed in the waiting area and I don't want to leave, in case we get called."

"Suit yourself," Rob replied and closed his eyes. Rob could sleep anywhere. It was the mark of a man who traveled for a living and slept in a different bed every night. Rhys just sat and stared at the wall.

The quality of the light outside changed as the afternoon wore on, the bright white light of early afternoon becoming softer and flatter as it painted oblong boxes on the linoleum floor. Rhys had managed to nod off but woke when Rob elbowed him in the ribs. "We're up, mate."

They were directed to a small office at the end of the hall, where a balding, middle-aged man in thick horn-rimmed spectacles sat behind a desk overflowing with files and reports.

"Thank you for waiting, gentlemen. As you can see, I'm a little busy," the man said, extending his hand. "My name is Farouq Durani. I'm the director of this facility."

Having lied about the purpose of their visit, Rhys could hardly get straight to the point. He spent a quarter of an hour quizzing Mr. Durani about funding, staff, mortality rates, and availability of supplies before finally broaching the subject of Ali Khan.

"Mr. Durani, the brother of a young man I've befriended since arriving in Kabul was brought into your facility several weeks ago. His name is Ali Khan."

"What about him? Did he not receive adequate treatment?" Mr. Durani asked, his eyebrows raised in obvious surprise.

"He did, but I need to know who brought him in."

"Why?"

"Because he wasn't alone when he got injured. He'd taken a colleague of ours into the mountains, and we've yet to find out what happened to her. If someone helped Ali, they might have found her as well."

"What is your colleague's name?"

"Jo Turing."

Mr. Durani clicked a few keys on his keyboard and stared at the screen. "No one by that name was brought in at any time in the last thirty days. I do see an entry for Ali Khan. He was admitted on December sixteenth. His left leg was shattered below the knee, he had a bullet wound in his right shoulder, and several other less serious injuries."

"That's correct."

The director shook his head, his expression one of profound sadness. "It's devastating for one so young to find himself disabled, especially in a country that doesn't look after its invalids."

"Mr. Durani, who brought Ali Kahn in?"

The man removed his glasses and pinched the bridge of his nose. He looked tired and defeated. Rhys thought he was about to reply, but he remained silent as he replaced the glasses on his face.

"Is there a reason you'd rather not tell us?" Rob asked, obviously frustrated by the man's reluctance.

"I have no wish to get involved, Mr. Malone. We operate on a shoestring budget and any mistake on my part could result in a decrease in funds and donations. The Americans are our friends," he said, giving Rhys and Rob a meaningful look.

"We appreciate your dilemma, Mr. Durani," Rhys said and got up to leave. "I will make a generous donation to your organization as soon as I return to London. You can count on that."

"Thank you, Mr. Morgan, Mr. Malone." Mr. Durani shook their hands and watched them walk out the door.

"So, Ali was brought in by Americans," Rob said as soon as they were back in the Jeep.

"They must have been military personnel."

"They'd have to be, given where the explosion happened."

"Do you know where their headquarters are?" Rhys asked.

"I do, but I also know a really good kebob place, which is where I'm going right now. I'm starving, and no self-respecting American officer will give you the time of day after five o'clock."

"Tomorrow, then?"

"Look, Rhys, I'm flying home tomorrow. I sent my cameraman

back several days ago. I only stayed on to help you out. I'm afraid you're on your own from this point on. I can leave you the Jeep, and you can return it at the airport when you're ready to leave. I strongly suggest you contact the British Embassy and have them make an appointment for you. You'll never get close to a U.S. Army base on your own, not even with your press pass."

Rhys clapped Rob on the shoulder. "I appreciate your help, Rob, and I'll take you up on your offer of both the Jeep and the kebobs. You must be thrilled to be going home."

"I am. I'm more than ready to get out of this hellhole."

"I've been here for less than a week, but it feels like a lifetime," Rhys said as he climbed into the Jeep and buckled his seat belt.

"This place has that effect on you. It also serves to remind us how bloody lucky we are to live in a country that protects our rights and our religious beliefs."

"I'll drink to that," Rhys said.

"No, you won't. They don't serve alcohol." The men laughed bitterly, neither one particularly given to mirth, and drove off.

TWENTY-ONE
JANUARY 2015

London, England

The snow came down in thick, heavy flakes, blanketing London in a pristine quilt of white and giving it a storybook appearance. Quinn pushed aside the net curtain and stared out the window, Alex in her arms. He watched the snow coming down with complete absorption, his eyes round with wonder as he held out a splayed hand, thinking he could catch the snowflakes.

"Snow," Quinn said to him. "Snow." Alex cooed happily, and Quinn kissed the top of his dark head. He had that intoxicating baby smell and her heart flooded with love... and guilt. When she'd gone to the shop yesterday, she'd purchased baby formula and infant cereal. She hadn't given it to Alex yet, but she would today. She'd planned to nurse Alex until he was at least six months old, but the past two weeks had been a challenge. Her milk had become less plentiful, something that had become obvious to her when she pumped, and Alex seemed dissatisfied and fussy when he finished nursing.

"I think he's still hungry," Quinn had said to Gabe after she'd nursed Alex last night. "I don't think he's getting enough. Sylvia said supplementing the milk with cereal will make him feel fuller."

"Perhaps she's right."

"I just want to do what's best for the baby."

"What about what's best for you? You're struggling, mentally and physically. You wince every time Alex latches on."

"My nipples are sore," Quinn confessed. "He's starting to teethe, and his gums are firmer. That boy has a death grip when he's hungry. I'm going to call the clinic and speak to his pediatrician. If he says it's all right, I will start Alex on solids and supplement my milk with store-bought formula."

"I think that makes perfect sense," Gabe agreed.

Quinn was grateful for Gabe's support, but she still felt as if she were failing her son. Some women nursed until the child was as old as eighteen months, while she'd only managed four. But there were other issues. Perhaps it was the stress of discovering that Jo was somewhere in Afghanistan, or the helplessness of only being able to stand idly by while Rhys went off to Kabul, putting himself in danger for her benefit. She had no illusions about Rhys's motives. He wasn't there for Jo, he was there for Quinn. She should have refused, should have dismissed his offer as soon as it had been made, but she simply couldn't bring herself to pass up the chance to find her sister.

And now everyone was on edge. Logan sent daily texts, asking if there was any news from Rhys, and Sylvia had phoned twice over the past few days. Her parents, her cousin Jill, and even Drew Camden, whom Quinn and Logan had hired to find Jo, called to check in. Their concern only made her more anxious. She was so desperate to find Jo, she'd allowed Rhys to go into a war zone, and if anything happened to him, it'd be her fault. As she told Gabe, Rhys had a hard shell, but inside he was soft and sensitive.

"You make him sound like a boiled egg," Gabe said. He tried to use humor to lift her out of her black mood, but she felt off-balance, weepy and depressed. Perhaps her current mood was to blame for the lack of milk.

Quinn turned from the window and walked into the lounge, where she set Alex down on his play mat. She'd been able to leave him there while she prepared dinner or packed a few boxes of kitchen utensils and dishes they didn't use on a daily basis, but Alex had recently learned to turn over, and when Quinn had returned to the lounge several days ago after peeling some potatoes, she'd cried out in alarm when Alex wasn't on his mat. She'd looked around in panic, finally spotting him by the sofa, where he'd rolled all on his own. Alex was full of glee, but Quinn had scooped him up and held him close, having had her first real brush with maternal panic.

"You little rascal," she'd whispered. "You gave Mummy such a fright." But Alex felt no remorse. He kept trying to pull away from Quinn, eager to get back to the floor, where he could practice his new skill.

"How does he roll so fast?" Emma asked, watching in amazement. "He's like a little round ball."

"It's a good thing we're moving," Gabe observed as he rescued the baby from rolling under the low coffee table. "There's no room for him to spread his wings."

"He doesn't have wings," Emma protested.

"They are not literal wings, Emma, but figurative."

"What?"

"I meant that he'll need more space and freedom as he gets older. He'll start crawling in a few months, and then will take his first steps. This is not a safe environment for him."

Emma pondered this information. "Did I roll like Alex?" she finally asked.

They were used to her questions, but the lack of information still bothered them both. They knew very little of Emma's first four years and there was no one to ask. Gabe had taken to simply telling her what she wanted to hear, not wishing to remind her day after day that he hadn't been a part of her life until her mother died in that motor accident.

"Of course, you did, only you weren't nearly as round as Alex. You were a tiny baby."

"Didn't I like to eat? I like to eat now."

"Well, since you couldn't have any pizza or ice cream when you were this small, I expect you weren't as pleased with your choices," Quinn interjected.

"I don't like milk," Emma replied.

"All babies drink milk. It's their first food," Quinn explained.

"When will Alex start eating real things?" Emma demanded.

Quinn was glad to see her finally taking an interest in her little brother, her jealousy receding now that she'd had an opportunity to choose her bedroom in the new house and settle on a color scheme.

"I will start mixing a little cereal into his milk once he turns four months. Once his belly gets accustomed to the cereal, he'll be ready to try some mushed vegetables and stewed fruit."

"Yuck!" Emma made a face. "I'm glad I'm no longer a baby, but I'd like to try new things. Maya says I should be more open to new experiences."

"Then perhaps you should tidy up your room. That would be a new experience for you," Gabe replied smoothly as he tried to suppress a grin.

"Dad! I meant I wanted to try new foods."

"Really? Such as?" Gabe asked.

"Maya says her family has international night every Friday. They eat a different cousin every week."

"Don't they like their cousins?" Gabe asked, teasing her. "I think you mean cuisine, darling."

"Yes, whatever. You know what I mean. Maya said they had sushi last Friday."

Gabe and Quinn exchanged glances. Emma liked only certain types of foods, and her pediatrician had advised them not to force the issue. "It's a form of control. She's lost her mother and had to deal with drastic changes, including a new baby in the house. Limiting what she eats allows her to feel a sense of control over her environment."

"All right, then. Friday night is sushi night," Gabe announced dramatically. "Ready or not, Emma McAllister Russell, you'll be eating raw fish come Friday."

"Eww," Emma cried. "Sushi is raw fish?"

"It certainly is," Gabe replied.

"Can we start with something less icky?" Emma asked.

"Of course. What shall we have?"

"How about kebobs?"

"Done," Gabe exclaimed.

"Where do kebobs come from?" Emma asked.

"From places like Iran and Afghanistan," Gabe replied. He glanced at Quinn, his gaze apologetic. "Sorry, I—"

Quinn waved the apology away. "You're all right."

But despite her cavalier attitude, she felt a knot of anxiety settling in the pit of her stomach. Rhys still hadn't called after being gone nearly a week. What if he had gone missing too? She knew she was being irrational, and the mere mention of the place was no reason to get upset, but her mind seemed to be on a track of its own.

Quinn handed Alex to Gabe and dashed to the bathroom, making it just in time. This was the second time this week she'd been sick. She rinsed out her mouth and pressed her forehead to the cool tiles of the bathroom wall, breathing deeply to prevent a second wave of nausea.

"Quinn, are you all right?" Gabe called through the door.

"Fine," Quinn replied, but she felt anything but.

TWENTY-TWO

Quinn was relieved when Gabe and Emma left for school and work early the following morning. Being alone with Alex allowed her to worry and brood without constantly having to account for her feelings. She knew she was all over the place, but for once in her life she couldn't force her emotions into an appropriate box. She felt weepy and hopeless one moment, angry the next. She wasn't even sure who she was angry at these days. She was angry with Sylvia for separating her from Jo, annoyed with Seth for calling her every few days to check on the progress of her search, and furious with Rhys for not calling her when he must have known she'd be going out of her mind. She was even angry with Logan for not being as obsessed with finding Jo as she was. That was probably why she hadn't been feeling well. She no longer felt nauseated, but her head ached, and her belly was cramping, as if she were about to get her period. She hadn't menstruated since giving birth because she was still nursing Alex, but as soon as she stopped, she was sure to get it soon. She actually looked forward to getting back to normal. It was time.

Quinn settled Alex down for his midmorning nap and put the kettle on. She was jittery, but she wanted a cup of coffee, and something to eat. She hadn't had any breakfast, and now her stomach felt hollow. Perhaps some buttered toast. And an egg, Quinn decided.

She'd just popped the bread into the toaster when the doorbell buzzed. Funny, that. When she'd lived with Luke at her little chapel, no one had ever come by. She supposed there really hadn't been anyone to come by in those days. She and Luke had led a pretty claustrophobic existence when it had been just the two of them. Now the flat was like the arrivals area at St. Pancras. Quinn pressed the button and saw Jude's sorrowful face staring into the screen.

"Hey, can I come up?" he asked.

"Sure." Quinn buzzed him in and shook her head in amazement. She'd thought she and Jude would never form any sort of relationship, but this was the second time he'd come to visit her. Perhaps there was hope for her siblings after all.

Quinn opened the door and let Jude into the flat. He was wearing his navy coat and a knitted cap, a thick striped scarf around his neck.

"You got a dog," he exclaimed as Rufus came trotting down the corridor, eager to greet the visitor. He gave Jude a cursory sniff, then let out a half-hearted woof, as if he wasn't sure if Jude was friend or foe. "He's sweet. What's his name?"

"Rufus."

"Right. Interesting choice."

"We let Emma name him."

"Now it all makes sense," Jude joked as he followed Quinn into the kitchen after divesting himself of his coat, hat, and scarf. "I gather Cecil was voted down. That was her initial choice, if I recall correctly."

"Yes, it was. Want some coffee?" Quinn asked as she took another mug down from the cupboard.

"Yeah, that'd be grand."

Quinn put her toast on a plate and moved it toward Jude. He accepted it and reached for the butter. "Want an egg?"

Jude smiled. "I'm actually hungry today."

"I'll take that as a yes." Quinn gave Jude one of her eggs, poured the coffee, and sat down across from him. "No work today?"

"My shift starts at two. Where's the little guy?"

"Napping."

"I was kind of hoping to see him. Emma too. I miss her."

"She's at school."

"Right, I forgot." Jude bit into his toast and stared at Quinn, his gaze inviting her to ask him why he was there. He looked pale and sad.

"Is something wrong?" Quinn asked gently. "You seem—I don't know—miserable, for lack of a better word."

Jude hung his head and sighed loudly. "I am."

"Want to talk about it?"

Jude nodded but didn't say anything. Quinn took a sip of her coffee and waited. Jude was obviously grappling with something and needed the space to approach whatever it was he wanted to say in his own time. He tapped on the egg and sliced off the top, then stared at the contents as if he'd never seen a boiled egg before. He took a spoonful of egg and swallowed it, grimacing. He sprinkled a bit of salt into the egg, then tried again. Finally, he spoke.

"I'm doing all the right things for my recovery, Quinn. I'm in a methadone program, I've got a job, I've chucked in my drug-using girlfriend, I spend my evenings under the watchful eye of my mother, and all I can think of as I sit there watching *Britain's Got Talent* is that I want to die. I've never felt so hollow, so joyless."

"Would drugs take that feeling away?"

"For a time." Jude's gaze slid toward the window, his expression as bleak as the colorless winter sky. "I hate my job, Quinn. It's soul crushing. How can anyone spend their days taking out the rubbish and sweeping the floors and be content? I can't even help myself to anything in the dispensary to make the days a little less dreary. It's locked up air-tight," Jude said, a sarcastic smile tugging at his lips. "And I miss Bridget. I know she was no good for me, but I miss her.

I'm supposed to be on the straight and narrow, but I feel like my life's gone completely tits-up. If I don't find an outlet for my frustration, I'll go starkers."

Quinn reached out and put her hand over his. Her heart went out to him. He was so young, and so unhappy. At this moment, he looked as if his soul was in someone else's body, trying to figure out how to live this new life.

"Jude, I know you're grateful to Logan for getting you the porter job, but surely there's something else you can do that'd make you happier."

"Making music makes me happy. Playing clubs, getting high, and shagging Bridget in the toilets after a show makes me happy. She liked doing it in public places. It turned her on," Jude added with a heavy sigh. "Is that too much information? Sorry, but I really have no one to talk to. Mum and Logan will lecture me on the evils of my chosen lifestyle, and my friends will try to drag me right back into the hole I'm trying to climb out of. Things are pretty bleak at the moment."

"Is there anything that appeals to you, career-wise?" Quinn asked, desperate to help in any way she could.

Jude shrugged. "I like kids," he mumbled, "but who's going to let me come within a foot of their child? One look at me and they'd start calling me a 'pedo.'"

"Just because you're a young man who likes kids doesn't make you a pedophile, Jude. I wouldn't recommend looking for employment as a nanny, but surely there are other things you can do. You're a talented musician. What about teaching music to kids? Or you can volunteer and see if you enjoy it."

Jude looked up, his expression thoughtful. "They have people who come to entertain the kids on the pediatric oncology ward."

"I'm sure those children would like a real-life musician to play for them."

"You think?" Jude asked, a spark of hope lighting his melancholy gaze.

"I think there are lots of options out there, but you won't discover any of them unless you stop feeling sorry for yourself. Nothing will give you the high you got from heroin, but that doesn't mean you can never be happy. There are other girls, other jobs, and other ways to nurture your love of music."

"Thanks, Quinn. I know you're right, I'm just rubbish at motivating myself. My band was the only thing I got excited over. I got us gigs, made arrangements, and generally kept everyone on their toes. Now they're touring without me. I hear they got a new bass player. I've been very quickly replaced."

"No one is irreplaceable, Jude. Just over a year ago, Emma lost her mum. She was shocked and devastated, but now she has a new family and she calls me Mum. Life goes on. If a small child can find the strength to move forward, so can you."

"I can't see that Emma had much choice in the matter," Jude replied.

"And neither do you. Not if you want to have a future. Maybe, once you've been clean for a while, you can go back to playing clubs and shagging in toilets, but now you have to stay strong."

"And resist the siren call of the heroin?"

"And resist the siren call of the heroin."

"You never stop hearing it, you know."

"I imagine not, and facing a lifetime without it must seem impossible. But if you take it one day at a time, you have a much better chance of success."

"Now you sound just like Logan," Jude complained.

"He's only trying to help," Quinn said softly.

"I know. I'm blessed to have so many people who care enough to give me a bollocking. Well, I'd best be going. I have a few errands to run before I have to report for another exciting shift at the hospital. Thanks for the food, and the talk."

"Jude, come back anytime. Emma would love to see you. She might even let you walk Rufus."

"Your husband won't be pleased to find me here." Jude still

hadn't forgiven Gabe for slamming him against the wall and threatening to call the police when he found Jude's heroin fold in Emma's possession.

"Gabe will be fine. Just come back. Promise me you will."

"Okay, I promise," Jude said. He gave Quinn a peck on the cheek, grabbed his coat, cap, and scarf, and walked out the door.

TWENTY-THREE
JULY 1620

Virginia Colony

Mary watched from her perch at the table as Travesty cut and buttered thick slices of cornbread, then wrapped them in a piece of muslin, buttered sides facing each other to avoid ruining the cloth. She poured ale into a stone bottle and set everything into the basket, which she was about to take to the men out in the field.

"I'll do that," Mary said, surprising herself. Travesty always brought dinner to John and Simon, while Mary busied herself with household chores. The sun was brutal when it rode so high in the sky, and Mary's fair skin turned an angry shade of pink whenever she spent too much time outdoors. Travesty wore a man's wide-brimmed hat over her cap when she went out. She'd never said where it had come from, but Mary suspected it had been her husband's. The first time Mary's skin had burned, Travesty had forced her to sit at the table and smeared buttermilk on her face. She said it soothed the sunburn and prevented the skin from blistering. Mary hadn't thought she'd enjoy having curdled milk all over her face, but Travesty had been right and the cool buttermilk helped soothe her burning skin.

I must make myself a hat, Mary thought as she made her way between rows of leafy tobacco plants. She'd borrowed Travesty's hat, but she didn't like the heavy feel of it, or the sweat stains that marred the brim. She saw the men's heads above the greenery, their shoulders bent as they went about their task. Simon was the first to spot her.

"Good day, mistress," he called out. "And I thought this day couldn't get any brighter, John." He wiped his brow with his shirt-sleeve and smiled hugely. "Is this a meal prepared by Travesty, or is this a special treat you put together with your own fair hands?"

Mary's eyes slid to John, who stood leaning on his hoe. She'd expected him to rebuke Simon for speaking to her so familiarly, but John appeared amused.

"I'm afraid you'll have to contend yourself with Travesty's cooking, but I churned the butter. I must confess I can't compete with Travesty's skill at making cornbread," Mary replied.

"It melts in your mouth," Simon agreed, giving her an insolent once-over that made her feel uncomfortably warm. "But I'm sure your butter is creamier than hers." His gaze caressed Mary's breasts, making his meaning clear. "I look forward to sampling it." He licked his lips, the action too brief for John to notice, but Mary could have sworn she saw John's jaw tighten and his eyes narrow as he turned toward Simon.

"Come now, Simon. Enough silly banter. I'm famished," John said and reached for the basket. He removed the bottle of ale and took a long pull, his Adam's apple bobbing as he drank. "Ah!" he said. "This heat breeds an insatiable thirst." He passed the ale to Simon, who drank deeply.

Mary had thought she'd offer to sit with the men while they ate, but now that she'd delivered the food, their attention strayed from her to talk of the weather.

"I think a storm's brewing," Simon said as he looked at the cloudless blue sky.

"'Tis likely," John agreed.

Mary wasn't sure what had led them to that conclusion but decided not to ask. She picked up the basket and accepted the empty bottle from John. "I'll be on my way, then," she said, hoping he'd ask her to stay a while longer and talk to her.

"See you at supper," Simon called cheerfully.

John raised a hand in farewell and went back to chewing his bread, his expression unreadable.

Mary had never lived in a household with servants, but she couldn't imagine any master would permit his indenture to speak to his wife in the manner Simon had spoken to her just then. Was John oblivious to the innuendo, or did he simply not care? Did he value Simon's regard so highly that he was willing to allow him unlimited freedom? It certainly seemed so. Simon behaved like an equal, and at times, Mary got the impression that he was the one who was master here, not John. John and Travesty had an indulgent attitude toward Simon, as if he were an amusing child who was the apple of his parents' eye.

Mary walked back through the field, her heart heavy. What would happen if Simon's playful words led to something more? Would John allow him to make free with her? Would he care? John didn't seem the jealous type. In fact, he didn't appear to have any passions at all where she was concerned. Last night, John had reached for her, and she, thinking he might finally desire her, wrapped her arms around his neck and pressed her lips to his. John's eyes had flown open in surprise, and even though he didn't pull away, he didn't return the kiss. Instead, he'd shut his eyes when she stared at him in the darkness, waiting for some response, then pushed apart her legs and slid inside her, moving silently for a few minutes, as was his ritual. Once finished, he'd risen from the bed and reached for his breeches.

"Where are you going?" Mary had asked.

"I just need a breath of air. I'll smoke my pipe and come back to bed. Go to sleep, Mary."

Mary hadn't gone to sleep but lay wakeful, waiting for sweet tendrils of pipe smoke to engulf her, but she hadn't smelled John's pipe. She'd waited for him to return but eventually fatigue overtook her and she fell asleep, only to wake in the night to find him stretched out next to her, his breathing even and relaxed in repose. Had her kiss upset him? Was it not natural for a wife to kiss her husband, especially during moments of intimacy? She hadn't known any marriages aside from that of her parents, and Uncle Swithin and Agnes. Her parents had been loving and devoted, equal partners, but Swithin and Agnes reminded her of a tomcat and a frightened mouse, the poor mouse always ending up squealing as the cat pinned its tail with its paw, eager to play with its food before devouring it.

Perhaps John thought kissing was sinful. Did he have Puritan leanings? It didn't seem likely. John was not what she'd call devout. He went to church because it was expected of him, and because it afforded an opportunity to speak to other settlers and get a much-needed break from the monotony of the six-day work week. With others, John was amiable and attentive, listening with his head bent toward the speaker as if he feared missing even a single word. He paid that same kind of attention to Simon, but Mary noticed that whenever John listened to her speak, his gaze was fixed on some faraway point, his mind already on something else.

Mary made a sharp turn and walked away from the cabin and toward the barn. She couldn't bear to spend the afternoon in Travesty's sullen company. She needed a bit of time to herself, but as Reverend Edison was fond of saying, idle hands were an invitation to the devil. Mary stuffed the basket full of straw and headed toward the creek. It was the only place she could be truly alone, the green coolness of the small clearing a balm to her weary soul.

She took off her shoes and stockings, hiked up her skirt, and waded into the water. Once she felt sufficiently cooled down, she returned to the bank and sat in a shady spot, her back against the trunk of a thick oak. She reached for the straw in her basket and began to braid the stalks, collecting the braided lengths in her lap. Once she had enough braided straw, she'd be able to fashion it into a hat, but she'd need a lot of braids if she hoped to make a brim wide enough to shade her face.

Mary was so intent on her work, it took her a while to realize she was being watched. Her head snapped up, her heart hammering with fear when she saw Walks Between Worlds on the other side of the creek. He waded in and was next to her in moments, water running down his long, muscled legs from the breechclout that clung to him in a most embarrassing fashion. He seemed completely unaware of her discomfort and squatted next to her, watching her hands fly over the straw.

"What are you doing?" he asked.

"Braiding straw for a hat." She suddenly realized she was no longer frightened. Nothing in the Indian's demeanor suggested that he meant her any harm. He looked mystified but nodded as if he understood.

"And what are you doing?" Mary asked. Why did he haunt this spot?

"Checking my traps."

"Don't you hunt?" she asked.

"Yes, for large game, but it's easier to set traps for smaller animals. Their meat is more tender, and the English like the fur."

"So, you trade with the English?"

"Of course."

"What do you get in return?" Mary asked.

She hadn't noticed the dagger at the Indian's hip, tucked into the side of his clout. He pulled it out and showed it to her, sliding the blade out of its sheath. It was a fine weapon, the handle and sheath intricately carved, the blade long and sharp.

"It's better than a stone blade, and lighter," he explained. He hefted the blade in his hand, showing her how light it was.

"Why do they call you 'Walks Between Worlds'?" Mary asked. The name had stayed with her, making her wonder if the Indian was adept at some form of devilry. "Do you commune with the dead?"

"No. The shamans can contact the dead, but I'm not a shaman." Up close, Mary noticed that his eyes weren't all gray. A bit of dark blue ringed the pupil and seemed to dissolve into the gray that lightened at the outer edges. His eyes were unique, as was his face, despite its nut-brown color.

"Why, then?"

The Indian's gaze slid away from her, fixing on something on the other side of the creek. "Because I am of two worlds. I'm neither one nor the other."

"So, what are you?" Mary asked, trying to comprehend what he was telling her.

"A half-breed," the man said bitterly.

"What worlds do you belong to?" Mary asked, curious to find out more about this strange man who seemed as fascinated by her as she was by him. He wasn't all that threatening, if one managed to ignore his near nakedness. He was just a man, and a very attractive one at that.

"My mother was English."

Mary felt as if he'd slapped her and instinctively drew back from him. "You must think me very gullible," she snapped, gathering up her braids and tossing them into the basket.

His brow furrowed with concentration. "I don't know that word."

"Daft. Stupid. Your mother couldn't have been English. There were no Englishwomen here until last year. Reverend Edison said so."

The Indian's eyes flashed with anger. "You think I'm lying?"

"Aren't you?" she demanded, staring him down.

"I don't lie, to you or anyone else," he spat out.

He sprang to his feet and was gone before she could form an adequate response. Mary stood up, shoved her bare feet into her shoes, and tossed her hose into the basket. She'd been having a perfectly pleasant time until that trickster showed up and ruined it all.

"Half English," Mary muttered. "And I'm English on one side, Moorish princess on the other." She huffed as she strode back toward the cabin. She'd allowed herself to be taken in by a pair of beautiful eyes and a disarming smile. He was a savage, a heathen, and a liar.

TWENTY-FOUR

By the time Mary returned to the cabin, the sky had turned an ominous shade of gray and any trace of a breeze had died down, leaving the air still and heavy. There was an atmosphere of expectation, as if nature were holding its breath, waiting for just the right moment to exhale. At long last, fat drops of rain began to fall, soaking the floor just beneath the windows.

Travesty dropped what she was doing and dashed across the cabin to affix the leather panels to the windows to prevent the interior of the house from turning into ankle-deep mud. Unable to concentrate on mending John's shirt, Mary set it aside and moved to the table. She was surprised to see Travesty produce two fat rabbits, which she laid out on the flat surface.

"Where did those come from?" Mary asked. It'd been at least a fortnight since they last had meat, and her mouth watered at the prospect of rabbit stew. Their diet consisted mostly of corn, beans, cheese, and the occasional serving of stewed fruit, picked from the wild fruit trees Travesty had discovered near the plantation. Meat would be a most welcome change.

"Simon came across some traps in the woods," Travesty replied. "Set by the savages, no doubt. So, he helped himself."

"That's stealing," Mary replied without thinking.

Travesty gave her a sharp look. "Concerned with fairness toward the godless, are you? They don't deserve your sympathy."

Mary didn't reply. She couldn't help wondering if the traps were the ones set by Walks Between Worlds. He had said he'd come to check his traps, but he'd been empty-handed. Perhaps he'd left what he'd collected on the other side of the creek. She was still angry with him, but she shouldn't have called him a liar to his face. He'd appeared genuinely hurt by the accusation.

Mary watched as Travesty hacked off the heads of the rabbits, sliced their bellies open from neck to tail, and began to clean out the innards. The Indian had told her his name meant he walked between worlds. It was a strange name, but it said something about who he was. She'd known many Marys, Annes, Elizabeths, and Margerys. She'd never known anyone whose name was utterly unique. Except Travesty.

Travesty grunted with effort as she separated the skin from the lifeless bodies, leaving behind nothing but shiny pink carcasses. She set aside the skins and began to cut up the rabbits, dividing each carcass into six sections. Her hands were covered in blood and gore, but she didn't seem bothered. Her eyes shone with the prospect of a good meal.

"By suppertime, these will have been simmering in the pot for several hours. The aroma alone will bring the men running back."

"Won't they return from the fields now that it's storming outside?" Mary asked. The rain was still coming down in a torrent, its hammering clearly audible even with the window coverings down.

"Nah. They'll keep at it. Working in the rain is probably more pleasant than toiling in the hot sun. And it's not as if there's lightning. To my knowledge, no one's been damaged by a little rain."

"What will you do with the skins?" Mary asked, watching as Travesty carefully washed off the blood and hung the skins to dry after getting the stew going.

Travesty's head spun around, her eyes flashing. "You can have them, not that you have need of them."

"I wouldn't know what to do with them," Mary replied, trying to pacify the woman. She was so easily roused to anger. "I only wanted to know what they can be used for."

Travesty had the decency to look contrite. "Forgive me, mistress. I shouldn't have snapped at you. I don't know what's got into me these past few days," Travesty said. "I was going to tan the leather and use it to make new shoes. Mine are worn right through."

Mary hadn't noticed that there was a cobbler in Jamestown, but perhaps Travesty would make the new shoes herself. Walks Between Worlds had been wearing soft leather shoes that didn't resemble any shoes Mary had ever seen, but they looked comfortable and seemed to make no noise when he walked.

"Travesty, have there ever been Englishwomen here in Virginia before now?"

"Not that I know of. I was one of the first to arrive on these shores. Why do you ask?"

"No reason," Mary lied. Travesty looked somewhat more amenable since her unexpected apology, so Mary seized the opportunity to keep her talking. "Is Travesty your real name?" she asked.

"Why wouldn't it be?"

"It's unusual, is all. Not the type of name you imagine a mother giving her child."

"I wasn't named by my mother," Travesty replied. She turned toward the hearth to stir the contents of the pot, releasing the appetizing aroma of cooking meat. After she finished, she turned back to Mary. Her expression was wary, but she sighed and allowed her shoulders to relax, as if she'd made peace with whatever emotions were raging inside her. Travesty sat down at the table and clasped her hands in front of her, her gaze directly on Mary.

"My mother and her brother, Jack, were orphaned at a young age. My mother was the elder and managed to look after Jack. She found employment for them in a tavern. My mother did the cooking during the day and served the patrons at night. Jack helped out in the stable."

"How old were they?" Mary asked.

"They were fourteen and eleven. They got along fine for about a year, until Jack discovered that my mother was with child. She wouldn't tell him who the father was, but he suspected it might have been one of the patrons, who was long gone and had no way of knowing he'd left something behind. Not that most men would care. He'd got what he wanted, and the rest was none of his concern. It wasn't one of the local lads, of that he was sure. It was an isolated place, and Jack had never seen anyone hanging around Holly." Travesty let out a deep sigh. "I haven't told this to no one but my husband, mind," she said. "I don't like talking about it."

"I'm sorry. I had no wish to pry."

"Hadn't you?" Travesty retorted. "Well, I might as well tell you the rest of it now. When Holly's pains began, she went to the stable, where no one would disturb her. She had no money for a midwife, and there wasn't one around for miles anyway. She labored for two days, during which time the landlord came into the stable and beat her black and blue for leaving him without help. The beating finally brought on the child. I was born in the dead of night, with just Jack to attend on my mother. She died before she even laid eyes on me. This was the worst thing that could have happened, so Jack named me Travesty, for I would always be a reminder of the sister he'd lost."

"Oh, Travesty. I'm sorry," Mary said softly and reached for Travesty's hand, but the woman yanked it away.

"So, twelve-year-old Jack was left with a newborn baby and no employment, since the landlord told him to clear off and refused to pay what Jack and Holly were owed. Jack took me and left. He never spoke of that time, but I know it nearly broke him. He managed to keep us alive, and when I was two, he left me with a family he'd come to know in London and went to sea. Whenever he came back, he paid Master and Mistress Harkness for harboring me, and he brought me little treats. He was the most important person in my life, Jack. Years later, when I married my Stephen,

Jack stayed with us whenever he was back in London. He was there when the Black Death came calling."

"He died with the rest of them," Mary muttered, recalling that Travesty had said her brother had died along with her family.

Travesty nodded. "Yes, he died with the rest of them. I'm the only one left. The thoughtless name he gave me is the only thing I have left of him and the life I knew. I've come to like it. It says something of who I am and where I come from."

Just like Walks Between Worlds, Mary thought.

"Don't feel sorry for me, mistress," Travesty said, her voice clear and sharp. "We've all had our share of troubles. But I mean to make something of myself in this new land. I won't be a slave forever."

"You're not a slave," Mary countered.

"As good as." Travesty gave Mary a look of pity. "But at least my enslavement will end."

The rain had tapered off while they talked, and a hazy sun now shone through the thin leather covering the window. Travesty opened the windows and allowed the fresh air to blow away the stale closeness of the cabin.

"After a storm, the sun always comes out again," she said, as if speaking to herself. "The sun *will* come out again."

TWENTY-FIVE
JANUARY 2015

Lingfield, Surrey

The sun had finally come out after several days of impenetrable gloom. The snow had melted, but the countryside was a study in brown and gray, the bare trees spreading their skeletal limbs toward the sky as if imploring spring to come.

Quinn turned into the narrow lane that led toward her house. A part of her was reluctant to arrive at her destination, her heart refusing to accept that this might be the last time she ever laid eyes on her sanctuary. She knew it was time. They'd be moving into their new house at the end of next month, or the beginning of March at the latest, but she still felt a bit sad at the thought of giving up her little chapel. She'd fallen in love with it the first time she laid eyes on it, and she loved it still, but keeping several residences wasn't practical, and the chapel wasn't large or modern enough to house a family.

It was a spiritual retreat, a bolt hole, but not really a home anymore. The chapel held many memories, but the happiest one was of the night Gabe had proposed to her, slipping an engagement ring onto her finger as they lay together in the large claw-footed tub, their bodies flushed not only from the heat of the water, but from the love they'd made just before getting into the bath. It was amazing to think how their lives had changed since that night—for the better mainly, but in some ways for the worse. People had been found, and people had been lost.

Quinn glanced at the beautiful antique ring on her finger. Her relationship with Gabe was no longer in the honeymoon phase. It had been tested, threatened, strengthened, and blessed in so many ways. They were no longer two individuals optimistically forging a path forward. They were a couple, a unit, and parents to two children. They were on the verge of a new chapter in their lives, and she was ready. Well, almost.

Quinn parked the car, extracted the key from her handbag, and walked toward the arched doorway. The interior of the chapel had been modernized and converted into a private home, but the building still looked like the medieval lady chapel it had originally been, built by a loving husband for his devoted wife. It had been ransacked during the Dissolution of the Monasteries, but it had survived, like so many other beautiful religious buildings. It had stood the test of time and was a silent reminder that some things weren't easily destroyed.

Quinn approached the iron-studded door, a replica of the original, and was about to insert the key in the lock when something made her pause. There was no other car parked in the drive, nor did she see anything odd, but she had the distinct feeling that the chapel hadn't been empty since she was last there. Uninhabited homes had an air of neglect, a forlorn look she always managed to spot.

Quinn stood still, listening for anything that might put her on full alert. Maybe she was just imagining things. The lock appeared intact, and there were no marks on the door that would suggest that it had been forced open.

She was just about to unlock the door when a loud crash came from inside, followed by a muffled oath. She couldn't quite make out the words, but she recognized the cadence and timbre of that voice. She'd heard it often enough during the past decade. Quinn slipped the key back into her pocket and raised her hand to knock on the door. Walking in would startle her unwelcome guest, and that was the last thing she wanted, given his unpredictable behavior of late.

She knocked three times and waited. No one came to the door. Well, he'd left her no choice. Quinn pulled out the key again and unlocked the door, opening it a crack. "I know you're there," she called. "I'm coming in."

When there was no answer, she pushed the door fully open and walked in. Luke stood leaning against the worktop, a tea towel in his hand. Shards of glass littered the floor at his feet and a brown stain was spreading slowly on the gray tiles. He must have dropped his cup of coffee when he heard the crunch of tires and Quinn's footsteps on the gravel path.

"Hello, Quinn," Luke said. He looked around furtively, no doubt wishing he were anywhere else. Signs of habitation were everywhere. A half-eaten sandwich lay on a plate on the worktop, his coat hung on the coatrack, and there was an open book lying on the sofa. A heap of ashes in the fireplace attested to a recent fire, and several empty beer bottles were heaped in the bin beneath the sink.

Quinn stood close to the door, unsure how to proceed. Then she returned the key to her pocket and took her mobile out of her bag.

"Quinn, don't," Luke begged, realizing what she was about to do.

"You're trespassing. You have no right to be here."

"I know, and I'm sorry, but please, don't call the police."

Quinn didn't make the call but kept the phone in her hand, should she need it. "What are you doing here, Luke? This is no longer your home."

"I still had the key," he replied.

"That doesn't make it all right for you to use it."

"I had nowhere else to go." He bent down, quickly wiped up the coffee, then threw the wet towel onto the worktop. "Can I make you a cup of coffee?" he asked. "I desperately need one. I can't function without caffeine in the mornings."

Quinn was about to refuse, but a cup of coffee sounded great just then. And Luke made good coffee. "All right," she said. She removed her coat, tossed it over a chair, and walked to the sofa, still clutching her mobile.

Luke made two cups of coffee and brought hers over to her. He'd made it just the way she liked it, with one sugar and a splash of milk. Quinn took a sip and set the mug down on the low table in front of the sofa. She didn't say anything. Luke hated long silences, and usually began to speak before the silence grew heavy and uncomfortable. He sat down at the other end of the sofa and positioned himself against the armrest, like a cornered animal.

He looked awful, she realized. Luke had always been proud of his looks and took time with his appearance, cutting his hair every six weeks and maintaining a sexy stubble that gave him that devil-may-care flair of academic nonchalance. Most of his shirts and jumpers were in various shades of blue, intentionally purchased to bring out the color of his eyes. At the moment, Luke's hair was unkempt and his stubble more of a shaggy beard. He wore a pair of jeans, beat-up trainers, and an old gray hoodie that looked like it could do with a wash.

"Quinn, I'm sorry. I really am," Luke began, not sounding sorry at all. His eyes flashed with anger, but he quickly adjusted his expression to one of self-pity. "Gabe sacked me from my job at the institute," he added, his voice flat.

"I know," Quinn replied. Gabe hadn't had much choice, and the decision to terminate Luke's employment hadn't been personal. In fact, it had been made by the board of trustees, not Gabe alone. Luke's behavior the previous term had been erratic, inappropriate, and downright aggressive.

"I don't blame him," Luke continued. "I did have it coming. I was angry and I was acting out. I never meant to upset anyone."

"Didn't you? You called Monty a poof and made offensive

sexual comments to half the female staff, as well as several students."

Luke nodded. At least he had the decency not to try to defend his behavior. He reached for his mug and took several slow sips of coffee, as if he needed time to formulate his next response. "I applied for several positions but, alas, no takers. What with Christmas around the corner, no one was hiring. My application for grants has also been denied."

"So, you could no longer afford your posh flat and decided that squatting at my house would keep you financially afloat that much longer," Quinn finished for him.

"You make it sound so underhanded."

"It *is* underhanded."

"If I'd asked your permission to stay here, you would have refused," Luke said, pouting theatrically.

"Damn right I would have refused," Quinn snapped.

"This was my home too."

"Last time I checked, my name is on the title to this property. And it's about to be sold. I'm meeting an estate agent here in half an hour. I only came early to tidy up a bit. You need to leave, Luke, right now. I won't charge you any back rent, but I will not allow you to remain here a moment longer." Quinn held out her hand. "Key, please."

Luke fumbled in his pocket and produced the key to the chapel. He slammed it into Quinn's palm, his face now marred by resentment. "You always were a heartless bitch," he hissed.

"Good thing you ditched me when you did, then. Now, get your stuff and get out."

"Quinn," Luke began, quickly realizing belligerence would get him nowhere. "Please, I need a bit of time to get something sorted."

"Call Monica Fielding. Maybe she'll put you up," Quinn suggested. She rarely saw Monica now, but the two women had never got on and never would. Some resentments went deep, and Monica had taken every opportunity to needle Quinn and try to undermine her professional standing as well as her relationship with Gabe.

"She's not speaking to me," Luke replied, his shoulders slumping in apparent misery. "I tried to apologize, but she never forgave me for the comments I made about Mark leaving her because she bored him in bed."

"You know, for once, I'm on Monica's side. The things you said were unforgivable."

"I was hurting, Quinn," Luke exclaimed.

"That's no excuse. You're not a child. You don't get to throw a temper tantrum and hurt everyone you know because taking them down makes you feel better about your failures. You have ten minutes to get out, Luke. If you're not gone by then, I'm calling the police."

Quinn stood and headed for the door. "I'll be in the car." She gripped her mobile, frightened Luke might try to take it away from her to prevent her calling for help.

Luke stood as well. "Do you honestly think you're not safe here with me?"

"I don't know."

"I would never hurt you. I loved you once, and I love you still. Leaving you for Ashley was the biggest mistake of my life. I know that. I also know that Gabe is the better man, and that he makes you happy. You look different since you've been with him." Luke's eyes grew misty as he looked at her, as if he might break down and cry.

"In what way?" Quinn couldn't help asking.

"Like there's a tiny flame burning inside you. The glow of that light is there for everyone to see. I suppose that's what real love looks like. I hope to find it someday," Luke said, his voice wistful.

Quinn nodded, unsure what to say. She was pleasantly surprised by Luke's observation, but not at all sure he wasn't trying to play on her emotions to manipulate her into allowing him to stay. "I'm sure you will," she said at last and headed out into the chilly morning, closing the door behind her.

Less than ten minutes later, the door opened, and Luke emerged, an old rucksack slung over his shoulder. He gave her a half-hearted wave and started down the lane toward the village. Quinn watched him for a few moments in the rearview mirror. She didn't know why, but she was suddenly sure they'd never meet again, and she was glad of it. Luke was a part of her past, but there was no place for him in her future. He'd been her first love, her first romantic disappointment, and a valuable lesson she'd needed to learn. Luke's betrayal had led her to Gabe, and on some level, she was grateful to him. Despite her earlier anger, she wished him well.

By the time the estate agent pulled up to the chapel, Quinn had tidied up and stowed some of her personal possessions in the boot of her car. This chapter of her life was over; it was time to leave. She signed several documents, giving the agent permission to list the house, and handed over her key. She would not be returning, but her earlier sadness had evaporated. She smiled as she sped down the lane, eager to get home.

TWENTY-SIX
AUGUST 1620

Virginia Colony

The church was stifling, the stagnant air reeking of sweltering bodies. Mary fidgeted on the hard bench, wishing the sermon would end. Reverend Edison was in the throes of preaching on the virtues of loving thy neighbor, a subject no doubt inspired by a brawl that had taken place in the tavern a few days ago, resulting in the death of a settler. Although the reason for the disagreement was still unclear, the two men responsible for the murder would be tried immediately after the service.

Mary fixed her eyes on the reverend, but her mind drifted out of the church and into the cool forest. She'd gone back to the creek numerous times after Walker, as she'd come to think of him, had stormed off. She bathed more than she ever had, washed everyone's undergarments, and having successfully made herself a straw hat, offered to make one for Travesty. Walker had not returned, and as time passed, Mary had begun to feel gnawing guilt in her gut. He'd seemed genuinely shocked when she accused him of lying. He hadn't looked like a man who'd been caught out, but rather a man whose pride had been wounded. Perhaps he'd never known his mother and had been told she was an Englishwoman. He was wrong, of course, but if he truly believed he was telling the truth, was it still a lie?

Mary shifted her bottom again, growing increasingly uncomfortable. She'd asked herself again and again why she longed for the Indian to come back. He was nothing to her, a mere curiosity, but given John's increasing aloofness, Simon's baffling over-familiarity, and Travesty's nearly impenetrable sullenness, Walker seemed like a ray of sunshine on a cloudy day. There was something in his gray gaze that lifted the spirit and offered a glimpse into another world, a world that was so unimaginably different from her own. There were so many questions she wanted to ask him, especially about native women. What were their lives like? Did they have choices that her countrywomen didn't?

At times it seemed that a woman's only mark on this world was the headstone she left behind. If she had no children, it was almost as if her life had never happened. She simply vanished from the world, quickly forgotten, like Mary's own mother. No one except Mary kept the memory alive, but after all these years, the image of her mother was fading from her mind, the sound of her voice receding into the mist of time that separated them. Mary wondered morosely if that would be her fate as well, as Reverend Edison droned on.

Who would care if she died? John certainly wouldn't, since he didn't seem to have developed any feelings for her. They had been married for only two months, a very short time, but Nell had been right when she'd said you just knew about a man. John was courteous and not unkind; that was the best she could say of him. She saw some of the other women she'd arrived with aboard the *Lady Grace*. They sat close to their husbands, looks of contentment on their faces. They weren't permitted to display any affection in church, but there were the warm looks, the casual touches of the hand, and the solicitous way the husbands escorted their wives from the church and to their wagons. John usually just walked out, assuming Mary would follow. If anyone tried to touch her, it was Simon, who never missed an opportunity to get too close, making her feel threatened rather than admired.

Mary's hand instinctively went to her belly. She'd had her courses only last week. When she'd seen the blood, she hadn't been sure if she was relieved or disappointed. A baby would give her life greater meaning, but did she want to be one of the first women to bring a child into this primitive place? There wasn't even a midwife to help the women of Jamestown when their time came. Of course, the Virginia Company, in their wisdom, hadn't thought to send out a midwife along with the dozens of women they were shipping to the colony.

Another shipload had arrived only a fortnight ago, the women comely and young, and frightened. Another spate of weddings had taken place, to the great delight of the governor, who was said to have made a pretty speech of welcome. Perhaps, in time, they would send out enough women for all the men, but according to Secretary Hunt, who also enjoyed making speeches on behalf of the Virginia Company—mainly after service on Sunday—the male population of the colony neared one thousand souls. Hundreds of men longed for wives and hoped that this was the beginning of a new policy of the Virginia Company. They prayed more ships would come.

John's face was tense with concentration as he listened to the reverend's words. He was one of the few people paying attention. Mary wondered why John had got a wife while hundreds of others hadn't. She could hardly ask him. Perhaps it was because his plantation was doing well, or maybe because he happened to have a good relationship with Secretary Hunt, who probably made the selection. Whatever the reason, there were men who truly longed for companionship and love, but John Forrester wasn't one of them.

The service over at last, Mary followed Simon and Travesty outside, while John remained inside for the trial. Mary took her place in line at the well, desperate for a cup of water. The sun beat down on her shoulders and she was glad of the hat shielding her face. She'd just taken a drink when she saw several Indians walking through the gate. Her belly fluttered with sudden nervousness, since one of them was Walks Between Worlds. His gait was relaxed, but she noted the rigid set of his shoulders and the thin line of his lips. He wasn't at ease. The other two men didn't seem similarly affected, but they walked in silence, their heads held high. They knew they were being watched by every colonist in Jamestown.

The men were headed for Governor Yeardley's residence when someone informed them that the governor wouldn't be able to receive them until after the trial. The Indians settled in to wait, their expressions stony as they watched the settlers, who milled around in eager anticipation. There weren't many trials in Virginia, according to the talk around the well, and there hadn't been a murder trial in years. Maybe not ever. Many of the settlers were relatively new to the colony, and this was the most excitement they'd had, save the arrival of the women.

"We should go back to the wagon," Simon said. "It's cooler beyond the gates and less crowded."

Mary would have liked to spend some time in the company of Nell and Betsy, whose husbands were also inside the church, but most of the women headed toward their wagons, uncomfortable in the presence of so many overexcited men. Simon was right. It was best they leave. Travesty fell into step with him, but Mary hung back as they approached the Indians, who were standing by the gate, talking quietly amongst themselves. Walker's eyes bore into her, his expression hard, his cheeks mottled with anger. He hadn't forgiven her the insult.

Mary dipped in front of him, as if taking a pebble out of her shoe. She looked up, glad he was still watching her. "I'm sorry," she whispered. "Please forgive me."

His expression changed little, but there was a thawing in his gray eyes. He didn't say anything but inclined his head a fraction, letting her know he'd heard her apology.

"Mistress, are you all right?" Simon asked when he realized she wasn't walking directly behind him. He returned for her and took her arm. "Was that savage bothering you?" he asked loudly.

"Not at all. There was a pebble in my shoe."

"I don't like the way he was looking at you," Simon growled.

"How was he looking at me?" Mary inquired as they walked toward the wagon.

"With insolence," Simon retorted.

Mary had to stifle a giggle. If anyone was insolent, it was Simon. He was still holding her close, a familiarity that was completely unnecessary, given that she was in no danger. She pulled her arm free and sat on the grass in the shade of Betsy's wagon. Nell joined them as well.

"My arse is numb," Betsy proclaimed, making them laugh. "If that pompous windbag went on any longer, I think I might have pissed myself. There's only so long a woman can hold her water."

"He is longwinded," Nell agreed. "Good thing you have padding, Betsy. Imagine how we bony-arsed girls feel."

Betsy patted her ample rump with a smile. "My Silas is inordinately fond of my padding," she said as she tried to stifle a giggle. "Says it's like sleeping on a cloud."

"Are you sure it's your arse he's referring to?" Nell asked, giving Betsy's overflowing bodice a meaningful look.

"Whichever it is, he's a happy man," Betsy replied. "And that makes me a happy woman. Never thought I'd enjoy having a man of my own so much," she confessed.

Nell nodded in agreement. "I like my Tom as well." Both women turned to Mary, awaiting her contribution. She simply nodded, as if agreeing with them.

"That Simon's a handsome devil," Betsy remarked. "I wager many a woman would overlook his questionable past to get him into her bed."

"What do you know of his past?" Mary asked. Simon never spoke of his life in England, and she hadn't asked, not wishing to encourage his interest in her.

"Oh, nothing," Betsy replied. "But most indentures have been sent down for some crime, haven't they? He might be a murderer."

Mary stared at Simon, who was talking to Travesty. He was smiling into her eyes and standing closer to her than an unmarried man should.

"I should hope not," Nell said, peering at Simon as if she could tell just by looking at him. "Mary, what was he sent down for?"

"I don't know. I never asked. I'm sure John knows."

"You should ask him," Betsy suggested. "You should know what type of person you're living with." She looked around in irritation. "I want my dinner," she complained. "How long does it take to try someone?"

"Not that long, apparently," Nell said when a commotion erupted within the settlement. "The trial must be over. Now the poor buggers will face their fate."

Mary stared at her. It hadn't occurred to her that the men might be executed. It was a tavern brawl, and by all accounts, the dead man had started it. Surely that counted in the accused's favor. Mary sprang to her feet when she saw John emerging from the gate. He bowed stiffly to Nell and Betsy and beckoned to Mary to return to their wagon.

"Let's go home," he said and climbed onto the bench. "I've done my part."

"Are they to hang, master?" Travesty asked from the back.

"Many called for execution, but the governor decided on leniency, given that they hadn't started the fight. They're to be flogged this afternoon, after the governor has his dinner and concludes his business with the Indians."

"The governor must have his dinner," Simon scoffed. "At least the man has his priorities straight."

"Simon!" John said sharply. Simon went quiet, but his mouth was still twisted in a sarcastic grin.

"I'm ready for my dinner," John said in an effort to lighten the atmosphere in the wagon. "And then I will go to the creek and have a well-deserved bath. It was stifling in that church. Join me, Simon. The afternoon service has been canceled, due to the flogging."

"With pleasure. If Reverend Edison will only make us sit through one sermon on Sundays, I hope they flog someone every week," Simon said. It was a blasphemous thing to say, but Mary suspected they all secretly agreed. Having to endure two services on Sundays was torture, especially since all the settlers worked their land six days a week and had animals to tend to.

"Oh, I do look forward to the weather cooling down," Travesty said as she pulled her hat lower over her eyes. "'Tis like the fires of hell, this heat. I'd never known anything like it before coming here."

"In England, they have fires burning in the grate all through the summer," Simon said, sounding wistful.

"Aye, it was cold and wet, but I miss it," Travesty said with a dramatic sigh. "I miss it all."

"As do I," John agreed. "I wonder if I'll ever see the shores of England again."

A silence settled over them as they contemplated their chances of ever going home, knowing it wasn't likely. For better or worse, their futures were tied to the fortunes of the Virginia Colony.

TWENTY-SEVEN

Mary waited impatiently for the men to leave for the fields come Monday morning. She completed her morning chores, then stripped off the bed linens and dumped them into her basket. She'd washed them only a week ago, but the sheets were grubby from their bodies sweating in the relentless heat and stained with her menstrual blood. Mary added John's hose and her own sweat-crusted chemise and stockings.

"Travesty, give me your bedlinens," Mary said. "I'm going down to the creek."

"Off to launder again?" Travesty asked, her lip curling with amusement. "I've never met anyone so cleanliness minded."

"I've never lived in such a hot place before," Mary retorted. Travesty made it sound as if she were shirking her responsibilities, but the laundry needed to be done. Today. Or so she told herself. In truth, it didn't make much difference. By tomorrow morning the sheets and the garments would be sweat stained again and smell like they hadn't been laundered in weeks. England had been damp, but it was the kind of damp that seeped into the bones and made her feel like she'd never be truly warm again. This damp heat made Mary feel as if her skin were sizzling over an open flame, the flesh roasting like that of a suckling pig.

Mary put on her straw hat over her cap and walked out of the cabin, grateful to be away from Travesty, who'd been in a particularly foul mood since their visit to Jamestown yesterday. Come to think of it, everyone had been subdued, especially Simon. On their way back to the plantation, he'd made rude jokes about the flogging the men were to receive, but she'd noticed a spark of fear in his eyes. What did Simon have to fear?

Mary stopped for a moment to adjust the basket on her hip. Perhaps Simon had been flogged for whatever crime had brought him to Virginia, she theorized, resuming her pace. She'd never seen Simon without his shirt, so perhaps he bore the scars to remind him of his punishment.

As Mary drew closer to the woods, she forgot all about Simon. The morning dew sparkled on the lush grass and the sky was dotted with fluffy clouds that floated lazily overhead, momentarily obscuring the sun and offering a brief respite from its searing rays. She breathed a sigh of relief once she reached the cool shade of the forest. It was filled with birdsong and smelled pleasantly of pine.

Mary kicked off her shoes. She no longer wore hose beneath her dress when at home. What was the point, especially since she only had the one pair? She wished she could give up wearing the long-sleeved chemise as well and wear just the bodice over her sleeveless shift. She'd look like a strumpet, but she'd be a lot more comfortable.

The water in the creek was higher after last week's rain, and deliciously cool. Mary positioned herself on the bank, took a sheet out of the basket, and began to wash it, using the hard soap Travesty had made. Soap scum swirled away when she rinsed out the sheet and floated downstream. Mary hoped no one would drink the soiled water. She washed all the items she'd brought and hung them on low branches to dry. She'd really thought Walker would come after her apology, but the forest was as quiet and peaceful as ever. Mary removed her hat and lay back on the grass beneath the great oak. It was shady and cool, and she closed her eyes, allowing herself a moment of quiet. There was no reason to rush back.

She woke with a start, aware, even before she opened her eyes, that she was no longer alone. Walker was sitting cross-legged on the grass, watching her sleep.

Mary sat up and smiled. "I didn't think you'd come."

"I can't seem to stay away," he replied, his eyes serious.

"I really am sorry," Mary said, noting the tense set of Walker's jaw. "I didn't mean to insult you."

He inclined his head, in that way he had, to indicate he'd heard her and accepted what she was saying, but didn't reply.

He is still angry, Mary thought. *I wounded him more deeply than I imagined.* Watching him from beneath lowered lashes, she wondered if all natives were so proud. They certainly appeared to be very arrogant, and fierce, from what she'd seen in Jamestown. She'd seen Indians many times now, but she had yet to see a native woman or child.

"So why did you come back?" she asked. "To check your traps?"

"I set new traps deeper in the forest. Someone was helping himself to my catch. Your servant, I think."

"Why do you think it was him?" Mary asked.

"He has no honor."

Walker's answer took Mary by surprise. She'd assumed a sense of honor to be a purely English trait, and to hear Walker accusing an Englishman of having no honor was unsettling. She opened her mouth to reply but closed it before she made the mistake of insulting him again. Perhaps the natives had their own idea of honor and weren't the savages the English believed them to be. And Walker was right. She'd had her doubts about Simon from the start and realized the Indian had simply verbalized her own feelings about the man.

She inclined her head, intentionally copying his earlier response to her apology, but didn't say anything more about Simon. Walker suddenly smiled, revealing straight white teeth. He must have realized she was mirroring his mannerisms.

"I came to see you," he said. His demeanor had changed. He

was no longer angry with her, and a wave of relief washed over Mary. She couldn't explain, even to herself, why it mattered to her, but it did.

"Why? Surely there are women in your village."

"Yes, but they are not like you." Walker reached out and caught a silky chestnut curl that had escaped from her cap. "You remind me of someone."

"Your mother?" Mary asked softly. He nodded.

Mary willed herself to remain quiet and refrain from questioning him. She knew with absolute certainty that there had been no women in Jamestown until 1619. Everyone said so, from Reverend Edison to Governor Yeardley and Secretary Hunt. Walker had to be a few years older than her, which would make him close to twenty-five. How was it possible that his mother had been English?

"Is your mother still alive?" Mary asked instead.

"She died when I was a boy. I could barely summon up her image in my mind until I saw you that day on the way to Jamestown. You were frightened when you saw me staring at you, but I was struck dumb. It was like seeing my mother's spirit come to life."

"Walker—I hope I may call you that, Walks Between Worlds is such a long name—where had your mother come from? What part of England, I mean," Mary amended, not wishing to sound as if she were doubting him.

Walker shrugged and plucked a blade of grass, crushing it between his fingers. His gaze drifted off, beyond the trees to a bird wheeling high above. It spread its wings, momentarily blocking out the sun.

"The Powhatan are not my people," he finally said. "I'm not of their tribe. I come from a place in the north, many days' walk from here. The Powhatan welcomed me and adopted me into their tribe, but I am different, an oddity. Just as I was among my own people."

Mary remained silent, enthralled by Walker's soft voice.

"Many summers ago, long before I was born, English ships came to a place called Roanoke. It was the ancestral land of the Croatoan, my people, but they didn't make war on the English. They were curious about them and wanted to study their ways. The ships brought men, women, and children, and they built a settlement and tried to make a life in a wilderness to which they weren't accustomed. They struggled against hunger and sickness. The Croatoan offered the English their help. They brought them corn to plant and showed the men how to set traps and hunt, but the settlement was not thriving. They did not try hard enough. They waited for their God to help them," Walker said bitterly.

"What happened to them?" Mary asked. She'd been told that Virginia was the first and only English colony in the New World, but what Walker was telling her sounded genuine, although she couldn't imagine that England would send ships full of women and children. The Virginia Company had sent out only strong, skilled men at first, and the colony had remained without women for over a decade.

"No one knows. Croatoan scouts reported that they hadn't seen smoke coming from the settlement in many days, and the chief sent a scouting party to investigate and offer help if it was needed. When the scouts walked into the settlement, everyone was gone. The houses had been knocked down and the well was covered. No possessions had been left. The scouts decided that a ship from England must have come to take the people away, and were glad for them. This land was no place for them. They didn't have what it took to survive," Walker said.

Mary stayed silent, afraid to interrupt his tale. He seemed lost in a private memory, and his voice was barely audible when he continued.

"One of the scouts carved the word 'Croatoan' into the fence-post. He was happy to see the English go. The scouts scoured the site, searching for anything that might be useful. The English had sharp blades and good cooking pots, but there was nothing. They were about to leave when they heard crying coming from below ground."

"Someone had been buried alive?" Mary cried, sucking in her breath when she realized she'd interrupted Walker's account. Walker shook his head.

"The English had dug a hole in the ground to store food. They thought it'd last longer down there. The hole was covered with a wooden door. One of the scouts pulled up the door and found a woman and child inside. The woman was insensible, but the child was frightened and crying, begging his mother to wake up."

"Why were they left behind?" Mary asked.

Walker shrugged and grew quiet, staring into the distance as if he could see that fateful day, despite the fact that he hadn't been born yet.

"Please, go on," Mary pleaded.

"The scouts helped the child out of the hole and carried the woman to a canoe. They brought her back to the village."

"Did she come to?"

"Yes, but she was terrified and couldn't communicate with anyone since she didn't speak the language. She refused to eat and rocked back and forth for days, moaning to herself and staring at nothing. After a time, she began to take a little food but still wouldn't respond, not even to hand gestures. She just stared into the fire or slept."

"What happened to her?" Mary asked.

"After many moons, she began to adjust to life in the village. She helped the other women and learned our tongue. When she gave up all hope of England, she was given a new name." Walker said something strange in his tongue.

"What does that mean?"

"Sad Eyes."

"What was her name before, in England?"

"Elizabeth Viccars. And her boy's name was Ambrose. After the seasons changed many times, she took a husband from among the village braves. Their first child died on the day of its birth. I was born the following spring. My mother died when I had eight summers."

"What became of her other child?" Mary asked.

"He grew up, took a wife, and had many sons," Walker replied. "He's my brother, and he's still with the Croatoan."

"Is that why you came here? To see the English?"

Walker nodded. "My mother retained her native tongue. She spoke to me in English and told me stories of her homeland. She sang strange songs. She said it'd benefit me to speak the English tongue when more men came across the sea. When I heard the English had built a settlement on Powhatan land, I came to see for myself. I wanted to learn about that part of my spirit."

"And have you?"

"The English are a mystery to me."

"In what way?" Mary asked, mystified.

"In every way. The English way is very contrary."

"I don't understand."

Walker's eyes locked with her own, his brow furrowed in concentration. "Your God created everything, so the Bible says. He made man in His image."

"Yes. What's so contrary about that?"

"If man is made in God's image, why does your God punish man for following his instincts, the instincts He gave him?"

"What instincts?"

"He gave people curiosity, then banished them from Eden for using it. He made men lustful, but your church says desiring a woman is a sin."

"It's not a sin to desire one's wife," Mary explained patiently. "God said, 'Be fruitful and multiply.' You can't multiply without lying together."

"No man can desire only one woman his whole life. That goes against nature."

"Do people not marry in your culture? You just said your mother took a husband, and your brother married and had many sons," Mary said, intrigued by this unusual logic.

"They do, but if they no longer make each other happy, they go their separate ways and find different partners. It's not a sin to love more than one person. The Indians have no concept of sin."

"How is that possible? If lust is not a sin, or adultery, how about murder? Surely that's the greatest sin of all."

"People kill because they must. Why should that be a sin?"

"It's wrong to take a life," Mary argued.

"The English take many lives. They have killed to conquer other people, to defend their own, to protect what's theirs, and to punish for everything from betraying their country to stealing a loaf of bread, all with the blessing of their God and king—and queen, whose name my mother shared," Walker added.

Mary stared at him. "How do you know?"

"I talk to the settlers. I ask questions about their homeland. They like to talk, especially when drunk on corn liquor."

"The English take lives for the same reasons as the Indians," Mary protested. She felt defensive, confused by Walker's strange arguments.

"Is it just to hang a hungry child who stole food to survive?" Walker asked. "Surely that's the greater sin."

"You said the Indians kill to punish," Mary argued.

"Yes, but the punishment has to fit the crime. To kill children is barbaric."

Mary bowed her head, considering Walker's point of view. The English claimed his people were savages, but he saw the English as savage, and given what he'd said, he had good reason.

"Do your people think the English are barbarians?" Mary asked, shocked to have put the thought into words.

"My people think the English are to be feared."

"And the English say the Indians are fearsome and blood-thirsty."

Walker laughed. "You see, that's why my people single me out. They mistrust the English, and the English mistrust the Indians. I'm the man between, the man who doesn't belong."

"You belong with the Powhatan now," Mary replied, trying to understand.

"I'm useful to the Powhatan."

"Will you return to your tribe?" Mary asked. The thought of Walker leaving made her unaccountably sad.

"Not yet. I've made a study of English men. Now I'd like to learn more about Englishwomen."

He leaned forward and brushed his lips against hers, shocking her with the intimacy of the gesture.

"I'm a married woman," Mary said sharply.

"Do you love your husband?" Walker asked. Judging by his neutral expression, he wasn't challenging or shaming her. He was simply asking a question to which he needed an answer.

"No," Mary conceded.

"Then you are free to follow your heart."

He leaned forward and kissed her again. The second kiss was more intimate, more demanding. It was the first time she'd been truly kissed, and it was confusing and wonderful all at once. For just a moment, Mary gave herself up to the kiss, desperate to feel affection and desire, but then she placed her palms against Walker's bare chest and pushed him away.

"I'm not free to follow my heart. Marriage is a sacred covenant between two people into which I entered willingly. I made vows before God. I made a promise to honor my husband and be faithful to him."

"But you don't love him," Walker protested. It was his turn to be confused.

"And is that what you're offering me? Love? You said yourself that I remind you of your mother. You're curious, and maybe lonely. You don't love me any more than I love you."

Walker smiled at her. She'd thought he'd be upset, but instead he looked amused, his eyes crinkling at the corners.

"The first time I saw you, you reminded me of my mother. She had hair like yours, and eyes the color of the sky. And her skin was like the petal of a flower from those trees you gather red fruit from.

But you're nothing like her. There was a profound sadness in my mother that never left her. I was a young boy when she died, but even I understood that death came as a relief to her. You are brave, Mary. You will not look to death to free you from your bonds. You will fight because you have a strong spirit."

Mary's eyes welled up, and she looked away from him, unable to explain what his words meant to her. No one had ever told her she was strong, or brave, or spirited. Ever since her parents had died, she'd felt invisible, inconsequential. Her only value lay in her ability to work. Even John, who had at first seemed so pleased with her, had lost interest. He looked at her, but he didn't see her. He never spoke to her the way Walker did, never explained anything or asked any questions.

"Why are you crying?" Walker asked, puzzled by her reaction.

"Because you see me," Mary replied.

"Of course, I see you. I have eyes."

Mary laughed through her tears. "You see me with your heart." She placed her palm over his chest. His skin was warm and smooth, and she felt the steady beating of his heart beneath her fingers.

Walker placed his hand over hers and tilted his head until she was forced to meet his gaze. "It is because I see you that I understand your struggle. Vows are important, as is honor. I will not trouble you again, Mary."

Mary gave him a watery smile. "I thought you were a savage," she said. "Hardly more than a wild beast. You're the most gallant man I've ever met."

"I don't know what 'gallant' means, but I know that you're a woman of your word." He took her hand from his chest and kissed her palm. "I wish you a good life, Mary Forrester."

Mary's eyes swam with tears. She didn't want him to leave. She liked talking to him. He made her feel beautiful and worthy of attention.

"What if I want to see you?" she whispered.

"Leave me a sign on that tree," he said, pointing to the oak.

"What kind of sign?"

Walker shrugged. "Tie a piece of cloth to the branch."

Mary nodded. "All right. I will. I mean, I won't, but just in case."

Walker cupped her cheek. "If you need me, I'll come."

She nodded and watched as he disappeared into the woods.

TWENTY-EIGHT
FEBRUARY 2015

Kabul, Afghanistan

Rhys had traveled widely before settling down to his job at the BBC nearly a decade ago, but he'd never felt as out of his element as he did in Kabul. His spirits quickly sagged once Rob departed for home, and they had already been low. There were other European reporters at the hotel, but Rhys had no desire to engage in conversation. The news about Jo had devastated him, but he couldn't leave until he learned what had become of her remains. It was the least he could do for Quinn, who'd now never meet her twin. She'd be shattered.

Early in the morning, when waiting for a call back from the British Embassy became unbearable, he made an impulsive decision. Given what had happened to Jo and Ali, driving into the mountains was probably the most irrational decision he'd ever made, but when he left the hotel, he reasoned that he wouldn't get far, since there were checkpoints on the outskirts of the city and a visible military presence. Rhys had asked for a map at the hotel and pinpointed the location Ali had drawn. He mapped out his route and set off.

The morning was cold and clear, the mountains rugged and

forbidding in the distance. He wasn't sure how long it'd take him to get to his destination, but it wasn't as if he was in a rush. Lack of purpose always made him feel restless and frustrated. At least this was something he could do. He sailed through the checkpoints, being a white, middle-aged man with a press pass, and continued toward the foothills. He'd expected to get overtaken by a military vehicle at any moment but found himself completely alone on the narrowing road that led into the mountains. He drove for two hours before finally nearing the place Ali had marked.

Rhys stopped and looked around. He didn't dare leave the road or step out of the vehicle. As long as he stayed put, he was safe, or so he told himself as he extracted the binoculars he'd borrowed from one of the other reporters, who was an avid twitcher, and brought binoculars everywhere he went. Rhys had never cared for birdwatching, but the glasses would come in handy.

He peered into the binoculars, scanning the area inch by slow inch. He wasn't sure what he expected to find. Surely if Jo's body was lying out in the open, someone would have seen it by now. The steeply rising mountain terrain offered up nothing. The dry, rocky mountainside was an unbroken vista of brown, occasionally dotted with a smudge of green from a particularly stubborn weed or sapling. Rhys saw craggy fissures higher up and assumed some of them were caves, but it was difficult to tell from his vantage point.

There were no signs of life, not even the orange blur of fox fur or the burrow of a groundhog, if they were native to Afghanistan. The sky was clear as well. Not a single bird had entered his field of vision, not even a pigeon or a sparrow. After approximately half an hour of staring at the unrelenting background of dun-colored dirt, Rhys set aside the glasses and made a very careful U-turn, scrupulously avoiding the sides of the road. That was where explosives were frequently buried, according to Rob.

The return trip to Kabul took much longer, since it was more difficult to enter the city than leave it. The line at the checkpoint was at least thirty cars long and moved at a snail's pace, but eventually Rhys made it back to the hotel, tossed the binoculars on the chair, and threw himself down on the bed, physically and mentally exhausted. What he'd done was so monumentally foolish, he could hardly admit it to himself, and he thanked his lucky stars for having returned to the hotel in one piece. A part of him was relieved he'd found nothing, but he was also disappointed. It was as if Jo had vanished into thin air. Rhys sank into the lumpy mattress and fell into an uneasy slumber.

It was late afternoon by the time he woke up. His back ached, and his emotional fabric was in tatters. He hadn't learned anything new this day, but he felt heavier somehow, more lethargic. He sat up slowly and ran his fingers through his hair. He wanted nothing more than to throw his few possessions into his case, drive to the airport, and get on the next flight out of Kabul, but he couldn't leave until he had something concrete to tell Quinn. He knew her too well to believe that she would simply accept Jo's death, especially when there was no body. Quinn would never find peace unless he could present her with irrefutable proof that Jo was gone.

Rhys stood and walked to the window, pushing aside the hideous apricot-colored curtains. The sky just above the distant mountaintops was a palette of pink, lavender, and gold, but the city spread out below was already shadowed with the deep purple of a winter evening. Rhys grabbed his coat and headed for the door. He was hungry but had no desire to eat at the hotel restaurant. The kebob place Rob had taken him to was a ten-minute walk from the hotel, and he felt like getting a breath of air. The tiny room made him claustrophobic and depressed.

The street was practically deserted. Darkness came early in February and people retired to their homes, undoubtedly safer behind their flimsy, bullet-strewn walls. Rhys walked along at a brisk pace, eager to get to the restaurant. The place was small, but lively, and although he'd resented the festive atmosphere so soon after learning of Jo's death, he longed for a little cheer this evening.

Rhys was a few minutes away from his destination when a windowless black van turned the corner. It was driving slowly, as if the driver were looking for an address or landmark. Normally,

Rhys would have ignored a passing vehicle, but something about the van's deliberate slowness and grime-covered plates made the hair on the back of his neck rise. He quickened his step, hoping it would simply pass him by.

As he neared the junction, the vehicle drove past him and disappeared around the corner. Rhys breathed a sigh of relief. He was overly anxious, his nerves on edge in this city that was like a violent video game, where the bad guys kept coming and the good guys kept trying to keep them at bay. What would anyone want with him? He was just another foreigner, a faceless dot in an over-populated metropolis.

Rhys stopped and waited for the light to change before he could cross the street. He saw the bright lights of the kebob restaurant just up ahead. The screech of tires startled him, and he looked back, surprised to see the van racing toward him. It must have made a circle and come back around. The vehicle stopped next to him, the side door slid open, and two men jumped out. They were dressed entirely in black, dark caps pulled low over their eyes. Rhys could have sworn they were European.

Rhys took a step back, but the men were upon him before he could formulate a coherent thought. They pulled a bag over his head, yanked his arms roughly behind him, bound them with a strip of plastic, and shoved him inside. Rhys fell onto his side and pulled his knees up to his chest to protect his vital organs. The floor of the van smelled sweet, a sickening odor that made his head swim. *Opium*, Rhys thought. He'd never actually smelled it but had seen its distinctive scent described several times in popular literature.

The van lurched as it pulled away, speeding down the street. The men talked quietly between themselves, but Rhys couldn't understand a word. He thought it was one of the Eastern European languages. They definitely weren't Afghans.

"What do you want with me?" he demanded, his voice muffled by the bag over his head. "I'm a British journalist."

"We know you are," one of the men responded.

So, it wasn't a mistake. He'd been taken deliberately. Rhys tried freeing his hands, but the plastic strips bit into his skin. They couldn't be loosened, like with rope. He'd seen those types of restraints used in action films. His feet were free, but there wasn't much he could do. Just when Rhys thought his kidnappers would take him out of the city, the van stopped abruptly. He tensed as he heard a set of footsteps somewhere above his head. The driver must have remained seated, ready to go at a moment's notice. This was Rhys's one chance to save himself. He opened his mouth to speak, desperate to engage his kidnappers in discourse, but strong hands yanked on his ankles, straightening his legs.

Rhys had a few seconds to react to this development before a heavy boot struck him in the stomach, making him cry out in pain. He gasped for breath, the dusty fibers of the bag making him cough as they landed in the back of his throat. Rhys sputtered, tears streaming from his eyes as he doubled over in pain. The boot kicked him in the knees, forcing his legs to jerk away and expose his stomach once again. Rhys was kicked several more times, each blow leaving him breathless and gasping for breath. The pain in his stomach was excruciating, and each breath was an agony on his bruised or broken ribs.

Rhys curled into a ball and his attacker allowed him to remain in that position. Moving behind, he kicked Rhys in the lower back, aiming for his kidneys. Rhys jerked involuntary, throwing his head back and lowering his knees. Another kick followed. Rhys heard a roar. It took him a moment to realize the sound had come from him. His mind seemed disconnected from his body, maybe because of the opium he'd inhaled, but the pain enveloped him like an iron shield, solid and impenetrable. He was crying and whimpering between coughs, but he wouldn't give his attacker the satisfaction of pleading for mercy. It'd probably just spurn him on.

Rhys closed his eyes tightly and saw the image of his daughter as he'd seen her on the antenatal scan. She'd been alive then, moving slowly, her feet like flippers making ripples in the amniotic fluid. She'd lifted her hand and moved it toward her face. Her fingers had been splayed, tiny and perfect. Rhys didn't care if she'd been his. She'd *felt* his.

Elizabeth, Rhys thought groggily, using the name he'd secretly picked for her. *My Elizabeth. I'm coming, sweetheart. We'll be together soon.* He braced for another kick, but the assault stopped.

"This is your one and only warning, Englishman. Stop asking questions about things that don't concern you and go home."

The van stopped moving and Rhys was unceremoniously tossed out. He couldn't break his fall with his hands, so he landed on his side, slamming his head against the pavement. His restraints were clipped, and then he heard the screech of tires as the van pulled away.

Rhys remained immobile for a few minutes, unable to gather enough strength to stand. He was vulnerable and exposed, but he needed to catch his breath. His back and stomach were on fire and he could barely draw breath. Finally, Rhys pulled the bag from his head and looked around. He'd been dumped in the same spot where he'd been snatched. He saw the lights of the kebob restaurant glowing warmly in the dark night, but he was no longer hungry.

TWENTY-NINE

"You are lucky to be alive, Mr. Morgan."

"I'm acutely aware of that," Rhys replied acidly. The pain had dulled to a steady throb, as long as he didn't make any sudden moves. He could only take shallow breaths, but thankfully, his ribs didn't appear to be broken.

"Do you require a doctor?"

"I'll be fine."

"You don't look fine, if you'll pardon my saying so. You'll need some painkillers at the very least to get through the next few days."

Rhys couldn't argue with that. He'd gladly take some pain tablets, a dose large enough to treat an elephant, if he could get his hands on it. He had a headache as well. He'd spent the past twenty minutes answering questions about his abduction, the sum total of his answers being "I don't know."

Eric Hallam, Attaché to the British Embassy in Kabul, was what Rhys liked to think of as an everyman. He was the type of person who was so physically average, he could blend into any crowd, penetrate any organization without ever being noticed, and melt away as if he'd never been there at all, but Rhys was sure that he was anything but ordinary when it came to intelligence. You didn't get to occupy this type of position if you were a middling bureaucrat.

"Where is Jo Turing, Mr. Hallam?" Rhys asked, tired of answering questions.

"Resting in a shallow grave, I imagine," Hallam replied. "And so will you, if you persist in conducting this investigation."

"Why aren't *you* conducting this investigation?"

"Because no one has reported her missing."

"Her agent has. Mr. Charles Sutcliffe."

"Mr. Sutcliffe called the embassy last month but didn't initiate a missing person's report. He simply indicated that he hadn't heard from Ms. Turing in several weeks and was concerned. He never rang back, so we assumed she'd turned up."

"I need to speak to the Americans," Rhys said. "Someone high up. I don't want to have to explain this to some low-level flunky." He took several careful breaths, playing hide-and-seek with the agonizing pain in his ribs.

"Good luck with that," Hallam replied.

"You can get me an appointment," Rhys said, leaning back in his chair to indicate that he wasn't about to be ushered out.

"I'll see what I can do," Hallam said, gathering several papers to indicate he was a very busy man and it was time for Rhys to take his leave.

"No time like the present."

"Mr. Morgan, I would strongly advise you to go home to London and leave the business of Ms. Turing to us."

"And I would strongly advise you to pick up the phone and call your American counterpart. Work the special relationship."

"It hasn't been especially fruitful of late."

"Make the call," Rhys growled, tired of the verbal fencing. If the Americans had found Jo, alive or dead, surely, they'd have no problem turning her over. Or perhaps they already had. Rhys suddenly had a thought that nearly made him laugh out loud. What if Jo was MI-6? Then real life would truly be stranger than fiction. "Mr. Hallam, is Jo Turing an agent of the Crown?"

"No."

"Are you quite certain?"

"I am." Hallam looked momentarily exasperated but picked up the phone and pressed a button. "Linda, get John Smith on the line for me."

"Is that his real name?" Rhys asked, trying unsuccessfully to suppress an eye roll.

"Believe it or not, it is. John, good morning," Hallam said into the phone. He sat down behind his desk and a bland expression slipped over his irate features. "Yeah, good. And you? How's the family? Right. Can't say I blame her," Hallam said, possibly commenting on something John Smith had said about his wife. "So, she's stateside? Lucky lady. I wouldn't mind taking a break from the wonders of Kabul myself."

After several moments of banal banter, Hallam finally got to the point. "Look, John, I have a bit of a situation here. Need your help. A British journalist has gone missing and is believed to have been a victim of an ambush in the mountains. I have it on good authority that your boys found her and her hapless guide. No, I don't know if she's alive. Is there someone who can fill in the blanks? Right, thanks a million. I owe you one." Hallam disconnected the call and turned to Rhys. "He'll make enquiries."

"And how long will that take?"

"As long as it takes."

"And what am I to do in the meantime?" Rhys asked. He knew his belligerent attitude was a defense mechanism. He was frightened, and the thought of being alone in Kabul for even one more day scared the wits out of him.

"Mr. Morgan, as a rule, most people don't get a second warning, or even a first, for that matter. They don't want to kill you, whomever they are, but they will if you disregard their message."

"And who are they, Mr. Hallam?" Rhys asked. He still had no inkling who'd want him out of the way, and why.

"Most likely, they're drug traffickers, who are protecting their turf. Going into the mountains on your own wasn't a smart idea.

Whatever Ms. Turing might have stumbled on had clearly upset someone enough to have her and her guide shot at. The IED was an added bonus, I should think, or maybe an intentionally planted deterrent."

"So, what am I to do?"

Hallam sighed. "You are to sit tight. Do not go anywhere until you hear from me. The hotel is the safest place for you right now. Do you understand?"

"I understand," Rhys replied.

Rhys made to rise, but Hallam held up his hand. "We have a doctor on staff." He made a call. "Giles, do you have a few minutes? Yes, I have someone here who's run into a bit of trouble with the locals. Right. I'll send him right over." Hallam hung up. "My PA will walk you over. Giles is an excellent physician. Nice chap too. He'll fix you up."

Rhys thanked the attaché and stepped out into the outer office, where Hallam's assistant was already waiting for him.

"This way, please, Mr. Morgan," she said pleasantly and began to walk. She slowed her pace when she noticed that Rhys was struggling to keep up. "You poor man," she said, shaking her head. "What have they done to you?"

What they had done to him was beat the *shite* out of him, as Dr. McCallum put it. He bound Rhys's bruised ribs after examining him extensively, then supplied him with a full bottle of painkillers. "Take as needed, but don't get carried away."

"Are these addictive?" Rhys asked, studying the label.

"Only if you start popping them like sweeties. Do not exceed three a day, and make sure there are at least four hours between doses. Here's my direct number. Call me if you don't feel better in a few days. I sincerely hope you will be back in England by then. See your own GP when you return home."

"Thank you, Dr. McCallum."

"My pleasure. Feel better, old son."

Rhys chuckled. Dr. McCallum was around thirty-five. He hadn't expected to hear the outdated expression from a man his age. "Will do," Rhys replied and left the doctor's office. He wasn't surprised to find Linda waiting outside. They would never allow him to wander the corridors on his own. He might be a spy. It was an amusing thought. Rhys followed Linda down to the foyer, where he said his goodbyes and left the embassy.

It was broad daylight and there were guards posted outside the gates, but Rhys's whole body tensed as he looked from side to side, almost expecting the black van to come racing around the corner. He hated the thought of being cooped up in his tiny room, but Hallam was right; the hotel was the safest place for him. Although, if someone wanted to get to him, a hotel full of foreign nationals wouldn't stop them. All they had to do was walk in, find his room, break down the door, and put a bullet in his head. They clearly knew where he was staying and had most likely been watching him to make sure he'd heeded their warning.

Dear God, Rhys thought as he drove back to the hotel, *I know I don't talk to you often, but if you allow me to get out of this hellhole alive, I promise I'll never ask you for anything again. Well, for at least six months. Maybe three. But please, don't let me die here*, Rhys prayed as he parked the Jeep in the car park and practically sprinted to the hotel entrance.

THIRTY
AUGUST 1620

Virginia Colony

The sound of the door closing jolted Mary out of a deep sleep. It had taken her a long time to fall asleep since the heat inside the cabin was so stifling, she'd felt as if she were being roasted alive. John liked to keep the windows uncovered overnight to allow the night air to vent the cabin, but the marginally cooler breeze brought with it a swarm of mosquitoes that feasted on Mary as if she were their last meal. For some odd reason, John never got bitten.

Mary scratched at a new bite on her arm and looked around groggily, wondering if it was time to get up, but the sky outside the small window showed no signs of dawn, and Travesty was still in her loft, snoring softly. Mary threw off the sheet covering her body. She was bathed in a sheen of perspiration. Even in the middle of the night, the air was thick with humidity. John had been having trouble sleeping the past few weeks, due to the heat, he'd said. He often woke in the night and went outside, sometimes to smoke a pipe, and sometimes to just sit on the bench and allow his body to cool until he was ready to return to bed. Mary allowed him these moments of privacy, not wishing to intrude. She usually turned over and went back to sleep, tired from a full day of household chores, but the cup of water she'd had after supper was making itself known. She got out of bed and walked to the door, letting herself out into the balmy night.

John wasn't by the cabin. She looked around, wondering where he might have got to, then thought he might have gone to the privy. Well, she'd find out soon enough. She knocked softly on the door, but there was no response from within. Mary pulled open the door. The outhouse was empty, the interior so suffocating after a day of baking in the hot sun that she momentarily considered relieving herself behind a bush. Who would know? But there could be something in the grass, like a snake, or some insect just waiting to bite her bottom.

She sucked in a deep breath and went into the privy, finishing her business as quickly as humanly possible. She released her breath once she stepped outside and looked around. She needed to go back to bed; tomorrow would be another long day filled with never-ending chores and mind-numbing boredom, but Mary couldn't bring herself to go back in just yet. The yard was bathed in silver moonlight, the night peaceful and still. She sat down on the bench and looked up at the velvety sky. The stars twinkled like a swarm of light bugs, the light distant and dulled by the humid air, the silence interrupted only by a chorus of cicadas.

Mary rested her head against the wall of the cabin and sighed. She hadn't seen Walker since the day he'd kissed her by the creek. That was well over a month ago, and although she prided herself on doing the right thing, some small part of her regretted her rashness in turning him away. She was lonely in a way she'd never been. When she was a child, she'd had her parents. When she'd lived with Swithin and Agnes, she'd had the girls and several neighbors she could call on when she had a few minutes to spare.

There had been one couple in particular, the Morelocks. Michael Morelock was a cooper, a trade highly valued in a port town. His wife, Susan, looked after the house and helped her husband by taking orders and negotiating the prices for his barrels.

But she was also a skilled midwife and was often called upon to help the women of the parish in their time of need. Master and Mistress Morelock, who were both in their sixties, had been parents to three sons, but by the time Mary had made their acquaintance, they no longer had any living children to care for. They were the closest thing Mary had to parents, and as Mary grew into a woman, Susan kept a watchful eye on her, worried that Swithin might take an unhealthy interest in his comely niece, particularly once Agnes passed. Mary was grateful for their company and sincere concern and made sure never to leave her encounters with Swithin to chance. Mistress Morelock warned her never be alone with him in his chamber or sleep in a place where he might have access to her without disturbing his young daughters. Sleeping with her cousins had been a trial at times, but it had kept her safe, and their innocent affection often made up for the lack of a more mature love in her life. She missed the girls and hoped Mistress Morelock was looking after them the way she had looked after Mary when she'd been orphaned.

Even on the ship to Virginia, she'd had constant companionship. The women were all different and often got into disagreements, but they'd also told stories, shared anecdotes, and had a few laughs, especially when they speculated on a wife's marital duties. The conversations started out seriously enough, but after a few minutes someone would say something bawdy and the women would dissolve into giggles, desperate for any kind of diversion to take their minds off the great unknown. As miserable as conditions had been, Mary sometimes missed her days aboard the *Lady Grace*, and she missed Nell and Betsy.

Mary had established early on that she would never have that type of easy relationship with Travesty; and Simon, although not as odious as Swithin, was motivated by something other than a desire for company. Mary had worked in a tavern long enough to recognize a glance of appraisal followed by a spark of lust. Simon's suggestive comments had grown bolder, so she made sure never to be alone with him for fear of finding herself in a compromising situation. Simon was handsome, to be sure, and very confident of his appeal, but there was something beneath the playful exterior that put Mary on guard. He was watchful and calculating, and although he seemed loyal to John, she didn't think he'd pass up the opportunity to grab something for himself, even if it went against the interests of his master.

Mary stood, somewhat reluctantly. She'd have liked to enjoy the beauty of the night a bit longer, but she needed her rest, and her eyelids were heavy. She was just about to open the door when she heard a noise. It sounded like an intake of breath, followed by another. She looked around. Where was John anyway? Could he have walked away from the cabin and hurt himself somehow?

Mary followed the sound. It came from the direction of the barn. She walked quietly, her bare feet making no noise on the packed earth. She peeked into the barn, but all was quiet, so she continued around the side. The yard was enclosed by a fence made of wooden rails to keep the farm animals in and wild animals out.

Mary stopped abruptly, concealed in the shadows. Simon was leaning heavily on the rail directly behind the barn. He wasn't wearing a shirt and his pale skin glowed in the moonlight. His head was bowed, and his breath was coming fast. His breeches were around his ankles and he was stroking himself furiously as John made free with his body, his cock sliding in and out of Simon's backside. Both men seemed to be lost in the act, completely oblivious to Mary's shocked gasp. She clamped her hand over her mouth and retreated, terrified of being seen.

She hurried back to the cabin and threw herself on the bed, turning her face toward the wall. Hot tears of anger and humiliation slid down her cheeks. She'd never seen two men together, but she knew enough to understand that what she'd witnessed was an act of sodomy. Perhaps that should have been the greatest shock, but what stunned her more was the look on her husband's face. No longer aloof, his eyes had burned with desire, his mouth partially open as he panted with lust. John's hands had gripped Simon's hips firmly, and he'd driven into him with a force that bespoke a total lack of control. She'd never seen ecstasy up close, but knew it when it slapped her in the face. John had never looked like that when he lay with her. He had the glazed eyes of a dead fish, and his mouth was usually pressed into a thin line, as if he found the act distasteful. Perhaps he did.

Mary buried her wet face in her pillow. Was that why John had married her? What better way to hide a sin of that magnitude than to conceal it beneath a guise of decency? She was his cover, his ticket to safety. Governor Yeardley had passed strict morality laws once women began to arrive in the colony. A man could be put in stocks if he so much as kissed his wife in view of others. What would the governor decree if he learned of John and Simon's transgression? Would they be put in stocks, flogged, or worse? She was sure it wasn't the first time they'd engaged in sodomy, and it wouldn't be the last. Was the pleasure they got from it worth the risk? Judging by what she'd seen tonight, the answer was a resounding yes.

Mary stuffed a fist into her mouth to muffle her crying as John came stealthily back into the cabin. He got into bed and was asleep within moments. She needn't have worried that he'd hear her crying. Nor would he care.

Mary inched further away from his hot body. She didn't love her husband, but she'd been prepared to honor and obey him. But now he repulsed her, as did the sharp reek of his sweat and spilled seed. John had betrayed their marriage. He had betrayed her, and she no longer owed him her obedience or respect. She had to think of herself now, and her future.

THIRTY-ONE

When morning came, Mary didn't utter a word of reproach. What was the point? It wasn't as if John would be repentant. He was in good spirits, enjoying his breakfast and talking to Simon about his plans for the day. Neither man paid much attention to her or Travesty, who went about her business with her usual efficiency.

Mary poured Simon more ale and watched him from beneath hooded lids. Simon accepted the ale and looked up to nod his thanks. As expected, his gaze slid to her bosom, taking in the sun-kissed flesh above the neckline of her chemise. John never looked at her bosom. As she turned away from the men, Mary wondered if John might be coercing Simon. Simon was John's to command until his indenture contract was up, and they had been on their own for a time, before Travesty joined them. Could this be all John's doing?

Mary bid the men a good day as they rose from the table and headed for the door. She was glad to see the back of them. She tore off the bedlinens and filled her basket. "I'm going to the creek," she told Travesty.

"I've never seen anyone spend so much time laundering," Travesty muttered but nodded and went back to what she was doing.

Mary walked to the creek and tied a scrap of fabric to one of the lower branches of the great oak before turning her attention to the linens. She hoped Walker would come, but it wasn't likely. Not this soon. She stripped off her clothes and took a dip in the creek to cool her burning flesh before reluctantly returning to the cabin to begin her other chores.

The despair of last night was gone, replaced by a steely determination to seize whatever joy she could from her life in this dreary colony. Unlike Simon and Travesty, she wouldn't be set free at the end of her indenture. She was bound to John for life, and the prospect of living that life filled her with dread that gnawed at her insides and hollowed her heart until it felt like an empty shell, completely incapable of feeling anything other than burning rage.

Mary went back to the creek several times over the next two weeks, but Walker was never there. The strip of fabric hung limply on the branch, its frayed edges as ragged as Mary's patience. She felt more despondent with every passing day, certain she would spend the rest of her days in this remote cabin with no one to talk to, and not even a child to love. She'd been married to John for nearly three months now, but there was no sign of a child growing in her womb. She bled regularly, and every time she got her courses, she was torn between relief and disappointment. The colony was a strange place, the settlement soulless without children or domestic animals. It was the home of tired, frustrated, rugged men, who'd lost whatever veneer of civility they'd once had after years of hard work and no female company.

Even the ruling class, which included the governor, the secretary, the marshal, and the reverend, had acquired something feral in this wild land. The governor could be seen striding about in nothing but his shirt and breeches, and the marshal was always on edge, his eyes constantly scanning his surroundings for signs of trouble. It would take no more than a spark of hostility to ignite a war in this dung heap of a colony. No wonder the Virginia

Company was sending out women. The women were the water to the flame, coming to douse the passions that were running high and were desperate to be satisfied.

When the next dozen brides arrived, the men stood about as the ship docked, tense and grim-faced, terrified that the woman assigned to them might have died during the crossing. It happened often enough. Mary, who happened to be in Jamestown for Sunday service, watched, enthralled, as the tired, dirty women came trudging into the settlement, led by a well-dressed man. He didn't appear to be the quartermaster and carried a curious wooden case that had many tiny drawers which were held shut by lengths of rope that encircled the polished wood.

Governor Yeardley came forward and shook the man's hand. "Glad to have you with us, Doctor. We're a hardy bunch, we've had to be, but having a physician among us is a step toward a civilized society and not just a settlement carved out of the wilderness. Secretary Hunt has prepared a surgery for you. I hope you'll find it to your liking."

"Thank you, Governor. I'm sure it will be most satisfactory."

The doctor was not yet thirty, in Mary's estimation. He had dark hair, and eyes so light, they reminded her of a sheet of ice reflecting the pale winter sky. He wore a neatly trimmed beard and was somberly dressed in russet and brown velvet. He was as tall as the Governor, who stood several inches above most men. The doctor was lean, and his calves, clad in remarkably clean hose of mustard yellow, were well muscled. Several women threw him admiring glances, but he ignored them and urged the ladies to adjourn into the church, where the next spate of marriages would take place shortly. The prospective grooms were already inside, waiting anxiously to face their future.

"He's a handsome devil," Betsy said softly as she came up behind Mary and Nell, who'd been allotted a few minutes by their husbands to socialize before returning to their wagons for the ride home.

"With an impressive codpiece," Nell added, her eyebrows nearly disappearing beneath the rim of her cap.

"Roll up a stocking and stuff it into your man's breeches," Betsy advised. "He'll be just as impressive."

Nell giggled. "My Tom wasn't blessed with razor-sharp intellect, but he doesn't lack distinction in that area."

"Lucky you," Betsy replied. "My husband's cod is more of a goldfish." Betsy glanced toward Mary and smiled. "You must really love your John, Mary," she said.

"Why do you say that?" Mary asked, stunned by Betsy's observation. Her gaze strayed to John, who was engaged in conversation with several men, one of them being the marshal. Simon stood off to the side, his gaze fixed on Secretary Hunt. He seemed to be studying the man as he welcomed the doctor to the colony and led him toward his new quarters. The secretary was dressed in a suit of dark blue velvet, the fine fabric set off to perfection with a stiff white ruff and hose of cream silk. He wasn't a handsome man, but he exuded an air of competence and authority. Simon saw her watching and looked away, fixing his glance on Travesty, who stood alone in the shade of a tree.

"You revere him. It must be true love," Betsy said, giving Mary a knowing smile.

"Come, Betsy. Leave Mary be. I think her pretty blush is admission enough," Nell said, saving Mary the need to reply. "John is a fine man, and a caring husband."

Mary glanced away, amazed by how far off the mark her friends were. It'd been several weeks, but she still couldn't get the image of John and Simon out of her mind. She'd endured John's attentions several times since that night and thought she'd be sick with disgust. She didn't blush because she was in love with her husband. She blushed because she was consumed with shame.

"Come, it's time we went home," John said as he startled Mary out of her reverie. "You've had your amusement for the day. Good day to you, ladies."

Mary followed John obediently as they walked past the group of newly arrived women. Had she looked that bedraggled when she came off the ship? Had she had the same light of hope in her eyes? She was cleaner and better dressed now, certainly better fed, but the hope had ebbed away day by day, replaced by a bitterness she hadn't realized she was capable of.

London, England

"Quiche Florentine," Logan announced, handing Quinn a covered dish as he entered the flat. "Compliments of Colin. He's taking a class, you know, and wielding a kitchen knife with as great a precision as he wields his scalpel at the mortuary. It's so sexy," Logan said with a wicked grin. "Every time he cooks a chicken, I almost expect him to give me the cause of death and enlighten me on the health of the victim before its untimely demise."

"Yes, he did mention it," Quinn said, returning Logan's smile. "Thank you. Would you like some? It's nearly lunchtime, or brunch, as Seth likes to call it."

"Thanks, but I'm all quiched out. A cuppa would be nice though. It's cold out there."

Quinn filled the kettle and set it on the hob while Logan divested himself of his coat and came to join her in the kitchen. "Where's my gorgeous nephew?"

"Sleeping. He'll wake up the minute I pour myself a cup of tea," Quinn said. "It's like he has a built-in sensor. I have yet to enjoy a hot beverage."

Logan settled himself at the kitchen table and leaned back in his chair, looking nonchalant, but Quinn could see the worry in his eyes. Now that she knew him better, she wasn't buying into his carefree act. It was all smoke and mirrors. Quinn took out two mugs and a bottle of milk, going about her tasks silently. Logan needed to talk, and like most people, he'd jump into the breach to fill the silence.

"Have you heard from Rhys?" Logan finally asked.

Quinn sighed with frustration. "Yes, but he told me exactly nothing. He sent me a brief email two days ago, telling me that he's all right and busy pursuing various leads."

"I don't like the sound of that."

"Neither do I, but he hasn't replied to my last email, nor is he answering my calls," Quinn complained.

"You think he's avoiding you?"

"Yes, I do." She hadn't realized it was true until she said it out loud. He couldn't blame his lack of communication on a spotty signal or no access to the internet. He'd managed to email not only her, but his PA, Rhiannan Makely, who'd been in touch with Quinn, per Rhys's instructions, as well as several other coworkers who worked on the *Echoes from the Past* series. Quinn's calls to Rhys went directly to voicemail, but his mobile was operational since he'd upgraded his plan before leaving for Afghanistan. Rhys was purposely ghosting her.

Logan nodded slowly. "Right. Did he say when he was coming back?"

"No, he didn't."

"If Jo were dead, Rhys would have no reason to hang around Kabul. Since he's not on his way back, he must have unearthed some useful information."

"You think?" Quinn asked, her voice buoyant with hope.

"Look, Quinn, if Jo were that easy to locate, Rhys would have found her by now. The fact that he is still there after a fortnight means he believes there's a chance. Do you think she might have been kidnapped? For ransom, I mean."

"Generally, when a person is kidnapped for ransom, a demand for payment is made. As far as I know, no one has come forward."

"Perhaps a demand was made of someone you're not aware of," Logan theorized.

"According to Charles Sutcliffe, Jo's agent, who's known her for years, Jo is something of a lone wolf. There's no husband or boyfriend, and no close friends that he knows of. He's the most likely person a kidnapper would contact."

"And he hasn't heard anything."

"No, he hasn't."

The kettle boiled and Quinn made the tea. She'd just added milk to hers when a thin wail erupted from the baby monitor. "Right on cue," Quinn said with an affectionate smile and set down her mug.

She returned a few moments later, Alex in her arms. He was still sleepy, his eyes hooded as he took in the new arrival. For a second, he looked as if he were about to cry, but seemed to change his mind as he pressed his face into Quinn's shoulder.

"He's hungry," Quinn said.

"May I feed him? Mum said you've stopped nursing," Logan added.

He reached out and Quinn handed him the baby, who eyed Logan suspiciously until he noticed the tattoos on Logan's forearm. The interesting shapes and colors distracted Alex long enough for Quinn to take out a bottle from the fridge, warm it up in the microwave, test the temperature on her hand, and pass it to Logan. Alex forgot his misgivings as soon as he saw his food.

Logan settled the baby comfortably on his lap and gave him the bottle. "There, you can now enjoy your tea."

"Thank you," Quinn replied as she took a sip of her still-hot tea. "Wonderful."

"How are you feeling?" Logan asked.

"I'm all right. Why?"

"I don't know. You look a bit peaky."

"I've been a little off, to be honest, but I think it's just stress."

"Off in what way?" Logan asked, instantly switching from brother to nurse.

"Tired, queasy, weepy, moody. I have an aversion to certain foods. Nothing I haven't felt before."

Logan's eyebrows lifted in surprise. Quinn knew what he was thinking, and she shook her head.

"I'm not."

"I think you should pay a visit to the clinic, nonetheless. Better safe than sorry."

"I'm all right, Logan. Really. Don't worry about me."

"I think I'm just on high alert these days, what with Jude and all," Logan replied. "Of course, you know best."

"How is Jude? He came round to see me last week."

Logan sighed and tilted his head, as if weighing his answer. "All things considered, I think he's doing well. What would make his recovery easier is a bit of fun, a pleasant distraction, but getting involved in a new relationship is not advisable so soon after starting the recovery program."

"Why is that? Don't you think a new girlfriend might help raise his spirits and give him something to look forward to at the end of the day? I know he misses Bridget."

Logan shook his head. "A new relationship can become an emotional crutch or a trigger. It can lead to him spiraling out of control. Jude is not ready for any emotional upheaval. What he needs is a comfortable routine and a strong support system, which we are trying to provide. He hates his job at the hospital, but having him there allows me to keep an eye on him, even when I'm not on shift."

"You mean you have spies?" Quinn asked, smiling over the rim of her mug.

"On every floor," Logan replied. He set down the bottle and lifted Alex onto his shoulder, patting his back gently until Alex belched.

"Hey, you're good at this."

"I love children. Maybe someday…"

"Have you and Colin talked about it?" Quinn asked. It had never occurred to her that Logan and Colin might want to start a family, but these days it was very possible for two gay men to have a child.

"We have." Logan sat Alex up in his lap and reached for his own mug of tea, which had now cooled. "Colin would like to adopt. He says there are too many unwanted children in this world, and if we could help even one of them, it would make him happy."

"And you?"

"I'd like a biological child. We could find a surrogate."

"Is Colin open to that?"

"He wouldn't refuse me the chance to become a father, but I think, on some level, he would feel like I would be more of a parent to that child than he would be. Adopting a child would put us on equal footing."

"There is that," Quinn agreed.

Logan took a sip of tea and made a face. "Stone-cold."

"I'll make you a fresh cup."

"Don't bother. I have to get going. I just missed you, that's all," he added shyly.

"I missed you too, Logan." Quinn set down her empty mug and came up behind Logan, putting her arms around him. "I love that you're in my life."

Logan leaned back against her and covered her hand with his own. There was no need to say anything. They were thrilled to have found each other, but now the specter of Jo loomed over them, reminding them that they might lose their sister before having found her.

Kabul, Afghanistan

It took several days to finally get an appointment with someone at Camp Eggers, a U.S. Military facility in Kabul. Rhys was issued a visitor's pass at the gate and had to navigate through several checkpoints before being finally admitted into the inner sanctum and allowed to meet with a two-star general, who hopefully had the power and, more importantly, the desire to help him.

Rhys was ushered into a waiting room and then invited into a utilitarian office dominated by a large desk and several cabinets. The papers on the desk were organized into neat piles, the exposed wood surface gleaming with polish. General Hewitt was a tall, trim man with the bronzed skin of someone who'd spent time in the field, and the gray hair of someone who'd lived to tell about it. His dark eyes gave nothing away as his gaze followed Rhys's approach.

"Mr. Morgan," the general said as he invited Rhys to sit down. "Can I offer you a cup of coffee... or tea?" he added, perhaps recalling that Rhys was British.

"Coffee, please," Rhys replied. He tried to relax, but his injuries were paining him, especially once he lowered himself into the hard chair. It'd been several days since the attack, and his bruises were beginning to turn a greenish yellow, a vast improvement on the angry black and blue of the morning after the beating, but his ribs still ached every time he took a deep breath, and his lower back was sensitive to the touch.

"So, what does the BBC want with us?" the general asked once the coffee had been served by his assistant. "I hear you pulled quite a few strings to get an appointment."

"I'm here on a personal matter, General."

"Oh?" General Hewitt leaned back in his chair, his dark gaze fixed on Rhys. He had the air of a man who was about to deny any request made of him, no matter how insignificant.

"General Hewitt, on December sixteenth, a young man by the name of Ali Khan was brought to the Cure Hospital of Kabul. He'd been severely injured when he drove over an IED. He was brought in by American military personnel."

"We don't treat civilians at military facilities," the general replied. "Protocol was followed."

"I've no doubt; however, Ali was a guide for a British photojournalist. Her name is Jo Turing. I checked with all the other hospitals in Kabul, and no British woman was brought in around that time, alive or dead."

"I see. Was she one of yours?"

Rhys nodded. "If your troops came across Ali, chances are they also found Jo. I need to discover what happened to her, sir. For the sake of her family. If she's deceased, then I would like to take her remains back to England, where she can be laid to rest by those who love her."

General Hewitt laced his fingers in front of him and stared at Rhys. Whatever he had been expecting to hear, it obviously wasn't a plea for remains. "Mr. Morgan, if you leave your contact information with my assistant, I will investigate and have someone get back to you."

Rhys was about to protest, when the general held up his hand. "Mr. Morgan, you have my word. I will make inquiries. It might take a few days, but you will be hearing back from this office."

"Thank you, General Hewitt," Rhys said as he got up to leave and accepted the general's outstretched hand. "I will wait to hear from you."

"You will."

Rhys was promptly escorted from the building and walked toward the gate by an armed guard, who remained in place until Rhys got into the Jeep and drove away. There wasn't much for him to do but return to the hotel and await word from Camp Eggers.

Rhys left the car in the car park and entered the hotel, his eyes straying to the INTERNET CAFÉ sign in the foyer. He knew Quinn was going mad with worry, but he'd emailed her once, telling her that he was well and following Jo's trail, and hadn't contacted her since. Gouging out his own eyes was more appealing than telling Quinn that Jo was most likely dead, but he had to prepare her for the news that was sure to be confirmed in a few days' time.

Rhys stopped at reception, purchased a Wi-Fi code, and proceeded to an empty computer station in the café. He opened a new email and began to compose a message to Quinn. Having deleted eight possible versions of the truth, he gave up and emailed Gabe instead:

Gabe,

All evidence points to the fact that Jo was killed in an explosion. I will try to bring back her remains for burial. It's the only thing I can do to give Quinn some peace of mind. Do your best to prepare her for the news. I should have more concrete information in a few days.

Regards,

Rhys

Rhys had time left on his session, so he checked his email, answered several communications from work, replied to Rhiannan's endless inquiries about his well-being, and sent messages to his mother and brother. Just before he closed the browser, a message from Gabe popped up:

Rhys,

Thank you for letting me know, and thank you for not telling Quinn just yet. I will do my best to prepare her, but please, allow me to break the news to her, if Jo is, indeed, deceased. Stay safe.

Gabe

Rhys logged out and headed to his room with a heavy heart. Jo was almost certainly deceased. The only question remaining was whether there was anything left of her to bring back to England.

THIRTY-FOUR
FEBRUARY 2015

London, England

Gabe deleted the email from Rhys and stared at the screen of his mobile. Until that moment, he'd believed Quinn would eventually be reunited with Jo, but the missive from Rhys had put an end to that highly unrealistic supposition. He knew he should have expected the worst, but he tended to reserve judgement until he had enough facts. How was he supposed to tell Quinn that Jo was dead? She'd be devastated. She truly believed Rhys would bring her sister back.

Gabe grabbed Rufus's lead and called out to the dog. He had to get out of the flat before Quinn correctly read his face and demanded an explanation, and he needed a little time to prepare a statement that would introduce the possibility that Jo was gone without conveying certainty. And, of course, he couldn't let Quinn know that Rhys had contacted him instead of her. Gabe pulled on his coat, wound a scarf around his neck, and attached the lead to the dog's collar, smiling wistfully at the excited puppy.

"You are so lucky your life is not complicated," Gabe addressed the dog as they left the flat. Rufus barked defensively, as if challenging Gabe's comment, as they exited the building and set off down the street.

"Don't even go there," Gabe replied. "I know dealing with Emma is not easy. Believe me, I know, but she loves you to bits, and you get to eat, sleep, and enjoy endless cuddles. And, you don't have in-laws," Gabe added, amused by the look of shock a passing pedestrian aimed his way.

"I'm having a conversation with a dog," Gabe muttered while he waited for Rufus to do his business against a tree. He fished out his mobile and dialed his mother. Since his dad's death, he'd rung her every morning to make sure she was all right, but he'd been remiss the past few weeks, busy with the children, packing, and Quinn's mercurial emotional state. He could hardly blame her, given what she'd recently discovered.

Damn Sylvia, he thought savagely as he turned for home, raging at the woman who seemed to have singlehandedly ruined so many lives. Quinn flitted from one emotional crisis to another, trying desperately to come to terms with her newfound family while raising two small children, headlining a television program, and preparing to move to their new home. She looked overwhelmed and had been pale and listless the past few weeks. She'd been sick several times, although she tried to hide it from him. The cases she delved into for *Echoes from the Past* were getting to her, using up her emotional reserves, and sapping her energy. Had no one in history ever died of old age after living a happy and meaningful life? Gabe mused.

He modulated his tone when Phoebe answered her mobile. "Hello, Mum. How are you?"

"Nice of you to call," Phoebe replied, her tone laced with sarcasm.

"Mum, I spoke to you only the day before yesterday," Gabe protested.

"And that's how it starts. First you call me every other day, then twice a week, and then the next thing I know, all I get is a phone call for my birthday and Christmas."

"Really, Mum!" Gabe exclaimed, caught between annoyance and amusement. "Surely *you* can ring me once in a while."

"I don't want to bother you with my geriatric problems," Phoebe replied coolly.

"I think you could teach a course on parental blackmail," Gabe said, trying to suppress a laugh.

"If that's what it takes to get a phone call from my son. If I play my cards right, I might even get to see my grandchildren sometime before Easter."

"Mum, you are welcome to come to London anytime."

"As if I could. I'm busy decorating. I think I've finally settled on a color scheme."

"So, you're happy with the new place?"

"I'm filled with glee," Phoebe replied, sounding anything but.

"Mum, what's wrong?"

"Why should anything be wrong?"

So, they were playing *that* game. Gabe stopped walking and pulled on Rufus's lead. This would take a few minutes. "Mum? What is it?"

"Nothing. Nothing at all. I will borrow a ladder and hang up the curtains, as well as the shelves Cecily and I bought the other day. I'm only seventy-four. Agile as a teenager, me."

"Mum, please don't climb any ladders. I will come up as soon as I can and hang up everything that needs hanging, fix anything that needs fixing, and plug every hole that needs plugging. Surely you can wait a week or two."

"I suppose. At least there's no body in the kitchen this time," she replied. She was still in a huff, but Gabe could sense the beginnings of a smile.

"Alex is rolling over," Gabe said, hoping to distract her from her list of grievances against him.

"Good lad," Phoebe cried. "He'll be walking in no time."

"He's four months."

"You were very advanced for your age," Phoebe replied.

"So I hear."

"That boy will surprise us all. Did you know Mozart began composing music by the time he was four?"

"Mum, I think you need to adjust your expectations."

"Aim high, I always say," Phoebe snapped. "Anyway, how's Quinn? She sounded a bit down in the mouth last time we spoke."

"I think her sister is dead."

Gabe listened to the shocked silence on the other end. "Damn Sylvia," Phoebe finally swore, making him smile. "I do wish she'd never found Quinn. How much happier that poor girl would be without all this endless drama. This will crush her."

"I know. Rhys is trying to sort out the question of Jo's remains. He'll have her shipped home, if possible."

"Who would bury her if that were to happen?" Phoebe asked.

"The Crawfords, I suppose."

"I though she's not on speaking terms with them."

"As far as I know, she has no other family. She's not married and has no children. Perhaps her agent has been made aware of her wishes."

"How sad. In my day, women that age were almost all married. They had husbands and children to look after. They didn't traipse around the world blowing themselves up for no good reason."

Gabe didn't interrupt the tirade. He knew his mother didn't really believe what Jo had been doing was meaningless. She'd been something of a socialist in her youth and chafed against the restrictions imposed on women, but she was upset, and this was her way of covering it up.

"Quinn is the closest thing to a daughter I've ever had. I can't bear to see her hurt again." Phoebe said with a sniffle. "First that homicidal bigot, then the heroin-addicted ne'er-do-well, and now this. The poor girl doesn't have a single normal relation."

Gabe couldn't argue with the truth. With one brother in prison for attempted murder and Jude's thoughtless behavior at Emma's *Frozen*-themed birthday party, Quinn could really do with a bit of familial support. "There's Logan."

"And he's a lovely boy, but he's really off with the fairies, isn't he?" Phoebe said.

"Mum, Logan is a gainfully employed man in a committed relationship. With a doctor," Gabe added for good measure.

"I know. I'm still not used to two men getting married, but times change, and we must change with them, mustn't we? Logan is handsome, I'll give him that. And his fiancé—like a young Peter O'Toole."

"Mum, I—"

"I really must go, dear. I have chair yoga in ten minutes. Kisses to Quinn and the children."

Gabe disconnected the call and looked down at Rufus, who was licking his balls with great concentration. Gabe sighed and pulled Rufus toward home.

"By the way, I forgot to tell you, Jude stopped by a few days ago," Quinn said when Gabe came into the kitchen. She filled Rufus's bowl with dog food and replenished his water.

"Should I check the silver?"

"Come on, don't be like that. He's struggling. He's really trying to get clean."

"Why do I feel like there's more?" Gabe asked. He knew he sounded like a world-class prick, but talking about Jude set his teeth on edge.

"I invited him to come back. He wants to see Emma."

Gabe opened his mouth to protest, but bit back his response, recalling Rhys's email. Quinn was going to need all the support she could get, and if trying to help Jude made her feel better, who was he to deny her that small bit of emotional satisfaction?

"Sure, of course," he said instead. "Bygones and all that."

"Really?" Quinn exclaimed. "You know, Luke always did call you St. Gabe to annoy me, but you're becoming saintlier by the day," she said as she slid onto his lap and wrapped her arms around his neck.

"I'm not a saint, Quinn. I'm a mere mortal who's trying not to—pardon the expression, I picked it up from an American student—lose his shit. If another relative comes out of the woodwork, I'll have to seriously rethink this marriage."

Quinn buried her face in his neck, but she was shaking with laughter. "No more long-lost relations. You have my word. If I find out that I'm a triplet, or my mother had another set of twins a year later, I will draw a line under the whole bloody family tree and walk away."

"And I'm next in line for the throne," Gabe replied, pulling her closer. He was about to kiss her thoroughly when Emma ambled into the kitchen and made a face when she saw them.

"You two are really embarrassing. Always at it, just like Maya's parents. Call me when you're done."

Quinn dissolved into giggles. She slid off Gabe's lap and leaned against the worktop, still grinning.

"Think we should meet Maya and her parents?" Gabe asked, looking as if he'd just been informed he needed a root canal.

"Perhaps not just yet," Quinn replied and was rewarded with a look of gratitude. "For some reason, I don't think the meeting would go well."

"I almost miss Aidan," Gabe joked.

"Me too."

THIRTY-FIVE
AUGUST 1620

Virginia Colony

The summer dragged on. Mary's flesh seemed to be melting off her bones as she sweated day after day in the airless cabin, clad in garments more suited to a colder climate, the ever-present flame in the hearth driving the temperature higher. By evening, her chemise was crusted with dried sweat and her hair was limp and lifeless. No amount of cool water relieved her relentless thirst, and her normally good appetite was all but gone, her body unable to hold on to anything but the simplest foods.

Travesty seemed to handle the heat better, her face set in grim lines as she baked bread, made pottage, and boiled milk before skimming off the curds to make cheese. She kept a bucket of water in the corner and splashed her face every time she grew too warm. Mary took to doing the same. The water warmed up after sitting in the cabin all day long, but it was still refreshing, especially after she'd been standing next to the hearth for so long.

Having seen to the animals, mucked out the stalls, and watered the vegetable garden, all before the sun rose well above the trees, Mary helped herself to a cool drink and settled in to churn the butter. In the meantime, Travesty had cleared up after breakfast, washed the crockery, and started on the day's bread. She was about to turn her attention to the wild turkey Simon must have pilfered from one of Walker's traps when the door to the cabin flew open.

John supported Simon as he helped him inside. Mary gasped at the sight of Simon's blood-soaked hose and pale, sweating face. His hands were shaking, and his eyes were half closed, as if he were barely conscious. Mary became flustered, unsure what to do, but Travesty simply instructed John to lay Simon on the bed and remove the hose. A deep gash that looked like a wide smile dissected Simon's shin. It was bleeding profusely and soaked the towel Travesty had placed beneath the calf in minutes.

"Elevate his leg," Travesty said as she brought the bucket of water from the corner.

"He cut himself with the scythe while harvesting the bottom leaves of the tobacco," John explained. He looked pale and nervous, his eyes darting from Travesty to Mary. "Shall I fetch the physician?"

"There's naught the physician can do here," Travesty replied. "The bleeding is slowing down already, now the leg is lifted. All he needs is a poultice to keep the wound from festering and a thick bandage. That'll fix him right up. It'll take at least a week for the wound to close properly. I can sew it up," she said, her head tilted as she studied the cut.

"No," Simon moaned. "Please, don't."

"Suit yourself," Travesty replied, as if she were offering him an extra helping of stew.

"Let's wait and see, shall we?" John said. "You might have to grin and bear it, Simon, if the wound is too deep."

Simon didn't reply. He closed his eyes and seemed to drift off, exhausted by hours of hard work, oppressive heat, pain, and loss of blood.

"You'll have to help me out in the field, Travesty," John said. "I can't afford to lose days of work."

Travesty looked none too pleased but nodded in agreement. "As long as the mistress can look after Simon."

"I'll do my best," Mary replied. She watched as Travesty washed out the wound, smeared it with the foul-smelling poultice she kept on a shelf by the hearth, and wound a length of linen around Simon's leg. Simon's eyes remained closed, and his breathing was ragged, but Mary was sure he was awake.

"What's in that?" John asked, taking a step back.

"Lard, wild garlic, and honey," Travesty retorted. "If you don't care for the smell, step outside."

John didn't leave but moved over to the table and sat down on the bench furthest from the hearth. "Simon will have to sleep here for the next few days," he said. "He can't climb a ladder to his loft in the barn."

"We can sleep in his loft," Mary offered. Perhaps it'd be cooler there.

"You go on. I'll sleep here with Simon, in case he needs anything during the night."

Mary inclined her head. Of course, John would wish to remain with Simon. Most likely, Simon had shared John's bed before Travesty came along and they'd had to begin hiding their relationship. How much easier it must have been when it'd been just the two of them. Not for the first time, Mary wondered if Travesty knew. She never let on, and Mary didn't expect any confidences. Travesty understood the value of silence and would do nothing to betray John. Her livelihood depended on him, and by her own admission, she owed him a debt of gratitude. She was biding her time until her indenture was up, and she could finally take her place among the free women of the colony.

Mary did sleep in the loft that night but returned to the cabin early in the morning to find John stretched out next to Simon, his arm across Simon's stomach. The opening of the door woke him, and he yanked his arm back, pretending it'd been an accident.

"How is he?" Mary asked.

"He slept well. I think he'll be all right," John replied, clearly relieved Simon's injury wasn't more serious. He touched Simon's cheeks gently. "He's not fevered."

"Thank God," Mary said. John needed Simon to work the land. He couldn't afford to lose a strong pair of hands during this crucial season.

Simon slept through breakfast but woke after John and Travesty left for the tobacco field. "May I have a drink?" he asked Mary.

"Of course." Mary poured him some ale and brought it over to the bed. Simon accepted the cup, drank the ale in one swallow, and handed it back to her. Mary nearly lost her footing when he grabbed her around the back of her legs to keep her from moving away from the bed.

"Come here then, fair Mary, and give me a kiss. It'll make me feel stronger."

"How dare you?" Mary sputtered. "What would John say if he found out?"

"Not too much, I suspect," Simon replied with a careless shrug. "Don't act so indignant. If you'd ever had a real man, you'd know what you're missing."

"And you are a real man?" Mary demanded. "I know all about you, Simon. I saw you and John together. You're a sinner and a sodomite."

Simon looked up at Mary's furious face and smiled. Even with his face flushed and covered with dark stubble, and his hair mussed, he was attractive. "I'm not a sodomite, but your husband is."

"Takes two to do what you were doing," Mary snapped.

"Yes, it takes two, but only one is doing the deed, and I'm not the one."

"What difference does it make?" Mary asked, confused.

"Oh, it makes a world of difference, my girl. I like women. Always have. But John can't get aroused by a woman. It's a glimpse of a hard, quivering cock that does it for him. It's me he thinks of when he lies with you. It's the only way he can do his duty by his comely wife. Now I wouldn't need much encouragement. Come here and I'll show you."

"I'm going to tell John you tried it on with me," Mary threatened. She found Simon's advances infuriating and repellent.

"You can tell him, if you like, but don't expect him to do aught about it," Simon replied.

"And why wouldn't he? He's my husband, like it or not."

"Because I hold his life in my hands, Mary dear. Sodomy is a crime, a serious one. If Reverend Edison, or the governor, for instance, were to get wind of our John's proclivities, things wouldn't go well for him. John has to keep me sweet if he wants to hold on to what's his."

"If you're not a sodomite, then why do you allow him to use you?" Mary asked, wishing she could slap the sly smile off Simon's face.

"Because allowing him to have his way with my body is a small price to pay for a master who treats me well and loves me above his own wife. And when my indenture is up, John will help me set myself up. I'll be wanting my own parcel of land to work, and John will see that I get it."

"You mean you will blackmail him, you heartless scoundrel?"

"Mary, the minute John unlaced his breeches and penetrated me, he put himself at my mercy. He knew it as well as I did. I allow him to make use of me. I even enjoy it from time to time, when he's in the mood to pleasure me, but I won't walk away from John without taking what's owed to me. I've suffered enough at the hands of people who had power over me. I like how it feels to finally have a bit of leverage over someone else."

"Is this what this is? Leverage?" Mary demanded, hands on hips.

Simon inched his hand up her thigh and grabbed hold of her bottom, cupping it suggestively. "I won't force you, Mary. I'm not a bad man. But know that I can have you any time I want, and John will not lift a finger to help you. Now that you're his wife, you belong to me as surely as he does. You can thank him for that. John thinks he's working for himself and his future children, but he's working for me and mine. Make no mistake, mistress, I won't let this opportunity pass me by."

"You're despicable," Mary gasped. She pressed down on his wound, making Simon cry out and let her go. She took a hasty step back, getting well out of his reach. To her, Simon no longer looked handsome. He was ugly and twisted, and she'd seen the eyes of the snake behind his innocent blue gaze. "What's made you so cruel?" she asked, shaking her head in dismay.

Mary was surprised to see Simon's features crumple. Gone was the manipulator, replaced by a man who wanted her sympathy. All the bravado seemed to go out of him, leaving behind a weak, injured man. Simon's eyes grew misty, as if he were remembering something painful.

"I wasn't always like this, Mary," Simon said at last. "I was an honest man, doing honest work. I served a fine lord, looking after his horses. My father was the head groom, but once he grew too old to do his duties, the position would pass down to me. My family had worked for Lord Denton's family for generations. My grandfather had been a serf, as was his father before him. My father was a free man, but he continued to serve the family, for a fair wage. My younger brother worked in the house, and my sister started in the kitchens when she turned twelve."

"So, what happened?" Mary asked, curious despite her anger.

"Lord Denton's wife, who had fulfilled her marital duty and produced three fine sons, ceased to interest him. He took a mistress in the village, a girl younger than his eldest son. The poor lass wanted no part of him, but her family didn't give her much of an option. Lord Denton owned the village, and everyone in it. If the girl dared to refuse, her family would suffer, and their only recourse, the minister, would side with his lord."

"Did you stand up for her?" Mary asked, hoping she'd misjudged Simon.

"There was naught I could do to help her. Besides, her family benefited nicely from having their daughter warm the master's bed. They never ate so well, nor had coin to spare on minor luxuries before he took a liking to her."

"So, how did any of this affect you?"

"Lady Denton, who was a proud woman, didn't take kindly to being set aside. She'd always been partial to me, but once her lord strayed, she took to coming into the stables, hoping for something more than a spirited gallop."

"People just can't keep their hands off you, can they?" Mary said bitterly. "So, did you service her and get caught by her husband?"

"I refused. Told her I was courting a girl from the village and we were to be married that autumn."

"Did she leave you alone?"

"She was angry and humiliated that a lowly groom would reject her. She told her husband I'd stolen a ring from her, and he turned me over to the constable. There was no proof. They found nothing on me, but her word was enough to convict me. I was to be hanged for a crime I didn't commit. The day before I was to be executed, Lord Denton petitioned the magistrate to commute my sentence to indentured servitude. I think Lady Denton had a change of heart and told him the truth of what she'd done."

"She told her husband you rejected her advances?" Mary scoffed.

"Of course not. Probably said I was insolent to her and she wanted to see me punished."

"Why would she change her mind?"

"Likely didn't want my death on her hands. She wasn't a cruel woman, just a scorned one."

"So, that's how you came to be here in Virginia?"

Simon nodded. "I spent two months aboard a ship, treated no better than vermin. All they fed us was gruel, and we weren't allowed up on deck, not even for a breath of air. Do you know what a hold with two dozen men who haven't washed in months and filled with slop buckets overflowing with shit and vomit smells like,

Mary? I swore to myself if I made it to Virginia alive, I'd do whatever it took to survive. Whatever. It. Took. I won't be leaving my service empty-handed."

"What Lady Denton did to you was cruel, but John doesn't deserve to be punished for her actions."

"I'm not out to punish him. He's a good man, John. He's been kind to me. But I've lost everything, Mary. Even if I had the means to return to England, I've nothing to go back to. My family was shamed. My father and brother lost their employment. And my beloved likely married someone else. My life was stolen from me. I just need a helping hand to start a new one, and after what I've been to John these past years, he owes me."

"He should help you because he wants to, not because you hold exposure over his neck like a sharpened ax," Mary argued.

"Mary, do you honestly believe John will simply give me a portion of his land, or enough coin to buy a plot of my own? You're more naïve than I thought. No one gives you anything in this life. If you want it, you have to take it."

"That's an awfully self-serving view."

"It's the self-serving people who prosper in this world. Now, if you won't give me a well-deserved kiss, then give me a piece of bread. I'm hungry, and all this talking's given me a mighty thirst. You promised John you'd take good care of me. And believe me, he will ask."

Mary returned to the table to fix a plate for Simon. She was angry with him, and wary of his advances, but what he'd said about John resonated in her mind. Was John a kind master who had romantic feelings for his servant, or was he a predator who took advantage of a man in no position to deny him and used him to satisfy his carnal urges? Had he done Travesty a kindness by purchasing her contract when no one else wanted it, or had he seen an opportunity to get her cheaply and taken a chance she wouldn't die? Had John married Mary because he longed for a family and companionship, or had he simply used the opportunity to hide his own proclivities and possibly produce an heir?

Sadly, she didn't know John well enough to answer those questions. John was an enigma to her, one she wasn't sure she cared to solve. She was bound to him for life, and whether he was the soul of kindness or a ruthless manipulator, she had no choice but to do his bidding.

Kabul, Afghanistan

A tremor went through the room, startling Rhys. The bed had moved several inches away from the wall, and the entire room shivered violently before the lights flickered off and on several times, and then went completely out. Rhys jumped to his feet, wondering if there was an earthquake. It was only when he yanked the earbuds out of his ears that he heard the screaming and the unmistakable sound of shattering glass.

He grabbed his wallet and mobile and raced downstairs. The foyer was crowded, and several people peered anxiously through the glass doors, or what was left of them.

"What happened?" Rhys asked an employee who stood calmly behind the reception desk, looking on with interest.

"There was a suicide bombing nearby," he replied, his tone as casual as if he were telling Rhys it had started to rain and he should take an umbrella.

Rhys stepped away from reception and looked around, unsure what to do next. Remaining in the foyer seemed pointless and, in this instance, there was no safety in numbers, but his lonely room didn't beckon, so he remained downstairs, taking the opportunity to chat with a few people he knew. After a time, the group of reporters adjourned to the hotel restaurant and ordered a round of drinks.

Ahmad set a glass of red wine before Rhys, his eyes anxious. "You find your friend?" he asked softly.

"Not yet. How's Ali?"

"Same."

"I'm sorry to hear that," Rhys replied.

Ahmad didn't answer but went on to take orders at the next table. The restaurant was doing brisk business in the wake of the bombing.

"This is retribution for the six militants who were captured in Nangarhar Province this week," said a reporter whose name Rhys didn't know. "They're responsible for the 2014 school massacre in Peshawar."

"How would you know?" asked an American reporter named Deborah Carter. "There are suicide bombings nearly every day. Are they all retribution for some specific act?"

"This bomber managed to get into the center of the city despite all the checkpoints. He must have had a network of operatives to rely on, unlike the amateurs who use homemade explosives and detonate themselves anywhere they find a large gathering of people."

"Jesus Christ, I can't wait to get out of this shithole," Deborah exclaimed. "I miss my kids."

"Worst assignment ever," someone from the next table said. "After this, I'll happily cover dog shows and bakeoffs. Hey, waiter, bring another round of beers."

Rhys tossed a bill on the table and left the restaurant, walking toward the internet café. While everyone was busy discussing the bombing, there'd be free stations. He only hoped the explosion hadn't disrupted internet service. He logged on and searched for a flight home. He would try to leave by the weekend. He still hadn't heard back from anyone at Camp Eggers and didn't really expect to. General Hewitt had probably forgotten all about him, just as he'd forgotten about Jo Turing. Rhys was just about to book a flight when his mobile vibrated in his back pocket.

"Yes?" He hadn't meant to sound brusque, but he was tired, frustrated, and scared out of his wits. The pulsating pain in his stomach and lower back reminded him every minute that he was lucky to be alive, and despite his failure to find Jo, his conscience was clear. He'd done everything in his power. It was time to go home.

"Mr. Morgan, it's General Hewitt."

Rhys sat up straighter, stunned the general had called him in person.

"I did say I would call," the man said, as though taken aback by Rhys's silence.

"I'm grateful, General. Have you any news?" Rhys felt his chest tighten as he waited for Hewitt to speak. He wasn't calling with good news—Rhys could tell from the tone of his voice and the lengthy pause. "General?"

"You were right, Mr. Morgan. Several American troops came across a burned-out vehicle on their way back to base on December sixteenth. They'd heard the explosion and assumed there would be casualties. They found the young man close to the site of the explosion. It was a crude device that wasn't nearly as deadly as a landmine, but still powerful enough to cause grievous injury. The young man was unconscious. He'd lost a leg, as you already know. They found the woman about fifteen feet away from the vehicle. She must have been thrown clear when the explosion went off. She was still alive."

"Where is she?" Rhys cried. "Where did they take her?"

"Mr. Morgan, when the IED exploded, the woman's bag caught fire and the contents perished. She had no identification, and the memory card in her camera had melted. The young man didn't have any identification on him either. Our boys had no idea who she was, so she was referred to simply as Jane Doe. They brought her back to base for an evaluation by our medical staff. Subdural hematoma, I'm told, as well as some other non-life-threatening injuries. Since Jane Doe was a civilian and we had no way to contact her next of kin, we flew her out to Landstuhl Regional Medical Center in Germany. It's located a few miles from Ramstein Air Base."

"Why was no one notified? Surely you had the resources to find out who she was."

"Mr. Morgan, as you know by now, we have a lot on our plate right here in Kabul. I gather you heard the explosion a few minutes ago. The bomber detonated very close to your hotel."

"Yes, I heard the explosion." *And felt it as well*, Rhys thought angrily.

"Perhaps someone in Germany has been working to identify your friend, but as far as I know, you're the only one who's come looking."

"Will they let me in to see her?" Rhys asked. He could hardly just waltz into an American military medical facility and demand to see Jane Doe.

"There's a flight leaving for Ramstein tomorrow afternoon. You can be on it. You will be provided with the necessary travel documents, and someone will meet you once you get to the medical center. I'm afraid that's all I can do."

"That's more than enough, General. Thank you. I'm very grateful."

"Someone will be in touch. Good day to you."

Rhys disconnected the call. Jo was alive, and she was at one of the best facilities in the world. General Hewitt had said nothing about her current condition, but Rhys was optimistic. He stared at the phone, wondering if he should call Quinn.

THIRTY-SEVEN
FEBRUARY 2015

Ramstein Air Base, Germany

Rhys zipped up his coat, slung his carryall over his shoulder, and followed Lieutenant McBain off the aircraft. It was bitterly cold, and a hazy winter sun shone from a nearly colorless sky. The light reflected off the silver airplane, making Rhys wish he'd worn his sunglasses. Two ambulances approached the newly arrived aircraft, the paramedics ready to transport the patients who'd been brought over from Kabul to the medical center.

Lieutenant McBain gestured to an army vehicle waiting at the edge of the airfield. "You're with me," he said to Rhys. "I'll drop you off at the hospital. I hope your friend's doing okay. I was there the day she was brought in. She was a mess, let me tell you. We all thought she was a goner. She must be a tough little thing." Rhys inwardly cringed at the insensitive words but didn't say anything. The young man meant well. "She was lucky to be alive. The kid that was with her took a beating. Lost a leg. He's lucky he didn't lose both."

"I don't think he sees himself as being very lucky," Rhys replied as he buckled his seat belt.

"Well, that's your 'glass half full' versus 'glass half empty' conundrum," Lieutenant McBain replied with a grin. "There's many a soldier that'll take losing a leg over getting blown to bits. Of course, there are injuries that make being blown to smithereens look appealing."

"Like what?" Rhys asked, genuinely curious.

"There've been a couple of boys who stepped on mines. The blast hit them right between the legs, blew their private parts off. It's bad enough to lose your legs, but to lose the family jewels is really adding insult to injury. They had to have reconstructive surgery, but from what I hear, their new equipment is nothing to write home about. Man, can you imagine having to tell your wife that bit of news? I'd rather be dead and buried."

"Are you married, Lieutenant?"

"Married, with two kids. This is my third tour, and if I sign up for another one, my Sherry will castrate me with a kitchen knife. Can't say I'd blame her. Our third is due at the end of May. I'll be home by then, God willing. It's a boy this time. I can't wait. You got any kids?"

"No."

"You don't know what you're missing, man. My heart melts when I see my girls. This is why I'm doing this. For them. I want to leave them a better world. Not sure I'm making any difference though. Sometimes it's hard to see the big picture when you see your friends dying and their families suffering. Well, here we are. Good luck, buddy. See ya round."

Lieutenant McBain dropped Rhys off in front of the medical center and drove away. The two ambulances from the air base were just pulling up, and medical personnel were already on standby outside the facility, ready to receive the wounded. Rhys walked in through the main entrance and approached the visitors' desk.

"Hello, I'm Rhys Morgan—"

"Mr. Morgan, you're expected. Just take a seat and someone will be with you shortly," the guard informed him. "Shouldn't be more than a few minutes. Oh, and you can leave your bag with me. You can't bring it inside."

Rhys took a seat and looked around. He appeared to be the only civilian. Everyone looked busy and purposeful, but there was a cheerful atmosphere that he found surprising. The medical personnel were relatively young, and everyone smiled and exchanged friendly comments as they went about the business of looking after their wounded comrades. Rhys gazed out the window. Gentle snow had begun to fall, huge snowflakes twirling merrily before settling on the ground in a blanket of pristine white.

Would Jo remember him? Rhys wondered as he studied the colorless sky. They'd met several times before, mostly at work functions, where one was introduced to countless people and forgot their names as soon as they walked away to speak to someone else, but he knew Jo, and she had known him. They'd chatted more than once, and had even walked over to the bar and had a drink together the night Jo was due to receive her award. She'd been nervous about making a speech, and Rhys had taken it upon himself to help her relax. She wasn't a woman accustomed to making speeches, she'd told him that night. She liked being on her own, with no one to tell her how to do her job or offer criticism or unwanted advice. He'd liked her, and he thought she'd liked him, but more as a fellow professional, not as a man. She'd been very attractive, he did remember that. Would she look the same?

"Mr. Morgan?"

Rhys hadn't even noticed the woman approach. She was in her thirties, with wide blue eyes and silver-blond hair pulled into a neat bun. She had a lovely smile, and those perfect teeth all Americans seemed to have. "I'm Dr. Stein. I've been looking after your friend. Shall we talk in my office?" she asked.

"Of course," Rhys agreed and followed her toward the lift. They made small talk about the weather until they reached their floor and walked down the bright, scrupulously clean corridor. Dr. Stein led Rhys to a well-appointed office that was flooded with sunshine.

"Please, have a seat. Would you like some coffee? I have a

Keurig," she explained, jutting her chin toward the coffeemaker. "Can't live without it."

"Yes, thank you. I'd love a cup."

"Choose your flavor," Dr. Stein said with a conspiratorial grin. "I like hazelnut, with a splash of milk."

"Hazelnut with a splash of milk it is, then."

Dr. Stein made two cups of coffee, added milk, and set one in front of Rhys. "Now we can talk. Mr. Morgan, I'm sure you understand that the situation is somewhat complicated, and not only health-wise. Since you are not Ms. Turing's next of kin, normally I wouldn't be able to divulge any details of her condition to you. However, Ms. Turing hasn't been able to provide us with any contact information, or even the name of a relative or a friend. Up until two days ago, we were still referring to her as Jane Doe. You're the first person to come asking after her, and we've had her at this facility for over six weeks. Can you help me out?" she asked. "Any information you can give me would be extremely helpful."

"Ms. Turing's attorney is Mr. Louis Richards, Esq., based in Leicester, England. I am here on behalf of Jo Turing's twin sister, Dr. Quinn Allenby. Ms. Turing has two other siblings, Doctors Karen and Michael Crawford, with whom she hasn't been in contact for some time."

"I see."

"Dr. Stein, I'm not asking you for confidential medical information. I simply want to see her, and talk to her, if possible. Surely she's allowed visitors." Dr. Stein nodded but didn't immediately reply. "I was told she suffered a subdural hematoma," Rhys tried again.

"Yes, that is correct."

"May I speak to her neurosurgeon?"

Dr. Stein smiled. "You are. I performed the surgery, and I had her in an induced coma for five weeks. A coma allows for the swelling to go down and proper brain activity to resume at its own pace. Ms. Turing was woken from the induced coma only two days ago. It was fortuitous that you helped us identify her before we woke her up. She responded to her name, which is always a good start."

"Will you send me away?" Rhys asked. He was trying not to get upset, but Dr. Stein's serene countenance was beginning to grate on his nerves.

"No, Mr. Morgan. You've come all this way in search of someone you obviously care about. I'm not going to send you away. If I were, I wouldn't have given you any information about Ms. Turing's condition. I think it will aid her recovery to see a familiar face and maybe be reminded of people back home, as long as you don't tell her anything that might upset her. You can speak to her for a few minutes each day, and we'll see how things go. Is that acceptable?"

"Yes, that sounds reasonable."

"Good. Shall we go see her, then?"

"Please."

Rhys followed Dr. Stein down the corridor. An unnatural hush permeated the entire floor, the nurses slipping by on silent feet as they attended to the patients, most of whom were hooked up to machines. They walked past several open doors before reaching Jo's room. From the doorway, Rhys could see Jo's lower body covered with a white hospital blanket, but he couldn't see her face.

"Just wait outside for a moment, please," Dr. Stein said. "I'd like to give her a heads-up."

"Of course."

"Good morning, Jo," Dr. Stein said cheerily as she walked into the room. "How are you feeling today?"

Rhys couldn't hear what Jo said. Her voice was barely audible. Dr. Stein checked her vitals while she continued to talk softly. "Someone's here to see you, Jo. Would you like to see your visitor?"

Jo must have agreed because Dr. Stein beckoned for Rhys to enter the room. He walked in slowly, not wishing to alarm Jo with his presence. She looked small and fragile, her pallor accentuated by the white walls and bedlinens. Rhys had expected her to be bald, given the head injury, but her abundant dark hair framed her lovely face, and the bandage at the top of her skull was clean and discreet. Healing cuts crisscrossed Jo's face, and the gauze of a bandage showed just above the neckline of her hospital gown. An IV line snaked toward the bed and into her left hand. The nightstand was depressingly bare. There were no flowers or get-well cards, or even a piece of fruit or a bar of chocolate.

"Jo, do you know who this is?" Dr. Stein asked carefully, once Jo had a moment to look at Rhys.

Jo's brow furrowed as she tried to place him. "Morgan. Rhys Morgan," she finally said. "Why are you here?"

"There are some people back home who are very worried about you. I was able to track you down using my press connections," Rhys replied, purposely vague. Now wasn't the time to spring news of a twin sister.

Jo's face dissolved into a grimace of sorrow and her eyes filled with tears. She turned to Rhys, her eyes pleading. "Did she send you?"

"Who, Jo?" Rhys asked softly.

"No, she couldn't have," Jo mumbled. "She wouldn't have." One of the machines started to beep, and Dr. Stein immediately checked the monitor. The green lines on the black background appeared to be spiking.

"Mr. Morgan, I think that's enough for today. Jo is clearly upset."

"Jo, may I come and see you again tomorrow?" Rhys asked. Jo nodded miserably.

"Out you go," Dr. Stein said more forcefully. "Jo, Mr. Morgan will come back, and you can talk some more. Now, you must rest."

Jo closed her eyes, but her face was pale and tense, her brows knitted in concentration. Her lips were moving, but no sound came out.

"Perhaps tomorrow you can show her some photos. I think that might help. Have you a place to stay?"

"No. I was brought here directly from the air base."

"There are several decent hotels in the area. I suggest you get a room and find something to occupy yourself with until you can see Jo again. You can come back tomorrow at ten, if that's convenient. I'll leave word with the front desk."

"Thank you," Rhys said. "I'll do that."

Rhys collected his case, thanked the guard for calling him a taxi, and stepped outside. The sun sparkled on freshly fallen snow, making the world look clean and fresh. Rhys took a deep breath and turned his face up to the sky, offering up a silent prayer of thanks. He couldn't wait to get to the hotel and call Quinn. Finally, he had something to tell her.

THIRTY-EIGHT
SEPTEMBER 1620

Virginia Colony

A brutally hot August finally gave way to a slightly cooler September. The days were still unbearably warm, but once the sun went down, a hint of a breeze moved through the trees and the smell of hay was fragrant on the air.

"How are things with John?" Nell asked as the two women sat in the shade of an old maple tree, enjoying a cup of ale.

"Much the same," Mary replied with a shrug. She hadn't told Nell the whole truth, but had been honest about her dissatisfaction with the marriage. "He's a cold fish, if I ever saw one."

"Some men just don't know how to talk to women. At least he doesn't treat you cruelly."

Mary leaned against the tree trunk and gazed up at the sky through the canopy of leaves. Cruelty wasn't always obvious, identified by a bruise or a harsh word. John's form of cruelty was much subtler. He'd robbed her of companionship and hope for the future. He'd denied her affection and understanding. "No, he doesn't," Mary said at last.

"Do you wish you'd remained in England?" Nell asked.

"I don't know, Nelly. Perhaps I do. This place is so wild, so remote. At times, I feel as if we're the only people in the world, toiling on this tiny bit of land, trying to avoid extinction. We could vanish off the face of the earth, just like that other colony."

"What colony?" Nell asked.

Mary instantly regretted her slip of the tongue. She hadn't meant to mention the colony Walker had told her about. And in any case, she didn't know what had happened to them, only that the settlers were there one day, gone the next.

"What about you, Nelly? Do you ever regret coming here?" she asked, hoping to distract Nell from her question.

"Never," Nell cried. "Mary, I have a home of my own, land, a man who treats me kindly, and soon, I will have a baby," she said, smiling happily. She placed a hand on her belly, caressing it as if the baby could feel her love.

"Oh, Nell, that's wonderful news," Mary gushed. "When?"

"Mid-April, I think. What about you, Mary? Any signs?"

Mary shook her head. "John has not been as diligent in his husbandly duties as your Thomas."

Nell laughed, the peals like silver bells. "Oh, Mary, you don't need diligence. Why, Tom comes in from the fields so tired, he can barely keep his eyes open long enough to have supper. I can count on one hand the number of times he roused himself long enough to finish what he started. But it took, and I'm so glad. Just think, a baby of my own. And now we have the handsome Dr. Paulson to look after us. He's quite something, don't you think? They say he has a wife in England. I wonder what brought him out here."

Mary shrugged. "I suppose he has a pleasant countenance, but there's something about the man that puts me off."

"You're too fanciful, you are," Nell chided. "Of course, he doesn't hold a candle to Simon. I don't know how you get anything done with that handsome scoundrel about. If the devil is temptation, then the rest of us have nothing to fear since he clearly lives at your house." Nell giggled happily. "And he's not indifferent to you, Mary. I've seen the way he looks at you in church."

Mary shrugged. Let Nell think Simon was sweet on her. It was certainly better than the truth.

"Don't despair, Mary," Nell said, laying her hand over Mary's. "This place is odd, make no mistake about that. What with the Indians, the wilderness pressing in on us, and not a child in sight to gladden the heart. But more ships are coming, bringing more women for the colonists. In a few years, this place will be unrecognizable. Jamestown will ring with the sound of children's laughter, and the wilderness will be pushed back as more homesteads are built and more fields are plowed. Someday, this part of the world will be as populated as England. There'll be towns and villages, and large, loud families to fill them."

"I like your vision, Nell. I'm just not sure I've the patience to wait for it to happen. I feel the isolation pressing in on me, chipping away at my resolve not to despair. I'm glad autumn is finally on the way, but what will winter be like in this desolate place? I think I shall go mad with loneliness."

"Winter always gives way to spring, Mary," Nell said. "And who knows, maybe soon, you'll have your very own baby to look forward to. Nothing fills a woman's heart like a child, and nothing keeps her as tethered. You'll have no time to feel lonely, or sad. You'll be too busy suckling a newborn."

"I hope you're right, Nell."

"Just you wait and see."

"I have to go back. There's too much to be done at the plantation."

Mary got to her feet and shook out her skirts. She wished she could stay a while longer, but Nell had supper to see to and Mary had her own chores to finish. Nell waved her off and Mary set off in the direction of home. Visiting Nell usually lifted her spirits, but today, she barely held back tears as she walked down the narrow path. She didn't begrudge Nell her happiness, but for some reason it made her own existence seem that much more barren. The golden afternoon only served to emphasize her loneliness as she trudged along.

An unexpected sound startled Mary out of her reverie. It was the unmistakable pop of a twig breaking beneath a man's foot. Mary stopped and looked around, suddenly frightened. She'd come this way many times and never encountered anyone on the path, but there were natives in the woods, and not all of them were as friendly as Walker.

Mary stood still for a few moments, listening, her mouth dry with fear. Everything seemed quiet and still, so she continued, but her sense of security had been shattered. She kept looking over her shoulder, expecting someone to step out of the woods at any moment.

Mary was relieved when she finally got home, so thirsty her tongue stuck to the roof of her mouth. She opened the lid of the barrel outside the door and filled a cup with water, draining it in one gulp. She was just refilling the cup when she heard Travesty's voice through the window.

"You've got to be more careful, Simon."

"I know what I'm doing."

"Do you?" Travesty challenged him. "If John finds out—"

"He won't."

"The consequences could be dire."

"There will be no consequences, Travesty. I've made sure of that."

"I hate that you're doing this," Travesty said with a deep sigh.

"It's a small price to pay," Simon replied. "I love it that you worry about me." Simon's voice had grown soft and silky, and Mary heard Travesty's sharp intake of breath.

"Go on with you," she said, her voice gruff. "One of them will be back any minute."

"John won't be back from Jamestown for at least another hour, and Mistress Mary's having too good a time with her friend."

"Still."

"I was only trying to please you, Travesty."

"If you want to please me, do the evening milking. I've supper to prepare."

"Won't you give me something by way of an incentive?" Simon purred.

Mary didn't hear Travesty's answer, but whatever it was, it made Simon laugh. She heard his heavy steps on the wooden floor and then the door was thrown open. Mary had just enough time to step out of sight, behind the corner of the cabin. She waited till Simon passed, then left her hiding place and approached the cabin, making sure to pass in front of the window.

"You're back early," Travesty observed when Mary came inside.

"Nell had chores to be getting on with." Mary tied her apron behind her back and turned to Travesty. "What needs doing?"

"Here. Shell these peas for supper."

"I thought I saw Simon when I came back," Mary said casually.

"He's doing the milking. He returned from the fields early."

"Where's John?" Mary asked.

"Had an errand in Jamestown. He'll be back in time for supper." Travesty turned her back to Mary and stirred the contents of the pot hanging over the flames. They worked in silence until they heard the hoofbeats of John's horse.

THIRTY-NINE

Mary shut the door and stood still for a moment, enjoying the silence. Travesty had been called upon to help with the harvest and left with the men directly after breakfast. She'd been reluctant to go, but didn't have much say in the matter. John and Simon had already seen to the bottom leaves of the tobacco plants and were now ready to harvest the rest of the crop. Once all the stalks were cut, they would hang them in the drying shed, which was now empty, since last year's crop had been sold. Mary was grateful to have some time on her own. She had numerous chores to attend to, but it was nice to work at her own pace and not feel Travesty's watchful gaze following her about, her mouth pressed into a thin line of displeasure.

Mary washed the breakfast dishes and set them on a shelf before turning her attention to the daily task of making cornbread. She was heartily sick of cornbread, but John never purchased wheat. It was too dear, and he couldn't justify the expense. Mary combined the ingredients in a large bowl, then filled two baking pots with the mixture, and covered them tightly before pushing them into the smoldering ashes in the grate. The cornbread would take a while to bake, which gave her time to peel and core the apples Simon and John had picked from a nearby tree. She wished they could make cider, but no one in Jamestown had a cider press, so apple jelly would have to do. It would come in handy during the winter months when they were desperate for a taste of sweetness on their tongues. She'd use some of the apples to make fritters. She had no idea how they would taste with cornmeal instead of wheat flour, but nothing containing grated apples and fried in lard could taste bad, in her estimation.

Mary's hands focused on the apples while she considered the conversation she'd overheard the day before. What exactly had Travesty been warning Simon about? Had she discovered Simon's plan to blackmail John? Simon had more than four years left on his indenture contract, so whatever he planned to do wouldn't happen for years to come. Perhaps Simon was stealing.

Mary set the knife down and stretched her back as she analyzed this new idea. She wouldn't put anything past Simon, but there was nothing to steal. Tobacco was the backbone of Virginia's commerce, supplemented by a healthy barter system. All goods were either paid for with bags of tobacco or traded. The blacksmiths were always ready to trade their services for a bag of beans or a basket of squash, since they lived in town and didn't have much room to grow their own vegetables. And Dr. Paulson would not say no to a jar of apple jelly, Mary decided, having heard that he had something of a sweet tooth. She'd keep one back in case they were ever in need of the physician's services.

John had nothing of value, save his tobacco and the cow, neither of which Simon could steal without getting caught and possibly executed. Theft was not looked upon lightly by the marshal, who took his duties very seriously. Given that most colonists toed the line, the marshal practically seethed with belligerence born out of inactivity. Over the past few weeks, the greatest crime committed in Jamestown had been Jonah Reed's failure to attend the mandatory church service last Sunday due to an upset of the stomach. The offender had been put in stocks for four hours, a punishment all the more effective because the poor man soiled himself on account of not being able to get to the privy. The marshal had practically glowed with satisfaction when Jonah was escorted into the church for the evening service, reeking of waste and humiliated beyond measure. Given the warmth of the day and the airless confines of the church, they'd all been punished that day.

Mary picked up a long apple peel that curled in her hand. She tore off small pieces and ate them, loath to waste such delicious goodness. Perhaps she could find use for the peels. She finished chewing and returned to the problem of Simon. Whatever he was doing had nothing to do with her, she decided. What she didn't know wouldn't hurt her, and it clearly wasn't hurting John. It was best if she put the conversation from her mind.

Mary transferred the cut-up apples to a clay pot and added a bit of water and honey, for lack of real sugar. She'd set the jelly to simmer as soon as she washed out the iron pot she'd had soaking since breakfast. The porridge, which had been reheated for the past three days, had burnt and stuck to the bottom. She'd just turned toward the hearth to rotate the cornbread when the door behind her opened.

"Did you forget something?" she asked, assuming it was Travesty returning from the field.

"No," a male voice replied.

Mary spun around, her heart racing at the sound of the familiar voice. Walker stood on the threshold, watching her. He was wearing his buckskin leggings and a loose linen shirt. A string of beads hung around his neck and several feathers were woven into a braid at the side of his head.

"I didn't think I'd ever see you again," Mary said. The scrap of fabric she'd tied to the branch was frayed and bleached by the sun. It hung limply, a sad reminder of a promise that hadn't been fulfilled. Until now. "You can't be here."

"They'll be gone for hours."

"Someone might return."

"Do you want me to leave?" Walker asked. His gaze darted

toward her nervously, his usual self-possession undermined by Mary's less-than-warm reaction.

"No," she admitted. "I'm glad you came. I thought you were angry with me." She cut a thick slice of yesterday's cornbread and poured a cup of ale. "Come, sit down. You look hungry."

Walker accepted the food but didn't sit. He leaned against the wall, breaking off chunks of bread and popping them into his mouth. "I was away."

"Where did you go?"

Walker's eyes clouded with despair and he bowed his head, fixing his gaze on the bread. "I went back to my village. I received word that my father was ill."

Mary was about to ask how one received word from a village that was several days' walk from Jamestown. Was there Indian mail? Did they write letters? Did they even have a written language? She supposed news traveled between settlements, with visitors passing on information, much as they did in England. "Is your father better now?"

"He's dead." Walker's voice was flat, but she noted the slight tremor in his hand.

"I'm sorry. I hope he didn't suffer."

"He did, terribly, but he hung on until I got there. He knew I'd come. He waited. I was there to hear his death song," Walker added.

"Death song?"

Walker didn't reply. Instead he took a sip of the ale and made a face.

"You don't like ale?" Mary asked. She had no idea what natives liked to drink.

"Tastes like piss."

Mary ignored the rude comment. "It must have eased your father's passing to have his only son by his side."

"There are others. My father had seen many winters, and had several wives, before and after my mother. His oldest children have many children. But he was glad to see me," Walker added. "He doesn't want me to help the Englishmen."

"Why?"

"He says they bring death."

"Whatever does he mean?" Mary asked, indignant. A stray thought suddenly sidelined her inquiry, and she walked up to the Indian and looked him in the eye. "Do you have a wife back in your village?"

"I did."

Of course, he would have been married, given his age, but his answer still came as a blow to Mary. She had no right to care, no right to feel any jealousy given her own situation, but the sudden possessiveness she felt toward this man left her confused and unsettled. She was probably better off not knowing, but something within her needed to hear the truth.

"Did she die?"

"No, she took another husband. She didn't wish to live with me anymore."

Mary opened her mouth to comment on the strangeness of such an arrangement but then clamped it shut. She'd gladly take another husband if such a thing were an option.

"Do you have children?" Mary asked. She tried to sound nonchalant, but the tremor in her voice gave away her sudden jealousy. She had no claim on him, but she didn't want him to belong to anyone else, to love anyone else.

"I had two daughters, but they both died at birth. My wife thought the fault lay with me."

"How is such a thing possible?"

"She consulted the shaman, who told her my spirit has been tainted by my English blood."

"But you said your brother Ambrose has many sons," Mary replied. She was trying to understand, but this logic made no sense to her.

"My brother is not of mixed blood. His parents were both English. His spirit is strong."

Mary shook her head, confused. "Does your wife have children with her new husband?"

"She has two living children. She made the right decision," Walker replied woodenly. "Her husband is a brave warrior, and a good friend."

"Do you still love her?"

"Why so many questions, Mary?" Walker asked, his anxious gaze holding her own. Talking about the past must have upset him. Either that, or he still loved the woman who had left him and placed the responsibility for their children's deaths squarely on his shoulders.

"I want to understand. I want to know you."

Walker nodded. His face was thoughtful, his expression pained. "Why did you summon me? What's changed?"

Mary hung her head to hide the sudden tears that sprang to her eyes. She couldn't tell him of her shame. Now that he was here, she wasn't sure what exactly she wanted from him. All she knew was that she felt safe in his presence, and the thought of never seeing him again made her feel desolate. "I was melancholy," she replied softly.

"What does that mean?"

"I was sad."

"And now? Are you still sad?"

Mary shook her head, but the tears threatened to spill down her cheeks. It wasn't until this moment that she realized how lonely she'd been. She'd learned to live with the loss of her parents, learned to live without love, without affection. No one in this world, except perhaps Nell and Betsy, would care if she were gone. No one else would mourn her. No one would miss her.

"I don't understand. You are no longer sad, but you're biting your lip and trying not to cry. Has your husband hurt you, Mary?"

"Not in the way you think."

"There are many ways to hurt a wife," Walker said. He reached out and traced the path of a single tear that slid down Mary's cheek.

"Sounds like you're speaking from experience," Mary choked out.

"I suppose I am. My mother was not a happy wife, nor was my own wife, even before our children died. I'm glad she found solace with someone else."

"It's not as simple as that for someone like me. I can't simply take another husband."

Walker nodded and allowed his hand to drop to his side. "I know. Your God doesn't want people to be happy."

"Why would you say that?" Mary cried, offended. "Jesus Christ was a peaceful and loving man."

"Maybe so, but your church doctrine is all about sin and punishment. It's about breeding fear and condemning all the things that make people happy."

"Such as?" Mary exclaimed, taking a step back from him in her outrage.

"Such as love, both physical and emotional. Love can never be pure as long as one person has dominion over the other. The partners must be equal, free to give and receive, and leave, if they feel they must. Your women are slaves to their men, and your men are selfish and brutal."

Mary stared at Walker. She wanted to be angry, to demand that he leave, but there was a kernel of truth in what he said. An Englishwoman had few rights, before or after marriage. She was at the mercy of her father or closest male relative until she wed, at which point she became the chattel of her husband. She had no say in anything, no possessions of her own, and no one to turn to should things become unbearable.

"Do your women have equal rights?" she asked, wondering if Walker had a legitimate claim to his high moral ground.

"Our women are respected and revered. They choose their own husbands and can end the marriage if they so desire. No one will punish them or threaten them with eternal damnation. Women are the embodiment of love. They create life and nurture it. They are more important than men."

Tears spilled down Mary's cheeks. What Walker said was so beautiful, and so true, but so far from the reality of her everyday life.

Walker pulled her into his arms, and she pressed her face against his chest, the soft linen of his shirt absorbing her tears like a handkerchief. Walker's heartbeat thumped against her temple and his solid arms made her feel protected and loved, something she could never hope to experience with her husband. He was so strong, so warm, and so gentle.

Mary raised her face to his and looked into his eyes. He looked at her with concern, his head tilted to the side as he studied her tear-stained face.

"How can I help you, Sad Eyes?" he asked softly, using his mother's Indian name as an endearment.

"You can't. I have no choice."

"There's always a choice."

"Is there?"

"If you're brave enough to make it."

"What can I do?" Mary asked, willing him to give her an answer. "Will you have me turn my back on everything I believe?"

"I can't make that decision for you, but I will wait for you by the creek tomorrow at midmorning. If you come, I will be very glad, and if you don't, then I will not trouble you again unless you summon me."

Mary nodded into his chest. Walker didn't pressure her or take advantage of her vulnerable state. He was an honorable man, the first she'd ever met. Strange that it should be someone the rest of the world saw as a savage.

London, England

Quinn set aside the comb and glanced toward Alex, who was still fast asleep, his mouth slightly open and his hands curled into loose fists. She hadn't been spending much time with Mary, given the amount of time she dedicated to the baby and the sporadic packing that had resulted in mountains of boxes taking up half the flat. Gabe's books alone filled several large crates, but thankfully, the end was near. They were down to bare necessities, which would get packed away in the days before the move. Quinn couldn't wait.

Today, however, she felt an overwhelming need to escape from her own reality. There'd been no word from Rhys since his brief message, and she was getting the distinct feeling that Gabe wasn't telling her something. It wasn't anything obvious, but she knew him well enough to sense that he was holding back. Perhaps he was having issues at work, but there'd be no reason for him not to share his concerns with her. He'd always done so in the past. Briefly, Quinn thought Luke or Monica might be making waves again but quickly dismissed the thought. No, it had something to do with Rhys. Every time she raged about Rhys not returning her calls, there was a fleeting expression of pain in Gabe's eyes. What did he know?

Last night, Quinn had finally lost her patience and cornered Gabe. "Have you heard from Rhys?" she had asked pointblank.

"Eh, no."

"Sure, are you?"

"Quinn, I know you're going out of your mind with worry, but Rhys will get in touch as soon as he knows anything."

"It's been two weeks," Quinn whined. "Surely he must have learned something by now." There was that look again. That furtive glance toward the door, as if he wished he could make a break for it. Quinn walked over to Gabe and placed her hands against his chest, looking up into his face. "Gabe, I can take it. Please, tell me what you know."

"Darling, I don't know anything for a fact. What I do know is that clearly Rhys has made very little headway in the time he's been in Kabul. Rhys is a resourceful man, and if he hasn't been able to track Jo down, there's a good chance—"

"Don't say it," Quinn cried. "Please, don't say it. I can't bear the thought."

Gabe nodded and wrapped his arms around her, pulling her close. "Quinn, whenever I was worried about something when I was a boy, my dad always said, 'Hope for the best, prepare for the worst, son.' I still think that's good advice."

"So, you think there's still hope?"

"There's always hope until there isn't. But you should prepare yourself for a tragic outcome. She's been gone a long time," Gabe reminded her gently.

Quinn's eyes filled with tears. "You think she's dead, don't you?"

"I think that's very likely," Gabe replied softly, stroking her back as if she were a colicky baby.

Bitter tears spilled down Quinn's cheeks as she laid her head on Gabe's shoulder. He didn't tell her not to cry; he simply held her while she sobbed, slowly allowing her hope of finding Jo to ebb away. Deep down, she knew the truth. Rhys wasn't calling because he had nothing good to tell her. He was stalling, hoping against hope that he'd stumble across something that might make the news easier for her to bear. Rhys cared for her and couldn't bring himself to break her heart until he was absolutely certain that every avenue had been exhausted.

"Quinn, I know you're hurting, but you must stay strong. Concentrate on the things you can control. Concentrate on us, on the children. On Mary. Rhys will be expecting a comprehensive report when he gets back."

"There's plenty of time. We haven't even started shooting episode four. The actor who was meant to play Guy de Rosel pulled out. Got a better offer."

"Isn't he in breach of contract?" Gabe asked. He was clearly trying to distract Quinn from thoughts of Jo, and she appreciated the effort.

"No. He never actually signed the contract. He was waiting to hear from his agent. He was perfect though. Now the part needs to be recast, which will put us behind schedule."

"You can sit in on the auditions. I'm sure Rhys would appreciate your input. After all, you've actually seen the man in your visions."

"I spoke to Rhiannan Makely. She said the auditions are already in progress. Rhys will make the final decision when he returns, which she believes will be imminently. I think he's been in touch with her."

"That's possible. You know how Rhys is when it comes to his projects. He's the consummate professional. He leaves nothing to chance."

"Which makes it all the more maddening that he hasn't called me. I'd rather know the truth than spend every day in this limbo of not knowing."

"Quinn, do you trust Rhys?" Gabe asked, wiping her cheek with his thumb.

"Yes."

"Then trust that he's doing what he thinks best," Gabe replied. "Give him a few more days."

Quinn nodded into his chest. "I will. Thanks, Gabe."

"You never need to thank me. I'm here for you, no matter what. We'll get through this together, whatever the outcome."

Quinn looked up at Gabe and gave him a watery smile. "You know what one of the best things about not nursing anymore is?"

"Tell me."

"I can have a glass of wine, which I sorely need."

"Coming right up. Red or white?"

"White. And bring the bottle."

She had felt better after two glasses of wine and a cuddle on the sofa, but now that she was on her own again, she needed to distract herself from her morbid thoughts.

Quinn slid off the bed and tiptoed out of the bedroom, closing the door softly behind her. A slim folder labeled MARY WILBY rested on the table. It had taken hours of research, but she'd been able to finally track down the manifest for the *Lady Grace* that proved Mary Wilby had been on board the ship. Quinn had also been able to find, more by sheer luck than persistence, a copy of the Virginia Company ledger that listed the names of the women who had gone out to Virginia, and their spouses. The list began in 1619 and covered the period Quinn was interested in. An entry from June of 1620 confirmed a marriage between John Forrester and Mary Wilby. The rest was still a mystery.

Quinn filled the kettle and set it to boil while she perused the file. The two entries she'd come across were the sum total of Mary's life. Nothing was left of the young woman whose remains now rested on a slab in Colin's lab. What had happened to her? How had she come to be in Cornwall, her remains hidden in a cave? Had she found a way to return to England when her marriage to John Forrester proved to be a sham? Who would have paid for her passage, and why, given that she was pregnant? And what had become of her husband?

The kettle boiled and Quinn made herself a cup of tea, which she took through to the lounge. She took a seat on the sofa and folded her legs beneath her as she considered what she knew so far. At first, she'd assumed Simon would come between Mary and John, given his obvious interest in her, but by now she was fairly sure that wasn't the case. Mary detested Simon and feared his ambition and lack of honor. And she didn't appear to hold Travesty Brown in high esteem either. The woman was an enigma. She was understandably angry with the hand life had dealt her, but her attitude toward Mary and her less-then-subtle defiance went beyond bitterness, making Quinn wonder if there was something in her circumstances that caused her fresh pain. Could she have been in love with John? Was that the source of her resentment toward Mary?

Surely, after living with Simon and John for over a year, Travesty would have been aware of their relationship. Or would she? Perhaps she didn't care. Had John married her, her indenture would have come to an end, and she would have been mistress of the plantation and a woman of property should her husband die. Perhaps she viewed Mary as a usurper.

That left Walks Between Worlds. Mary was drawn to him, there was no question about that. Walker was a very attractive man, but Mary had been taken in by his attention and kindness. Would she really consider going off with him, a decision that might cost her her life if she were caught and brought back? It seemed unlikely. Life in an Indian village would go completely against the grain for a young woman reared in England and indoctrinated in the ways of the Church. Like Walker's mother, Mary would never find peace among people she could never hope to understand, people who would always view her with suspicion. Perhaps Walker longed for someone who'd be as much of an outsider as he felt himself to be. After all, what man wouldn't be tormented with guilt if he'd been blamed for the death of his children, especially given that the accusation came from the tribe's spiritual leader? He might have feared taking another Indian wife and risking the lives of their future offspring.

He felt a kinship with Mary, but could he have really loved her? Could Mary have loved him? Sipping her tea, Quinn sighed when she recalled a quote from a book by Joseph Stein. "A bird might love a fish, but where would they build a home together?" Where, indeed? There'd be no happy ending for Mary and Walker, Quinn knew that. But what had led to Mary's gruesome death on the beach of St. Just?

FORTY-ONE
FEBRUARY 2015

Ramstein-Miesenbach, Germany

Rhys kicked off his shoes and stretched out on the bed, enjoying the firm support beneath his back. Hotel Europa looked like something straight out of a Grimm fairy tale, and after the spartan accommodations of the Mustafa Hotel, he was enjoying the amenities. Rhys acknowledged to himself that he was way too attached to his creature comforts, but the private bath that smelled of pine cleaner and boasted excellent water pressure made him doubly happy. He plugged in his iPad to charge—another luxury—and reached for his mobile. He'd go down to the bar and have a beer later, and if the appetizing smell coming from the restaurant was anything to go by, he'd be having a good dinner. But first, he'd call Quinn. It was just past three o'clock, so she'd most likely be on her own.

Rhys swallowed back his nervousness as he made the call. Quinn picked up on the second ring.

"Rhys, I left you a dozen messages. Where have you been?" she cried. Rhys heard the fear in her voice. Perhaps Gabe had done too good a job of preparing her for the worst.

"I'm sorry," Rhys replied in his most soothing tone. "I know you were worried, but I had to be sure of my information before I rang you."

"And? Are you sure now?" Quinn asked in a small, quivering voice.

"Yes, I am. Quinn, there's good news and there's bad news. I'll start with the bad, if you don't mind. Jo and a local guide took a trip into the mountains. They drove over an explosive device, which detonated beneath their vehicle. The guide survived, but when he woke up in hospital, he had no idea what had happened to Jo."

"Rhys, please, just tell me. I can't bear this," Quinn moaned.

"I'm sorry. I thought you'd want to know what happened. Jo, who was badly hurt, was lucky enough to be picked up by American troops who were in the area. They took her to a military facility in Kabul, then flew her out to their base in Germany, which is where I am now."

"You're in Germany?" Quinn exclaimed.

"I arrived this morning on a military transport."

"Have you seen her? Have you seen Jo?"

"Quinn, Jo suffered a subdural hematoma, as well as some other injuries. She's been operated on and is on the mend. I saw her this morning. She recognized me."

"Oh, thank God! Did you tell her about me?" Quinn asked, her voice small and shaky.

"Jo's doctor warned me not to upset her. I couldn't just blurt out that I'd been sent by the twin sister she'd never heard of. It'll take time, Quinn. You must be patient. The worst is over."

"Rhys, where exactly are you?"

Rhys heard the determination in Quinn's voice and smiled. He knew exactly where this was going, but this was the Quinn he knew and loved, and he'd expect nothing less. "Perhaps you should give it a day or two," he suggested, knowing his advice would be completely ignored.

"Absolutely not. I will be on the first flight to Germany, as soon as you tell me precisely where you are."

"All right. I'm in Ramstein-Miesenbach, and Jo is at the Landstuhl Regional Medical Center. She's in the best of hands, Quinn."

"Rhys, did her doctor indicate when she can come home?" Quinn asked.

"No, she didn't. Jo was in an induced coma for several weeks. She's not going anywhere just now. Okay?"

"Okay."

"Quinn, how's our case going?" Rhys asked, his mind switching momentarily to work.

"I'll fill you in when I get there. I have to go. I can't wait to tell Gabe, and I need to call my dad, and Logan. Not sure if I want to tell Sylvia though," Quinn mused. She sounded lighter, and full of purpose. "Perhaps Logan can pass on the news."

"Text me your flight information. I'll see about hiring a car."

"Rhys, I can't thank you enough," Quinn said, her voice soft and breathless again. "What you've done for me..."

"It was my pleasure. Now, I have a date with a wiener schnitzel and a stein of local lager, and if you'd spent a fortnight in Kabul, you would understand just how exciting that is. I will see you soon."

"Enjoy your schnitzel, Rhys," Quinn said with a chuckle.

Rhys disconnected the call and stared at the blank screen for a moment, wondering if he'd made a terrible mistake by calling Quinn so soon. How would Jo react, in her current state, to a sister she'd never met, and would Dr. Stein object to Quinn putting Jo through such emotional upheaval so soon after waking her from a coma? Perhaps he should have waited until he'd spoken to Dr. Stein and had a clearer picture of what to expect, but at this stage, nothing would keep Quinn away. Even if she weren't allowed to visit with Jo, she'd sit outside her hospital room, happy in the knowledge that they were finally in the same place at the same time.

The shower beckoned, and Rhys set aside his mobile and stripped off his clothes, which still smelled of the musty room in Kabul. He hoped Hotel Europa had laundry service. He stepped beneath the blissfully hot spray and inhaled the pleasant smell of lavender soap. He'd allow himself one evening of indulgence: a long, hot shower, followed by a good dinner, and a film or two, if he couldn't find a cooking program. He'd never thought he'd be this excited to see a television. Tomorrow, Quinn would arrive, and they'd deal with whatever circumstances arose together.

FORTY-TWO

Quinn tossed her mobile onto the sofa and sprang to her feet. She wasn't the type of person who paced when she was anxious, but she couldn't have remained immobile if her life depended on it. She prowled the length of the room, her mind going over her conversation with Rhys again and again in an effort to determine if he'd held anything back. She knew him well enough at this stage to notice when he was being evasive or trying to deftly maneuver her onto another topic, but he'd seemed completely upfront. Jo had been badly hurt, but she was all right—or would be once she had time to recover. Quinn would see her tomorrow.

TOMORROW! her mind screamed. She would meet her twin tomorrow. Quinn increased her pace to match the racing of her heart at the giddy thought. Never had she been this excited and nervous, not even the day before her wedding.

She longed to shout the news from the rooftops, but a small part of her wanted to hold on to this moment for just a little longer, to hug the knowledge to her chest like a wonderful gift that she wasn't quite ready to show anyone just yet. She finally sat down and wrapped her arms about her legs, resting her chin on her knees. Her initial burst of excitement was beginning to wear off, while anxiety settled in, and all the questions that had been gnawing at her for the past several months reared their ugly heads. Why hadn't Jo responded to her letter? She must have received it before leaving for Kabul. Why had she severed ties with her brother and sister and chosen not to attend their father's funeral? Why had she not been in contact with Charles Sutcliffe? Surely he'd be one of the first people she'd call. What if Jo refused to see her?

Quinn reached for her mobile. She needed to talk to Gabe, but the call went straight to voicemail. She glanced at the time on the screen. Of course, Gabe had a staff meeting at three, and it was now half past. He wouldn't be available for at least another half hour, and then he'd go directly to Emma's school to collect her. Quinn would tell him about Jo when he got home and was able to give her his full attention. She'd tell Seth once she had more information. Seth was the type of person who'd get on the next flight to Germany, and Quinn wasn't at all sure it'd be a good idea to spring him, or his unsavory past with their mother, on Jo this soon. One surprise at a time was probably all the poor woman could handle in her present situation.

Logan. She had to tell Logan. He would be as excited as she was but wouldn't do anything rash. Logan understood that although Jo was his sister as well, Quinn was her twin and needed to be the first to speak to her. Logan would be supportive and talk her through this without making the situation all about himself, as Sylvia would if she got wind of the news. Quinn selected Logan's number and pressed the call button. He answered on the first ring.

"Logan, I'm so glad you picked up. I have to talk to you. Something's happened," Quinn blurted out. Now that she had Logan on the phone, she couldn't wait to share the news.

"How did you find out, Quinn?" He sounded tense and upset, not at all like his usual happy-go-lucky self.

"I just got the call a few minutes ago."

"From whom?" Logan demanded. "Please tell me you didn't tell Mum."

"No, I rang you first. Why are you so upset?" Quinn asked, taken aback by Logan's reaction.

"I'm sorry, sis. I'm just really scared right now."

"Of what?" Quinn asked. "It's really good news, under the circumstances."

"I know it could have been worse, but it's touch and go at the moment," Logan replied. "We'll know more in the next few hours. I wish Colin would get here. I could use the support."

"Logan, what are you talking about? What's happened?" Quinn asked, realization dawning that Logan wasn't speaking about Jo.

"I thought you knew," Logan replied. "I assumed Colin rang you." He sounded confused as well, and distracted. Quinn heard hospital sounds in the background. Someone was being paged.

"No, Colin never called. I wanted to tell you about Jo," Quinn explained. "Rhys called from Germany."

"Jo?"

"Our sister. Logan, what on earth is going on? You're scaring me."

"Jude was brought in about an hour ago," Logan said. He sounded as if he were about to cry. He *was* crying, Quinn realized.

"Why?" Quinn's excitement fizzled, instantly replaced by an icy dread spreading through her chest and chilling her heart.

"He overdosed, Quinn. He's in a bad way. I thought he was doing well. I thought he had a chance this time."

"Was he alone when it happened?" Quinn wasn't sure why it mattered, but she supposed she wanted to have someone to blame.

"Bridget was with him."

"Was she the one who called an ambulance?"

"Not exactly." Logan sniffled loudly, then blew his nose. He sounded a wreck.

"Logan, please tell me."

Logan took a shuddering breath. "Quinn, as you probably know, Jude is into erotic asphyxiation. Sometimes, he did it on his own when he wanked off, but he also did it with Bridget. He had her tighten the belt around his throat when he came. He said it took the orgasm to a different level."

"I thought you said he overdosed."

"He did. He had a seizure and lost consciousness. Bridget was flying high on heroin and thought she'd pulled the belt too tight. She was too terrified or too strung out to call for help. Her flatmate found them when she came home. Bridget was huddled in the corner, and Jude was on the bed, the belt still around his neck. He'd been unconscious for some time. They won't know for certain till he wakes up, but he might have suffered brain damage from lack of oxygen."

"Oh God. I'm so sorry, Logan. Sylvia doesn't know?"

"I don't know how to tell her this, Quinn. She'll be devastated. She tried so hard to help him get clean. I'll never forgive myself if he dies," Logan sobbed. "It's all my fault."

"How can this be your fault?"

"We argued last night. I should have listened to him, but I got angry and gave him a right old bollocking instead. I told him to get his shit together and stop blaming everyone else for his failings. I told him I'd never forgive him if he cocked up this chance."

"So, he was upset and broke down and rang Bridget."

"Exactly. I should have stayed and talked to him. I should have taken him out for a coffee or a film. I should have never left his side, Quinn. I should have known he'd self-sabotage. Instead, I rushed home because Colin was making dinner for me and I didn't want to keep him waiting."

"Logan, you can't be by Jude's side every minute of every day. Jude's an addict. You can't save him from himself. Only he can do that."

"I must. He's my baby brother, and I let him down. And now Mum will blame me too. She always does. She says Jude might have never started using had I not abandoned him."

"You didn't abandon him."

"No, but I should have been there for him when our dad died. I should have paid more attention to what he was going through. I was too busy with my new relationship and my job. I chose Colin over Jude."

"Logan, you did nothing wrong. You're allowed some personal happiness in your life. You can't be held responsible."

"But I am," Logan moaned miserably.

"I will be there shortly. We'll talk then."

"Thanks, Quinn."

"No need to thank me. You're my brother and I love you." And she loved Jude and would be devastated to lose him, she realized, as she threw things into Alex's baby bag. She added a bottle of formula and went to get Alex. He'd be cranky at being woken, but she couldn't afford to wait. Logan needed her, and so did Jude.

FORTY-THREE

Quinn found Logan in ICU, sitting next to Jude's bed. Jude's skin looked gray in the pale light of the winter afternoon. His eyes were closed, and his lips had a blue tinge that added to his corpse-like appearance. Ugly purple welts decorated his neck where the belt had been tightened. It must have been very wide, since the bruises fully covered his Adam's apple.

Quinn let out an involuntary sob, her hand flying to her mouth. Surely, they weren't going to lose him. Logan stood and faced her. His eyes were red-rimmed, and he was almost as pale as his brother. Quinn put her arms around him, offering silent support. Alex, who was now between them, thought it a fun game and smiled with delight.

"Is there anything I can do?" Quinn asked as she removed the baby carrier and unzipped Alex's snowsuit.

"Just sit with me for a while," Logan replied.

"You have to tell Sylvia, Logan. She'll never forgive you if anything happens and she wasn't here," Quinn said gently.

"I know. I've tried ringing her several times but couldn't go through with it."

"Would you like me to do it?"

Logan shook his head. "It has to come from me. Just give me a few more minutes." He buried his face in his hands. "I can't bear it, Quinn."

"It's not your fault, Logan," she assured him but knew her argument was falling on deaf ears. Logan would always blame himself if Jude died, or worse, remained a vegetable for the rest of his days.

"Even if it isn't my fault, which is a big if, he's still here, unconscious, fighting for his life. He's my brother. Losing him would be like losing a limb."

"Logan, he's young and strong."

"Plenty of young people die every day, some because they have no choice, and others because they're stupid bloody wankers who take their life for granted and would sell their soul for a hit."

There wasn't much Quinn could say to that, so she pulled up a chair and sat next to Logan. He reached for Alex and held the baby against his chest, burying his face in Alex's silky hair. "Don't ever do anything stupid, you hear me?" Logan whispered to him. "Don't ever destroy the people who love you."

Alex raised his hand and tried to grab Logan's nose, making him smile despite his misery. He sat the baby in his lap and kissed the top of his head. "Jude was so sweet when he was a baby. I hated him something fierce, of course, but he was just like Alex, always smiling and wanting to play. Mum had me watch him when she went out to the shops and Jude wouldn't give me a moment's peace. I had to mind him every minute or he'd fall on his head or poke out his eye. He was such a pest," Logan said quietly. "I'd gladly watch him now if he'd let me. I'd keep him safe."

Logan suddenly turned toward Quinn, giving her a piercing look. "What were you going to tell me when you called?"

"I was going to tell you that Rhys found Jo. She's in Germany, Logan. She's been seriously hurt."

"Oh God. I'm sorry, Quinn. You must be beside yourself with worry. Have you told Seth?"

"Not yet. You were the first person I called."

Logan reached out and took Quinn's hand. "You must go to her."

"I won't leave you, not when Jude is in critical condition."

"Quinn, I know what this means to you. She's my sister too, but she's your twin. You must go to her. I will look after Jude, I promise."

"I know you will, but a few more days won't make that much of a difference. Jo is in good hands and she's recovering. Rhys is with her. What he's done for me is amazing," Quinn said, her voice breaking with emotion.

"He loves you, and he needs something to give him a reason for being now that he's lost the baby and his girlfriend. His world tilted on its axis, and helping someone is the best way to forget your own troubles."

"Yes, I suppose it is. Isn't it amazing how that one night thirty-two years ago resulted in all these tangled, unexpected relationships?" Quinn mused.

"Yeah, Mum sure knows how to cock things up. If my dad were alive right now, I think he'd die all over again, from shock. Are you still angry with her for what she did?" Logan asked.

"I'm angry with her for lying to me, but I'm not angry with her for what happened. It's not for me to condemn her. It would have been just another night had she not fallen pregnant and decided to hide the birth of her children. She should have used better judgement and turned to people who could help her, but she was young and frightened."

"And incredibly stupid," Logan added. "It's strange to think that my mum, who I always thought was so conservative and restrained, willingly shagged three blokes, got pregnant, and managed to deliver twins without anyone knowing. She's a sly old thing, isn't she?"

Quinn nodded. Sylvia was sly and endowed with an incredible gift for self-preservation. Her actions had hurt so many people, including Rhys, who'd lived all those years with the guilt of believing he'd taken advantage of Sylvia against her will in his eagerness to lose his virginity. He deserved to be happy. They all did.

"Quinn, go to Jo," Logan said again. "I want you to."

"Will you ring me the minute anything changes?"

"Of course, I will. I will not leave Jude's side until he wakes or—"

"Don't even say it. He will wake up. He will recover."

Logan nodded. "As you say." He took the monkey hat from Quinn and carefully slipped in on Alex's head, then handed the baby back to her.

Quinn zipped up his snowsuit and placed him in the baby carrier. She kissed Logan's cheek. "Ring me any time of day or night."

Logan nodded. "Say hello to our sister."

"I will. Ring Sylvia."

Logan took out his mobile and held it up, indicating his intention to make the call. "I love you, Quinn," he said softly.

FORTY-FOUR
SEPTEMBER 1620

Virginia Colony

Mary spent a sleepless night after her encounter with Walker, tossing and turning in her lonely marriage bed. On the surface, her choice was simple. She'd made a promise before God when she married John. He wasn't the man she'd expected him to be, but that didn't mean her vows were invalidated by his acts of betrayal. If she remained in the colony—which wasn't really a choice given that she had no money for a return voyage, nor would anyone take a woman abandoning her husband aboard their ship—she had to stay married to John.

Mary traced a finger along the wall, feeling the rough grain of the wood. She could never marry Walker in the true sense of the word, even if she were free to wed, but he was an antidote to her loneliness, a balm to her soul. He offered her not only companionship, but affection, tenderness, and a true partnership, something she could never have with John. But at what cost, and was she willing to pay it?

Yes, a soft voice in her head replied. A life without affection or hope wasn't worth living. When she envisioned her future with John, she felt as if she were buried alive, forever sealed off from air and light, left to suffocate in an all-encompassing darkness. Perhaps she was being overly morbid, but after these past months, she knew with unwavering certainty that John was a castle she could never breach, not emotionally and not physically. He noticed her less and less as the weeks went by and had lain with her only once since she last bled, proving to her that begetting an heir wasn't high on his list of priorities.

"Why, Simon?" Mary had asked Simon after their conversation when he'd been hurt. She'd cornered him in the barn, desperate to vent her anger and frustration. "Why did John marry me?"

Strangely, since that unexpected encounter, Simon appeared to be the only person in the household to whom she could speak openly, since neither of them needed to bother with the pretense any longer, and despite Mary's obvious distrust and dislike of him, Simon seemed to feel some sympathy for her.

"Secretary Hunt read out the list of men who were to get brides before the entire congregation one Sunday. Refusal would have singled John out for suspicion and ridicule. He never meant to hurt you, Mary. He had no choice."

"But he *is* hurting me. As are you."

Simon shrugged. "We all have our crosses to bear. I mean you no harm, Mary, but I must see to my own interests."

"And what about Travesty? Why does she hate me so?" Mary demanded, her fury nowhere near extinguished.

"She doesn't hate you; she envies you," Simon replied as he continued mucking out the stall, as if they were exchanging pleasantries or talking about the weather.

"This union was none of my choosing," Mary snapped.

"Travesty thought to wed the master, and instead she got a new mistress, one she thinks is spoiled and naïve."

"Spoiled?" Mary sputtered. She had been naïve, yes, but spoiled? She was hardly that.

"Mary, let me give you a piece of advice, and remember that it's kindly meant. Make the most of your lot, bide your time, and seize an opportunity with both hands if it comes your way."

"Is that what you're doing? Just waiting for your opportunity?" Mary asked. She hated the bitterness in her voice and the tang of tears at the back of her throat.

"You know I am," Simon replied, indifferent to her pain.

"And do you not care who gets hurt through your schemes?"

"Not a bit. And neither should you."

"You're despicable," Mary cried.

"No, my darling girl, I'm just honest. A rare quality in most folk, in case you haven't noticed."

Mary had stomped from the barn, wiping the tears away with the back of her hand, but made a sharp turn and went to check on the vegetable patch when she saw Travesty emerging from the cabin with a bucket of slops. She'd be damned if she let that woman see her tears.

Now, weeks later, Simon's advice returned to her, and she turned it over in her mind as she stared at the darkened ceiling of the cabin. The way she felt now, even a few stolen moments of happiness would be worth the risk. What was the worst that could happened? Who'd know? Walker would be waiting for her by the creek tomorrow. She could either go to him and willingly embrace a life of sin or remain a virtuous wife and embrace a life of bitterness and secret shame. Either way she was damned, either in this life or the next.

Mary ran her hand along the cool sheet on John's side of the bed. He'd snuck out as soon as he thought her asleep. She knew where he'd gone and what he was doing. Even John had love, or something that passed for it. He had a companion, someone who accepted him for what he was and was willing to keep his secret. John's relationship with Simon was sinful and based on lies, but it was a relationship nonetheless, one that seemed to satisfy both parties for the time being.

Mary sighed. Was it wrong to crave love? Was she unnatural in wishing for a soft touch in the night, or a tender kiss? The church preached against lust, but was this lust or a basic need to be cared for? Would she still long to be with Walker if he could never consummate their relationship? Yes, she would. She felt whole in his presence, and visible.

Mary squeezed her eyes shut and slowed her breathing as John tiptoed into the cabin and crept toward the bed. He lay down and turned onto his side, his back to her. She could smell the sweat on his skin, and a tang of something else, something she preferred not to name. She stole a peek at John once he fell asleep. He was smiling.

London, England

A peaceful winter night settled over London. The sky was strewn with stars, and a crescent moon hung over the city, its points sharp as a sickle. Gabe poured himself a drink and settled on the sofa. It was late, but he knew he wouldn't sleep, not yet. The house was quiet around him, only the sounds of late-night traffic barely audible in the stillness of the night.

It'd taken Quinn hours to get to sleep. She'd been weepy and excited at the same time, overcome with worry about Jude and anxious about finally getting to meet Jo. Gabe was genuinely sorry about Jude. He'd never been driven by a self-destructive impulse himself but wasn't at all sure he'd be strong enough to resist a desperate need like Jude's if he were. It was easy to say, "Get clean" or "You have to stop using," but so hard to do. Jude was an addict, and even if he was lucky enough to ride out this crisis and regain control of his life, the desire and impulse would always be there, stalking him like prey, hounding his every waking hour. Jude would need the support of his family if he recovered, and Gabe would have to set his own feelings aside and encourage Quinn to offer whatever assistance she could.

And then there was Jo. She was either really brave or spectacularly stupid to go traipsing through such a dangerous region with nothing but a teenage guide for company. No photo, no matter how amazing, was worth losing one's life over. Had Jo been inspired by her desire to tell a story or driven by a need to glorify her own name in the photojournalism circles? Gabe couldn't rightly say without getting to know her, but if her twin were anything to go by, then Jo had probably only wanted to shine a light into the darkest corners of humanity's lust for power. Whether she'd been after photos of Taliban hideouts or looking for hidden stashes of opium, she would be showing the world once again how the cruelty and greed of a few destroyed the lives of many. How much of the heroin Jude had ingested came from Afghanistan? Probably a good bit. How would Jo feel when she learned of her brother's addiction?

Gabe took a sip of Scotch and felt the fiery liquid slide down his throat, warming him from within. He wished the alcohol would take the edge off and help him get to sleep, but he was wide awake, his mind not ready to set aside his troubled thoughts. Would Quinn ever find inner peace? The meeting with Jo would go a long way toward helping her if it went well, but despite trying his best to be supportive, he was deeply worried. His mind buzzed with speculation, persistent as ever despite a refill of Scotch. What if Jo rejected Quinn and wanted nothing to do with her? Or what if Jo welcomed Quinn into her life but turned out to be nothing like the sister Quinn hoped for? Gabe genuinely liked Logan and was glad Quinn had a brother she loved, but, given her history with Brett and Jude, the situation with Jo could go either way. Gabe drained the glass and eyed the bottle affectionately before screwing on the cap and putting it away in the kitchen cupboard. Enough. He could control himself, and he would. Two drinks were his limit.

Gabe returned to the sofa and lay down, propping his head with a decorative pillow as his thoughts returned to Jo. Which parent did Jo take after, Sylvia or Seth? Those two were an unlikely pair if there ever was one. Now that he'd got to know them both, he was glad Quinn was more like her father, direct and practical—well, to a point. She did tend to get overly emotional and deeply involved, not only with the people in her life, but with the individuals whose lives she saw playing out in her mind day after day. And he loved her for it. He loved that she cared, even though centuries had passed since those poor souls had walked the earth. Quinn's voice shook and her eyes blazed with indignation when she spoke of the injustices they'd had to endure and the unfair treatment of women in centuries past. Her heart broke when they suffered, and she mourned their deaths as if they had been her friends and not mere holograms she saw in her uniquely wired brain. Quinn had been unusually tight-lipped about Mary Wilby, possibly because the state of Mary's remains had affected her so deeply, or maybe because she couldn't focus on Mary when Jo was constantly on her mind.

Gabe had tried to dissuade Quinn from ringing Sylvia, given her emotional state, but Quinn had felt she owed it to Sylvia to share the news about Jo and refused to wait. She thought the knowledge that Jo was safe might ease Sylvia's suffering as she waited for news of Jude. Sylvia had sounded surprisingly calm on the phone. Gabe had heard her side of the conversation since Quinn's mobile was only inches from him when she spoke to her mother. Sylvia had persuaded Logan to go home and get some rest while she kept vigil over her youngest child. Quinn had waited until an appropriate moment presented itself to tell Sylvia about Jo, but Sylvia hadn't asked too many questions or expressed an immediate interest in seeing her daughter. All her attention was focused on Jude.

A noise from the bedroom startled Gabe out of his reverie, and he looked up to find Quinn padding toward the sofa. She looked tired and sad, her mouth turned down at the corners. Her hair was mussed, and there were dark smudges beneath her eyes. Gabe sat up and opened his arms, and Quinn slid onto his lap and pressed herself against him, like a small child.

Gabe wrapped his arms around her and held her close, not

saying anything. After a while, Quinn's lips found his and she slid her hand down his track pant bottoms, her fingers closing around him with obvious intent. Gabe cupped her breast, but Quinn pushed his hand away and wiggled out of her knickers as she pulled him down on top of her.

"No foreplay. And do it hard," she commanded.

"Are you sure that's what you want?" Gabe asked, mystified by her mood.

"I want to feel something other than sorrow right now."

Quinn wrapped her legs around Gabe as he drove into her, giving her what she'd asked for with single-minded determination. He didn't bother with kisses or endearments, and she slammed her hips against his with unexpected force. He had to be hurting her, but she clawed at his back and ground against him, urging him not to pull back. Gabe closed his eyes and allowed himself to let go, pummeling her until she arched her back, cried out, and went limp beneath him.

He pressed his forehead to hers, looking into her clouded gaze. "All right?"

Quinn nodded and pushed him off. She left as suddenly as she'd come, leaving him alone on the sofa with his troubled thoughts.

FORTY-SIX
SEPTEMBER 1620

Virginia Colony

Mary took out the freshly baked bread and covered it with a muslin cloth to keep the flies away, then looked around the cabin, searching for something more to do. She'd milked the cow and let her out to pasture, mucked out her stall, washed the crockery from their morning meal, picked some runner beans from the vegetable patch and set them to soak, ground enough corn to bake fresh bread for supper, and swept the floor. She sank onto the bench and folded her hands in her lap. She was stalling, she knew that, but it was time to decide. She could either go to the creek and meet Walker or let him walk out of her life, and she didn't think she could bear that. Deep down, she'd known what she would do. She untied her apron, hung it up on a hook by the door, and left the cabin.

The late-morning sun caressed her flushed face as she hurried toward the creek, hoping Walker would still be there. What if she'd waited too long? Mary stopped to catch her breath. The day was truly glorious. The sky was a robin's-egg blue, the thick canopy of leaves above her head still green and lush, and the babbling of the creek in the distance inviting and soothing. Birdsong filled the air, and Mary soaked up the peacefulness of the forest, grateful to be away from Travesty's prying eyes. What would they see in her face right now—hope, fear, desire, anticipation? She felt all those things as she rushed into the clearing by the creek and stood still, looking around.

The rag she'd tied to the branch had been removed, but there was no sign of Walker. He must have come and gone, or maybe he'd changed his mind and never showed at all. He was handsome and unwed. There had to be plenty of young women he could choose from, women who would make him their priority, tend his home, and bear his children. Why should he need Mary, a woman who was married to another, and who could never be free to follow her own heart?

She didn't believe all that nonsense about the deaths of his daughters for a minute. Children died all the time, not only at birth, but at any time thereafter. Their deaths had nothing to do with incompatibility of two spirits, but with disease, poverty, and ultimately, God's will. Walker might not believe in her God, but surly the Creator he worshipped was no less fickle and vengeful. Some people lived, some died, some suffered all their lives, while others lived a life of comfort and security, blessed by an accident of birth. If there were any sensible women in Walker's village, they'd figure out this simple truth and snap up a good man while he was still free—at least that was what her mind told her. Her heart, on the other hand, felt sore with disappointment that he hadn't come.

Mary sank to the ground and stared at the sparkling water of the creek. The water rose higher than it had at the height of summer and wasn't as warm. The nights were cooler now, the days shorter, the winter stealthily approaching. Mary wrapped her arms around her legs and rested her chin on her knees, staring intently into the trees on the other side of the creek. She knew she should return to the cabin and put Walker from her mind once and for all, but some internal need to stay kept her rooted to the spot. She bowed her head, pressed her forehead to her knees, and closed her eyes, allowing the peace of the place to wash over her and fill her with strength. This wasn't her first disappointment, and it most certainly wouldn't be her last. This was for the best.

What made her think she deserved to be happy? She was alive, fed and clothed, and in good health. Countless women would change places with her, even if they knew the truth. They would gladly settle for the security John provided and turn a blind eye to the other aspects of marriage. Some would probably even be grateful to be spared their husband's carnal demands. There had been women in Plymouth who gave birth to one child only to get pregnant with the next within a few weeks or months. They bore babies every year, children they could ill afford, didn't want, and were too exhausted to care for. With John, that'd never be her fate. She had to be thankful for what she had. She had to accept the hand life had dealt her.

Mary finally pushed to her feet, brushed the grass off her skirts, tucked a stray curl into her cap, and turned to leave. She cried out in surprise when Walker stepped out from behind the wide-bellied oak. He had an unnerving way of blending in with his surroundings. He came toward her, his gaze smoky and serious.

"I didn't think you were coming," Mary said by way of greeting. Her heart was hammering in her chest and she felt as if a heavy weight had been lifted from her shoulders. She felt all aflutter, like a bride in love on her wedding day. Her resolve to have nothing to do with Walker evaporated like morning dew at the sight of him.

"I was here all along."

"Why didn't you show yourself?" Mary asked, stung by his admission.

"I wanted to watch you for a while."

"Why?" Mary exclaimed, hurt boiling over.

"Because I needed to be sure."

"Sure of me?"

"Sure of myself," he replied.

"And what does that mean?"

"It means I want you to come with me," Walker replied. He

still hadn't touched her or even smiled at her. His gaze was intense and unrelenting.

"Come where?"

"To the Powhatan village."

Mary stared at him. What exactly was he asking her?

"Mary, you will be treated with kindness and respect. You will be accepted as my wife. No one will hurt you."

Mary shook her head. "I can't. I'm not one of you."

"But you can be. My mother learned to be happy again. She married and had children."

"They called her Sad Eyes," Mary reminded him.

"Mary, my mother had endured something dreadful. Something she couldn't bear to speak of, not even to my father. She was sad because she missed her homeland and her friends, and because she knew she'd never see any of them again."

"But given the choice, she would have returned to England," Mary argued.

"Perhaps. But there was no choice. She made the best of her situation. You have a choice."

"Do I?"

"Yes."

Mary looked into his opaque eyes, trying to understand what was driving him to suggest this to her. She'd never been one to ask for kindness or reassurance, but she had to know. "Walker, why do you want me to come with you?"

The question seemed to surprise him. "Isn't it obvious?"

"Not to me."

"I love you, Mary. I want to care for you and protect you. I want to have a family with you."

"You love me," she repeated stupidly.

"Is that so difficult to believe?"

"No one has loved me," she said. "Not since my parents died. I'm not sure I even recognize the feeling."

Walker closed the space between them and drew her into his arms, kissing her hard. This wasn't a kiss of seduction—his kiss was a brand. He was claiming her as his own, letting her know that if she felt the same, he was hers for the taking.

Mary kissed him back with all her innocent passion. She had no idea what was expected of her, but she needn't have worried. Walker drew her away from the clearing and into a thicket of trees. No one would see them there, not even if they came looking. He put his hands on her shoulders and looked down at her, silently asking for permission, and she gave it. She pulled off her cap, releasing her hair. It tumbled to her shoulders, framing her face. Walker ran his hands through the tresses. His eyes were clouded with desire, and he reached for the laces of her bodice, tugging on them impatiently. Mary untied her skirt and let it pool around her ankles as Walker pulled her chemise over her head.

She stood in front of him, naked and vulnerable. No one had ever seen her like this, except him. The first time, he'd stolen the privilege, but this time she was offering it willingly. He cupped her breast and lowered his head to flick his tongue over her nipple as he pulled her against his almost-naked body. He was so warm and solid, so sure of what he was doing. Mary surrendered herself to him, allowing him to lay her down on a bed of soft earth.

Walker untied his breechclout and lay down next to her. His skin blended into the colors of the forest, unlike her milky whiteness that was in stark contrast to the green carpet beneath her. Mary expected him to take her, like John did, but Walker was in no rush. He kissed and caressed every inch of her, making her cry out as waves of red-hot pleasure washed over her, leaving her trembling with an urgent need. She clung to him, terrified he'd stop, but he was just getting started.

"Walker!" His name escaped from her lips. It sounded like a breath on the wind, a prayer to a benevolent deity. And he responded in kind, worshipping her as if she were a goddess, and doing things that left her weak with desire. She grabbed a fistful of his hair when his tongue slid inside her, exploring her with an intimacy that heated her cheeks and stirred her blood.

"Walker, please," she pleaded, unable to stand it any longer.

When Walker finally joined his body to hers, it was nothing like her awkward couplings with John. It was exquisite. She clung to him and ground her hips against his, desperate to take him in deeper and let him fill the emptiness that had been a part of her for so long. He answered her need by thrusting harder and faster, making her gasp with every stroke until something inside her uncoiled and burst forth, like a rosebud finally opening to the sun, its petals unfurling in all their scarlet glory. Her body shuddered around him as he reached his own peak, spilling his seed into her. His mouth stretched into a sensuous smile as he gazed into her heavy-lidded eyes.

"Come with me," he whispered. "Let this be our life."

Mary closed her eyes to block out his seductive invitation. Her body was damp with perspiration, and her insides still quivered with the aftershocks of their love. She'd never known anything like this, and she never would again if she allowed Walker to leave her. Mary's thoughts swirled in incoherent patterns, the threads escaping as she tried to tie them together. She wanted to go. She needed to stay. She wanted him to protect her. She needed to protect him.

Mary forced herself to concentrate. She needed to make sense of what she was thinking. "I need a little time," she finally said, unable to put into words what was in her heart. "Please, give me time."

Walker kissed her softly, his eyes glowing with love. "Take time, Mary. There's no rush. I will wait."

"What would my Indian name be if I came with you?" she asked, allowing herself a moment to fantasize about a life with Walker.

"Man Eater," he whispered into her ear as he slid into her again. Mary's eyes flew open in surprise, but Walker was smiling.

"Why?"

"Because you are hungry," he replied, precluding further questions by feeding her hunger until she was sated.

FORTY-SEVEN

Mary returned to the cabin just in time to get started on supper. John, Simon, and Travesty would be back from the fields soon, and they'd be hungry and tired. Mary went about her tasks, her hands moving of their own accord, unconnected to her jumbled thoughts. The hours she'd spent with Walker were the happiest she'd ever known. He hadn't pressed her to give him an answer or spoken of what their life together might be like. He'd simply gloried in spending time with her.

After making love for a third time, Walker pulled her to her feet and helped her dress. Her hands trembled, and she couldn't manage to tie her laces. He gently moved her hands aside and laced up her bodice, as if she were a little girl, then ran his fingers through her tangled tresses and expertly braided her hair, pinning it up so she could put her cap back on.

"I want to show you something," he said. "Come."

They followed the creek until Walker spotted a fallen log. He lifted it easily, held it up and allowed it to fall across the creek, forming a crossing. The log wasn't thick, but big enough to hold their weight if they crossed one by one. Walker went first, then turned and beckoned for Mary to join him on the other side. She followed.

"Where are we going?"

"You'll see."

They walked for about a mile toward the Kirby plantation, then Walker took a sharp turn and pulled Mary deeper into the woods. There, nestled among the trees, was a small shack. The roof was covered with pine boughs and the walls green with moss, making the tiny dwelling almost impossible to spot.

"What is this place?" Mary asked as she followed Walked toward the narrow door.

"I came across it some time ago while setting traps. Some Englishman built this years ago, but it's been abandoned for a long time."

Walker pushed open the door and invited Mary to come inside. The interior of the shack wasn't nearly as ramshackle as the outside. There was an old wooden cot covered with a blanket of fur, along with other signs of habitation.

"Do you sleep here?"

"I did once, when I got caught in a terrible storm while hunting with two others. We were here for two days. I've never seen a storm like it before or since."

"So, why did you bring me here?" Mary asked.

"It's not safe for us to meet by the creek. Once the harvest is in, your husband and his servant will spend more time at home. And the woman, she is not to be trusted. She sees more than you think. We can meet here. And you can come here if you ever need a safe place."

Mary nodded. "All right. But I must go back now. I have supper to prepare."

"I went to see the physician yesterday," Walker said as he walked Mary back to the spot where they'd met earlier.

Mary's eyes flew to Walker's face. "Are you ill?"

He flashed her a grin. "I am well."

"Why did you go, then?"

"My mother was mistrustful of tribal medicine. She said the

English knew more about healing. I want to learn about English ways."

"And did you?" Mary asked.

"Dr. Paulson was happy to show me his medical tools and some of his potions. He was amused by my interest. He spoke to me like I was a curious child," Walker said, chuckling. "His tools seem more appropriate to butchering meat. He showed me a saw for cutting off limbs."

"Sometimes it's necessary to remove a limb to save a life."

Walker shrugged. "It's barbaric. A body should not be desecrated. There are other ways."

Mary would have liked to know what those ways were, but they'd reached the turnoff toward the plantation.

Walker gathered her into his arms and kissed her tenderly. He held her face in both his hands and smiled into her eyes. "I will wait for you."

"I will come," Mary replied.

That night, when John slipped out of bed, Mary didn't care. Her body still thrummed with desire, and she could hardly wait to see Walker again.

FORTY-EIGHT
FEBRUARY 2015

London, England

Quinn threw some clothes into a suitcase, then took half out and added several warm jumpers. She had no idea what she'd need, or how long she'd be staying, but it was sure to be cold. Her insides quivered every time she imagined her first meeting with Jo. What would it be like to finally meet her face-to-face?

Quinn sat down heavily on the bed and stared out the window. Even after all these months, she knew next to nothing about her sister and had no idea what to expect. Would they have something in common? Would there be an instant spark of recognition between their souls, or would it be like meeting a complete stranger? Would Jo be welcoming or wary of her, resentful that Quinn had forgiven their parents for abandoning her? Would Jo want to be a part of Quinn's life?

All these questions would get answered soon enough, but Quinn couldn't leave for Germany without making sure Gabe and the children would be all right. Gabe would take a few days off work, but he'd have his hands full. Emma went from being sweet and cuddly to bristling with defiance at the drop of a hat, and Alex drooled incessantly, his gums red and swollen with incoming teeth.

He didn't seem to be suffering too badly at the moment, but the pediatrician had warned that Alex might run a low-grade fever and experience periods of severe pain when the teeth cut through. Gabe was a hands-on dad, who didn't shy away from any task, but he might need a helping hand all the same.

Quinn picked up her mobile and selected Jill's number. She hadn't spoken to Jill since shortly after the New Year, when Jill was in the midst of running her post-holiday/going-out-of-business sale. Her cousin put on a brave face about closing her vintage clothing shop, but Quinn knew she was bitterly disappointed. The shop had been a cherished dream, a mad gamble for a person who, having trained as a forensic accountant, did not easily leap into the unknown. Jill wasn't a risk-taker; she was someone who liked lists and balance sheets, a person for whom every column had to add up. And now she was walking away from something that had been important to her and planning her return to the world of corporate accounting. Quinn didn't expect her to be in good spirits and felt a twinge of guilt for not calling sooner.

"Hey there, Quinny," Jill exclaimed when she answered the call. "How's the new year treating you?"

"Not too badly. You sound surprisingly chipper," Quinn replied with an amused smile.

"No wallowing in self-pity for me. What's done is done. I've given it my all and failed miserably, but I was wise enough to admit it and make the decision to move on. I embrace this experience and see it as a learning opportunity."

"That's a very healthy way of looking at it."

"Not really. I'm just trying to sound like a New Age guru and talk myself into seeing this as a positive experience. I'm utterly gutted and want to drown myself in a vat of Malbec."

"Now, that's the Jill I know and love," Quinn said with a chuckle.

"Yeah, New Age positivity lasts for about thirty seconds before I remember that I have to start interviewing for a new job come March. How are things with you?"

"Rhys has found Jo," Quinn said, a catch in her voice.

"Blimey. Where is she?"

"She's in a military hospital in Germany. She was hurt in an explosion while on assignment in Kabul. She was lucky enough to be picked up by some passing Americans. They saved her life."

"Oh, Quinn, will she be all right?"

"According to Rhys, she's on the road to recovery. I'm flying out to Germany tomorrow morning. I would have gone today, but Jude's overdosed. He's still unconscious. Logan's with him. I feel awful about leaving at such a difficult time. Logan needs me," Quinn said. "And so does Sylvia."

"Quinn, you can't be in two places at once. Jude has his mother and brother to look after him. Jo has no one. She hardly knows Rhys."

"She doesn't know me at all," Quinn replied, her anxiety returning. "She might not want me there."

"She might not know you, but you are her sister. You should be by her side whether she wants you there or not."

"Thanks, Jill. I needed to hear that."

"How will Gabe cope on his own while you're gone?" Jill asked, her practical nature making itself known.

"Actually, that's why I called," Quinn admitted. "Purely selfish reasons. Is there any way you can give Gabe a hand while I'm away? I've weaned Alex, so he's on the bottle now, but he's teething, poor mite. And Emma's been a right little madam. Sometimes I forget she's only five."

"No problem. I'm a free agent till the end of the month. The shop's closed, the inventory has been disposed of, and I have nothing to occupy my time besides updating my CV and fretting about what comes next. I can even take the children for a night or two if that will make things easier for Gabe."

"Will Brian not mind?" Quinn asked. Jill and Brian had just moved in together at the beginning of January, a marked step toward formalizing their relationship, according to Jill.

"The way I see it, Brian will either get on board or run for the hills and stay at his brother's flat until it's safe to come home. It will make for an interesting experiment."

"I'm glad you see my children as a means to an end," Quinn joked.

"I don't. It's just that Brian seems to be on the ten-year plan when it comes to starting a family. I wish he were more like Gabe."

"Gabe was on a ten-year plan as well. I just wasn't aware of it," Quinn replied. Gabe had waited eight years for her while she wasted her time with Luke.

"Hm, that's true. Well, he did get what he wanted in the end."

"So did I. And so will you, Jill. Brian is getting there. Slowly, but steadily."

"Yes, at the rate we're going, he'll pop the question by the time I'm forty. Did you know that if you get pregnant past the age of thirty-five, it's referred to as a geriatric pregnancy?" Jill's sigh sounded like a deflating balloon.

"Jill, you're thirty-one. You're a long way from a geriatric pregnancy. Give him time. He loves you, it's obvious to anyone who cares to look. I have no doubt you two will end up together."

"As a wise man once said, 'There's many a slip betwixt the cup and the lip,'" Jill intoned theatrically. Had Shakespeare still been alive, Jill would have been a fawning groupie.

"Yes, there is, so hold on to your cup with both hands," Quinn replied, making Jill laugh. "Brian isn't going anywhere, even if you subject him to my children. I bet he'll surprise you."

"Thanks, Quinn. You always make me feel better about things. Have a safe flight and good luck with Jo. I can't wait to meet her."

It was Quinn's turn to sigh. "What if she wants nothing to do with me, Jill? What if she doesn't like me? I wish I could just teleport myself there right now because I can't wait another minute, but then I wish I could put off meeting her until I'm truly ready."

"'Time is very slow for those who wait, very fast for those who are scared, very long for those who lament, very short for those who celebrate, but for those who love, time is eternal.' William Shakespeare."

"All right, I see where this is going. Parting is such sweet sorrow, but methinks I really must go now before I starteth speaking in iambic pentameter."

Jill giggled. "See you tomorrow, coz. I'll come by before you leave."

Quinn was still smiling after she ended the call. That was how it was with Jill, even when they were girls. They'd start off upset, moaning about their teenage sorrows, but after a few minutes, they'd be laughing like they didn't have a care in the world, their silliness a shield against reality.

A loud whine came from the direction of Alex's cot, and Quinn set aside her mobile and reached for the baby. He pressed his warm cheek against her neck, still sleepy, but ready to fill his belly. "I don't want to leave you, but I have to go away for a few days," Quinn whispered into his ear. Alex seemed to sense her mood and whimpered, grabbing a fistful of her hair.

"I'll be back soon. I promise." Quinn spoke softly, hoping to comfort him, but Alex began to cry in earnest. "Daddy will take care of you. And Emma."

Alex wailed louder, but the sound of a key in the lock seemed to quiet him. Did he really understand the sound meant the arrival of Gabe and Emma? Was he that aware at only four months? Alex turned his head toward the door, his bad mood forgotten. Quinn felt him holding his breath as he waited for the sound of Gabe's voice. "You clever little lad," she said, holding him tighter as his little body leaned forward in his eagerness to see his father.

"We're home," Gabe called out.

Emma burst into the room, her cheeks ruddy with cold. "It's snowing outside. Rufus loves snow," she exclaimed. "He had so much fun."

Alex leaned even further forward, his gaze fixed on the door.

"He knew you were coming," Quinn said as Gabe walked into the room. "He was waiting for you."

"That's because he's brilliant. I saw that, Emma," Gabe said as Emma made a face.

"He's not brilliant. He's just a silly baby."

"He's not silly. He's adorable," Gabe said as he reached for Alex, who was smiling at him and holding out his arm. "You're adorable too," Gabe said, kissing Quinn over Alex's head. "All right?" he asked carefully, watching her to see if anything had changed since he'd left an hour ago.

Quinn nodded. They'd spoken at length last night, but it was their lovemaking that had made her feel more balanced. No matter what happened with Jude or with Jo, Gabe would still be the center of her world, and as long as her center was intact, she would remain whole. Her only choice was to take things day by day, or in the case of Jude, hour by hour. She'd spoken to Logan earlier and he said there'd been no change during the night. Jude wasn't better, but he was no worse, which she supposed was something to be grateful for.

"When do you think you'll be back?" Gabe asked, his gaze travelling to her open suitcase.

"I really couldn't say."

"Why are you leaving again?" Emma demanded. "It's not fair."

"I'm sorry, darling, but it's only for a few days. It's important."

"What's more important than us?" she demanded as her eyes filled with tears. "I don't want you to go."

"I will call you every day, and you can tell me all about school and how Daddy and Alex are doing," Quinn promised.

"No! I don't want you to go," Emma screamed.

"I have to go, but Jill said you can have a sleepover at her new flat. Would you like that?"

"I'd rather have a sleepover with Maya."

"Maybe we can arrange that once we move into our new house. I'll ring Maya's mum and work out the details with her. In the meantime, Jill is looking forward to having you over," Quinn said in her most convincing tone.

"Does Alex have to come?" Emma asked, her eyes narrowing with suspicion.

"Alex is too little for sleepovers. He'll stay right here with me," Gabe said.

"All right," Emma conceded. "I suppose a sleepover at Jill's will be fun. We can play dress-up with some of her weird old-fashioned frocks, and Brian makes pineapple pizza. But you'd better come home soon," Emma warned.

"I will."

FORTY-NINE

After dinner, once the children had gone to bed, Gabe poured them both a glass of wine and they settled comfortably on the sofa. Quinn tucked her feet beneath her and took a long sip, enjoying the full-bodied flavor of the wine. The last two days had been an emotional roller coaster, but despite Gabe's willingness to listen and offer support, she had no desire to talk about either Jude or Jo.

"Tell me about Mary," Gabe said, taking Quinn by surprise.

"What? Now?"

"Yes, now. Talking about Mary will allow you to focus on something other than what will happen tomorrow. Tell me what you know so far. It will help. Besides, you've hardly spoken about her, and I'd love to hear her story."

Quinn flashed Gabe a grateful smile. He was right, of course. She needed to calm her mind if she hoped to get any sleep tonight. The wine would help, but so would redirecting her attention toward something other than her hapless siblings.

"Mary was not in a good situation," Quinn began.

Gabe smiled. "I'd be surprised if she was."

"She was an impulsive young woman, a little rebellious. Those are admirable qualities in our world, but in the seventeenth century..."

"They could be a death sentence," Gabe supplied.

"Exactly. Mary's husband, John, was homosexual. He'd consummated the marriage and done his best to fulfil his conjugal duties, but he had no interest in Mary, and his lack of attention was hurtful and confusing. Mary wasn't prepared to settle for that sham of a marriage."

"Can't say I blame her. Although, she's not the first woman to be duped into marriage with a homosexual man. A wife is the most effective cover in a society where homosexuality is seen as a crime against God. But, given the law of the colony, what could Mary do?" Gabe asked. He refilled Quinn's glass, but not his own. "I'll get Alex if he wakes during the night. Don't worry," he said, following her gaze. "I just want you to feel relaxed tonight."

"Thank you. I do feel much better." Quinn considered Gabe's question. "There was nothing Mary could do. The only thing that would release her from the marriage was death. If John were to die, Mary would be free to remarry, and I'm sure she'd have no lack of suitors, being an attractive widow with a sizeable plantation."

"Could that have happened?"

"I really can't say. I don't know precisely when Mary died or who fathered her child. But given her feelings for Walker, I'm not sure she'd rush into another marriage."

"Walker? Who's Walker?" Gabe asked.

"Walker was Mary's name for a Native American called Walks Between Worlds. And this is really interesting: Walker claimed to have been born to one of the women who vanished from the Roanoke colony. He was half-English."

"Is that even possible? To this day, no one knows what happened to the colonists of Roanoke Colony. They simply vanished."

"Walker told Mary how his mother and older brother came to live with the tribe, and his story sounded plausible. He said his mother's name was Elizabeth Viccars, and his half-brother's name was Ambrose. I checked against the names of the colonists who settled on Roanoke, and both Elizabeth Viccars and Ambrose

Viccars appeared on the list. Besides, Walker's appearance suggests that he was, indeed, of mixed race. Because of his English mother, Walker was something of an oddity among the natives. It seemed they trusted him and treated him like one of their own, but he never truly felt like he belonged. He saw a kindred spirit in Mary, and she found his sensitivity and kindness hard to resist."

"I can't imagine that a liaison between them would end well, given the time and place they lived," Gabe speculated. "The governor of the colony would never allow a British woman to marry a native, even if she were free to marry again, unless Mary simply ran off with him."

"I agree, but what I don't understand is how Mary wound up in that cave in Cornwall. She would have left Virginia some time in her third trimester. Why did she leave? Where was she going? What happened to force her to return to England, and who paid for her passage? And who hid her coffin in that cave, and why? There are so many unanswered questions."

"And you don't really want to find out, do you?"

"No, I don't. Whatever happened to her was awful. She was a young woman who'd known very little happiness in her brief life, and to see how she ended up breaks my heart. Something truly unexpected must have occurred."

"How do you mean?" Quinn suspected Gabe knew exactly what she meant, but he wanted to keep her talking, to keep her mind on Mary and off Jo. And she appreciated the effort.

"Mary would not have returned to England unless she was widowed and had no wish to remain in Virginia."

"What makes you think Mary left Virginia alone? She might have been traveling with her husband. Also, you're assuming Mary was already pregnant at the time of her departure, but there's nothing to support that," Gabe replied, his tone thoughtful. "It's possible that she returned to England with John and became pregnant here. You did say John consummated the marriage, so it's entirely plausible that she could have conceived with him. Or, she might have remarried and been expecting a child with her second husband."

"That's an interesting theory," Quinn said. "I haven't considered that. I need to go back and search for any mention of Mary or John Forrester in Devon and Cornwall between 1620 and 1625. Given Colin's age estimate of Mary's skeleton, she wouldn't have lived past that."

"No, that doesn't seem likely. Is there a record of colonists who died in Virginia during that period? Perhaps it would shed some light on Mary's marital status at the time of her death."

"Yes, there should be a record. If John Forrester died before 1625, then I'd be able to establish a credible timeline of Mary's actions."

"I think you need to get some sleep," Gabe said, pulling Quinn to her feet. "You have a big day tomorrow."

"Yes. I do. Will you hold me until I fall asleep?" Quinn asked, suddenly feeling like a frightened child.

"As if you even have to ask."

FIFTY
SEPTEMBER 1620

Virginia Colony

Mary breathed a sigh of relief when the door closed behind Travesty and she was left blessedly alone. She'd hardly seen Travesty these past weeks, busy as the other woman was with the harvest. Travesty alternated between hanging tobacco in the shed and collecting corn and stacking it in the corn crib. Mary's "exalted" position as the mistress of the house spared her the field work. She was left in charge of all the chores: cooking, laundering, seeing to the animals, mucking out the barn, tending the kitchen garden, and even chopping wood. Mary didn't mind. She welcomed the solitude and breezed through the work, eager for a few hours with Walker.

She'd seen him several times since his declaration of love in the thicket, and their every meeting brought them closer together. Walker had let go of some of his natural reserve, and Mary, starved as she had been for affection, opened up to him like a flower, eager to please and overwhelmed by the attention he paid her. Walker was constantly in her thoughts, not only when she longed to feel his arms around her or a quiver of desire struck her like a bolt of lightning, but also when she longed for someone to talk to and laugh with. There wasn't much laughter at the Forrester house. In fact, there was hardly any conversation. Travesty, tired and disgruntled after a full day of hard labor, barely managed to keep her eyes open long enough to eat supper, and the men, used to the work but having no interest in conversing with the women, ate their meals and went outside, leaving Travesty to rest and Mary to clear up.

Mary washed up and prepared for bed, hoping to be asleep by the time John came back inside. He'd barely touched her these past weeks, and for that she was grateful. The thought of him inside her repulsed her now that she knew what love was meant to feel like, and his acrid sweat forced her to turn away and press her nose to the wall, which smelled pleasantly of pine and woodsmoke. It wasn't until she'd blossomed under the caress of Walker's tender gaze that she'd realized how much she actually hated John. He'd robbed her not only of a chance at a real marriage, but also of choice. She was bound to him, and she despised her captor.

Mary often woke when John slid out of bed to go to his lover. Did he really imagine she didn't know what he was up to? Or maybe he simply didn't care. But once awake, Mary's mind went round and round, unable to find peace. She stood on a precipice, forced to decide whether she wanted to honor her marriage vows or follow her heart, and she'd never faced a more difficult decision. Had Walker been a Christian, he might have understood her dilemma, but his mind couldn't grasp the chains that bound Mary to John. She was his wife before God. She was a Christian woman. She couldn't simply walk off with another man. But ,unlike her, Walker didn't seem to feel any moral reservations about stealing another man's wife and couldn't even begin to fathom the concept of damnation.

I'm an adulteress. A sinner, Mary had thought as she stared at the low ceiling of the cabin after John had slipped out last night. *Every time I go to Walker, I make the choice to betray my marriage vows all over again, compounding my sin. I should repent and beg God for forgiveness.*

But when morning came, her dark thoughts evaporated like the morning mist. How could her feelings for Walker be wrong when he made her so happy? For the first time in her adult life, she experienced joy, and pleasure. The almost unbearable anticipation of what was to come when she saw him made the chores go easier, and her heart fluttered with excitement as she rushed toward the shack, knowing that Walker would be there, waiting for her. He always brought her something: a pretty flower, a handful of berries, or an exotic feather. He'd even made her a beaded necklace, but she couldn't bring it back to the cabin. If someone found it, she'd have a lot of explaining to do. So, she left the necklace at the shack, hidden beneath the fur, to be taken out and admired in private. Mary had run her fingers over the smooth red and blue beads. Walker had said they represented her and him. She was the blue: peaceful, loving, and kind. And he was the red: hot, passionate, and jealous.

"I can't bear the thought of sharing you with that man," Walker had said the last time they were together two days before.

"You're not sharing me, Walker. You have me, body and soul."

"You lie next to him every night. He can have you whenever he chooses. He dishonors you with his lies and his unnatural desire for that man."

"He's my husband."

"He's your jailer," Walker snapped. "I want to wake up next to you and know that you will be there when the day is done. I want you to be the mother of my children. I want you for my wife."

"And I want you for my husband, but I can't have two husbands, Walker. As long as John is alive, I'm not free. I made vows before God." Her words were made ludicrous by the fact that she was lying naked on the soft fur of the cot, her limbs intertwined with Walker's, her body sated and languid after their lovemaking.

"So, unmake them," Walker replied with the air of a man who was suggesting the only obvious solution to someone who was too dim to see it for herself.

"How does one do that?"

"The same way one vows to do something, by speaking the words. You tell your God that you are no longer able to honor the vow you made."

"Or not willing. There's a difference."

"Do you want to be with me, Mary? Yes or no?" Walker asked.

Mary was sometimes taken aback by his direct approach to every situation. There was no slyness or untruth with Walker. He said what he meant and did what he promised, and expected others to do the same. He couldn't understand Mary's reservations. To him, the matter was simple. She was wed to a man she didn't love, a man who preferred another; therefore, there was no reason not to end the marriage and take another husband, one who suited her better. Walker was thoroughly confused by the notion of hell and couldn't comprehend why any God would punish a woman for leaving an unhappy marriage. Mary gave up on trying to explain this basic tenet of Christianity and tried another tack.

"Walker, I would be putting you and your people in grave danger if I agreed to leave with you," Mary said, trying to get him to see sense. "The marshal and his men would hunt us down. He's a violent man, by all accounts, and would like nothing more than to have a reason to make war on the Indians."

"Mary, your marshal would never find us, and he'd have no reason to believe you were taken against your will."

"Do you think I can simply vanish without anyone noticing?"

"My mother's people vanished one day, and no one came looking for them, not until years later. The English did not make war on the Croatoan when they came. They had no reason to."

"This is different."

"You are right. It is," Walker agreed. "The English are here to stay this time. They sent their men to work the land and build a settlement, but now they are sending women. A generation of children will be born here, and they will see it as their home. They will have children, and their children will have children. They will push us deeper into the woods, force us to flee. The English have guns and ships. The English are not our friends, even if they pretend to be. It will not be the loss of one woman that starts a war."

"That's a very grim view."

"It's what I see coming to pass."

Mary sighed. She didn't want to think of the future, but she suspected Walker wasn't far off in his estimation of the situation. Perhaps it wasn't the loss of one woman that would start the war, but it might bring it closer, and the war for her eternal soul was already raging.

"Will you come with me, Mary? You must decide before the winter comes."

"Why?"

"Because the mountains up north will become impassable once the snow comes. We won't be able to reach my village, and if we try, our tracks will be that much easier to follow."

Mary sighed, oppressed by the growing heaviness in her heart. She needed time to think. Whatever she chose to do, she had to be at peace with her decision. Walker had nothing to lose and everything to gain. She was the one who'd be condemning herself for eternity.

"I love you, Mary," Walker said, sensing her sadness.

"And I love you. I just wish things were simpler."

"Are they ever?"

"I suppose not. Please, be patient with me."

"I will wait for as long as you wish me to. There's no other woman for me. But, please, promise me you'll decide soon."

And she had promised, seduced by his love for her, but she was no closer to a decision. She longed to be with Walker, but could she face a lifetime of living among people who were as foreign to her as Chinamen and would expect her to give up her faith? She would never be able to return if she found her new situation unbearable. She'd have to adopt the ways of the natives: dress like them, think like them, and worship like them, or she'd forever remain an outcast.

And she hadn't been exaggerating when she told him her decision could start a war between the Indians and the colonists. Relations were coolly civil, but there was an underlying tension that could easily explode into open conflict. How would the governor and marshal react to an Englishwoman vanishing into the wilderness? They would never believe she'd gone off on her own and immediately assume she'd been abducted by savages. What would they do if they discovered, as they certainly would, that a native had claimed one of their women for his own? Would Walker's tribe protect him, or would they sacrifice him to keep peace with the English? She couldn't bear to be responsible for his banishment or death. And even if they managed to get away and reach his tribe, would the Croatoan welcome her as they had welcomed Walker's mother, or would they see her as an interloper and a liability? Walker seemed to believe they would accept her, and Mary had to trust him on that score, but her fear of the consequences made her decision even more difficult to make.

Mary finished her morning chores, washed her hands, and ran a comb through her hair, which she left uncovered. She then made sure Travesty was nowhere near and left the cabin, hurrying toward the woods. She couldn't wait to see Walker.

I will decide soon, Mary thought as she approached the shack. *But not today.*

FIFTY-ONE
FEBRUARY 2015

Ramstein-Miesenbach, Germany

Having collected his rental car, Rhys made several stops before going to the hospital to see Jo. He bought a bouquet of flowers, the brightest he could find to offset the sterile whiteness of her surroundings, and a bunch of grapes. He also picked up a box of *paczki*, round pastries stuffed with a fruity filling and dusted with powdered sugar.

Rhys drove to the medical center, parked the car in a spot designated for visitors, and made his way inside. He had to admit he was nervous. He hardly knew Jo Turing, and since Dr. Stein had expressly forbidden him from upsetting her, he could hardly spring a long-lost twin sister on her or ask about what had happened in Afghanistan. They could always chat about mutual acquaintances, since they were bound to have a few, but that conversation would only get him so far, and this was his last chance to prepare Jo for Quinn's imminent arrival.

Dr. Stein met Rhys at the nurses' station and smiled at him warmly. "Mr. Morgan, good to see you again. Jo is awake and in good spirits. I think she's looking forward to your visit."

"May I offer her a pastry?" Rhys asked, opening the box to allow Dr. Stein to examine the contraband.

"Only if you offer me one as well," she replied with a wicked grin. "I've been on call for the past twenty-four hours and I'm desperate for a sugar rush."

"There's plenty. Please, help yourself."

Dr. Stein reached for a pastry and took a bite. She rolled her eyes in ecstasy. "Delicious. Thank you. Ask the nurses to page me if you need anything. No more than fifteen minutes, please."

"Understood," Rhys replied. Fifteen minutes was a long time to make small talk.

Jo was propped up by several pillows, her face pale in the morning light that streamed between the slats of the plastic blinds. Her eyes lit up when Rhys walked into the room and she smiled, making Rhys's heart turn over with a sudden realization that her smile was exactly like Quinn's: warm, impish, and genuine.

"Rhys, thank you for coming to see me. Are those for me?" she asked, noticing the flowers. There was a catch in her voice, as if no one had ever brought her flowers before.

"I thought the room could do with some brightening up." Rhys had borrowed a vase from the nurses' station and filled it with water, setting the bouquet on Jo's nightstand.

"Oh, they're gorgeous. Thank you." For a moment, Rhys thought she might cry.

"In my opinion, these are so much better than flowers." Rhys handed Jo the box of pastries.

She opened it and inhaled the mouthwatering aroma. "Mm. You're right. I'll have one now and save the rest for later. Would you like one?"

"No, I've already indulged. I have a weakness for pastries, but I prefer baking them myself," Rhys confessed. "It's something of a hobby."

"Funny thing, that. I'm exactly the opposite," Jo said, smiling again. "I prefer instant gratification." She took a bite and chewed slowly, savoring it.

"Jo, is there anyone I can call for you? Charles Sutcliffe?" Rhys suggested.

"There's no need, but thank you for offering."

"Surely there must be someone who's worried about you."

Jo's face clouded and she looked away, staring at the window, the pastry in her hand forgotten. "Sadly, no."

"What about your brother and sister?" Rhys persisted.

"Especially not them." Jo turned back to face Rhys, her dark eyes searching his face. She looked like a woman desperate to find an answer to a question that had been haunting her for some time. "You know her, don't you?"

"Whom do you mean?"

"You work with her. You produce her program." Jo spoke rapidly, breathless with anxiety.

Rhys sat back in his chair, completely taken aback by Jo's sudden intensity. "Jo, Dr. Stein asked me not to upset you."

"I'm not upset. Please, answer me. Do you know Quinn Allenby?"

"Yes, I do."

"Did she send you?" Jo whispered, her eyes shimmering with tears. "Oh, please say she did."

Rhys nodded and reached for Jo's hand. "She did, Jo. She raised hell to find you."

"Really?" Jo's voice was barely above a whisper, but a light shone out of her eyes, a light of life-altering hope.

"So, you know about Quinn? You got her letter?"

Jo nodded. "I received it the night before I left for Kabul. I tried to reply. I must have scrapped a hundred different versions, but I just couldn't get it right. It was such a shock. Such an unexpected gift. I was terrified of cocking it up, so I decided I'd just meet with her once I got back. I had to do it face-to-face, because no words could express what I was feeling. I couldn't get to sleep that night. I must have watched a thousand videos on YouTube, anything that featured Quinn. I feel as if I know her face as well as I know my own. Rhys, what is she like?" She looked like a lovesick teenager, hoping for any sign of interest from a boy she liked. Jo was desperate for affirmation that Quinn was the woman she hoped she'd be.

Rhys smiled widely and covered her hand with his own. "She's amazing, Jo. She's smart, and funny, and so generous of spirit. She's searched desperately for you these past few months. She was convinced you needed help."

"I did." Jo used the back of her hand to wipe away her tears. "Rhys, all my life I felt as if something was missing. I couldn't put a name to it, it was just this hollow place inside my chest, as if a vital organ had been removed. I thought it must be the lack of knowledge about my birth parents, but I realized long ago I really didn't care to find them. They'd abandoned me, left me ill and alone, with nothing more than a scrap of paper with my name and date of birth. I have no use for them. But a sister. A twin sister." Jo's face was radiant with love.

"She's on her way, Jo," Rhys said softly. "She'll be here today."

"Oh God," Jo sobbed, overcome.

"What's all this?" Dr. Stein demanded as she walked through the door. "I specifically told you not to upset her."

"I'm not upset," Jo moaned. "I'm elated."

"You don't look elated to me. In any case, you need to rest now. Mr. Morgan can come back tomorrow and continue elating you then," Dr. Stein said sternly.

"Rhys, please bring her," Jo begged as Rhys was ushered out the door. "Please."

"You have my word."

The last thing Rhys heard as she left the room was Jo's muffled sniffling.

He returned to the car but didn't immediately start the engine. Instead, he leaned back against the headrest and stared at the expanse of pristine snow just beyond the car park. So, Jo knew. She'd known for months. That would certainly make things easier for Quinn. Rhys glanced at his watch. His first impulse was to call Quinn immediately, to relieve some of the gnawing trepidation she felt at the prospect of meeting her sister, but Quinn would still be in the air. His news would have to wait until he collected her from the airport later today.

Rhys started the car, and the engine sputtered into life. There was no other word for it. He'd have happily paid a premium for a better vehicle, but this two-door economy hybrid in bright yellow was the only thing he could get. He cringed and pulled out of the parking space. He hoped Quinn would use her time on the flight to learn more about Mary instead of fretting needlessly.

FIFTY-TWO
OCTOBER 1620

Virginia Colony

Once the harvest was in and the haying was done, it was time to start preparing for the winter in earnest, which made getting away unnoticed that much harder. Mary was once again under Travesty's watchful eye, and John and Simon went out hunting in the woods nearly every day, which made meeting Walker there more dangerous. Mary pined for him but was too afraid to put him in danger. If John or Simon saw her with Walker, they might shoot him, thinking he'd accosted her.

Walker came to her once a week, when she went to the creek to do the laundry, but their meetings were brief and tense. Mary was terrified of being discovered, and Walker's patience was running out. If they were to leave, they'd have to leave very soon. Every week, Mary told Walker she'd have an answer for him soon, but when the time came, she simply couldn't bring herself to commit to a course of action. At least she had a good reason to do the wash so often, so no one questioned her forays to the creek. Her clothes reeked of smoke and were stained with blood.

Every time John and Simon brought back a fresh kill, they butchered the carcass in the yard and left the preparation to Mary and Travesty. Large joints were hung up on hooks in the smoking shed, where a low fire had to burn day and night, preserving the meat. Mary and Travesty took turns feeding the fire or dousing it with wet leaves if it got too hot. In between their runs to the shed, they concentrated on making sausage, using the washed-out intestines and stuffing them with a mixture of meat, fat, blood, and oats. The sausages were also hung up in the shed, in preparation for the winter months.

"Do we really need so much?" Mary asked as she stretched her back after mixing yet another batch of sausage filling. She felt tired, queasy, and lightheaded.

"And what do you think will happen when the stores run out, mistress? Think you'll just go to town on market day and buy what you need? 'Tis not England. The ships will stop coming once the weather turns, and then we'll be on our own in the wilderness until the first ships come in the spring. What we make and store now will feed us till then."

The idea that no help would come for at least four months gave Mary a panicky feeling. What if they ran out of food? "Has anyone ever starved to death out here?" she asked.

"I'm sure they have, especially during the early years. We must plan ahead and make do. Anything we can preserve, we will."

"What about foraging?" Mary asked, thinking she could escape and spend a few hours with Walker.

"For what? We've already collected all the apples and berries we could find."

"Mushrooms," Mary suggested.

"And do you know which mushrooms are safe to eat?" Travesty asked, her voice dripping with contempt. "Do you want to poison us all? If you are so desperate to go to the woods, then just go. You don't need to make up an excuse."

Mary balked. Did Travesty know? She didn't say anything, but Mary wouldn't put it past her. Walker had warned her not to trust Travesty. "I was only trying to help. I've never had to prepare for the winter before, living in Plymouth," Mary retorted. She knew she sounded defensive, but Travesty's comment had put her on guard.

"Well, I wasn't exactly smoking joints of venison in London either," Travesty replied, "but we do what we must."

"Come, and bring a bucket," John commanded as he threw open the door to summon Mary outside. A deer was already hanging off a stout tree limb, with Simon ready to cut its throat once the bucket was in place to collect the blood, then clean out its entrails.

The sight turned Mary's stomach, and she bolted toward the nearest bush and retched until there was nothing left in her belly. Her forehead was covered with a sheen of cold sweat and she panted as she tried to catch her breath. A cup of water would have been nice, but no one thought to offer her one, so she leaned against the nearest tree and closed her eyes, breathing deeply through her nose until she felt more normal.

"I didn't realize John married such a lily-livered madam," Travesty said nastily. "Come here, there's work to be done."

"I can't—" Mary gasped as bile flooded her mouth again. She ambled to the privy. Even the suffocating smell of human waste was better than the tang of fresh blood. Mary shut the door and pressed her forehead to the rough wood. She normally got her flux at the end of each month, but they were well into October and she hadn't bled. She was about three weeks late. Her breasts felt tender, and she experienced strange twinges in her lower belly, different from the pains she normally got on her worst menstrual day. Mary slipped out of the privy and walked toward the creek. She needed some fresh air, or she'd be sick again.

The creek sparkled in the autumn sunshine, the water fresh and cool. Mary wet the hem of her apron and pressed it to her forehead, then her cheeks. The nausea had receded somewhat, but she couldn't bear to return just yet. Mary sat down on the grass and wrapped her arms around her legs. There was only one reason her courses would be late. She had to be with child. The thought excited and terrified her. She had no way of knowing whose child she was carrying, but neither option would make her decision any easier to make. If the baby was John's, she'd do it a terrible disservice by going off with Walker. John's offspring would inherit the plantation he'd worked so hard to keep going. Nothing in this world gave a person more status than owning land, and the child deserved the best start in life it could possibly get.

If the baby was Walker's, she'd be putting it in terrible danger if she chose to remain in Jamestown. Any indication that the baby wasn't born of white parents would rouse intense suspicion. What would Reverend Edison and the marshal do to her if they discovered the child's father was a native? What would they do to her child?

Mary buried her head in her hands. She had no idea what to do. Whether the child was John's or Walker's, she wanted it with all her heart. Having a baby of her own to love and cherish was her heart's desire. She'd love her baby no matter what, even if she didn't love its father. As she laid a hand on her still-flat belly, Mary wondered if she'd know whose child it was once it was born. The only thing that'd truly give its paternity away would be the skin color. John was white as milk in places that never saw the sunlight, while Walker was nut-brown, like saddle leather. Despite the obvious danger, she wanted it to be Walker's. She wanted a baby that had been conceived in love, not the result of John's sporadic assaults on her body.

Mary rested her forehead on her knees as tears of despair rolled down her cheeks. She had no one to talk to, no one to confide in and ask for advice. She trusted Nell, but even Nell, kind as she was, would condemn Mary for her actions. Nell feared the savages as much as anyone and never ventured past her dooryard on her own, terrified she'd be attacked. To admit to her that she'd willingly lain with an Indian would put an end to their friendship. Nell would keep her secret, Mary was sure, but she couldn't risk telling her the truth. She couldn't risk telling anyone.

Having come to a decision, Mary got to her feet and began walking toward home. She'd keep the pregnancy a secret from

Walker for as long as she could. If he discovered she was with child, he'd put pressure on her to leave immediately, but she couldn't bring herself to deny her baby its inheritance or the salvation of Christ. She'd remain with John until the child was born, then if it was obviously Walker's and she and the child were in danger, she'd take the baby and walk into the forest and away from civilization. If the child was white, she'd stay with John and have it baptized. That was the only logical plan she could think of, so she wiped her eyes and adjusted her cap. She had a child to think of now. Her own desires were no longer relevant.

Frankfurt, Germany

Quinn wound her scarf around her neck and zipped up her coat before exiting the terminal. A steady stream of humanity flowed past her as she looked around, trying to spot Rhys. The access road in front of the terminal was thronged with cars, mostly taxis, picking up and dropping off their fares, the scene reminiscent of every airport Quinn had ever flown into. A gentle snow fell, the snowflakes twirling gracefully before settling on the pavement. There was a stillness in the air, but it was much colder than it had been in London, and Quinn shivered, hoping Rhys would get there soon. She smiled widely when a yellow Honda Fit nosed into a space just vacated by a taxi.

"Welcome to Germany," Rhys said as Quinn wrapped her arms tightly around him. He winced, then instantly rearranged his features into a bright smile.

"Are you all right?" Quinn asked.

"Absolutely fine."

She knew Rhys wasn't being truthful but didn't press him. He was a private person and wouldn't appreciate her prying. She smiled back and surrendered her case to Rhys, who stowed it in the boot before getting into the driver's seat.

"Can we go directly to the hospital?" Quinn asked, breathless with nervousness and excitement.

"Sorry but visiting hours will be over by the time we get there, so you'll have to wait till tomorrow morning," Rhys said as he eased the car into the flow of traffic. He seemed surprisingly comfortable with driving on the right side of the road. "For tonight, you're stuck with me."

"I could do with a drink," Quinn confessed. "I'm so nervous. I keep wondering what Jo will make of me."

"Do you wonder what you'll make of her?" Rhys asked.

Quinn turned to look at him, surprised by the question. "What do you mean?"

"You keep worrying about her reaction to you, but what about your reaction to her? Is there anything that might put you off?"

"Why would you ask me that?" Quinn demanded, suddenly worried that Rhys wasn't telling her something vital.

"I'm just curious," Rhys replied, his tone light.

"Rhys, what are you not telling me?"

Rhys didn't answer immediately. He drove for a few minutes until he spotted a bar on the side of the road and pulled up in front. He got out of the car, opened Quinn's door, and invited her to follow him inside.

The bar was cozy and dimly lit, most of the tables unoccupied at this early hour. A few old-timers sat at the bar, enjoying their drinks and chatting with the barkeep. Quinn's heart sank when Rhys motioned her toward an empty table in the corner and went up to the bar to place an order. He returned with an espresso for himself and a glass of wine for Quinn. She took a healthy gulp in anticipation of whatever it was Rhys was about to impart. He took a delicate sip of his coffee and set the cup down, watching Quinn with an air of amusement.

"Whatever it is, tell me this instant or you will live to regret it,"

Quinn threatened. She was thrumming with nervous energy and what Rhys was doing was absolute torture.

"I didn't want to tell you in the car," Rhys replied. He was smiling, so whatever he had to tell her couldn't be too awful. "Quinn, Jo knows all about you. She's watched videos of your interviews and the first season of *Echoes*. She received your letter before she left for Kabul. She can't wait to meet you."

"She knows?" Quinn whispered. "She's looking forward to meeting me?" A wonderful, warm feeling spread outward from her chest, cocooning her in a delicious sense of well-being.

Rhys nodded. "She's fragile, Quinn. And lonely. There doesn't seem to be anyone waiting for her back in England."

"How can that be?"

Rhys shrugged. "I don't know. Maybe she'll tell you."

"Have you told her about Logan and Jude, and Sylvia? What about Seth?"

"No. I thought it would be better coming from you. How is Jude?" Rhys asked carefully.

Quinn sighed and took a long sip of wine. "He's still unconscious. I spoke to Logan just before I boarded. Sylvia hasn't left his side."

"There's no greater tragedy than losing a child," Rhys said quietly.

Quinn reached across the table and placed her hand over his. No words were needed. Rhys turned his hand over and took hold of hers, squeezing it gently. His gaze misted over with unshed tears and he looked away, staring at the snow falling outside the window.

"Rhys—"

"I'm fine. Tell me about Mary," he invited. It was a distraction tactic, but Quinn was happy to play along. They both needed a moment to collect themselves, and Mary was a safe subject, having been dead for nearly four hundred years. "Have you learned anything that might explain what happened to her? Have you brought the comb with you?"

"Yes, I have," Quinn replied sadly. "I think it won't be long now until it all kicks off."

"How can you tell?"

"Mary became pregnant but didn't know who the father of her baby was. She was torn between her love for Walker, a Native American of mixed blood, and her duty to John. If the baby she was carrying was the one we found in the coffin with her, then she only has a few more months to live."

"But how did she wind up in Cornwall?" Rhys asked as he took a sip of his coffee.

"That seems to be the million-dollar question," Quinn replied.

"You sound like an American," Rhys said with a chuckle. "I think your father is beginning to rub off on you."

"I find some of his turns of phrase very amusing, and he thinks some of the things I say are absolutely hilarious."

"Ah, the joys of having a multicultural family," Rhys quipped as he took a last sip of his espresso. "Would you like another glass of wine?"

"No, I'm all right."

"So, do you think John Forrester might have decided to return to England?"

"John was doing very well for himself in Virginia. He had no reason to leave Jamestown," Quinn said.

"Unless he was forced to," Rhys countered.

"Unless he was forced to," Quinn agreed.

"Have you been able to locate any records to back up our narrative?"

Quinn shook her head. "There's tangible proof that Mary Wilby went out to Virginia in 1620 and married John Forrester. And, of course, Elizabeth and Ambrose Viccars are on the list of colonists who went out to Roanoke Island and vanished along with the rest of the settlers sometime between 1587 and 1590. That's all I have so far. I've been a little preoccupied."

"I know. Sorry. Have you told Seth about Jo?"

"I was going to call him last night but decided to wait until I saw Jo for myself and had something more concrete to tell him. Knowing Seth, he'd be on the next plane to Germany, and I wanted to make sure his presence would be welcome. I think meeting one long-lost relative might be enough for Jo to handle for now."

"I think you made the right call. She needs time, Quinn."

"Why did she never respond to my letter? Did she tell you?" Quinn asked.

"She was nervous, same as you. She thought it might be better to speak in person. She was going to get in touch when she returned from Afghanistan."

"I don't think I'll sleep a wink tonight," Quinn said. "I'm too wound up."

"What you need is a hot bath, a good dinner, and another glass of wine. Or six. You'll sleep like a baby. Rest in the knowledge that tomorrow you will finally meet your sister, and it will be a happy reunion," Rhys said. "Now, let's get you to the hotel. It's starting to snow heavier, and I don't fancy driving on the Autobahn in this clown mobile."

"It is kind of ridiculous," Quinn agreed.

"It was the only one available on such short notice and in the size I requested."

By the time they got to the hotel, it was fully dark, and Quinn was ready for a meal despite her nervousness. After she ate, she took a long, hot bath, and got into bed. She was asleep within minutes despite her earlier misgivings, because morning couldn't come soon enough.

FIFTY-FOUR

The next day dawned bright and cold. Quinn pulled on her warmest jumper and a pair of jeans, then made her way to the dining room to meet Rhys for breakfast. There was no reason to rush, since visiting hours at the hospital didn't start till ten. Rhys was already seated, a steaming cup of coffee in front of him.

"I hope you're hungry. They do an excellent breakfast," he said, watching her intently. "Sleep all right?"

Quinn nodded. "I don't think I can eat."

"You should. We have at least an hour to kill, and you're going to feel pretty silly sitting there watching me as I demolish a gargantuan German breakfast." He was teasing her, but Quinn appreciated his concern.

"All right. I'll have something light."

"I don't think they know the meaning of the word," Rhys replied, studying the menu with single-minded concentration.

He chuckled when Quinn ordered a boiled egg and some toast. She understood why when her order arrived. The boiled egg sat in pride of place, surrounded by slices of cheese, salami, ham, cucumber, several olives, and a basket of bread with a dish of butter. There were also several tiny jars of jam and honey.

"Bon appétit," Rhys said as his own heaping plate was placed in front of him. "I love this country!"

"I'm starting to like it as well," Quinn replied, suddenly hungry. She rolled up a slice of salami and popped it into her mouth. "Mm, this is good," she said.

"Everything is homemade," Rhys said. "They get all their food from local farmers."

"How do you know?"

"I had a chat with the owner last night. It's no fun drinking alone, so he joined me for a pint. It was a quiet night."

"Making friends wherever you go?" Quinn joked.

"I know; it's a curse," Rhys said with a grin and tucked into his breakfast.

Quinn burst into a fit of giggles when they finally left the hotel after finishing their meal. Rhys's car was almost entirely buried in a snow drift. Only the top of the yellow roof was visible.

"Stop laughing and start digging," Rhys growled.

Several shovels were stacked against the hotel's side door for guests to use. Quinn grabbed a shovel and began to clear the snow. It felt good to be out in the fresh air, expending some of her nervous energy. By the time they finished, her cheeks were numb with cold and she felt better than she had in days.

"I hope this marvel of modern engineering starts," Rhys muttered as he slid into the driver's seat.

It did, and they set off for the hospital. It wasn't a long drive, but it felt like an eternity to Quinn. "Should I bring something?" she asked, suddenly realizing it was rude to show up empty-handed.

"Everything you need is on your mobile," Rhys replied.

"How so?"

"She has plenty of treats, I saw to that," Rhys clarified. "She'll want to see photos."

"Do you really think so?"

"Of course. Even if she never wants to set eyes on Sylvia and Seth, she's sure to be curious what they look like. And, of course, there are her brothers, and your own family. Don't you want to show off your babies?"

"Of course. I don't want to make her feel bad though," Quinn said, remembering that Jo seemed to be all alone.

"Quinn, you don't need to apologize for your life. We all make choices, and if Jo is alone, that's on her."

"I suppose you're right."

"Of course I'm right. I'm always right," Rhys joked as he pulled into the car park at the hospital. "Now, put on a brave face and let's go meet your sister."

Rhys and Quinn were intercepted by Dr. Stein when they got off the lift on the appropriate floor. "Good morning," she said. Her lab coat was clean and crisp, as was her manner. "I'm very happy to meet you, Dr. Allenby. Jo was very excited when she told me her sister was on her way. I'm sure I don't have to remind you that Jo had brain surgery. She is doing very well and shows every hope of being able to return home in the near future, but right now, we need to keep her from getting overly worked up. She's still recovering."

"I understand," Quinn replied.

"I realize this will be an emotional moment for you both—Mr. Morgan has explained the situation—but please try to refrain from upsetting her. I understand your brother is, eh... unwell?"

"Yes."

"If you can avoid telling her that, I'd be grateful. Only good news today." Dr. Stein smiled widely, revealing perfect teeth. "You look like you're going to jump out of your skin, so I won't detain you any longer. Have me paged if you need me."

"Thank you, Doctor. And thank you for looking after my sister."

"It's my pleasure."

"It's the third door on the right," Rhys said as soon as Dr. Stein walked away.

Quinn bowed her head, closed her eyes, and took several calming breaths, but the time-tested technique didn't work. She followed Rhys down the corridor toward Jo's room, her heart exploding in her chest, her stomach in knots.

"Are you all right?" Rhys asked.

"I'm shaking. I feel like I'm going to faint."

"You are going to be just fine," Rhys said in his most soothing tone. "Come, your sister is waiting."

Quinn approached the open door to the room but paused just short of going in. Her legs felt as if they'd just turned to water. She couldn't seem to get enough air into her lungs and felt like she might black out. *I've survived being locked in a tomb overnight without any hope of rescue,* she thought. *Compared to that, this is a walk in the park.*

"Quinn, I'm going to go to the cafeteria and get you a cup of tea. By the time I return, I expect to see a tear-jerking display of sisterly love that will choke up even an old cynic like me. Got it?"

"Got it." She sucked in a deep breath and stepped into the room.

Her heart nearly stopped when she saw Jo. Her sister was lying against the pristine white of the hospital pillow, her face criss-crossed by healing lacerations. Her hand lay on top of the blanket. It looked small and vulnerable, her nails cut short like those of a little girl. Jo had been looking out the window, but at the sound of footsteps, she turned her head and their eyes met.

Quinn sucked in a shuddering breath. She'd planned to go slow, to give Jo, and herself, a moment to absorb what was happening, but now that they were in the same room, all reserve melted away. She rushed toward the bed and wrapped Jo in her arms, holding her like she would never let go. Jo's arms went around Quinn, and she pulled her even closer, pressing her cheek to Quinn's. Quinn's face was wet with tears, but she wasn't sure if the tears were hers or Jo's. They were both crying and trembling with the overwhelming poignancy of this moment.

At long last, Quinn let go and sat on Jo's bed. Even a chair seemed too great a distance to put between them. Jo clasped her hand, unwilling to break the contact.

"Quinn," Jo whispered. "Oh, Quinn. When that explosion went off, my only thought was that I would die without ever meeting you, and I was heartbroken." Tears were sliding down her pale cheeks, but her eyes shone with wonder. "Tell me everything I've missed."

"I don't know where to begin," Quinn confessed through tears. "I've imagined this moment so many times, but now that I'm really here, I can't seem to remember a single thing I meant to say."

"There's time to remember," Jo replied. "We've time. We have the rest of our lives."

That brought on fresh tears. "When you didn't reply to my letter, I thought you didn't want to know me."

"The promise of meeting you was the only thing that kept me going when I woke up in this hospital, scared and alone. Knowing I had a sister waiting for me made me feel less frightened. And then Rhys appeared, like some sort of guardian angel."

"He'll adore that description," Quinn said with a chuckle. "Rhys took a great risk to go to Afghanistan to look for you, and for that, he will always have my undying gratitude."

"He must really love you," Jo said wistfully.

"He does. And I love him in a way I never thought possible."

"Is he...?"

"Oh, no," Quinn replied, laughing and shaking her head. "It's not what you think. Rhys is a friend—a very dear friend, and my boss. I have a family of my own, and then there are the others."

"Tell me," Jo said, her eyes huge with anticipation. "Please, tell me."

"I was adopted shortly after we were born. My parents, Susan and Roger Allenby, are wonderful people, the best parents I could have asked for. But despite that, I always longed to know where I came from. I'm a historian, after all; I needed to know my own story," Quinn added. "I met our birth parents only recently. Our mother's name is Sylvia Wyatt, and our dad's is Seth Besson. He lives in New Orleans."

"He's American?" Jo gasped.

"Yes. He's a good man, Jo. He never knew about us. He'd never have allowed us to be abandoned or separated if he'd known Sylvia had his children. He'd have looked after us."

"Why did she do it? Why did she leave me like that?" Jo asked, her voice full of anguish.

"She was seventeen, and she wasn't sure who the father of her children was. She panicked, especially when she realized you were ill."

"Have you forgiven her, then?" Jo asked, cocking her head in just the way Quinn had seen Sylvia do.

"Not completely, but I'm working on it. She's certainly not what I expected."

"Is Seth what you expected?"

"Lord, no," Quinn replied, laughing. "He's the exact opposite, in fact."

"Do they have families?" Jo asked.

"Sylvia is widowed and has two sons, Logan and Jude. Logan is lovely. Jude is a bit—shall we say—troubled. Seth is divorced and has one son, Brett."

"What's he like?"

Quinn thought about that for a moment. She'd promised not to upset Jo. Now wasn't the time to spring Brett's heinous crime on her. "Also troubled," Quinn finally said. "He's getting the help he needs." Well, that was sort of true, Quinn told herself as she quickly changed the subject. "I'm married to Gabe and have two wonderful children, Emma and Alex." Quinn's smile spread from ear to ear. "Everyone is so excited to finally meet you."

"Do you have photos?" Jo asked shyly.

"I certainly do." Rhys had been right, as usual. Putting faces to names was the best gift Quinn could offer Jo at that moment.

"Start with Gabe and your children. Oh, I can't wait to meet them. To think I have a niece and nephew. Are there others? Are our brothers married?"

"Logan is engaged. He and Colin plan to get married this summer. They're a great couple. Jude and Brett are single."

Quinn took out her mobile and began to show Jo photos. She grinned broadly when she saw Gabe and the children but became more somber once Quinn got to photos of Sylvia and Seth.

"Does Seth know about me?" Jo asked, lifting her gaze away from the screen.

"Of course. I didn't tell him you were here because he'd have been on the first flight he could get. He can't wait to meet you."

Jo stared at a photo of their dad. "He's handsome, in a very American way. I look like him, don't I?"

Quinn nodded. "You do."

"And who is that?"

"That's our grandmother Rae. She passed away recently. I wish you could have met her. She was lovely," Quinn said.

"Brett and I look alike," Jo said, her voice filled with wonder as she studied a photo of her half-brother. "Dad," she whispered as she gently touched Seth's face in the photograph.

"Do you want to speak to him?" Quinn asked.

"What? Now?"

"Why not?"

Jo's eyes filled with tears. "Yes," she whispered.

Quinn selected Seth's number and pressed the call button. Seth's deep voice came on the line almost immediately.

"Quinn, how are you, sweetheart? Is everything all right?"

"More than all right. Dad, there's someone here who wants to say hello."

Quinn heard a sharp intake of breath from Seth as the implication of her words sank in. "Put her on."

Quinn handed Jo the phone. Jo looked like she was about to faint, but she took the mobile and held it to her ear. "Hi, Dad," she said softly.

Quinn couldn't hear what Seth said to her, but she saw Jo's

face break into a huge grin. "Yes, it's all right with me," she said. "Yes, of course."

They spoke for a few more minutes and then Jo handed the phone back to Quinn. She was glowing. "He's coming, Quinn. He's coming here. Maybe even as soon as tomorrow. I'm going to meet my dad."

"Would you like to speak to Sylvia?" Quinn asked carefully.

"No, not yet."

"I told her I'd found you. I hope you don't mind."

Jo thought about that for a moment. "I have no objection, but I don't want her here. I'm not ready to face her. I may never be."

"You don't have to do anything you don't want to do," Quinn said. "It's your decision."

Jo nodded. "Until a few days ago, I was in no rush to go home, but now…"

"I won't leave until you're released," Quinn promised. "I will take you home."

Jo smiled, and her gaze moved toward Rhys, who'd sidled into the room, carrying two steaming cups. "Rhys, I will never forget what you've done for me. I know you need to return to London and your own life, but I hope we can see each other again."

Rhys's smile was luminous. "Of course, we can. I will come and see you as soon as you're settled at home. And I will keep on seeing you until you ask me to stop."

"I'll never ask that," Jo replied.

"Then I think this is the beginning of a beautiful friendship," Rhys joked, putting on his best Humphrey Bogart accent.

"Here's looking at you, kid," Jo replied.

"I hate to break up this lovely reunion, but Jo needs to rest now," Dr. Stein said as she briskly entered the room. "You can return in the afternoon, if you like. I think you're the best medicine," she added, smiling at Quinn.

"Will you come back?" Jo asked softly, her expression pleading.

"Of course, I'll come back. We both will," Quinn replied. She gave Jo a hug, and Rhys kissed her tenderly on the forehead.

"See you later." Jo was beaming as they took their leave.

Virginia Colony

Mary's first Christmas in Virginia turned out to be quite memorable, but not in any way she might have anticipated. There was a dusting of snow on the ground, and a brisk wind blew off the river as they rode into Jamestown for the Christmas service. Mary wrapped her threadbare cloak tighter about her, wishing she weren't so cold. After the brutally hot summer, she hadn't expected to ever mind the cold again, but she shivered as she sat next to John on the bench of the wagon. John, in his usual fashion, didn't notice Mary's discomfort and stared straight ahead, focused on the lane in front of him as if he might encounter another wagon on the deserted road.

The church was packed, but unlike most Sundays, when the mood was somber, there was a festive atmosphere among the colonists, and even Reverend Edison permitted himself a genuine smile as he welcomed his parishioners. Mary had hoped to sit close to Nell or Betsy, but they'd made a late start and only the back pew was still unoccupied, so she sat between John and Travesty, grateful for their body heat since there was a cold draft so close to the door.

No one lingered after the service to talk and exchange news and bits of gossip. Everyone was eager to return home, to enjoy their Christmas dinner and a few hours of rest. In England, tomorrow would be Boxing Day, but here in Virginia, no one bothered with the tradition since there were hardly any servants to give gifts to and everyone would treat it as just a regular working day.

Mary and Travesty had prepared a venison stew flavored with onions and wild garlic and baked an apple cake for their Christmas dinner. They were careful with their provisions, given that the winter had just begun, but this was a special occasion and they'd made enough for everyone to have seconds. John set a jug of ale on the table, inviting everyone to help themselves. Usually, they were allowed one cup, since John had to purchase barrels of ale from the tavern and they came dear, but today, they could have their fill.

Mary sipped gingerly from her cup. The ale soured her stomach, but there wasn't anything else to drink except cold water from the well. She was hungry though. The queasiness she'd felt for the past two months was beginning to pass and she found herself ravenous, especially around midday. Mary tucked into the stew, enjoying the rich gravy that soaked into the cornbread she'd crumbled into her bowl. Even Travesty, who normally didn't have much of an appetite, ate with relish and downed two cups of ale in quick succession.

John and Simon drank cup after cup, and Mary was surprised to see some of John's natural reserve melt away. After the meal, he began to sing and was soon joined by Simon and Travesty, who was more unguarded than Mary had ever seen her, probably due to the ale. Her eyes glowed with warmth, and her slightly unfocused gaze seemed to be trained on Simon, who was flushed with merriment and goodwill.

The traditional Christmas songs, which were meant to be festive, brought tears to Mary's eyes. They made her ache with homesickness for England and days gone by when her parents had been alive, and she'd felt safe and loved. And for Walker, whom she hadn't seen in several weeks. The lack of him weighed heavily on her heart, but it'd been difficult to get away. Travesty always seemed to be just behind her, and John and Simon were never far from home now that there was no field work to be done and they had enough meat to last them until spring.

Mary bowed her head so no one would witness her distress. She wished she could walk out of the cabin and go to the shack in the woods. Of course, Walker wouldn't be there, even if she could manage to get away, but she longed to see him with a need that was almost painful. She had to tell him about the baby. It wasn't right to hide the truth from him, and she was desperate to share her news now that she was sure. She hadn't told anyone, not even Nell. Nell was about five months along, and her rounded belly was just becoming noticeable beneath her apron. Several women in the colony were pregnant, but not a single child had been born yet, since the women who'd arrived the year before had mostly been indentured servants. Some of the first babies were due in the spring.

Mary was about three months gone, in her estimation, and although her stomach was still flat, it felt different, more solid somehow, her skin stretched tight. Her breasts strained against the bodice of her gown and felt sensitive to the lightest touch, and she tired easily, desperate to lie down and sleep for an hour by midafternoon. Mary tried to resist the urge but found herself swaying with fatigue. She settled to easier tasks, such as sewing, to mask her weariness, but her usually nimble fingers grew clumsy as she darned hose or repaired a torn hem. Travesty was sure to have noticed the changes in Mary, but hadn't asked her outright, for which Mary was grateful. She had no wish to share her news with the other woman.

John finished a song and lit his pipe, closing his eyes with pleasure as he inhaled deeply. His normally tense face was relaxed, and he'd moved closer to Simon and was now leaning against his shoulder. Their proximity was not unusual for two men who'd been drinking, but Mary saw it for what it was, and it repelled her. She had been John's wife for six months now, but the distance between them was as wide as the ocean she'd crossed to get to this wild place. Today, when snow covered the ground and the forest was silent and dark just beyond the boundary of John's land, she felt like she was on the edge of the world, and if she walked too far she'd simply fall off and keep falling, until her humanity was stripped away and her soul flew away like a bird, singing its heart out in anguish because she'd never found the words to express her feelings as a woman. She had no voice, and no rights. She was John's property, and the knowledge enraged her.

"Well, this has been a fine Christmas celebration," John said. His words were slightly slurred, and he looked ready for bed despite the early hour.

"And it's not over yet," Travesty said, smiling at John as if she were about to give him the greatest gift. "Mistress, why don't you share your news with us? You've waited long enough."

Mary's eyes flew to Travesty's face, but the other woman smiled blandly and patted her hand. "Come now, John has a right to know." When Mary still didn't say anything, Travesty stepped into the breach. "Our Mary is going to have a baby. Around June, I think. What say you, master?"

"My congratulations to the expectant parents," Simon exclaimed, filling the heavy silence that followed Travesty's announcement. John seemed shocked by the revelation, but Mary seethed with anger. How dare Travesty take it upon herself to divulge her news? She was a servant, but just like Simon, she didn't know her place and acted like the mistress of the house.

"Yes, congratulations." Travesty's lips pressed into a thin line, while her eyes narrowed with malice. "May your child take after its father." Travesty raised her cup in a toast.

John finally roused himself enough to reply. "We have been truly blessed," he said, fixing Mary with a direct gaze for the first time that day. What Mary saw there was not happiness at his impending fatherhood, but sheer relief. A baby would add a layer of legitimacy to their marriage and shield John from unwelcome scrutiny. A man who had a child lay with his wife and did his duty. No one could accuse him of not being a proper husband.

"I need some air," Mary croaked as she sprang to her feet and bolted for the door, grabbing her cloak as she passed. She pulled it on and kept going until she reached a stile and leaned against it, gazing at the woods beyond. The sky was a dusky lavender, dotted with pale stars that twinkled like a swarm of light bugs on a summer night. A huge, pale moon was rising, its rounded belly skimming the treetops in the distance. For just a moment, the world seemed to stand still, the air fresh and fragrant with the smell of snow and pine, the color of the sky deepening to a rich purple as night approached.

Mary tried to drink in the beauty of the Christmas twilight and allow it to soothe her soul, but Travesty's words filled her with dread. Had Travesty guessed the truth, or was Mary's guilty conscience perceiving a threat where none was meant? Mary scoffed to herself. Of course, Travesty knew, just as she was sure to know John's secret. Travesty and Simon held the power of life and death over them both, but John was too blind to see that. He seemed to have all the awareness of a stick of wood.

Mary stood at the stile for a long time. She was shivering and her feet were cold in her thin-soled shoes, but she couldn't bring herself to return to the warmth of the cabin. She had no wish to face the three people she trusted least in the world, the three people for whom she was nothing more than a pawn in their scheming. Somewhere in the distance, an owl hooted, and a stealthy wind moved through the trees. Somewhere out there was a man who loved her and was willing to risk his own place among his people to make her his family. And suddenly she knew with unwavering certainty that the child she carried was Walker's, because the love she felt for it was so intense it took her breath away. She'd never feel this way about a child sired by John. Her mind might not know for sure, but her heart knew. It had always known. She closed her eyes and took a deep pull of the frigid air, enjoying its freshness. And the sound in her ears was no longer the wind, but a gentle voice whispering, bringing her to her senses, and giving her permission to be free.

"I love you, Walks Between Worlds," Mary whispered toward the heavens. "And I will go to the ends of the earth with you if that means we can be a family."

FIFTY-SIX

Mary eventually returned to the cabin. She hung up her cloak on the peg and took off her shoes. The fire had burned down low, so she threw on a few more logs and stood in front of the hearth, warming herself until she felt a pleasant somnolence steal over her. Travesty had already cleared the table and retired to her loft, and John and Simon were still at the table, too drunk to pay her any mind. They went out shortly after, John mumbling something about taking a walk. He never came to bed at all, but Mary didn't care. She turned her face to the wall and went to sleep, grateful not to have to endure his ale-soured breath.

When Mary awoke the following morning, she tied on her apron and began going about her chores, her mind on her half-formed plan. She couldn't simply walk off into the wilderness. She had no way to contact Walker and she didn't know where his village was. The only thing she could do was tie a rag to the branch of the oak and hope Walker saw it and came to her. He'd find a way. By midmorning, she was ready. Mary grabbed a strip of linen from her work basket and stuck her feet in her shoes.

"And where are you off to?" Travesty asked.

"I'm going for a walk."

Travesty mumbled something about people who shirked doing

their share of the housework and thought they could get away with it, but Mary ignored her and left the cabin. She walked to the creek and tied the scrap of linen to the branch, then turned to go back, but her feet wouldn't move. She didn't want to go back. She wanted to see Walker. Now. Today. She knew he wouldn't be at the shack, but that was the only place she could feel close to him. It was their place, their sanctuary. Mary turned on her heel and walked along the bank. The snow of the previous day had melted, so no one would see her footprints and figure out where she'd gone. She'd simply say she took a walk in the woods.

The cabin was cold and dim, the ashes from the fire acrid in the ring of stones arranged in the center of the shack just beneath the vent hole in the roof. Mary sat on the cot and caressed the fur where she and Walker had lain, but it was damp and cold. She reached beneath and brought out the necklace. It felt warm in her hand and she held it close, wishing she could summon Walker with the sheer power of her need. Why had she waited so long to decide? Now the woods would be impassable in the north and they wouldn't be able to leave until the spring thaw. Walker had told her as much, but she'd thought she had time.

Mary got to her feet and was about to hide the necklace beneath the fur when she changed her mind. If Walker came, she wanted him to know she'd been there looking for him. She arranged the necklace on the three-legged stool that held a single candlestick with a nearly burned-down stub of a candle. He was sure to see it there. She then pulled the door closed behind her and turned for home. She had to hurry back before anyone became suspicious of her absence. This wasn't the time to draw attention to herself, especially since she'd need to find a way to sneak out again soon.

Mary reached the fallen log and stepped onto the wood, eager to get across quickly. From here, it was only a quarter of a mile or so back to the plantation. She was almost at the other end of the log when her foot slipped on the damp bark. Mary wobbled and threw out her arms to steady herself, but the sudden motion made her lose her footing completely. She cried out in alarm as she went over the side and fell into the creek with a loud splash, her woolen skirts instantly soaking up the icy water and dragging her under.

The creek wasn't too deep, but the shock of the fall and the frigid water momentarily stunned Mary and she began to sink. Her waterlogged skirts swirled upward, making it impossible to get her bearings in the murky water as the heavy fabric closed in around her head. Mary struggled, trying to push the wool out of her face. Once she managed this small victory, she was able to stand on her feet and push off from the bottom, coming up to the surface, sputtering and dripping water.

The bank was slippery and steep, with nothing to grab onto to help her haul herself out of the water. Mary reached for the log and hoisted herself up before crawling the last few feet to the bank. Her clothes were sodden, and her hair was plastered to her head. She'd lost one shoe while struggling to get purchase on the muddy bottom and her cloak was torn where it'd snagged on a branch as she fell.

Mary forced herself to her feet and hobbled along the bank. She was shivering so hard her teeth rattled, but she had to get home. She yelped as she stepped on a pine cone with her stockinged foot. Her one shoe squelched with mud and her wet clothes weighed her down. She'd never been so cold in her life. Mary ran the last few yards before yanking open the door and falling into the cabin.

"What happened to you?" Travesty exclaimed when she saw the state of her. "Good heavens, you'll catch your death. Get out of those wet clothes." She tore the blanket off the bed and came toward Mary, holding it open. "Take everything off and wrap this around yourself."

Mary undressed quickly and grabbed for the blanket. The wool felt rough against her chilled skin, but at least it was warm and dry. Travesty pushed one of the benches close to the fire and told Mary to sit down. She did as she was told, while Travesty put some water on to boil and hung Mary's clothes on the other side of the bench.

The fabric began to steam, and the smell of wet wool filled the cabin. Travesty poured some hot water into a basin and set it on the floor.

"Put your feet in," she said.

Mary stuck her feet in the water and sighed with pleasure as a wonderful warmth spread through her. She was still shaking, and her hair was wet, but at least her teeth were no longer chattering. She sat hunched beneath the blanket, her head drooping with sudden fatigue.

Once the water in the basin cooled, Travesty took it away and gave Mary an appraising look. "You'd best get yourself to bed."

Mary didn't argue. She climbed between the sheets, still wrapped in the blanket. Travesty climbed to her loft and returned with her own blanket, which she used to cover Mary. Travesty seemed to be saying something, but Mary couldn't hear her over the roar in her ears. Her limbs felt like tree trunks and she shivered violently now that she was away from the fire. She tried to say something but couldn't seem to get the words out. Her teeth were chattering again, and cold ropes of hair wrapped themselves around her neck, the water soaking into her pillow. Mary pulled the blanket over her head and buried her face in its warm folds. She needed to sleep. She was so tired.

FIFTY-SEVEN

Mary looked frantically from side to side. The cabin was on fire, the flames licking at the thick logs of the walls. She gasped for air, desperate to fill her sizzling lungs. She was panting, searching for a way out, but she couldn't make out the shape of the door in a wall of fire. She was burning, suffocating, unable to move. She was trapped on the bed, which would go up like a torch at any moment. Mary screamed, or she thought she screamed. All she heard was a desperate whimper. Someone was trying to pin her down, and she thrashed in an effort to save herself.

"Drink, you stubborn fool," Travesty said from somewhere above her head. "Take a sip."

Mary felt cold water trickle down her chin as Travesty held the cup to her lips. She drank greedily, desperate to douse the inferno raging inside her. A cool compress was applied to her head and she dozed off again, returning right back to her awful nightmare. When she came to again, she heard a different voice.

"Mary, can you hear me? It's Dr. Paulson." Mary tried to nod, and he replied to her kindly. "Good. That's very good. You've been very ill."

Have I? Mary thought groggily. Dr. Paulson laid a cool hand on her brow and then took her wrist between his fingers.

"Continue with the compresses. Make sure to apply them not only to her head, but to her armpits and to the soles of her feet to keep the fever down. Give her this tincture once a day, but try to get her to drink some broth or boiled milk. She needs nourishment."

"Yes, Doctor." That was John. "And the child?"

Dr. Paulson did not reply, and Mary became agitated, trying to open her heavy eyelids to see his face. The light in the cabin blinded her and her eyes grew moist with tears. She felt as weak as a newborn kitten.

"Don't worry about that now," Dr. Paulson finally said. "I will come back tomorrow."

"Thank you, Doctor. You have been most kind," John said.

"I'm a physician, Master Forrester. I'm not doing this to be kind."

Mary heard Simon's smirk. "Shall I take you back to Jamestown?" he asked.

"If you please, Master Faraday."

Mary heard the door close and John's footsteps retreating. She sank deeper into the mattress, her body already succumbing to the need for sleep. She felt as if she were falling, but it wasn't an unpleasant sensation. She landed on something soft and clean, and she allowed it to envelop her as she drifted off.

Mary slowly opened her eyes. They were no longer sensitive to the light and she didn't feel as if she were on fire. She lay in a tangle of sheets, the blanket about to slide off the bed. She pulled it back with some effort and covered herself. She was cold. Mary looked around. It had to be morning, but of what day? Her stomach rumbled with hunger and she tried to recall the last time she'd eaten, but couldn't. She appeared to be alone in the cabin. She tried to raise herself on her elbow, but couldn't find the strength, so she lay back down, wondering how to get herself to the privy.

A few minutes later, Travesty came in, carrying a bucket. She must have just done the milking. "You're awake," she said, setting the bucket on the floor and coming over to check on Mary.

"I need to go to the privy," Mary croaked.

"Well, that's a good sign, I suppose. You were sweating so much these past few days, it's a wonder there's any water left in you. I'll get you a bucket. You're not strong enough to go out, and it's cold out there."

Mary didn't argue. She didn't think her legs would carry her to the door, much less to the privy. She tried to get up, but a wave of dizziness overtook her, and she slumped back down, closing her eyes until the vertigo passed.

"Here, let me help you."

It took several minutes, but eventually Mary was able to return to bed, having accomplished what she set out to do.

"You need to eat something." Travesty propped her up with several pillows and settled on the side of the bed with a wooden bowl and spoon. She lifted the spoon, but Mary forestalled her hand.

"The baby," she whispered. "What about my baby?"

Travesty tilted her head and smiled, not unkindly. "Dr. Paulson said the little mite is as stubborn as you are. Anyone would have been laid out in a pine box by now, but not you, Mary Forrester. You're a survivor."

"Am I?"

"That you are. Now, stop blathering and open your mouth."

Travesty began to spoon a thin porridge into Mary's mouth, and she swallowed obediently again and again. She felt full after a few spoonfuls, but she needed nourishment for her baby, so she forced herself to eat. She had just about finished all the porridge when John and Simon came in, bringing the smell of cold and pine with them.

"The wagon is hitched," Simon said.

"I'll stay back from church and look after Mary," Travesty said.

"There's no need," Mary replied. Her voice was hoarse, but she made herself heard. "Go on, Travesty. I will be fine."

"You're not fine," Travesty snapped. Mary wondered if she were trying to avoid going to church, but it wasn't her concern. She just wanted to be left alone for a few hours.

"I feel much improved. I just need to sleep."

"Leave Mary some food and water, Travesty, and get yourself in the wagon," John commanded. "I won't have you put in stocks for missing church."

Travesty sighed with irritation but didn't argue. She set down a muslin-covered plate and a cup on the trunk by the bed. "Buttered bread and a cup of ale for your dinner. Don't try to get up," she admonished.

"I couldn't even if I wanted to," Mary reassured her.

"I'm glad to see you feeling better, Mary," John said awkwardly.

Mary gave him a watery smile. "Thank you, John."

She breathed a sigh of relief once everyone left. So, it was Sunday. She'd fallen in the creek on Tuesday. She'd been insensible with fever for four days. Mary brushed the tangled hair out of her face and sank deeper into the pillows. She was no longer fevered, but she had no strength to even sit up, so she closed her eyes and rested her hands on her belly. Her baby had survived. It was a miracle, and a sign. Surely God didn't condemn her for her actions if he'd allowed her and her child to live. Mary was smiling as she sank into a deep, peaceful sleep.

The hand on her cheek was gentle and loving. "Mary, wake up."

Mary forced her eyes open. She was still tired, but whoever was trying to wake her was quite persistent.

"Mary." Walker was leaning over her, his eyes filled with worry. "Mary, can you hear me?"

Mary nodded. "Yes. I was ill."

"I know."

"How do you know?"

"I saw the beads in the shack and came to find you. I heard your husband talking to his man. He thought you were going to die." Walker's voice caught on the last word. "I was desperate to see you."

"How did you know I'd be alone?"

"I saw them leave. I've been watching the house for days."

"I fell in the creek. I slipped."

"My poor love," Walker said, stroking her hair. "I wish I'd known sooner."

"Did you go home again?"

Walker shook his head. "I was needed by Chief Opitchapam. There was a meeting of the chiefs of the Tsenacommacah tribes. There are some who are in favor of war. Opchanacanough, the chief's younger brother, wants to drive the English from these shores before more people come and force the Powhatan to abandon their ancestral lands. The chief wanted my opinion on the motives of the English."

"What did you tell them?" Mary asked.

"The truth. More ships will come. The English will take more land and drive the Indians deeper inland."

"Are you in favor of war, Walker?"

"I'm in favor of living side by side with the English, but given what I've seen and heard, I'm not so sure that's what the English want. We have a peace, but it's a fragile one."

Walker reached for the cup of ale and helped Mary drink. "You are so pale, like a white dove. Why were you looking for me? Did you miss me?" he asked, smiling happily.

"Yes. I miss you every day. I came to tell you that I'll go with you to your people. I made up my mind. But what will happen to me if there's a war with the English? Will I be treated as the enemy?"

"Mary, you will be welcomed and adopted into the tribe. You needn't worry."

"But I do. I worry about our child," Mary said, smiling shyly.

"Our child?" Walker's hand went to her belly and he splayed it over the tiny bump. His face broke into a joyful grin.

"When can we leave?" Mary asked.

"It's a long walk to Croatoan lands, and the paths will be snow-bound until the beginning of what you call March. You need to get your strength back, Mary. Then you can come to the Powhatan village and stay there with me until we're ready to go. I will come for you soon."

"All right."

Walker leaned down and kissed her forehead, his lips soft and gentle. "I love you, Mary. Now, rest and get better. I will see you very soon." He extracted the necklace he had given her from his pack and slipped it over his head. "I will keep this for you until then."

Ramstein-Miesenbach, Germany

Quinn had expected Rhys to engage her in an analysis of the reunion once they got in the car and exited the car park, but he remained silent, allowing her time to process her feelings. That particular undertaking would take much longer than the drive to the hotel, but it was a start. Quinn's emotional circuit board was firing on all cylinders. She was elated, weepy, and excited beyond words, but also frustrated and angry. So much time had been stolen from her and Jo. Thirty-one years during which they could have been the best of friends, and the closest of confidantes. Thirty-one years during which they could have been there for each other and continued to nurture the bond that had begun in the womb.

"You might have hated each other," Rhys suddenly said, startling Quinn out of her reverie.

"What?"

"Your emotions are all there on your face," Rhys replied with a smile. "Don't look back, Quinn. What's done is done. You've found each other, that's what matters. Move forward, build on that."

Quinn reached out and squeezed Rhys's arm. He was speaking

from experience, and she appreciated his insight. He was moving on from his own tragedy, and she had to as well.

"Want to grab some lunch?" Rhys asked as he glanced at the dashboard. It was just past noon. Quinn wasn't hungry, but she could tell that Rhys longed for some company and couldn't bear to deny him.

"Just give me an hour, Rhys. I have to call Gabe, and Logan, and then we can go anywhere you like."

"Of course. Ring me when you're ready." Rhys parked the car and got out with a grimace of pain, which he instantly tried to cover up.

"I must have pulled a muscle when cleaning off the car this morning," he said, easing his back theatrically, but Quinn knew he wasn't telling the truth. She'd seen his careful movements and the way he paled when he took a deep breath. She'd also seen him taking painkillers when he thought she wasn't looking. Rhys was in pain, and whatever was hurting him was the result of his time in Kabul. Quinn felt a stab of guilt. It was all her fault, and Rhys cared about her too much to tell her the truth and make her feel accountable.

"Rhys, please tell me you're all right," Quinn said, facing him across the bonnet of the car. "I know you're hurting."

Rhys didn't bother to deny it this time, for which she was grateful. "I'm on the mend. I had a bit of a run-in with some thugs in Kabul. Don't worry, I was seen to. I'll live."

Quinn smiled, amused by Rhys's unwavering stoicism. He'd never admit to being in pain or needing help. He'd accept aid grudgingly, as if he were bestowing a great favor. "If there's anything I can do—"

"I'm fine. Now, go make those calls before I expire of malnourishment," Rhys said, ushering her into the lobby.

"Right. Sorry. You haven't eaten since breakfast. You must be on your last reserves," Quinn joked. "I'll see you in a bit."

Quinn shut the door to her room, shrugged off her coat, and extracted her mobile. She would call Logan, just as she'd said she would, but first, she needed to hear Gabe's voice. He'd be at work, but she hoped he'd be able to spare her a few minutes.

Gabe picked up on the first ring. "Quinn, are you all right, love?" he asked.

"I'm more than all right. Oh, Gabe, I just met her." Quinn had had every intention of providing Gabe with a measured and descriptive account, but instead she burst into tears at the sound of his voice, overcome by her turbulent emotions.

"That's wonderful, isn't it?" Gabe asked carefully.

"It is," Quinn said, sniffling. "Gabe, it was amazing. It's as if we've known each other our whole lives. There was this connection, this bond."

"I'm glad it went well. Will you be seeing her again tomorrow?"

"Of course. I'll stay for a few more days at the very least. It'd be nice if I could take her home."

"When will Jo be released?"

"I don't know yet. But she's doing really well."

"Quinn, one day at a time. You have your whole lives ahead of you. No one will ever come between you and Jo again."

"That's what Rhys said."

"Rhys is very good at staging the lives of others," Gabe joked. "I'm glad he's with you. How is he?"

"He seems more at peace," Quinn replied. "He's still hurting, and will be for some time, but I think he can see a way forward now." She decided not to mention Rhys's physical injuries. He wouldn't want her to.

"I'm glad to hear it. Have you spoken to Logan?" Gabe asked, his voice gentle.

Quinn sighed. "Not yet. I rang you first. I needed to hear your voice."

Quinn could almost hear Gabe smile. "Go on and call him. I must get back to work. I'll ring you once I get home and you can fill me in on all the details."

"Kiss my babies for me."

"Will do. I love you."

Quinn finished the call and stared at her mobile. She had to call Logan and tell him the news, but she was terrified of the news he might have to share. Or lack of news, in this case. She set aside the mobile and sat down in a wingchair by the window. Her head had begun to ache, and her uterus contracted with painful cramps. She pressed her hand to her lower belly. She'd had aches and pains for the past few weeks and her breasts felt tender to the touch, but her period still hadn't arrived. Quinn sighed heavily. What if she was pregnant? There'd been several times when she and Gabe had foregone protection in the heat of the moment.

Quinn stared miserably at the colorless winter sky outside her window. Did she want another baby? She loved Emma and Alex and loved being their mum, but in truth, she simply wasn't ready to have another child. Not yet. She should have done the test, but she'd been too afraid to find out the truth. Quinn slid her hand into the waistband of her jeans and massaged her belly. It didn't feel taut or tender, but the cramps that twisted her insides felt real enough. She pulled her hand out and touched her breasts. They were a bit swollen. "Please, God, no," she whispered as she consulted the calendar on her phone. It'd been nearly three weeks since she stopped nursing. Her period should have come by now. She'd do the test as soon as she returned home, but by that time there might be no need for it. The cause of the delay would be obvious enough.

Quinn dragged her mind away from her possible pregnancy and called Logan. It took him a while to answer, but he finally came on the line, sounding irritable and tired.

"Quinn, how goes it?"

"You first."

"Nothing's changed. The longer Jude remains unconscious, the greater the possibility that he's suffered permanent damage. I'm scared for him, Quinn." The tremor in Logan's voice betrayed that he was trying not to cry.

"Try to stay positive."

"I'm trying, if only for Mum's sake. She hasn't left Jude's side. It's not looking good, Quinn."

"Is there anything I can do?"

"You can tell me about Jo. I need a bright spot in my life right now."

Quinn spent the next half hour telling Logan about her meeting with Jo. By the time they ended the call, Logan sounded a bit more cheerful and excited at the prospect of meeting his sister. Tomorrow he and Jo might even get to speak in person.

Quinn glanced at her watch. Rhys would be waiting for her. She sent him a text and went downstairs to wait for him.

Rhys wasn't there when she arrived in the lobby, so she found a comfortable spot to sit down and decided to use the time to check her email. There were over fifty messages in her inbox, but only two caught her attention. There was one from Colin. It read: *Quinn, the Winthrop Lab has reopened, and I had them run newly collected DNA samples twice, just to be sure. I think you'll find the results surprising. Ring me.* Quinn thought she could guess what he was referring to and would ring him as soon as she was able.

The second email was from an acquaintance at the National Archives. Joanna Lang had helped Quinn on several occasions and often scanned the information and emailed it to save Quinn having to visit the Archives in person. Quinn was eager to take a look at the document but would have to do it on her laptop, since it was awkward to scroll through pages of entries on her phone. Whatever information the document held, it could wait another few hours.

"Anything interesting?" Rhys asked as he joined her.

"I think so. Colin has some news regarding the DNA analysis, and Joanna Lang has emailed me the information I requested. I'll fill you in later. So, where are we off to?"

"I found a quaint little place I think you'll like," Rhys said. He seemed eager to get going.

"Quinn, I've booked a flight home for tomorrow," he said once they were in the car.

"You're leaving?" Quinn asked. Rhys's news took her by

surprise, but she supposed it was only natural that he'd want to return home.

Rhys turned to her and smiled as one would at an adorable child. "Darling, you don't need me anymore. You've found your sister, and you two have much to talk about. I need to return to London and would very much appreciate it if you'd give me a lift to the airport tomorrow after you visit with Jo. I'm needed back at the office. Apparently, more than two dozen actresses have applied for the part of Valentina Kalinina, and I, for one, can't wait to audition them. According to Rhiannan, some of them are actually Russian." This bit of news seemed to make Rhys very happy.

"Have you ever noticed how everything sounds menacing when said with a Russian accent?" Rhys joked as he pulled out of the car park. "You can say something as simple as 'Get in the car,' and it sounds as if I'm taking you hostage."

"Is that why you can't wait to get back? You want to be menaced by dozens of Russian women?"

Rhys grinned. "That's the thing with Russian women, you don't know if they'll take you home and feed you borsht or put you over their knee and spank you like a bad little boy."

"Please, don't tell me which one you prefer. I don't need that particular image in my already traumatized brain."

Rhys laughed and merged onto the Autobahn. He floored the gas pedal and the little car lurched into action. "I suddenly feel much lighter," he said, turning to smile at Quinn. "And it feels good."

"I'm glad. I'll miss you."

"No, you won't," Rhys replied wistfully. "You have what you need right here. By the way, have you asked her?"

Quinn shook her head. "That's not the kind of question you just blurt out, is it? Brett possessed the same gift and we are half-brother and -sister. Jo and I are twins. She must have the gift. It's only logical that Jo should."

"I would think so too," Rhys agreed. "You must take it slow with her. She seems so fragile."

"Rhys, how can it be that she has no one to turn to at a time like this? I know there's been a rift with her siblings, but surely, there must be someone in her life she feels close to."

"Well, these are the things you'll have to ask her," Rhys replied.

"What about you? Are you through asking questions?" Quinn asked. Rhys seemed to have removed himself from the equation.

"I've done my part. I have a job to return to, and it's time I picked up the pieces of my life. Haley is gone. The baby is gone. I have to move on."

"Rhys, I'll never forget what you did for me," Quinn said. "And for Jo."

"I did it for myself as well. I needed something to lift me out of my misery. Kabul was the ideal place to remind me just how blessed I am and how much I have to be thankful for. I know what I want now, and I will have it. I've still got a few good years left in me."

"Rhys, no one deserves to be happy more than you."

"No one deserves anything," Rhys replied. "Life owes us nothing. It's all about what we make of the opportunities we're presented with. I've wasted several excellent chances, but I'm older and smarter now. I intend to make the next relationship count."

"I know you will."

"I'll leave you the car," Rhys said, turning to practical matters. "You'll need it to visit Jo."

"Thank you," Quinn said as she covered Rhys's hand with her own. "For everything."

"Anytime you need a knight in shining armor and Gabe's busy changing nappies, I'm your man," Rhys joked, as he parked. "Now, let's get inside. I'm famished."

FIFTY-NINE
MARCH 1621

Virginia Colony

The days passed slowly, filled with inactivity and frustration. The fever had taken a toll on Mary and her recovery was slow. The simplest tasks left her tired and dizzy, and she needed to lie down for an hour in the afternoons just so she could remain awake till suppertime. Travesty was surprisingly sympathetic, encouraging Mary to rest and offering her little snacks between meals. From time to time, Mary saw a softness in Travesty's eyes that had never been there before. It was as if she were in another world, another time, and she likely was, recalling the life she'd had before it had been snatched from her.

"You should sit outside for a bit," Travesty advised. "You need fresh air. Go on with you."

Mary obediently put on her cloak and went to sit on the bench. Travesty was right, it felt good to be outdoors. The fresh air was brisk and invigorating and dispelled some of Mary's lethargy. By the second week, she began to take short walks to regain her strength. First, she walked around the yard, but after a few days she ventured toward the forest. It was during one of those walks that she noticed a stealthy movement beyond a scrim of trees and pushed herself to walk further. Walker materialized from behind a thick tree trunk and took her in his arms.

"I'm so glad to see you up and about," he said, taking her face in his hands and kissing her gently.

Mary didn't bother to ask how Walker had known she was on the mend. He was like a shadow, a restless spirit that moved unnoticed through the trees. She wouldn't be surprised if he'd come to the plantation to check on her. He had a way of melting into his surroundings and standing so still that not even the sound of his breath gave him away.

"Are you ready to come away with me?" Walker asked, studying her.

"I need a few more days," Mary replied. "I don't think I can walk through the woods for hours just yet, especially not in these shoes." Having lost her shoe in the creek, Mary had to wear homemade shoes that Simon had fashioned for her. They looked like canoes, the left and right shoe identical, pointy and narrow. The soles were too thin to walk over pinecones and twigs, since Mary could feel every pebble and acorn through the leather.

Walker smiled. "Don't worry, Mary, you will have no need of your shoes or your cumbersome clothing. The village women have made you clothes and shoes. You will be comfortable and warm. I will bring everything with me to the shack, where you will be able to change before we leave."

Mary was sure she'd be comfortable, but she had doubts about being warm. Walker didn't seem to feel the cold. He wore no woolens or even a cloak, and his feet were bare inside his soft moccasins. The natives didn't wear hose or petticoats to keep out the chill wind, and Walker's head was always bare.

"I will keep you warm," he assured her with a smile that did indeed warm her insides.

"When do we go north?" Now that she'd made up her mind, she couldn't wait to leave. The trek to Walker's people no longer seemed frightening, but an adventure they would undertake together. She was ready to embrace her new life, as long as he remained by her side.

"You need to be able to keep pace," Walker replied. "In case your people mount a search for you. Let's wait for the new moon. You will be stronger then, and the snows will have begun to melt. I will come for you."

"All right," Mary agreed.

"Stay at the plantation," Walker warned.

"Why?"

"There's been some unrest."

"Between the colonists and the natives?" Mary asked, suddenly frightened.

"No, between the colonists."

Mary hadn't heard anything, but then she hadn't left the cabin in nearly three weeks, grateful to be excused from church services on account of her illness. She wished she could ask John, but how would she explain having come by the information? And John, in his usual taciturn fashion, hadn't mentioned anything. Perhaps Travesty would be a better source. Mary spent a few more minutes with Walker, then turned for home. She couldn't allow Travesty to grow suspicious. She returned to the cabin and lay down, tired out by the walk.

"Here, have a cup of warm milk," Travesty suggested. "It's good for the baby."

"Thank you. I hope I can come with you to church on Sunday," Mary said, as she sipped the milk. "I miss seeing my friends."

"I suppose you'd better. It isn't safe for you here alone."

"Why?"

Travesty continued working the crank of the churn, her mouth set in a grim line. "There have been a number of thefts. Marshal Craddock is beside himself, since he has no idea who's responsible."

"What has been stolen?" Mary asked. Was this the unrest Walker had been referring to?

"Food stores, mostly. Not like there's much else to steal in this

Godforsaken colony. I reckon some were not well prepared for the winter, and they've run out of supplies. 'Tis hard for unmarried men to see to their crops and take the time to stock up on provisions. Bags of grain, corn, and dried peas have been taken."

"Has anyone been hurt?" Mary asked.

"Not that I know of. They're stealthy, these blackguards, and quick. Marshal Craddock reckons 'tis not the work of a single man. They must work in gangs."

"Desperate men will do desperate things," Mary replied. "Has anything been taken from us?"

"No, but there are two men here, which increases the odds of the thieves getting apprehended or shot. Don't worry, we have enough food to last us till the spring."

Mary nodded and closed her eyes, suddenly exhausted. Travesty's voice washed over her as she drifted to sleep.

SIXTY

As the day of Mary's departure drew closer, she was torn between breathless excitement and unbearable anxiety. She dreamed of the day she'd walk out of the cabin for the last time and begin her new life with Walker. Strangely, a small part of that life had already begun. John had not slept with her since her illness, making himself a pallet on the floor instead. He insisted that he sleep apart so as not to disturb her during her convalescence, but in truth, she knew he was as repelled by her as she was by him, and now that she was carrying what he presumed to be his child, he no longer felt the need to bother with the pretense of being a true husband. He was still solicitous when the situation called for it, but he was, if such a thing were possible, even more distant and aloof, while Simon was watchful and preoccupied.

Mary didn't know what Simon was up to, but something in his demeanor had changed over the past few months. Travesty carried on as if everything was just the same, going about her chores and biding her time until her indenture contract expired. She still had years to go until she could even begin to make plans for the future, but it was the dream of something better that kept her going.

"I won't always be a slave," Travesty told Mary hotly one

morning while grinding corn with surprising aggression. "There are some as would be happy to have me, if I were free."

Mary had no doubt. Travesty was an attractive woman and still of childbearing years, but only just. Mary could understand her frustration at being held captive as what was left of her youth slipped away. "I will have a home of my own," Travesty said through gritted teeth. "I will be my own mistress."

"I've no doubt you will," Mary assured her, wondering what had brought on this bout of anger. Travesty slammed the pestle on the table and stormed out of the cabin, presumably to go to the privy. Mary picked up the pestle and continued grinding the corn.

Only a few more days, she thought happily as she wielded the tool. *A few more interminable days.*

The time would go by faster if there were something for her to do to prepare for her journey north, but Mary had no belongings to pack, and nothing but mundane chores to occupy her time and mind; however, there was one thing she meant to do before leaving —she had to see Nell. She couldn't share her plans with her friend, but Nell had been a true friend, and she couldn't leave without saying goodbye.

Mary set down the pestle and wiped her hands on her apron. It was a beautiful day for the beginning of March. The sun was bright and gentle as it shone from a cloudless blue sky. The air smelled of loamy earth and wood smoke, and birds sang happily, heralding the coming of spring. It was the perfect day to take a walk, and Mary was in sore need of friendly company. She donned her cloak and tied it at her throat, adjusted her cap, and prepared to leave. She wished she had something to bring Nell, but stores were running low and she didn't dare take something without asking John's permission. He and Simon were in the field, fixing a broken fence post, and she had no desire to seek him out.

"I'm going to see Nell," Mary called out to Travesty, who'd emerged from the privy, looking ill.

"Fine," Travesty barked and made for the house. *Must be her time of the month*, Mary thought as she walked out of the yard. Travesty was always more irritable while she bled.

Mary strolled along, enjoying the pleasant day. For the first time in weeks, she was at peace. Her belly had grown round and firm over the past month, and she'd finally felt the baby move only a few days ago. It had been a strange feeling, and she'd almost dismissed it, thinking it might be wind in her belly, but then it had happened again and again, and she'd finally recognized it for what it was—life.

She had a feeling the child would be a boy. She had nothing to support this supposition, but she embraced it. It would be nice to have a strong son who'd grow up to be as fierce and smart as his father. Of course, at first, he'd be a sweet baby. Mary tried not to dwell too much on the things Walker had told her, like how the mothers in the village strapped their babies to a wooden cradleboard. It seemed a strange thing to do, but Walker assured her the babies were quite comfortable and warm. She'd have to get used to the strange ways of his people, but the prospect no longer frightened her. Having seen her own people through Walker's eyes had been an illuminating experience.

Mary smiled broadly when she saw Nell's rounded form waddling into the yard, a basket on her hip. Nell set down the basket, put her hands on her lower back and stretched, then began to hang the newly washed garments on the line. She spotted Mary and waved, her round face breaking into a joyful grin. Mary quickened her steps and was with Nell in a matter of minutes, embracing her friend as their bellies pushed against each other, making them laugh.

Nell reached out and put a hand on Mary's stomach. "You're not too far behind me, Mary."

"How are you, Nell? You look just about ready to burst."

"I am. I can't sleep. I spend half my time in the privy, and I can barely get out of bed unassisted. I'm ready, Mary," Nell said with a grimace.

"Who will assist you when the time comes?"

"Tom will go for Betsy. She delivered her younger brothers. I do wish there was an experienced midwife here."

"Are you frightened?"

"Yes," Nell replied in a small voice. "Makes it worse, it being my first."

"Because you don't know what to expect?" Mary asked as she followed Nell into the house.

"Because I do. I've seen my ma birth my siblings. It's an ugly business, Mary, and a deadly one."

Mary nodded. She was frightened as well, but Walker had assured her she would receive competent help when her time came.

When they came indoors, Tom was seated at the table, carving something out of a hunk of wood, but he excused himself and went out, giving Mary and Nell a chance to visit.

"Tom's making a toy for the child," Nell explained as she swept up the shavings. She then set two cups on the table and poured them some ale. "He's already made a cradle. He can't wait to be a father. How is John taking the news?"

"The same way John takes everything," Mary replied, leaving Nell to draw her own conclusions.

"So, nothing's changed, then?"

Mary shook her head. "He's not unkind to me, but he doesn't treat me like a wife, Nell. I may as well be another servant. There's not a word of affection or a moment of closeness between us. We are two people who share a bed, but sleep facing away from each other." Mary thought it prudent not to mention that John no longer slept with her. It wasn't her intention to expose John, but simply to leave him.

"'Tis a shame, that," Nell said. "I must admit that Tom and I have grown closer, especially during these last months. He loves me, Tom does, and I care for him. This child is a blessing, and I pray there will be more to come."

"I'm glad for you, Nell, and I hope life will always be kind to you."

Nell took a sip of ale, a thoughtful expression on her face. "You make it sounds as if we won't see each other again."

"Do I?"

"Well, never mind," Nell said, refilling Mary's cup. "The spring is almost here, and it will be the start of a new life for this colony. Come autumn, there will be at least a dozen children in Jamestown, a new generation, and the first to be born in Virginia. Will they still be considered English, do you think, or will they be known as Virginians?"

"I don't know. I suppose since they'll still be His Majesty's subjects, they'll be considered English."

"Well, that's for the best anyhow. Who'd want to be known as a Virginian? They'd sound as if they're savages. My Tom says that in time, the English will drive all the savages out, so we'll have nothing to fear from the likes of them. Good riddance, I say," Nell said, her gaze fierce. "An extinct savage is a good savage."

Mary didn't reply but felt a sudden urge to leave. Several months ago, she would have wholeheartedly agreed with Nell, but she could no longer condone such sentiments. She didn't know many natives, but they were people just like the English, and they'd been on this land for generations. This was their home. What right did the English have to come and drive them off, and worse, hope for their extinction?

Mary got to her feet. "Well, I'd best be going."

"I might have a little 'un the next time you see me," Nell said, beaming. "Oh, I do hope I survive the birth."

"You will. You are strong, Nell—the strongest woman I know."

Nell wrapped her arms around Mary. "See you on the other side, my friend."

Mary returned the hug and hurried from the cabin. She would never see Nell again. She'd miss her company, and her support, but it was time to go. If all went according to plan, she'd be gone in a few days' time, and just like Nell, she was ready.

Mary was halfway home when she spotted three men walking toward her. She didn't recognize them, but then she only knew the colonists who went to church in Jamestown. There were over a thousand people in the colony now, and several other churches had sprung up to accommodate the overflow. The men were strolling along, looking for all the world as if they were simply enjoying the fine weather, but Mary noticed the black kerchiefs around their necks and the bulging sacks they carried. Two of them had muskets slung over their shoulders and a third had a wicked-looking knife, the kind John used to cut the tobacco.

Mary felt a twinge of unease as the men drew nearer. She had nothing worth taking, but that didn't mean they wouldn't detain her and try to check for themselves. Mary hoped they would move aside and allow her to pass, but as soon as they approached her, they spread out to block her on three sides—not that there was anywhere to run. On her left was the forest, and on her right an open field. If she ran, they'd catch her in moments.

The men were smiling at her as though enjoying her discomfort, their eyes glinting with amusement. Mary stood still, meeting their smiles with what she hoped was a stern expression, but her innards were quivering with fear. Up close, she saw that the men were young and fit, but their unkempt clothes and torn hose suggested they had no women to look after them.

"Good day to you, sirs," Mary said civilly. "Please allow me to pass."

"Good day to you, mistress," one of the men said. He was broad and stocky, his thick blond hair hanging to his shoulders in greasy sheets. "Where are you bound?"

"Home," Mary replied. The men still hadn't moved, and she was growing more nervous by the minute.

"And where might home be?"

"I'm the wife of John Forrester. I live about a mile down the road."

"Oh, aye, we just passed your homestead, didn't we, lads?" the blond man said.

The other two nodded. They seemed to have no interest in John or his plantation, probably because three men against two didn't make for good odds, and Travesty could make for a formidable opponent if armed with a hoe or scythe. The man cocked his head and studied Mary with interest, no longer smiling. Mary took a step back as he advanced toward her, but there was nowhere to go. The man standing behind her didn't budge, so by moving away from one, she moved closer to the other.

"I don't have anything of value," Mary cried, now terrified.

"Don't you?" the blond man said. The smile was back, but it was ugly and sly. "I'd say you have something even more precious than corn and beans, Mistress Forrester."

He grabbed her around the waist and pulled her toward him, pressing himself against her. The other two chuckled as they watched. Mary felt the bristle of her assailant's beard against her cheek. He reeked of sweat and onions, and she nearly retched when he brought his face close to hers as if he were going to kiss her. She knew he was toying with her, but she wasn't courageous enough not to show her fear.

"Please, let me go," she pleaded.

"You heard the lady, Anselm. Let her go," one of the men said, and the two laughed uproariously.

"Please—" Mary begged, but he silenced her with a hard, punishing kiss. The man who stood behind her slid his arms around her to cup her breasts. He weighed them in his hands as he ground his stiff rod into her buttocks. "Nice pair of tits on our Mistress Forrester."

Mary struggled, but the men had her surrounded. They were fondling her roughly, their hands all over her body. She cried out as Anselm bunched up her skirt and forced his hand between her legs, his fingers probing her in a most intimate way.

"Please, stop," Mary pleaded. "I'm with child."

"We don't mind if you don't." Anselm laughed mirthlessly and the other two cackled, as if he'd given them permission to be amused. "Hands off," he suddenly barked, and the other two took a step back, surrendering her to their leader. He pushed Mary onto the side of the path, where last year's grass covered the hard ground, and stood over her. "I haven't had a woman in six long years, mistress. I don't care if you're in your throes, I'll have you anyway. And then my companions will too."

He began unlacing his breeches. The other two were clearly willing to let him have the first go, happy to get a turn at all. They were rubbing themselves, mesmerized as they watched Anselm pin Mary to the ground and free his throbbing cock from his breeches. Mary thrashed, desperate to throw him off her, but he was too strong, and too eager.

"Quit fighting and I'll go easy on you," Anselm promised as he forced his knee between Mary's legs. "I mean you no harm. I just want to get my stones off with a real woman, not my calloused hand," he joked.

He moved his head closer to Mary, his ear only an inch from her mouth. Mary bit him. Hard. Anselm yelped and grabbed at his injured ear, giving her just enough leverage to throw him off.

Mary scrambled away from him on her behind, her teeth bared as she glared at him, glad she'd been able to inflict pain. She had no illusions—these men weren't going to let her go, not if she could identify them to the marshal. They were going to use her and kill her. Even if her body were found, no one would know who'd committed the crime. No one would hang.

Enraged, Anselm threw himself at Mary and pinned her to the ground with his body, shoving his knee between her legs again. He slapped her hard, then again, until her teeth rattled in her mouth. He was cursing at her, but Mary couldn't make out the words over the ringing in her ears. She swiveled her hips as Anselm tried unsuccessfully to guide his cock inside her with one hand. He grabbed her breast and squeezed hard, making her cry out in pain.

She heard a strangled cry, and then something hot and thick blurred her vision, but she couldn't wipe it away. Anselm's body drove the breath from her lungs as it slumped on top of her, heavy and immobile. Mary wiped her face against the linen of Anselm's sleeve and managed to open her eyes. An Indian tomahawk protruded from the top of his skull, the handle pointing toward the cloudless sky.

Mary screamed and tried to push Anselm's body off her, but he was too heavy, and she was pinned to the ground. She heard a swishing sound and watched in astonishment as an arrow lodged itself in the throat of one of the men. He raised his hand in disbelief and clutched at his neck as crimson blood ran over his fingers and dripped onto his shirt. His eyes rolled wildly as he rasped a plea for help, but the second man had no time for him. He fired his musket just as an arrow found its mark in his shoulder. The man roared with pain but tried to reload his musket regardless, his hands shaking and clumsy. He gave up and threw the musket to the ground just as his friend sank to his knees and then keeled over in the dirt.

"Walker!" Mary cried as he erupted from the woods.

Walker hauled Anselm's body off her and threw it to the side as if it were a corn dolly, his eyes roaming over her to assess the damage.

There was a look on his face she'd never seen before, and she found herself speechless, frightened by the bloodlust burning in his eyes. He was enraged, and murderous. He spun around, aware of danger before she saw it coming. The second man had torn the arrow out of his shoulder and tossed it aside. Blood poured from his mutilated shoulder, but he didn't seem to notice. His skin had turned a sickly shade of green, but he was shaking with rage, his eyes wild as he looked around for a weapon. He yanked the knife out of his friend's belt and came at Walker, his teeth bared in an evil grin.

Walker grabbed his own knife and tried to jump out of the way, but the man lunged with all his strength, knocking Walker to the ground and delivering a vicious stab to his stomach. He raised the knife again, but Walker drove his blade into the man's groin, taking him by surprise. The man roared like a wounded beast, startling the birds in the nearby trees. They took flight, their wings flapping loudly over Mary's head. The man wrapped his hands around the handle of the knife and drove it into Walker's chest before collapsing next to his attacker. He twitched as his life ebbed away, then went perfectly still.

Mary was beside Walker in seconds. He lay sprawled on the ground, his buckskin shirt shredded by the slashes of the knife. Mary didn't need to lift the garment to know the wounds were severe. Blood trickled into the dirt next to him, and he'd loosened his grip on the knife, allowing it to fall from his hand. The murderous rage had gone out of his eyes, replaced with pain and shock, and sorrow for what would now never be. His gaze seemed to be fixed on the sky, the blue of the heavens reflected in his pupils.

"Walker, please, don't go," Mary pleaded. "I'll go for help."

"There's nothing anyone can do for me now," Walker whispered. His voice was hoarse as though speaking took a great deal of effort.

"I'll get Dr. Paulson," Mary cried.

"No."

"Walker, please, let me help you."

"Help me by leaving. I need to know you're safe."

"I'm safe." Mary took Walker's hand and laid in on her belly. "He's safe too. You must live for him."

Walker's smile became dreamy, his gaze unfocused. "Tell him about me. Tell him I loved him."

"You'll tell him yourself. Please, don't leave me."

"My life is a small price to pay to keep you both safe," Walker whispered.

"How can you be so selfless?" Mary cried. She was always taken aback by the purity of Walker's emotions.

"Love is patient, love is kind. It does not envy, it does not boast, it is not proud. It does not dishonor others, it is not self-seeking, it is not easily angered, it keeps no record of wrongs. Love does not delight in evil but rejoices with the truth. It always protects, always trusts, always hopes, always perseveres," Walker rasped.

"How do you know that?" Mary gasped. Walker had never given any indication that he'd read the Scripture.

"My mother used to say that to me when I was upset. She said that love has the power to conquer all fears, all hate. Go, my Mary. Go home. Leave me. I don't want you to see me die."

"No, I won't leave you."

"Please," Walker pleaded. "Do this one last thing for me."

Mary kissed him tenderly on the lips and forced herself to rise to her feet. She took one step, then another, until she was walking toward the plantation. Tears streamed down her face, and she could barely see where she was going. She heard Walker's voice as it carried on the breeze, singing a song that tore at her heart. His death song.

She stopped walking and doubled over, seized by a pain so intense she couldn't go on. She couldn't breathe, couldn't think. The only person she loved was dying, bleeding out on the side of the road, alone and untended. Mary took a deep breath and resumed walking. Before she knew it, she was running for her life. She didn't care what Walker had asked of her. She was going for help.

Virginia Colony

Mary sat perfectly still, her hands folded in her lap and her eyes downcast. She couldn't bring herself to look at the men who filled the cabin, their voices harsh and loud, and their stances aggressive and intimidating. They were arguing, throwing out ugly accusations, and pointing the finger at her.

"Tell us again what happened, Mistress Forrester," Marshal Craddock demanded, towering over her, his eyes as hard as flint.

"I've told you already," Mary replied. Her thoughts were like threads that kept slipping away from her, her fingers not nimble enough to grab the ends and tie them together.

"Please, Marshal, she's clearly distressed," Secretary Hunt argued. "Just look at the state of her. Surely you believe her."

His words reminded Mary that her gown was still covered in blood—Anselm's blood, and Walker's. She laid a gentle hand over the dark brown stain on her skirt. The blood from the wound in Walker's stomach had leaked onto her skirt as she bent over him. *Walker!* her mind screamed. All she wanted was to cower in some dark place where no one could see her. She wanted to cry until she had no tears left, scream till she lost her voice, and rage at the cruel

God who had taken away the man who'd saved her from a terrible fate. Walker had died so she could live.

"I believe Mistress Forrester was there when the attack took place. Whether she was physically molested is unclear. My men and I have examined the scene. There are butchered remains of three colonists. One has a split skull, one took an arrow to the throat, and the third was stabbed in the groin and had half his shoulder gouged out. This attack was perpetuated by an Indian—a blatant attack on Englishmen, on England itself."

"Do you have any of the weapons?" Secretary Hunt asked. He wasn't nearly as incensed as the marshal, his face thoughtful and calm.

"No. He made sure to remove any trace of his involvement."

"Mistress Forrester claims the man who came to her aid was fatally wounded," Secretary Hunt pointed out. "What became of him?"

"He was nowhere to be found," the marshal replied. "Surely this proves he wasn't acting alone."

Mary breathed a small sigh of relief. The Powhatan must have removed Walker's body, as well as his weapons and broken arrows. They'd have wished to avoid an armed conflict with the colonists but had no way of knowing that there was a witness to what had taken place. Marshal Craddock had been interrogating Mary for two hours, and he was baying for Indian blood, ready to declare war on the Powhatan nation. It wasn't in Mary's power to prevent a war, but knowing that Walker's remains would be treated with dignity and respect made his passing a little easier to bear.

"Did you know this Indian who came to your aid, Mistress Forrester?" Secretary Hunt asked softly. He made a pretense of being sympathetic, but Mary knew he only wanted to avoid bloodshed. The Virginia Company was interested in profit, not revenge.

"I've seen him in Jamestown." Mary's voice sounded flat, disinterested. She didn't want anyone to think Walker had meant something to her. It was none of their business.

"Master Forrester, if you have no objection, Dr. Paulson will examine your wife," Marshal Craddock said. "We must be certain that she was indeed attacked, as she claims. If this Indian slaughtered three men with no provocation, there *will* be retribution."

Mary stared at the marshal, unable to believe what she was hearing. Not only did the men question her claim of being attacked on the road, they believed Walker had ambushed the men as they walked and had killed them savagely without any reason.

"Now, see here, Craddock. Those men had sacks filled with corn and grain. They'd been thieving, which is a crime punishable by death," Hunt interjected.

"And we would have dealt with them in our own fashion. If this Indian killed our men, the crime will not go unpunished. Master Forrester?" The marshal turned to John, his tone indicating that asking John for his permission to examine his wife was a mere courtesy. John would be a fool to refuse.

"I have no objection," John replied. No one had asked Mary if she objected to an examination. No one cared that she'd been attacked, frightened out of her wits, and forced to watch the man she loved butchered. Mary folded her hands in her lap and bowed her head in abject misery.

"Gentlemen, if you'd all step outside," Dr. Paulson suggested as he took a step toward Mary. Marshal Craddock opened his mouth to protest, but Dr. Paulson held up his hand to forestall him. "I will examine Mistress Forrester most carefully and report back to you in a few minutes. Now, please, step outside, Marshal."

He waited until the men left, then turned to Mary. "Will you please lie down for me, Mary? I won't hurt you. You have my word."

Mary nodded and reclined on the bed, lying as still as an effigy while Dr. Paulson examined her. He was gentle and kind, and his sympathy nearly undid her. She bit her lip hard, so as not to howl with grief.

The men trooped back in after the doctor completed his examination. "It's as she says. Mistress Forrester has bruises on her wrists and thighs. Her cheek is swollen where she was struck, and one of her teeth is loose. The blood on her bodice corroborates her story of the man being struck with a tomahawk while he was atop her."

"There's no proof she was assaulted by an Englishman," Marshal Craddock argued. "She might have just as easily been attacked by the Indian. For all we know, the men came to her aid, instead of the other way around."

"That's not consistent with the wounds inflicted on the men," the doctor pointed out. "If the Indian had Mistress Forrester pinned down, he could hardly loose an arrow or split someone's skull. Besides, the handle was pointed away from the face. The tomahawk had been thrown from behind."

"There you have it, Craddock," the secretary chimed in. "It's as she says. There's no call for retaliation."

"And why did this Indian feel the need to come to your aid?" Marshal Craddock asked. "Why should this savage care if you were attacked?"

Mary slowly raised her head and looked up at Marshal Craddock. Hatred for this belligerent and ignorant man pulsed through her veins. "He came to my aid because he was a man of honor."

"That's preposterous!" the marshal exclaimed. "The Indians have no honor. He saw an opportunity to give in to his savagery and availed himself of it."

"Secretary, may I have a word outside?" Travesty asked, surprising everyone into silence. She'd been sent up to her loft while the men questioned Mary, but she'd come back down unnoticed.

"If you have something to say, say it, woman," Marshal Craddock barked.

"Secretary?" Travesty continued, as if Craddock hadn't spoken.

"Very well."

While Secretary Hunt spoke to Travesty outside, Craddock's men helped themselves to ale. They were restless, their blood up, and their good sense overpowered by the desire to act and inflict the maximum amount of damage. Mary shrank against the wall, wishing she could disappear. She looked at John, but he kept his face averted, his eyes fixed on something beyond the window. Simon leaned against the wall by the hearth, his eyes warm with sympathy when his gaze met hers. He gave Mary a watery smile, but she didn't return it.

At long last, Secretary Hunt and Travesty returned to the cabin. Travesty's eyes burned with something akin to satisfaction, while Secretary Hunt was white to the roots of his hair.

"Marshal, arrest Master Forrester, his wife, and his servant."

"On what charge?" Marshal Craddock asked, clearly taken aback by this turn of events.

"On the charge of adultery and sodomy. Have your men spread the word throughout the colony. The trial will be held tomorrow at noon, and I want every plantation owner present."

Mary was too overcome with shock to protest as a soldier grabbed her arm and led her outside. The corpses of the three men who had assaulted her had been piled in the wagon, their sightless eyes staring up at the sky. John and Simon had to share the wagon with the dead, while Mary was permitted to sit on the bench next to the driver, on account of her condition. Travesty stood in the doorway, watching as the men mounted their horses and cantered out of the yard.

Once in Jamestown, Mary and John were locked in a shed that was hardly big enough for the two of them to stand in side by side. Simon was taken to a different location. At least they hadn't been put in irons. Mary sank to the ground, too weary to stand. She hadn't eaten since breaking her fast that morning and she was lightheaded. She leaned her head against the rough wood, wishing she could go to sleep and never wake up. John sat down beside her. He was as stiff as a board, his breathing shallow and rapid.

"Mary, do you know what Travesty said to Secretary Hunt?" he asked at last.

"I do not."

John sighed. "Mary, I—" He hung his head in despair, unable to go on.

"Don't, John," Mary replied, too overwrought to talk. She closed her eyes and tried to distance herself from the tiny, dark space and the sharp smell of John's fear.

THE CONCUBINE

SIXTY-TWO

Mary blinked as she was led out of the shed into bright sunlight. She felt lightheaded with hunger, and her mouth was dry as a bone.

"May I have a drink?" she asked the soldier who pulled her toward the church.

He didn't bother to reply, but Prudence came alongside her and handed her a cup of ale and a hunk of bread. Mary drank deeply and nodded her thanks before biting into the bread.

"Don't worry, Mary. All will be well," Prudence called out. Mary had serious doubts about this farce of a trial turning out well, but all she could do was face whatever was about to come her way.

John walked behind her, escorted by two of Craddock's soldiers. He hadn't said much during the hours they'd been locked in the shed, and Mary hadn't bothered to engage him in conversation. What was there to say? Travesty had made an accusation against all of them, but what Mary couldn't begin to understand was why. What did Travesty hope to gain by exposing John and Simon? She still had years left on her indenture contract, and if the trial went as Mary suspected it might, Travesty's contract would simply be sold to another settler, who might not treat her as kindly as John had or might take advantage of her vulnerable position and make free with her. Perhaps that was what she hoped for, but this course of action was a great risk, and Travesty was not a foolish woman. There was something Mary wasn't seeing. Perhaps it would come to light during the trial.

The church was full, every pew occupied and dozens of colonists standing against the walls for lack of additional seating. There were no women, save Travesty, who sat in the first pew, her head held high. Governor Yeardley, Marshal Craddock, and Secretary Hunt sat behind a makeshift table erected in front of the pulpit. Reverend Edison sat off to the side, not part of the tribunal, but an important witness to the proceedings. Mary, John, and Simon were made to stand before the table. John and Simon's hands were bound, but Mary's were left untied.

Secretary Hunt rose to his feet and held up his hand, calling for silence. "Thank you all for coming. Today, we are here to try John Forrester, his wife, Mary Forrester, and their indentured servant, Simon Faraday. The charges are adultery, sodomy, and coercion. Travesty Brown, John Forrester's indentured servant, has shared vital information with me, at great risk to herself, I might add. I applaud her bravery."

There was a general murmur of approval, and although Mary couldn't see Travesty, she could imagine her preening with self-importance.

"Mistress Brown, will you kindly repeat what you told me in confidence yesterday?" Secretary Hunt asked.

Mary turned to glare at Travesty, who ignored her accusing stare and got to her feet. She faced the three men and spoke in a clear and confident voice.

"John Forrester and Simon Faraday have been involved in an unnatural clandestine relationship for at least as long as I've been a servant at Master Forrester's house."

There was a gasp from the assembly, but Secretary Hunt held up his hand to silence the crowd. "Mistress Brown, when you refer to an unnatural relationship, what exactly do you mean?"

"I mean sodomy, sir."

"And do you wish to make an accusation against Mistress Forrester?" Secretary Hunt asked.

Mary's stomach clenched with foreboding. Was Travesty going to accuse her of covering for John? She could hardly have given him up to the authorities. Besides, she could claim ignorance. There was no proof that she had known about John's relationship with Simon.

Travesty took her time answering. She made eye contact with each man in turn to make sure she had their full attention before she spoke. "Mistress Forrester has been carrying on an adulterous relationship with a native, meeting him in the woods and lying with him freely. The child she carries is most likely his, since her husband wasn't interested in performing his conjugal duties. The savage who killed three colonists yesterday was not there by accident, but by design. It is my belief that Mistress Forrester intended to run away with him in the near future."

Mary's knees buckled as Travesty's cruel words sank in. She wasn't just condemning John and Simon, she was including Mary in the charges and ensuring she couldn't possibly mount a plausible defense in the face of the accusation. What had happened yesterday was enough to give Travesty's claim validity and imply that Mary was complicit in the deaths of her attackers.

A soldier grabbed Mary by the shoulders to keep her from falling, but she wasn't permitted to sit down. As she slumped against the man, welcoming blackness beckoned to her, offering oblivion and temporary peace, but Mary fought to stay alert. She had to hear what was being said. This was her only chance to fight for herself and her baby, and she'd make the most of the opportunity, if she were given one.

Secretary Hunt turned to John, who stood, head bowed, before the tribunal. "Master Forrester, have you had sexual congress with your servant Simon Faraday?"

John refused to answer, which was as clear an admission of guilt as if he'd shouted about his couplings with Simon from the rooftops.

"Master Faraday, is what Mistress Brown says true?"

Mary turned her head just enough to get a glimpse of Simon's face. Simon was no fool, and unlike John, he wouldn't go down without a fight.

"Sirs, I've been an indentured servant to Master Forrester these three years. During that time, my master has indeed used me to satisfy his unnatural urges. I was not a willing party to his lust, but being wholly in his power, I felt I had no recourse."

"Why did you not make a complaint?" Reverend Edison demanded, outraged.

"I was afraid no one would believe me, and I would have to not only bear the assault on my person, but also suffer punishment for betraying my master."

"How many times has Master Forrester made free with your body without your consent?" Governor Yeardley asked.

"Too many to count, sir." Simon looked like he was about to weep, and a murmur of sympathy went through the crowd.

"Has he hurt you?" Governor Yeardley asked.

"Frequently, sir," Simon said, his voice trembling. "He used me most brutally." John threw him a look of pure loathing, but Simon ignored it. "I was entirely at his mercy, good sirs."

"And you, Mistress Forrester, were you aware of this relationship between your husband and Master Faraday?" the governor asked.

"I was not," Mary lied. She wouldn't be party to this.

"Have you had an adulterous relationship with a savage?" the governor asked, watching her with narrowed eyes.

"I have not," Mary said. She held her head high and looked directly into the governor's eyes. She would not cower before these men.

"Liar!" Travesty called out. "I've seen you with him."

"I have spoken to the Indian known as Walks Between Worlds on several occasions. He set his traps not far from our cabin. He was courteous and respectful and never made any improper advances toward me," Mary replied, her voice clear and calm. She didn't care what happened to her, but she had to protect her baby, and she had to protect Walker's reputation. She would not give the tribunal any ammunition to hold him responsible for the massacre on the road.

"Mistress Brown, do you have any proof that Mistress Forrester did indeed engage in an adulterous relationship with this savage?" Secretary Hunt demanded.

"I saw them together several times," Travesty persisted.

"Have you witnessed an act of sexual congress?"

"I have not," Travesty admitted.

"So, what were they doing?" Marshal Craddock snapped. "Making daisy chains?" He looked angry and disappointed. He'd clearly hoped for more.

"They were talking," Travesty replied after a slight pause. "But they were too close to each other, their heads bent in a most intimate way."

The three judges conferred between themselves, their faces grim as they prepared to pass judgement. Secretary Hunt stood, waiting patiently until the noise died down and he was able to speak uninterrupted.

"Master Faraday, for allowing yourself to be violated and for not reporting the offense to the governors of this colony, you are to be put in stocks for a period of twelve hours. Once your punishment is complete, you will no longer be bound to Master Forrester. Your indenture contract will revert to the Virginia Company."

Simon pretended to look horrified, but Mary saw the relief in his face. He let out a sigh and addressed the court. "Thank you, sirs, for freeing me from this sinful man."

Secretary Hunt went on. "Mary Forrester, for the crimes of consorting with a savage, shielding your husband from justice, and for your involvement in the deaths of three colonists, you are to be banished. You will return to England on the next outbound ship. Until that time, you will remain incarcerated."

"But I have nothing back in England. I have no home or family to return to," Mary cried.

"That is of no concern to us. Only women of good character can be sponsored by the Virginia Company. Were you not with child, we'd consider a more stringent punishment. We have been merciful."

Mary began to shake. She hadn't expected this. "I am a married woman. You cannot separate me from my husband." It was a feeble attempt to change their minds about banishing her, but Mary had to try. She had nothing to go back to, no means of supporting herself and her baby, and no hope of a different future if she were still married to John.

"You are about to become a widowed woman," the governor replied. "Master Forrester, for the crimes of coercion, sodomy, and adultery, you are to be hanged by the neck until you are dead. The sentence will be carried out immediately."

John's head shot up, his eyes pleading for mercy, but the governor had already turned his attention to Travesty. "Mistress Brown, as a reward for your diligence and selflessness in bringing this matter to our attention, your indenture contract is now fulfilled. You are a free woman. You may remain at the Forrester plantation until you make arrangements for your future."

Travesty smiled happily. "Thank you, sir. I'm overcome by your generosity."

Numb with shock, Mary watched as John and Simon were removed from the church, Simon to be put in stocks, and John to be hanged. The soldier who'd helped her took her by the arm.

"Come. Back to the shed with you," he said, not unkindly. He escorted Mary down the nave and toward the door.

Travesty was already outside, surrounded by several men who were congratulating her on her good fortune and doing their hardest to ignite a spark of interest. Until the next shipload of women arrived, Travesty was the only marriageable woman in Jamestown, and she was already in high demand. She would receive several offers of marriage by the time John breathed his last.

You sly witch, Mary thought as she glared at the woman. Travesty had waited for the perfect moment to betray them, and now she would benefit handsomely from her cunning. John shook with fear as two soldiers seized him by the arms and dragged him toward the gate, where one of the marshal's men was already fashioning a noose. He tossed the rope over the crossbar and it hung there, swinging like a pendulum in the spring breeze.

"No, please," John begged as Governor Yeardley approached the place of his execution, but the governor ignored him.

Mary hoped she'd be spared the horror, but Marshal Craddock called out to the soldier who was about to lock her in the shed. "Bring her here. Faraday too."

The soldier turned her around and gave her a gentle shove toward the gate. "Looks like they're not through with you yet, mistress," he said softly.

A crowd had already gathered by the gate, men elbowing each other out of the way, eager to get an unobstructed view of the proceedings. Travesty stood at the edge of the crowd, flanked by several men, her eyes fixed on the noose, her mouth partly open. There was an odd look in her eyes, part satisfaction, part horror at what she'd done. She noticed Mary's hard stare and turned away.

Simon was brought to stand next to Mary. His breathing was shallow, and he looked pale and sick. Mary turned to him, but he wouldn't meet her gaze. In truth, she didn't blame Simon. Had he not accused John of coercing him, he'd have ended up swinging next to him. Mary briefly wondered what would happen to him once he was released from the stocks.

Reverend Edison approached John and invited him to pray. John's lips moved silently as beads of sweat appeared on his brow. He looked terrified, and Mary felt searing pity for him as his eyes darted from Governor Yeardley to Secretary Hunt. John probably still hoped for a reprieve, an eleventh-hour miracle, but it wouldn't come. There wasn't a single sympathetic face in the crowd. Everyone seemed to be waiting with bated breath, excited by the day's entertainment. The noose was pushed over John's neck, and he blanched with fear.

"John Forrester, do you have any last words?" Reverend Edison asked him.

John stared out over the crowd until his gaze alighted on Mary. "I'm sorry, Mary," he muttered. "I'm sorry for what I've brought you to."

Mary nodded. She couldn't speak. Her throat felt swollen shut, and her hands trembled with shock. She wanted to shut her eyes when the marshal gave the order to pull the rope but couldn't look away. A cry of satisfaction went up from the crowd as John's feet left the ground and he kicked his legs as the air to his lungs was cut off. His eyes bulged and a grotesque expression came over his face as he began to slowly suffocate. A stain appeared on the front of his breeches.

"He'll soil himself next," someone said, his voice quivering with excitement. He was right.

Had John had devoted friends, they might have pulled on his legs to break his neck and end his suffering, but no one came near him. His death throes went on for some time, but no one budged. Everyone stood by and watched, their eyes glued to the dying man.

"Serves him right," someone finally said once John's body went limp.

"It's been some time since I've seen someone doing the Deadman's jig," another person said with a snigger. "This one took a while." There was no sympathy in his voice, only satisfaction at having enjoyed a good show.

Mary cried softly as the soldier gripped her arm. "Come," he said.

"Will they cut him down?" Mary asked.

"Not likely. They'll leave him to hang for a while. Always a good deterrent for anyone who's planning on stepping out of line."

"That's barbarous," Mary replied.

"So is buggering a man," the soldier replied with feeling. "He got what was coming to him, and make no mistake." He opened the door of the shed and pushed her inside.

"Wait," Faith cried as she ran toward the shed, a bundle in her arms. "Here. Take this, Mary."

"God bless you, Faith," Mary said as she accepted the food and a blanket. "I won't forget your kindness."

Once she was locked in, Mary wrapped herself in the blanket and sank to the ground. The shed was drafty and dark, the only light coming through the gaps between the boards, which also let in the cold. She fixed her gaze on a whorl in the wood, staring at it until her eyes watered. She simply couldn't bear to think of what had taken place this day, nor could she allow herself to dwell on what would happen to her and her child. If she did, she'd go mad. Mary huddled against the wall, rested her head on her bent knees, and closed her eyes. Eventually, sleep overcame her.

SIXTY-THREE
FEBRUARY 2015

Ramstein-Miesenbach, Germany

Quinn took a sip of tea and settled back in her chair. The dining room was empty except for her and Rhys, who was all packed and ready to go. After breakfast, Quinn would take him to Frankfurt and drop him off at the airport before going to visit Jo. She'd ordered only toast, but Rhys was about to tuck into his gargantuan breakfast. The smell of the sausages made her feel slightly ill.

"You all right?" Rhys asked as he studied her across the table.

"I couldn't get to sleep last night. I kept going over my meeting with Jo, and worrying about today, so I thought spending a bit of time with Mary might help. I was wrong," Quinn said hotly.

"Tell me."

She quickly filled Rhys in on what she'd seen, from the attack on Mary to John's execution. "It was awful, Rhys. It was as if I was right there, watching the breath being choked out of him."

"I'm sorry. I can't imagine what it's like for you to be thrust into these situations. It must all feel frighteningly real."

"It does."

"Well, at least we now know how Mary came to be back in

England," he commented as he lifted a forkful of fluffy egg to his mouth.

"None of this makes any sense," Quinn protested.

"How so?" Rhys was a television producer, not a historian. What he saw was good drama, but Quinn was disturbed by the irregularities that jumped out at her when she considered what she'd seen.

"It's historically accurate that John would have been executed for the crime of sodomy. I'm not questioning that. Simon got off awfully easy with only twelve hours in the stocks, but what puzzles me is the rest of it. The information Joanna Lang forwarded raises questions that I have no answers to."

"Like what?"

"Joanna was able to find a record of John's death. March eleventh, 1621. Dead by hanging. That checks out; however, she also found a deed to his plantation. After John's death, the land passed to Simon Faraday."

"What?" Rhys asked, putting down his fork with undue force.

"Exactly. Mary was John's wife, and she was pregnant, with his heir, presumably. There wasn't a shred of evidence, besides Travesty's self-serving testimony, that Mary had been carrying on an affair or that her child wasn't her husband's. There was also nothing to indicate that she was in any way responsible for the deaths of the men who attacked her. The plantation should have gone to Mary, and in turn, her child. Instead, it had passed on to Simon Faraday within weeks of John's death. Simon still had several years on his indenture contract, which should have reverted to the Virginia Company. Secretary Hunt, who was the representative of the company, would have sold the contract to another colonist. Instead, Simon was not only freed, but rewarded with a thriving plantation."

"You think Simon was up to something? Rhys asked.

"He must have been, because this is clear proof that he had some powerful friends in that colony."

"Like who?" Rhys asked, taking a sip of coffee. "Did Simon ever leave the plantation?"

"I couldn't tell you," Quinn replied. "I can only see what Mary did. What Simon did behind the scenes is a mystery to me. I would assume he wasn't allowed to simply wander off."

"He was John's lover. Perhaps he enjoyed greater freedom than other indentures."

"Perhaps, but where would he go?"

"Into Jamestown."

"To have a glass of port with the governor or a game of dice with the marshal?" Quinn joked.

"Anything is possible. We've learned that from your forays into the past. Besides, Travesty Brown was freed as well," Rhys pointed out.

"I think Travesty negotiated a deal with Hunt in exchange for her testimony, but I don't see how Simon came to benefit so handsomely from the situation. Within a year of taking possession, Simon purchased two African slaves, which means he was doing very well for himself."

"There were slaves in Virginia that early on?" Rhys asked, his interest piqued. This would add an unexpected angle to the episode.

"The first Black slaves were brought to Virginia in 1619. By 1620, there were almost three dozen slaves working the plantations. Given that there were about one thousand colonists who might have wished to purchase a slave, the fact that Simon was able to acquire two would indicate that he had the means and the connections."

"What about the Virginia Company? Did it not go under?"

"It did, but not until 1624. In 1621, the Virginia Company still governed the colony, which made Secretary Hunt as influential as the governor."

"Do you have any theories?" Rhys asked.

"No. All I can say with any certainty is that Mary's banishment was utterly unjust."

Rhys resumed eating, his gaze fixed on the gentle snowflakes falling outside the window as he chewed thoughtfully. "Do you think Mary was murdered?" he finally asked.

"I really couldn't say."

Rhys pushed away his plate and poured himself more coffee from the French press. "Whatever happened to Mary, the end is in sight."

Quinn nodded. She felt terribly sad for Mary and her baby, whose fate appeared to have been sealed the day Walker died. "Yes, I think Mary died mere weeks after Walker and John."

"Do you think Mary would have been happy with Walker had they managed to get away and make a life together?" Rhys asked. "It's an angle I might wish to explore toward the end of the episode. As in, would Romeo and Juliet have actually made it work had they lived long enough to be together?"

Quinn shook her head. "I don't believe so. Virginia was only a year away from the Indian Massacre, which took place in March of 1622. The Powhatan wiped out a quarter of the colonist population. Some of Mary's friends might have died, as well as their children. I can't imagine that Mary wouldn't have been affected by that or wouldn't have felt as if she were living among the enemy."

"But she would no longer have been in Virginia at the time of the massacre," Rhys pointed out.

"No, probably not, and I don't think the Croatoan were part of the Powhatan nation, but I can't imagine she would have felt entirely at home among the natives, no matter how much she loved Walker or how welcoming his tribe was to her. She was an Englishwoman and a Christian, and that's something that would always stand between her and her new life. I think a part of her would always long to be among her own kind."

"Yes, I agree with you. Well, let's try to wrap this up quickly, then," Rhys replied. "Mary's story will make for an excellent season finale. And I have it on good authority that season three has already been approved. What say you, Dr. Allenby?" he asked, smiling at her across the table.

"I say, ask me again in a few weeks."

"Come on, Quinn. I know you have a lot on your plate just now, but this is great news. Isn't it?"

Quinn was about to reply when a wave of nausea drove her from the table. She rushed to the nearest bathroom and made it just in time to avoid being sick all over the floor. She wiped her mouth and leaned against the wall. Her legs felt like jelly and she'd broken out in a cold sweat. Quinn's hand went to her belly. "No," she whispered. "Please, no."

SIXTY-FOUR
MARCH 1621

Virginia Colony

After the first few days, Mary lost track of time. She sat huddled in the corner of the shed, her arms around her knees, her gaze fixed on the opposite wall. It was cold, but she was grateful for the draft as it cleared away some of the foul air inside her prison. She hadn't been provided with a bucket for her personal needs and was forced to use the corner of the shed. Once a day someone brought her food, but it was always the same: a cup of ale, a hunk of bread, and a wedge of cheese. She'd heard raised voices outside on what must have been a Sunday. Betsy had asked to see her but hadn't been granted permission. The soldier who brought her food had been kind enough to pass on Betsy's parcel. She'd brought some sausage, fresh cornbread, and a clean shift.

"Your friend was very persistent," he said as he handed Mary the food. "She also asked me to tell you that Mistress Kirby had a girl and they're both well."

"What did they name the baby?" Mary asked, her lethargy momentarily forgotten.

"How should I know?"

"She's the first baby born in this colony," Mary pointed out. The man shrugged. It made no difference to him.

"Thank you," Mary called after him as he left the shed. He didn't respond.

Mary tore into the sausage, desperate for something other than cheese. She could have easily eaten the whole thing in one sitting but forced herself to eat only about a quarter. She'd make the rest last for several days. Mary set aside the food and the shift. She'd beg the guard for some water to wash with next time he came. It made no sense to put a clean shift on a filthy body.

Mary rested her head on her knees in despair. It could take weeks, or even months, for a ship to be ready to leave for England, and then what? What was she to do once she got back? She had no money, no possessions she could sell, and no one to turn to. She'd have to beg Uncle Swithin for mercy, but knowing his mean-spirited nature, she didn't really expect any. He might take her in, but there'd be a price to pay, and she feared for the future of her child, especially if it displayed signs of being of mixed blood. Perhaps the Morelocks would take her in. They were kind people, but they barely had enough to sustain themselves. She'd thought she might receive at least a small portion of John's assets, if not the plantation, but Secretary Hunt had made it clear that her right to the land was forfeit.

In her solitude, Mary's thoughts sometimes turned to John. She'd thought she might mourn him once the shock of his execution wore off, but the tears never fell. She regretted his death, but deep down, she felt no real sense of loss. John had made his choice and it had become his undoing—unlike Walker, who'd died defending her. Grief for Walker tormented her day and night, her heart squeezing painfully at the thought of never seeing him again or hearing his beloved voice. How unfair life was, how cruel. Their future had been snatched away from them, and snatched away from their baby. Never would it have a loving family or know the security and peace of life in Walker's native village. Their baby would be born fatherless, sentenced to a life of penury, bound to a mother who was disinherited and disgraced.

Mary closed her hand around the bone comb, making sure it was still there. She'd come to this land with nothing but this comb, and she'd leave it the same way. She'd survive. She had to, for her baby. Mary's head snapped up when the door of the shed opened. It wasn't time to eat, so maybe someone had come to see her. She was surprised to see Dr. Paulson. He gasped and covered his nose and mouth with his hand as the overwhelming stench hit him. He stepped back out of the shed but didn't leave.

"Come with me, Mistress Forrester," he said.

Mary got to her feet. She felt shaky and confused after days of being in near darkness, but the doctor took her by the arm and led her across the way to his surgery. He invited Mary to sit at the table and offered her a cup of ale and a bowl of fresh, hot stew. Mary tried to eat slowly, but the delicious food weakened her resolve. She hadn't realized how hungry she was. Dr. Paulson was about to sit across from her but wrinkled his nose and moved to stand by the window instead.

"Am I to go back to the shed?" Mary asked once she finished eating. "May I wash before I go?"

The doctor smiled at her benignly. "Mary, I've had a word with the governor on your behalf. I see no reason you should remain locked up until such time as you can leave the colony. I am sure there's nothing you could have done to sway your husband from his chosen course, and the accusations against you are insubstantial at best, made by a person who had much to gain from being believed. I've asked the governor to allow you to bide with me. I have a spare cot, and you can make yourself useful by looking after my needs. I've been relying on Mistress Marsh, but she has her hands full these days, what with her husband ill."

"Thank you, Dr. Paulson. That's very kind of you."

"I will be leaving the colony with you, as it happens," Dr. Paulson said.

"Will you? Why is that, sir?"

"I am to be married in the summer, and I don't think my wife will care to live here permanently. I told her I'd give it six months and see how things stand, but truthfully, I think we'll both be happier in England. A new physician will be coming out to replace me."

"I see," Mary said. "Where will you settle with your wife?"

"I'm originally from Dorset, so that's where we'll make our home."

Mary pushed away the empty bowl and got to her feet. "I'll begin right away, sir."

Dr. Paulson shook his head. "There's no need. Mistress Bass has started her pains, so I'll be gone for several hours at least. With no competent midwife to attend the births, I'm afraid it falls to me to assist these poor women. Take the time to see to your own needs."

"Thank you, sir. Did you attend on Nell Kirby?"

"I did, indeed. Your friend Betsy was there as well. Mistress Kirby had a fine, healthy girl. Adelaide is the name. Both Nell and Betsy had asked after you and begged me to speak on your behalf. They're good friends to you, Mary."

"I know," Mary replied tearfully. "I wish I could see them one last time."

"I'll ask them to come by and see you after church on Sunday," the doctor promised. "Now, I'll be off."

Mary sprang to her feet as soon as the door closed behind Dr. Paulson. She poured some water into a basin, stripped off her filthy clothes, and unbraided her hair. The water was cold, and the soap was coarse, but she didn't care. To have a full belly and be clean again were the extent of her desires at the moment. Dr. Paulson's kindness brought tears to her eyes, more so because Walker had admired him. She sighed and wiped away the tears with the back of her hand. All she could do at this stage was take life one day at a time, and today was a good day.

Ramstein-Miesenbach, Germany

Quinn strolled down the sunlit corridor toward Jo's room. This was her third visit to the hospital, but already the place felt familiar. She nodded to the nurses she'd met on previous visits and returned Dr. Stein's wave as the doctor disappeared into another patient's room.

Quinn knocked softly on the doorjamb and entered the room. Jo was sitting up in bed, her hair brushed and woven into a braid that snaked over her left shoulder. She wasn't wearing any makeup, but there was color in her cheeks and her gaze was alert and full of anticipation. Her face broke into a radiant smile when she spotted Quinn.

"I've been waiting for you," she said.

"I brought you some chocolate," Quinn said, her voice conspiratorially low.

"Bless you. I'm sick to death of hospital food, and with Rhys gone, there's no one to bring me treats." Jo accepted the small box of chocolate and tore off the plastic. She held out the box to Quinn, but when Quinn refused, she popped a piece into her mouth and rolled her eyes in ecstasy. "I love chocolate," she said through a full mouth.

"Me too," Quinn confessed. "All right, give me one."

Quinn bit into a piece of chocolate and studied Jo while she enjoyed her treat. Jo was as happy as a kid on Christmas morning, but Quinn was about to bring her a bag of coal. So far, they'd spent several hours together, talking, laughing, and trading anecdotes, but neither one had touched on the weightier issues, instinctively avoiding topics that would spoil their long-awaited reunion. But the unanswered questions pushed into the room like two-thousand-pound elephants, making it more and more difficult to pretend they weren't there. They couldn't keep from delving into the past forever, and Quinn wanted to have a private conversation with Jo before Seth arrived that afternoon.

Quinn swallowed her chocolate, which suddenly tasted bitter, and faced her sister. "Jo, I've no wish to upset you, but there are things I'd like to ask you, and I feel this might be my last chance to speak to you privately."

Jo didn't immediately respond but replaced the lid on the box of chocolates and set it on her bedside table. Quinn waited patiently, but Jo avoided her gaze, turning her face toward the window instead.

"Jo, there are things I learned while searching for you," Quinn tried again.

Jo finally faced Quinn. The look in her eyes could only be described as haunted. "I know. You've been very patient with me. I would have blurted out what was on my mind right away; diplomacy has never been my strong suit. You can ask me anything, and I will answer. You've been so open with me about your own life."

Not really, thought Quinn. *Not yet*. But this wasn't the time to interrogate Jo about her psychic abilities, if she possessed any. First things first. "Jo, why did you go to such lengths to disappear?"

Jo's eyes widened in surprise. "I wasn't trying to disappear. Quite the opposite, in fact."

"So why did you change your name and cut ties with your family?"

A look of deep sadness filled Jo's eyes, but she didn't flinch away from the question. She smiled ruefully as her fingers pleated the crisp white duvet cover. "My childhood wasn't as happy as yours, Quinn. My father was an impulsive man, a selfish man. He made decisions that affected others without a moment's hesitation or consideration for how they might feel. He decided to adopt me and made a statement to the press without ever consulting his wife, a callous move she never quite forgave him for. You see, everyone thought he was the soul of kindness and compassion, but in truth, he was vain and self-aggrandizing. As soon as the adoption went through, he lost interest in me because the newspapers lost interest in the story."

"How do you know?" Quinn asked.

"Oh, my mother accused him of neglect often enough. My brother and sister plugged their ears with headphones, but I always listened in on their arguments. I thought I might learn something about my birth parents, but it turned out they didn't know any more than I did."

"What about your mother? What was she like?" Quinn asked, hoping Jo had at least one loving parent.

"My mother was a kind woman and did her best for me, but she hadn't wanted another child, especially not an infant. Karen and Michael were in their late teens by the time I came along, and she was looking forward to having a bit of freedom to finally pursue her own interests. My father dumped me in her lap and went on with his life as if nothing had changed. I spent a large portion of my childhood with nannies. Some of them were very kind, but I wasn't their daughter. I wasn't theirs to love."

"That sounds lonely," Quinn said, recalling her own family. It was small, but they'd been very close, and her parents' lives revolved around her. And there were relatives and friends, and especially Jill, who was her honorary sister.

"It was. I spent a lot of time reading, which is when I developed a love for history. I liked all those romantic stories of maidens in distress and strong, handsome men coming to the rescue, but as I got older, I became obsessed with World War Two. I hero-worshipped Alan Turing. To my mind, he singlehandedly won the war with his Enigma machine. And what a wonderful thank-you he got from our esteemed government. Prison or chemical castration—those were his choices," Jo added bitterly.

"But why change your name?"

"My father was a big fan of honesty. He felt it would be a disservice to me to withhold the truth of my origins, so I knew from the earliest age that my mother had abandoned me, left me struggling for breath in a hospital chair and walked away without a backward glance, leaving me with nothing but a name scribbled on a scrap of paper. I wanted no part of her. I didn't want that woman's one choice pertaining to my future to define who I was. Quentin sounded so pompous, so cumbersome, and impossible to shorten. Some of my friends tried calling me 'Q,' but I hated that. I wanted a name that was airy and light, and fun. I couldn't imagine some stodgy, humorless woman being called Jo. Jo was the name of a hippy, a world traveler, a woman who got to pick and choose rather than wait to be noticed. I wanted to be that woman."

"And you are," Quinn said, smiling.

Jo shook her head. "Not really. I'm still the same person, only I have a different name."

Quinn reached for Jo's hand and they sat in silence for a moment, each one focused on her own thoughts until Quinn finally spoke. "There's more, isn't there?"

Jo nodded. "Yes, there's more." She exhaled deeply. "When I was sixteen, Michael moved back home. He was going through an ugly divorce and needed a place to stay for a while. His wife left him for a friend of his and he was devastated. I felt sorry for him, and for the first time in my life I felt like I had a real sibling. We began spending time together. We went walking in the park, and out for pizza and a film. We went bike riding, and he took me to the hospital to show me where he worked. It was nice. I felt close to him and hoped that in time I might build a relationship with Karen as well. Karen had never been unkind to me; she simply took no notice of me. I wasn't a part of her reality. She was older and had her own life, and even if I'd been her actual sister, I think she might have treated me much the same. But she was close to Michael and even thanked me for trying to help him through a difficult time."

"So, what happened?" Quinn asked, a sinking feeling in the pit of her stomach.

"One night, several weeks after Michael moved back, we were alone at home. Our parents went to some charity function. We had dinner and watched a film, and then I went to my room. I thought Michael had gone to bed, but then I heard him on the phone. He and his wife, Kayla, were having a massive row. He was shouting at her and I thought I heard him crying. Eventually, I fell asleep." Quinn nodded. She could see where this was going, and her heart broke for Jo.

"Michael got stinking drunk. I woke up to find him in my room. He was a mess, blathering about Kayla and whimpering like a child. He said she'd emasculated him. I didn't know what that meant. He said he needed a hug, so I gave him one. He held on to me, refused to let me go. He started kissing and touching me. I tried to push him away, begged him to stop, but he wouldn't. He was too far gone."

"Did he...?"

Jo nodded. "I locked myself in the bathroom and told my parents what happened as soon as they got home. I expected them to comfort me, to take control of the situation, but instead, their first instinct was to protect Michael. If word got out, his life would be ruined. He could be struck off the medical board and even go to prison. My mother tried to calm me down, but my father began making accusations. He said I'd sent Michael the wrong signals, led him on. Michael was thirty-four and I was sixteen, and somehow this was my fault. He ordered me to go to my room."

Jo sighed and turned to gaze out the window, where a gentle snow was falling from a nearly white sky. "By morning, Michael was gone. My father booked him into a hotel and told him to lie low. When Karen came home a few days later, she called me names and said I'd tried to ruin her brother's life. I'd have left then, but my mother revealed she'd been diagnosed with breast cancer and begged me to stay." Jo turned back and faced Quinn.

"By the time I graduated, Mum had died, and there was nothing to keep me from leaving. I moved in with my boyfriend Jesse. He was a photographer. He taught me everything he knew, and I found myself falling in love with photography. It became a passion."

"And Jesse?"

"Jesse asked me to marry him," Jo said softly. "Perhaps I should have. He really loved me and would have probably made me happy, but I wasn't ready to make a lifelong commitment. I was too young. So, I took off and went to Paris. I had a grand time there, and for the first time in my life I felt truly comfortable in my own skin. I was no longer Quentin Crawford, unwanted brat. I was a new person, one I could be proud of. When I returned to England, I legally changed my name, since I wanted nothing more to do with the Crawford family. My father set up a trust fund for me through his solicitor, but I've never touched it. I wanted to make my own way in the world, and I have."

"I'm sorry, Jo. It must have been awful for you. Did you ever see Michael again? Has he even tried to make amends?"

"He tried to reach out to me while I still lived at home, but I refused to speak to him. What could he say that would make me hate him less? He was upset? He was drunk? He didn't know what he was doing? He knew. He heard me begging him to stop, telling him I was still a virgin. He saw me crying. He wiped the blood off his cock after he was done with me. He committed a crime for which he should have been prosecuted, but he had parents who loved him enough to sacrifice me for the good of his future. They made a choice that night, all of them."

Quinn moved closer and wrapped Jo in a fierce hug. All her life she'd felt incomplete because she was adopted. There'd been a hole in her sense of self, a giant question mark. It was only now that she understood how lucky she'd been, how blessed. Her parents loved her fiercely and would have protected her no matter what. Her father would have torn any man who tried to hurt her limb from limb, even if that man was his own son. She had been cared for and adored, while her sister had spent her childhood in a gilded cage, surrounded by luxury, but never truly loved. Quinn was suddenly glad she'd never met Michael Crawford. She never wanted to see his face or hear his name mentioned again.

"Jo, is there no one waiting for you back home? Friends, a boyfriend? Surely, someone must be missing you."

Jo shook her head. "I've spent the past decade traveling, focusing on my work. I've had encounters, but not relationships," Jo confessed. "It wasn't until I got your letter that I realized how lonely I was."

"So, what now?" Quinn asked. At present, they were isolated in their little cocoon, but soon enough real life would intrude on their idyll. They would return to London and resume their lives. What would their future be? Would Jo cling to her once she was back on her feet, or would she hide behind her career and keep Quinn at arm's length?

Jo seemed to misunderstand the question. "I will take on a new assignment once I'm well enough to travel," she replied. "Maybe a local one to start with, but those rarely interest me as much as the foreign ones. I'll probably return to the Middle East, or Africa."

"Jo, what were you doing in those mountains? Didn't you realize how dangerous that was?" Quinn exclaimed, stunned by Jo's cavalier attitude.

"I did, but I thought I'd be all right with Ali. He knew those mountains like the back of his hand."

"Were you looking for a Taliban hideout?"

"I was looking for the opium farms. I wanted the world to see where the heroin comes from. Those drug lords supply death, and they are a lot more dangerous than the Taliban. With them, it's not about religion or politics; it's all about profit, and they don't care who ingests their product, be it an adult or a child. Their only religion is profit."

"You could have died," Quinn admonished her.

"I'm glad I didn't, and I'm relieved to know Ali survived the explosion. I will make sure his family is looked after," Jo promised.

Quinn was about to ask something else when she heard a familiar voice from somewhere down the corridor. She grinned. "I think you have a visitor, sis."

A moment later, Seth stepped into the room, a huge bouquet of flowers in his hand. He was smiling, but his posture was tense, and his dark eyes were wide with anxiety. "May I come in?" he asked softly.

"Yes," Jo whispered. She was drinking him in, her eyes aglow with wonder as she took in the golden tan, the short dark hair, and the gleaming smile.

Seth set the bouquet on a chair and came closer. "Would it be all right to give you a hug?" he asked.

Jo nodded. Her eyes shimmered with tears and she opened her arms and welcomed Seth into them as she buried her face in his chest. "Dad," she whispered.

Seth held her tight and kissed the top of her head. "Jo, my baby, this is such a happy day," he said. "I didn't think it was possible to be happier than when I met your sister, but this is—"

"I'm so glad you're here."

Jo finally let go of Seth and he turned his attention to Quinn. "And how is my other little girl?" He caught Quinn in a bear hug. "I'm so happy to see you. Both of you. I feel like the luckiest man in the world."

Quinn's phone vibrated in her pocket as Seth let her go. "Here, take my chair. I'll give you two a few minutes to get acquainted. I think Gabe is trying to reach me."

Quinn went out into the corridor and found a quiet place to sit. She felt emotionally drained and physically unwell. Her head ached, and there was that persistent cramping in her lower belly. She felt queasy and tired, despite the early hour. Quinn pulled out her mobile and checked her missed calls. The call had been from Logan. She stared at the screen, reluctant to ring him back. Logan wouldn't be calling her just to check in. He was calling with news. Quinn braced herself and pressed the call back icon. Logan answered right away.

"How are you, Quinn?"

"I'm all right. I'm with Jo, and Seth just arrived. How are things on your end?"

"Not bad. Not bad at all," Logan replied happily.

Quinn exhaled the breath she hadn't realized she'd been holding. "Tell me."

"Jude woke up during the night. He feels weak and a little confused, but the prognosis is good. He's been diagnosed with diffuse cerebral hypoxia."

"In English, please," Quinn said. The name sounded ominous, but Logan didn't seem upset, so it couldn't be too bad.

"Basically, it's a minor impairment of the brain due to the lack of oxygen Jude suffered. It could have been so much worse, Quinn."

"What will this mean for Jude long term?"

"Hopefully, nothing. Worst case scenario, he'll need some rehabilitation therapy. He's fully aware of everything that's going on, and his motor skills appear to be intact. It will take him several weeks to get back to some sort of normalcy, but the worst is behind him."

"Thank God," Quinn breathed. "Sylvia must be relieved."

"She is. I sent her home to get some rest."

"Are you alone?"

"Colin is with me. He sends his regards. Wants to know if you got his email."

"I did. Thank you," Quinn replied, smiling. Colin could never put work aside, much like herself. "Tell him I'll ring him later today. I've been a little preoccupied."

"Colin says there's no rush," Logan replied. "Whenever you're ready."

"Logan, give Jude my love, and tell him I'll see him very soon."

"When are you coming back?" Logan asked.

"In a couple of days, I think. Jo is not ready to be released, but Seth is here now, and I need to get back. I miss my family."

"And they miss you. Gabe is feeling so forlorn, he even called me," Logan joked. "Have you told Jo about Jude and me?"

"Of course, I have. She can't wait to meet you."

"What about Mum? Will she meet her?" Logan asked carefully.

"That's up to Jo."

"I understand. One day at a time, eh?"

"With this family, that's the only way to go," Quinn replied, chuckling. "I'll see you soon."

She finished the call and stowed her phone away. She was about to return to Jo's room when she saw Dr. Stein walking down the corridor. She didn't seem harried, for once.

"Dr. Allenby, good morning," Dr. Stein called.

"Good morning. Dr. Stein, I was wondering when Jo might be released."

Dr. Stein looked thoughtful for a moment. "If we were in London, I'd release her in a few days, but given that she must travel home, I don't feel she is ready. I wouldn't feel comfortable with her getting on a plane so soon after brain surgery. The changes in cabin air pressure could result in a brain bleed, to put it simply."

"What if we were to drive?"

"What, to London?"

"Our dad's arrived. He and I can take turns at the wheel. I know Jo wants to go home, and truthfully, I can't stay much longer. I have a baby I need to get back to."

Dr. Stein nodded. "As long as Jo gets plenty of rest on the drive, I don't see a problem. I wouldn't recommend driving straight through though. That would be too much for her to handle."

"Let me discuss it with my father, and I'll get back to you."

"Sounds like a plan," Dr. Stein replied. "I was actually on my way to see Jo."

"Eh, Dr. Stein. May I ask you for a favor?" Quinn said. She felt embarrassed to ask, but simply couldn't put this off any longer.

"Of course. How can I help?"

"I think I might be pregnant," Quinn blurted out. "And I need to know for sure."

A knowing smile tugged at Dr. Stein's lips. "Don't worry, I know the feeling. When you realize you might be pregnant, you can't wait another minute to find out. I'll ask one of the nurses to get you a pregnancy test. I can refer you to an obstetrician here at the hospital, if you wish, or you can wait until you get home and can see your own doctor."

"Thank you. I'll take you up on that."

Less than five minutes later, Quinn found herself tensely watching the plastic stick. She went to the public restroom instead of using the one in Jo's room. For this, she needed privacy, and a few moments to recover, whatever the result. Quinn leaned against the wall of the stall and willed the test to work faster. She couldn't take the uncertainty any longer. She held her breath as the symbol in the little screen began to materialize. It was too soon to tell what it was, but in about a minute she'd know if her life was about to change once again.

A pink minus filled the tiny window, and Quinn breathed a sigh of intense relief. Not pregnant. Perhaps her symptoms were caused by all the stress she'd been experiencing the past few weeks and weaning Alex off breastmilk. Silent tears slid down her cheeks. She hadn't realized just how frightened she'd been it would be positive. She wanted to have another baby, sooner rather than later, but not in seven months' time. Alex and Emma needed her full attention, and she and Gabe were still figuring out how to maintain the delicate balance between being parents and partners. Neither of them was ready for another high-risk pregnancy or a difficult post-natal period.

Quinn threw the test away, washed her hands and face, and let herself out of the bathroom. Now that she could think more clearly, she had a road trip to plan.

<h1 style="text-align:center">SIXTY-SIX</h1>
MARCH 1620

Virginia Colony

Mary rose laboriously from her pallet, got dressed, and reached for her comb. She wound her braid around several times and pinned it into place before covering her hair with a cap. It was time to get breakfast going. She stretched her aching back and tiptoed toward the hearth, mindful of waking Dr. Paulson. The room was almost completely dark, and Mary banged her knee on a bench on her way to the hearth. She stifled a cry and hobbled over to the shelf where the tinder and flint box were kept. It took a while to get the fire going, but once it took hold, Mary stood before the hearth for a few moments, warming herself. The weather was pleasant during the day, but the nights were still cold, and the glazed windows of the doctor's surgery were covered with a thin layer of frost. Mary added a bit of water to the congealed porridge left over from the day before and set it over the flames to warm. Having done that, she threw a shawl over her shoulders and let herself out of the house. She needed to use the privy desperately.

By the time she returned, Dr. Paulson was already up and dressed. He sat at the table, looking morosely into the flames. "I heard you weeping last night," he said without any preamble.

"I'm sorry if I disturbed your rest, sir," Mary replied.

"It is I who am sorry. You have every right to weep for your husband."

"I weep for the man I loved," Mary corrected him.

Dr. Paulson nodded, taking her meaning. He never asked any questions or passed judgement on her. He was a kind man, one who understood the complexities of the human heart. Had it not been for him, she'd still be in that stinking shed, freezing, and starving half to death, but no amount of kindness could heal her heart. She grew more and more despondent as the days went by. She tried to hide her grief from the doctor, but when night came and she was alone in her dark corner, memories of Walker flooded her mind and she stuffed her fist into her mouth to stifle her crying. She felt the loss of him keenly, and the pain of his death gnawed at her insides every day.

She went out to fetch the water, did the laundry outside, and peeked out the window a hundred times a day in the hope of spotting visiting Indians. If she saw Walker's companions, she'd go up to them and ask outright what had become of Walker's remains. She needed to know that he was at peace and not rotting somewhere in the woods, his body devoured by animals, his bones sinking into the softening earth. But no one came. The incident had fanned the flames of resentment between the natives and the colonists, and trade seemed to have virtually come to a halt until goodwill could be restored.

"We are to leave shortly," Dr. Paulson announced as he spooned porridge into his mouth.

"Are we?"

"A ship was spotted on the horizon yesterday. It might be with us as soon as today."

"Will it?" Mary whispered. She'd known this day would come, but now that it was upon them, she was completely unprepared. She rested her hand on her stomach. It had grown bigger over the past few weeks, and the baby was more active, cavorting inside her day and night and making her belly heave like a restless sea. Mary was frightened of the coming birth, but she looked forward to meeting her child. She would no longer be alone. They would be each other's family, each other's support. She would do anything to give her baby a good life, even if it meant sacrificing her own happiness and well-being. She tried not to envision what her life might have been like had she left with Walker when he'd first asked.

Oh, Walker, what a fool I was not to go with you, Mary thought. *I'd give anything in the world to hear your voice again and feel your arms around me. Please, come to me, if only in my dreams*, she begged silently. *Let me see your face one more time.*

By the following day, the new arrivals had begun to trickle in—tired, bedraggled women who looked grateful to be on solid ground again and terrified of what awaited them in this colonial paradise, as Mary and her companions had been when they arrived nearly a year ago. John's body had been cut down and buried. After all, it wouldn't do to greet newcomers with a rotting corpse.

Exited bridegrooms had already gathered at the church, eager to meet their future wives. Mary could see Dr. Paulson through the window, conversing with a finely dressed middle-aged gentleman who must be the new physician, come to take his place. Soon, crates and sacks would get carried up to the settlement: tools, supplies, and letters from home, eagerly received and much discussed.

Mary turned away from the window and sat down on the bench. If only she could talk to someone besides the doctor, but she had been banned from church and wasn't permitted to walk outside. She hoped Nell and Betsy might come to see her, but the marshal had forbidden them to visit and she doubted he'd changed his mind.

Mary sat at the table and rested her head on her folded arms as silent tears flowed. She felt so frightened and alone now that she was truly on the verge of the unknown. A kick from within startled her out of her misery. Then another. It was as if the baby were telling her that she wasn't alone. It was there, just waiting to be born. Mary used the back of her hand to wipe her tears and sat up. "I'm sorry," she said to her belly. "I will be stronger. I promise."

She pushed her despair aside and got started on her afternoon chores. The new physician would stay with Dr. Paulson until his departure, so she had to make sure there was enough stew to go around. She added a few more sliced root vegetables to the pot and pushed a baking dish filled with cornbread dough into the ashes at the side of the hearth. Having seen to dinner, she prepared fresh linens to make up a bed for the new doctor, dusted the vials and jars containing various roots and potions, and then went to fetch some water. The new man would be wanting a bath after his long sea voyage.

Mary tried not to look toward the dock as she fetched the water, but her eyes had a mind of their own. She set the bucket on the ground and stared off into the distance. All she could see over the curtain wall and the treetops were the tall masts of the newly arrived ship, the middle mast flying a British flag. By this time next week, the ship might be ready to return to England, taking her away from these shores forever.

SIXTY-SEVEN

The day was heartbreakingly beautiful. A gentle sun shone from a benevolent sky and a gentle breeze brought the smell of spring, of things growing and bursting into life. Mary stood on deck, her cloak wrapped around her shoulders. The hustle and bustle of loading the vessel and preparing for departure had been replaced by crisp commands from the captain as the ship glided away from the dock. It would cruise along the James River before heading out into the Atlantic Ocean and sailing to England.

Mary stared toward Jamestown, an oppressive heaviness in her chest. She no longer belonged to this place, but England felt as distant and foreign to her as the shores of Africa. The future seemed utterly bleak, and even the baby in her belly seemed to be affected by her mood. It had remained quiet and still since Mary boarded the ship. Maybe the rolling of the deck beneath her feet had put the child to sleep. Mary rested her hand on her belly, wishing the babe would wake up. She felt unbearably alone, and even the slightest movement would remind her that life still had something to offer and this wasn't the end.

The ship moved slowly down the center of the river. Through the still-bare trees, Mary caught glimpses of brown fields and wooden cabins, blue-gray smoke curling from their chimneys into the cloudless sky. After a time, the plantations gave way to unsettled wilderness. The woods became dense and impenetrable, the only signs of life the squawking birds that perched high in the branches. Mary leaned on the rail and peered into the trees when she spotted movement on the shore. A man hobbled out of the woods and stopped to watch the passing ship, his hand pressed to his side, as if he were in pain. He wore buckskin breeches and a shirt, his feet in moccasins. His dark-brown hair rippled in the breeze, and the beads he wore around his neck were blue and red.

Their eyes met, and Mary let out an involuntary cry. Walker looked pale and thin, and lines of pain were carved into his hollow cheeks, but his eyes were just the same, the eyes that loved her. His gaze was full of despair and disbelief when he realized that Mary was lost to him forever. Walker raised a hand in farewell, then laid it over his heart, his gaze never leaving her face.

Mary was too far away to see clearly, but she thought he was weeping, and tears of bitterness and unbearable hurt spilled down her cheeks as she looked upon his beloved face for the last time. His people had saved him and brought him back from the brink of death. He still loved her. He would have come for her. They could have been a family. But now it was too late. They would never meet again, of that she was certain. Even if someday she managed to find her way back to Virginia, he could be long gone, returned to his own tribe and wed to a woman who was glad to walk along his divided path.

Mary stared at the shore until Walker faded from view, the place where he stood becoming a smudge on the horizon. Mary cried out as something soft rubbed against her legs and bent down to pick up a cat. It was smoky gray with a white patch on its throat, and she held it to her bosom, grateful for another living thing to share her sorrow with.

SIXTY-EIGHT
FEBRUARY 2015

Near the French Border

A shimmering purple dusk descended over the snowbound landscape, the windows of picturesque cottages set back from the road glowing warmly in the gathering darkness. There were few motorists on the road and the car chewed up the miles as it sped toward England. Seth had taken one look at the tiny yellow Fit and pronounced it unfit (no pun intended, he'd assured the women) for the drive to England. He'd rented a BMW SUV that was roomy and comfortable.

Jo, who sat in front next to Seth, had been animated for the first few hours of the journey, but now her head rested against the reclined seat, her eyes closed in deep sleep. She was bundled up in warm clothes and wore a dark-blue knitted hat, which had accentuated her extreme pallor when they stepped out of the hospital into the blinding brightness of the snowy morning. Quinn had been pleased to notice that a little color had crept into her cheeks after they'd stopped at a rest area to get some tea and use the restroom. Jo had asked to spend a few minutes outside, enjoying the sun on her face as she leaned against the car. She hadn't been outdoors since the day she got hurt, and the fresh air was doing her good.

She'd picked up a handful of snow and made a snowball, weighting it in her hand as if she were planning to hurl it at someone. Instead, she'd pressed it to her lips and grinned like a mischievous child when it began to melt.

"Would you like me to take a turn?" Quinn asked Seth. "You must be tired."

"Give me another half hour and then you can take over. I don't like driving in the dark. My eyesight's not what it used to be," Seth replied.

"I think we should stop for the night around seven. Jo needs rest and a decent meal. She barely ate anything when we stopped for lunch."

"I won't say no to a decent meal myself. I hate fast food," Seth agreed.

Quinn smiled. Seth loved good food and all manner of comforts. He wasn't a man who enjoyed "slumming it," as he put it.

"Want a Coke?" Seth asked. "There's one left."

"No, I'm all right. You have it."

Seth opened the can and took a long swallow. "I know soda's bad for you, but I just can't resist. There's nothing like a cold Coke when you're thirsty and tired. I'm not much used to driving on icy roads." His profile was tense as he gripped the wheel, wary of hitting an invisible patch of black ice.

"Quinn, there's something I want to talk to you about," Seth said. His voice was low so as not to disturb Jo, but Quinn could hear the sudden intensity in his tone. Whatever he wanted to tell her was important.

"What is it, Dad?"

"Kathy and I hired a crack-shot criminal attorney. She's going to file an appeal for Brett. There are certain issues in the case that bear scrutiny."

"Brett locked me in a vault and left me to die. Is that one of the issues you hope she'll scrutinize?" Quinn asked, angry despite herself.

"What Brett did is unforgivable, but he's very young, Quinn. I won't allow him to spend the best years of his life in prison. I'm his dad. I have to do everything in my power to help him."

"So, you hope to get him off on a technicality?" Quinn asked bitterly.

"In a nutshell, yes."

"And what technicality would that be?"

"I beat a confession out of him. Ms. Jackson says it should never have stood up in court."

Quinn felt a cold rage at the thought of her half-brother walking free after serving only a few months of his sentence but said nothing. She could sense Seth's nervousness. He'd been keeping this from her for a while. "You must do what you feel is right."

"Would you abandon Alex?" Seth asked.

Quinn was about to reply but paused. Would she? Alex was only five months old, so it was difficult to imagine him as an adult, especially one with criminal tendencies, but Seth's question was legitimate. She loved both Alex and Emma with her whole being, and the thought of turning her back on them in their hour of need went against the grain. Would she be able to still love a child who'd tried to kill someone, in this case a pregnant woman and a half-sister? Would she be able to forgive Alex if he'd tried to kill Emma? No, she wouldn't forgive him, but she would not abandon him either. Seth was right—Brett was still young. He was only nineteen. There was still a chance for him to turn his life around. He wasn't a hardened criminal, just a foolish young man who'd allowed his prejudices and fears to rule his head.

They'd shared a bond and had been on the verge of establishing a solid relationship when he'd turned on her. What would have happened had Quinn never told him the truth and threatened to expose their shared history on her television program? What if Brett had never discovered they were descended from a Trinidadian slave? His prejudice and fear had driven him over the edge, but was she partly to blame for what happened? Would Brett be here right now, come to meet his other sister, if Quinn had never stumbled on the truth about Madeline?

Quinn sighed. The situation wasn't as black and white (*no pun intended*, Quinn thought with a smirk) as she liked to believe, and Seth could hardly disown his son, the only child he'd known since birth and raised in a way he'd hoped had been right. What would her grandmother Rae advise her now if she were still alive? Quinn had met the old woman only twice, but Rae had left an impression on her, and she wished she'd had an opportunity to get to know her paternal grandmother better.

"Seth, are you asking for my permission to appeal the case?" Quinn asked at last.

"No, but I am asking for your understanding. I love you, Quinn, and I would give my life to keep you and yours safe, but Brett is my son—my teenage son. He deserves another chance, and I will do everything in my power to give it to him. I would like to know that I have your blessing to try."

"I'm not sure I can give you my blessing, but I do understand where you're coming from, as a parent. I would do the same for one of my children. I won't hold it against you, Seth, but I don't think I can be in the same room with Brett ever again."

"I would never ask that of you, but he is sorry, Quinn. He truly is. Have you read the letter he sent you?"

Quinn shook her head. "I couldn't bring myself to."

"Read it. Please."

"Seth, no amount of remorse can undo what Brett's done. Another few hours in that vault, and I would have miscarried Alex. I might have survived, but I would have lost my baby. I'm sure Brett believes he had good reason to do what he did. I realize that having grown up in the South, his prejudices run deep, and his fears were legitimate in his mind, but I simply cannot offer him forgiveness. I'm not that generous of spirit."

"I understand, and I thank you for not forcing me to choose between my children," Seth replied.

"We've all spent enough time apart, I think. This is our chance to rebuild, to heal. Jo needs you, and I need you. And so does Brett. If you can help him, then you mustn't pass up the chance."

"Thanks." Seth reached back between the seats and squeezed Quinn's hand. "I love you, kiddo. And I'm so grateful you brought us all together. I never imagined being so blessed with children, and grandchildren. I'm a lucky man, in more ways than one."

"You and Kathy are all right, then?" Quinn asked. Seth and Kathy had been divorced when Quinn first met them, but Brett's incarceration had brought them together in their shared pain, and they seemed to have recaptured something they'd lost all those years ago.

"I'm going to ask her to marry me again," Seth said, smiling into the darkness. "I was a fool to let her go, a stupid, arrogant fool. Kathy is the best part of me, and regardless of what happens with Brett, we belong together. We are a unit, and always were, even when we were apart."

"I'm happy for you, Seth. Kathy is a wonderful woman. I couldn't ask for a better step-mum."

"Funny how things turn out, isn't it?" Seth said as he peeked at Jo, who was dead to the world. "A year ago, I had no idea I had a daughter, and now I have two." Seth met Quinn's gaze in the rearview mirror. "Quinn, will you be putting your London apartment on the market once you move?"

"Yes, that's the plan."

"I'd like to buy it," Seth announced.

"What?"

"I'd like to buy your apartment. I want to be a part of your lives, and I can't do that from New Orleans. I need a base in London, and the apartment is perfect. It's large enough for Kathy and me, and it has a spare bedroom should one of our lovely grand-children wish to have a sleepover," Seth replied, grinning. "What do you think?"

"I think that's a great idea. I'd love it if you were closer."

"Well, I wouldn't be closer all the time. I still have a business to run, and I'm nowhere near retirement age, but I would like to have a permanent address in London. A foothold, I should say," he amended.

"I'll tell Gabe. He'll be pleased. Now, pull over and let me drive. You're tired, and I'm feeling useless."

"All right," Seth conceded. "We wouldn't want you to feel useless."

SIXTY-NINE
MAY 1621

Aboard the *Constance*

Mary lay back on the hard berth and closed her eyes. The ship seemed to be rolling beneath her, and her stomach was rolling right along with it. She thought she was going to be sick again, but there was nothing left for her to vomit into the bucket that was her constant companion. She'd expelled everything she'd eaten, and then some. Her face was hot to the touch, blood pounded in her veins, and her heart thudded in her chest. She gulped air like a landed fish, but only a small portion of it seemed to reach her lungs.

The sickness had set in shortly after they left Virginia and had grown worse over the past few weeks, making Mary's life aboard a living hell. She'd lost weight, and her normally wholesome shape had been reduced to her round belly and stick-like arms and legs that ended in grotesquely swollen ankles and feet. Her only respite was sleep, which thankfully came easily enough. Dr. Paulson had been kind enough to give up his berth after seeing Mary struggle to get into her hammock. He now slept in the hammock, and swore he preferred it as the motion lulled him to sleep.

"Mary, can you hear me?" Dr. Paulson asked as he reached for her wrist. He held it between two fingers, checking her pulse. He did this several times a day and his face grew grave as his suspicions were confirmed again and again.

"Yes," Mary muttered.

"Mary, I'm going to have to bleed you again."

"No, please," Mary whimpered. She felt so listless she could barely lift her head off the pillow.

"If I don't do something to relieve the pressure, you'll suffer an apoplexy."

"Doctor, please. I feel so weak."

Dr. Paulson nodded. He'd attended her day and night, and he looked weary and frustrated with his inability to help. He put a cool palm on her forehead. "You rest now. I'll have Collins bring you some broth. Let's see how you feel toward the evening, shall we?"

"The baby," Mary mumbled.

"The baby does not seem to be affected by your illness."

"I don't want to lose the baby," Mary pleaded.

"It's you I'm worried about," Dr. Paulson replied kindly. "I only wish to help you."

"I know and I'm grateful," Mary said. Her voice faded out as her eyes closed of their own accord. She felt as if she were falling, spinning in slow motion as she was sucked into some great vortex that threatened to swallow her whole. Strange images danced before her eyes and John's face loomed before her just as she began to drop off to sleep, his eyes bulging, and his tongue protruding, the rope still around his neck. His wild gaze seemed to be fixed on her, accusing her of allowing him to be executed. She couldn't see Travesty, but she heard her laughter. It was coming from a spot just behind Mary, and she knew with absolutely certainty that Simon was with her, chuckling with mirth as the rope tightened around John's throat.

"It's not my fault," Mary muttered. "It's not my fault."

"Of course, it's not your fault," Dr. Paulson replied in his deep, reassuring voice. "Try to sleep."

Mary moved her head on the pillow, unable to chase away the horrid image. "Go away, John," she mumbled. "Go away. There was nothing I could have done."

But John wouldn't leave. He seemed to be haunting her from the grave, tormenting her. Mary's mind conjured up an image of Walker, but when she tried to get to him, he moved out of her reach. Blood trickled from the wound in his side and a crimson stain bloomed on his chest, like a deadly bud opening its petals to the sun. He seemed to be hovering between life and death, between reality and fantasy.

"Walker," she mouthed. "Walker, come back. Please, don't leave me." But Walker hadn't left her, she'd left him. She was halfway across the world, the distance between them growing with every mile. He was alive, but he was dead to her now, just like she was dead to him.

"Mary, who is Walker?" Dr. Paulson asked gently.

"A spirit that walks between worlds," Mary muttered.

"You can see spirits?" She heard alarm in the doctor's voice, but it didn't matter. Nothing mattered. The baby was the only thing keeping her tethered to this world.

What will happen to it if I die? Mary thought desperately as she fought the encroaching darkness. *I must not leave my baby.*

Dr. Paulson slipped his arm beneath her shoulders and lifted her so she could take a drink. She tasted the cloying sweetness of laudanum on her lips and welcomed the oblivion it would soon bring. Dr. Paulson had a limited supply, but he gave her a few drops from time to time when she was particularly agitated and couldn't settle down.

"You sleep now, Mary. I will watch over you."

Mary tried to answer, but the opium was already taking effect. The all-consuming vortex seemed to have become a puffy cloud. Mary relaxed into its comforting folds and its softness enveloped her. She began to drift, her anguish forgotten. She felt so peaceful, so free. If only she could feel this way forever.

SEVENTY

A bracing wind tore at Mary's skirts and freed tendrils of hair from her cap. She turned her face into the gust, eager to feel the wind's cool breath on her face. She'd come up on deck early in the morning, desperate for a breath of fresh air after being confined to the cabin for nearly four days. Dr. Paulson had slept on the floor instead of retiring to his hammock, fearful of leaving Mary on her own. He genuinely wished to help, but Mary felt like she was drowning and the hand that tried to pull her out of the water was slippery and too feeble to hold on to her for long. She had no fever, and no symptoms of any known illness. There were times when she felt well, and then quite suddenly, her face would become suffused with heat and her heart would start to hammer in her chest, rendering her almost breathless with the force of its beating. Her head often hurt to the point where her vision became blurred, causing her to rub her eyes in the hope of clearing away the fog.

"Mary, you shouldn't have left your bed," Dr. Paulson chided her when he came up on deck, looking tired and disheveled. "You're not well."

"I was desperate for fresh air. I feel better," she added.

The doctor nodded. "Don't stay too long. You're not strong enough. I think I can use a shave," he added, running a hand over the coarse stubble shadowing his jaw. "Are you up to eating something?"

"I think so."

"Excellent. I'll wash up and then we can break our fast together." He smiled and patted Mary's shoulder in a fatherly way.

"I don't know what I would do without you, Dr. Paulson."

"I'm glad to be on hand. I must admit, I've never encountered a case such as yours. It's most perplexing."

"Am I going to die?" Mary asked. Her voice trembled with fear.

"Mary, I will do everything in my power to prevent that from happening. You have my word."

"Thank you."

Mary leaned on the rail and gazed out over the endless ocean. The sun was just beginning to rise, a shimmering semicircle of brightest pink skimming the horizon in the east. The sky, which had been a murky gray only a moment ago, blazed with crimson and gold as the new day dawned, bright and clear. Mary couldn't tear her eyes away from the awesome sight, buoyed by the thought that she'd survived long enough to greet another day. She was certain her sickness would miraculously disappear as soon as she stepped ashore. A silky ribbon wound itself around Mary's ankles, and she bent down and scooped up the little cat.

"There you are," Mary crooned. "I haven't seen you in days. Where have you been hiding, you naughty kitty?"

The cat purred and burrowed deeper into Mary's arms, frightened by the wind. Mary's fingers stroked its head gently in an effort to comfort the frightened creature.

Mary remained on deck for another half hour, enjoying her brief spell of well-being, then she joined Dr. Paulson for breakfast, which she ate with relish. She was hungry—no, ravenous. That had to be a good sign.

Folkstone, Kent

Quinn set aside Mary's comb and glanced at Jo, who was sleeping peacefully in the next bed, her dark hair spread over the pillow like Medusa's snakes. Seth's room was just down the corridor, but he'd gone down to the pub to have a pint and something to eat. Jo had been tired by the time they arrived in Kent, having crossed the channel from France, so they'd decided not to continue their journey until tomorrow and give her time to rest. Jo had taken a shower and fallen into bed, too weary to go down for dinner. Quinn had decided to remain with her. She hadn't been that hungry, and truth be told, she was tired as well after all those hours in the car. It had felt good to take a hot bath and stretch out on the bed, a soft pillow propped behind her head as she sank into the surprisingly comfortable embrace of the mattress. She hoped they'd get home tomorrow. She was desperate to see Gabe and the children. She longed to hold Alex in her arms and looked forward to spending some quality time with Emma. Quinn suddenly had an idea and grabbed her mobile off the nightstand. She googled "One Direction tour dates." Eureka! They would be performing in

London in September, shortly after Emma's sixth birthday. Quinn set a reminder on her phone to purchase tickets once they went on sale.

Concert tickets would be the ultimate birthday present. Maybe Emma was a bit young, but Quinn would be an absolute rock star in her eyes if she took her to see One Direction. Maybe she'd even get an extra ticket and offer to take one of Emma's friends. Maybe Maya, if they were still best friends. Emma would be so pleased—no, ecstatic. Quinn grinned to herself and congratulated herself on her proactive thinking. She was getting the hang of this mothering thing.

Quinn set aside the phone and glanced over at Jo again. After several hours of rest, she no longer looked so wan, but they should have insisted she have something to eat before going to bed. She didn't seem to have much of an appetite. Quinn wondered who would look after Jo once she got home, her heart squeezing with worry. Once they arrived back in London, she and Seth would take Jo to her flat and leave her on her own. Seth had booked into a nearby hotel, but he wouldn't be with Jo round the clock. He'd decided not to offer to stay at Jo's flat in case it made her uncomfortable. They seemed to be getting along and were getting to know each other, but Jo, by her own admission, was a woman who liked privacy and enjoyed her space. At least Seth would be on hand to take her to see her GP next week and escort her to a London-based neurologist to follow up on the surgery. Dr. Stein had sent over Jo's file before releasing her and personally made the appointment, to make sure that Jo received proper post-operative care.

Quinn slid off the bed and tiptoed into the bathroom, where she filled the tiny in-room kettle with water. She could use a cup of tea, and thankfully, there were several packages of complimentary shortbread on the dresser; she was hungry now. Quinn made herself a strong brew and settled in a chair by the window, looking out over the twinkling lights of the town. She wasn't at the end of Mary's story yet, but the latest vision had been eye-opening. She didn't need to consult a physician to understand what Mary was going through. Only six months ago, she'd been experiencing similar symptoms herself, but thankfully, they hadn't been as severe as Mary's. Mary was suffering from preeclampsia, possibly even combined with toxoplasmosis, which was carried by cat feces and could cause serious birth defects if the unborn baby became infected.

High blood pressure, headaches, vomiting, and swelling of the ankles would all be telltale signs for a modern doctor, but Dr. Paulson wouldn't have been familiar with the condition or its causes. He appeared to be doing his best to treat Mary, using methods available to him, such as bleeding and purging to relieve the pressure building up within his patient. Lowering Mary's salt intake, drinking plenty of water, and getting fresh air and exercise would have helped, but like everyone onboard, Mary consumed mostly salted pork and hardtack, and drank ale, and not enough of it to keep her hydrated. She barely left her cabin, told by Dr. Paulson that she needed rest more than exercise. She also came into direct contact with the cat frequently enough to get harmful toxins on her hands, which she wouldn't have washed regularly.

Quinn sighed. The ship would arrive in England in a few weeks' time, setting the stage for the gruesome final act of Mary's life, which would play out either onboard or in the barely noticeable crevice in the Cornish cliff face where Mary's mortal remains had been discovered.

"Oh, Mary." Quinn sighed deeply. Her heart went out to the young woman. What a short and unhappy life Mary had lived. The only bright spot had been Walker's love for her, but fate had other plans for the star-crossed lovers. Walker had survived his injuries, probably because someone got to him in time to stop the bleeding, but timing was everything, and Walker and Mary's timing had been off from the start. Perhaps he would have come for Mary once he was sufficiently recovered to undertake the long walk to North Carolina, or perhaps he would have sent someone to fetch her had he known she was about to be sent back to England, but given the frosty relations between the colonists and the Indians following the murders of the men who had accosted Mary, he likely had no inkling time was running out. He must have assumed that Mary was safe where she was until he could come for her, never imagining that he'd never see her again.

Had his presence on the shore been pure coincidence, or a planned goodbye? Quinn would never know since she could only see events play out from Mary's perspective. It was even possible that Walker had known of Mary's imminent departure and chose not to intervene. Perhaps he'd realized the danger he'd be in if accused of kidnapping a white woman, or perhaps he'd been ordered by the Powhatan chief to abandon his plans. Within a year, the Indians would massacre a quarter of Jamestown's population, an act of war that was likely already in the making at the time of Mary's banishment.

Quinn swore softly under her breath. She'd completely forgotten to ring Colin. She didn't think the DNA results would come as a surprise, but she needed scientific data to back up her suppositions. The combination of storytelling by a respected historian, lush and detailed visual presentation, and irrefutable science had made the program a runaway success. Quinn slipped from the room and walked to the end of the corridor, where she could speak privately. She called Colin and hoped he'd pick up.

"Quinn," Colin greeted her. "Excellent timing. Just finished my last cookery class. Duck à l'orange served with wild rice and asparagus, and crème brûlée for dessert. It was très magnifique, if I say so myself."

"That sounds delicious," Quinn replied, suddenly wondering if Colin had carved the duck the same way he dissected a corpse. "I've been so focused on Jo, I completely forgot to ring you back regarding the DNA results on our mother and child."

"Ah, yes. The results were rather surprising. The woman was of Anglo-Saxon descent, born and bred on the coast of England, based on the analysis of the isotopes in her bone collagen, which gives us a snapshot of the person's diet. The child, however, was of partially Native American descent. I'm not at all sure how a young woman whose remains were discovered in Cornwall might have copulated with an American Indian. Seems incongruous. Perhaps the samples were cross-contaminated, but I can't imagine that there'd be many samples at a London-based lab containing the DNA of a Native American. The only conceivable explanation would be that our girl came into contact with one of the Native Americans who accompanied Pocahontas to England. Pocahontas visited England at the beginning of the seventeenth century, which ties in with the approximate timeline of our remains. Oh, and it was a boy," Colin ended with a sigh. "A full-term baby boy."

"Was it healthy?" Quinn asked.

"As far as I can tell, yes."

"Thanks, Colin. I'll ring you when I get back."

Quinn disconnected the call and pondered the information Colin had shared with her. Even if the child had been infected with toxoplasmosis, the effects might not have been immediate, and as far as Quinn knew, the risks were mostly brain damage and blindness, not something that would show up in skeletal remains, since all soft tissue had decomposed centuries ago. In truth, the results would have been more surprising if the child had been John's, but Mary had been right, the baby was Walker's son.

Quinn returned to the room and resumed her seat by the window. She'd suddenly come up with a plausible theory of what happened to Mary and how her remains had wound up in the cave in St. Just, but needed to verify her hunch before presenting her findings to Rhys. A soft knock distracted Quinn from her thoughts and she went to open the door. Seth stood on the threshold, a bulging shopping bag in his right hand.

"I brought you girls sandwiches, chips—I mean crisps—and some mineral water. If Jo wakes, you should encourage her to eat something," he said. "And you should eat too. You must be hungry."

"I had some tea and biscuits."

"Cookies are not food," Seth admonished her. "Okay, I'm off to bed. Good night, sweetheart."

"Good night, Dad," Quinn said. She accepted the bag and grinned at Seth. Somehow, being paternal didn't really suit him, which made her appreciate his concern all the more.

SEVENTY-TWO
FEBRUARY 2015

London, England

Alex's face looked peaceful and rosy in the warm glow of the nightlight. He'd been asleep in her arms for nearly an hour but cried every time Quinn tried to put him down in his crib. His hand was wrapped around her finger, as if to make sure she was still there, holding him close. He'd reached for her the moment she came home and hadn't let her go since, and Emma had been on her best behavior as well, filling Quinn in on everything she'd missed and asking endless questions.

"They missed you," Gabe said when he came into the bedroom, having read Emma a bedtime story.

"I missed them too. I hate being away from them."

"But this was important. How's Jo settling in?" Gabe asked.

"She's glad to be home. Seth was still with her when I left. He'll stay in London for as long as Jo needs him. I'm so glad to see them getting on," Quinn said. "There were several times when I caught them wearing an identical expression. Funny how they'd never met until a few days ago, but they are so similar in some ways."

Gabe nodded. "I see Jenna in Emma when I least expect to.

There are times when she'll tilt her head a certain way or her eyes will flash with annoyance, and I get a sudden flashback of her mother."

"I can't wait to see what Alex will be like once he's older."

"He'll be an absolute rascal," Gabe replied with a soft smile. "Try to put him down. I think he's sleeping soundly now."

Quinn nodded and lowered Alex into the crib. He allowed her to put him down this time but retained his grip on her finger. Quinn carefully unfolded his tiny fingers and covered him with his fluffy blanket. Alex instantly raised both arms, assuming his favorite sleeping position that made him look as if he were surrendering.

Quinn and Gabe tiptoed from the bedroom and closed the door before settling together on the sofa. Quinn leaned against Gabe and rested her head on his shoulder as he wrapped his arm around her, pulling her close. It was good to be home.

"Has Jo spoken to Sylvia?" Gabe asked.

"No. She's not ready."

"How much did you tell her?"

"I told her everything, including the bit about Rhys and the part he played in our family drama. Now it's up to her to decide how she wants to proceed. She was angry with Sylvia for a long time, and I'm not at all sure her feelings will ever change. She blames her for everything. I do think it would be good for them to meet, even if they will never have any sort of relationship. It would give Jo an opportunity to say her piece and maybe find some closure."

"Is she angry with Rhys? Discovering that he might have been her biological father must have tainted her rosy view of him."

"I don't think it has. What Rhys did when he was a misguided teenage boy cannot possibly tarnish what he's done for her now. He risked his life to find her and followed her to Germany, when he could have simply shared the information with me and Logan and returned to his cushy life. Gabe, I think Rhys got badly hurt in Kabul, but he didn't want to talk about it."

Gabe sighed. "I must admit that I was wrong about Rhys. I always thought of him as a selfish prig."

"He feels guilty about the part he played in Sylvia's life," Quinn replied.

"He might have at first, but he's no longer motivated by guilt. He cares for you, Quinn."

"And he cares for Jo. I think Rhys is surprisingly sentimental beneath that crusty exterior. He and Jo recognized something in each other, something deeply personal."

"And speaking of deeply personal matters, have you asked her? Does she share your psychic ability?" Gabe asked.

"I don't know. I wanted to ask, but something held me back. It's not easy to blurt out, 'I see dead people. Do you?' The foundation I lay with Jo now will influence our relationship for the rest of our lives. I don't want her to think I'm a nutter."

"Perhaps she is one too."

"Not necessarily. Brett is psychic, but Seth isn't. And I have no way of knowing how many people along my ancestral line were endowed with the same ability. I will ask her—soon."

Gabe lifted Quinn's face with his finger and brushed his lips against hers. "Tomorrow, you can find out if Jo has the gift, but tonight, I'd like to show you how much I missed you."

"Not as much as I missed you," Quinn replied as she wrapped her arms around Gabe's neck and pulled him down on top of her. She hadn't told him about the pregnancy scare. There was no point now that the danger had passed, but tomorrow, she'd make an appointment to see Dr. Malik. She wasn't ready for another baby, and she was fairly sure Gabe wasn't ready either. They had a perfect family, and she didn't want to upset the balance by throwing an unplanned pregnancy into the mix. There were ways to avoid that, and it was time she took care of business.

SEVENTY-THREE

JUNE 1621

Aboard the *Constance*

White hot sun flooded the deck, making Mary squint against its brightness. It was unseasonably hot, and she felt too warm in her woolen gown as she leaned against the rail and peered out over the tranquil sea. It was hard to tell where the water ended and the sky began. She thought she might catch sight of land today, but the ocean stretched before her, just as it had for the past two months.

Mary's hand flew to her belly as a particularly vicious kick startled her out of her reverie. The baby could come any day now, according to Dr. Paulson, and despite her fear for the future, she was ready. She was uncomfortable and hot, even when the temperature dropped after sunset, and had to use the pot so frequently there was almost no point in trying to sleep.

Mary stepped away from the railing. She was terribly thirsty. Her mouth was so dry her tongue stuck to the roof of her mouth. She closed her eyes as a terrible headache began to build just behind the forehead, the pain reverberating into her temples. A telltale flush began to creep from her neck and into her face, her cheeks aflame within seconds.

Mary wet her hands in a barrel of water and patted them

against her flushed face, but the warm water did nothing to cool her down. She began walking toward the ladder that would take her down below, but her vision blurred, and terrible vertigo knocked her off balance. The deck rushed up to meet her and Mary fell hard, landing on her left side and slamming her head against the planks.

Rough hands lifted her, and she was transported to the cool sanctuary of the cabin. She heard Dr. Paulson's voice floating somewhere above her, its cadence distorted and muffled by the roaring in her ears. She couldn't open her eyes, and her whole body seemed to quake as the blood rushed in her veins and pounded in her temples, leaving her nearly insensible with pain.

"Mary, can you hear me?" the doctor was asking. Mary tried to reply, but all that came out was a pitiful moan.

"Mary. Mary," Dr. Paulson called. She felt his fingers on her wrist and his palm on her forehead. "I need to do something to relieve her blood pressure, or she'll suffer an apoplexy," he said, addressing someone in the cabin with them.

"Will you bleed her again?"

"No, that will take too long and isn't guaranteed to help. Unbearable pressure is building in her head. Look how flushed she is, and the whites of her eyes are tinged red from broken blood vessels. I must save her."

"What will you do?" the voice asked.

"Make a hole in her skull to relieve the pressure on the brain. I will trepan her."

Mary heard a sharp intake of breath. "Will she survive the procedure?"

"If I don't do something, she won't survive the day. And even if she does, the physical strain of delivering a child will surely kill her. I will do what I can to help, then find her lodgings once we come ashore. She will need ample time to recover."

"You don't expect her to survive the birth, do you?"

Mary didn't hear Dr. Paulson's whispered answer, but she didn't need to. It was obvious enough. What would happen to her baby if she died? Would someone look after it or just throw it into the gutter? Mary desperately tried to marshal her thoughts, but the pounding in her head obliterated every coherent thought, plunging her into a thick fog as she began to lose consciousness. The fog grew heavier, pressing down on her chest and suffocating her. She struggled to breathe but fought the darkness with every last reserve of her energy.

"Help me," Mary whispered. "Please, help me."

"Mary, I'm going to do everything in my power to save you," Dr. Paulson promised.

"The baby."

"I will make sure your baby will be looked after if you're not there to look after it yourself. You mustn't worry. Try to relax and breathe deeply."

Mary tried to respond, but her brief spell of awareness was swallowed by the ever-encroaching fog. She seemed to be floating on it, enveloped in its soupy thickness.

"Will you not give her some laudanum?" the voice asked.

"I'm afraid I don't have any left," Dr. Paulson replied. "She'll have to do without."

Mary cried out when a sharp pain roused her from her stupor and nearly sent her flying off the berth. She would have sat bolt upright, but strong hands held her down as Dr. Paulson leaned over her and bored into her skull. The pain was like nothing Mary had ever experienced. It was sharp and relentless. She convulsed in agony and screamed for the doctor to stop, but he only increased the pressure, rushing to get the job done.

"I'm almost done," he assured her in a breathless voice. "You'll feel much better once it's all over."

She couldn't respond. She was whimpering and crying like a wounded animal, her heart contracting from the pain as if it would burst.

"Hold her still," Dr. Paulson barked.

"No," Mary moaned, but no one seemed to be listening to her. They didn't seem to understand that her head felt as if it were being cleaved in two by a very sharp axe. At least that would have been a quick death. This was torture.

"Just a little longer," Dr. Paulson was saying. "I'm almost there."

Suddenly, the pain vanished, leaving behind a strange feeling of peace. Mary no longer cared about anything. She'd only wanted the suffering to end, and now it had. She floated on a gossamer cloud of tranquility.

"There now. She's feeling better already. Mop up the blood, will you," Dr. Paulson said above her head.

Mary heard a gagging sound. "Dear Lord in heaven, is that her brain?"

"It's nothing to be frightened of, Master Halsey. The pressure has been relieved, and a natural balance will soon be restored. We will leave her this way until she's out of danger and then replace the skull cap." Sounds of retching reached her from far away.

Mary felt the welcoming embrace of oblivion as darkness descended on her battered senses. She was no longer floating, but falling, falling into an abyss. She tried to fight it, but she was too weak, so she gave in and allowed the darkness to take her.

SEVENTY-FOUR
FEBRUARY 2015

London, England

Quinn stared at the white-painted ceiling of the bedroom, her heart heavy with unbearable sadness. She could never forget the horror she had just experienced, or erase Mary's suffering from her memory. She'd heard of trepanning, of course, but had never witnessed anything as barbaric or inhuman as this. Surprisingly, many patients had survived the procedure, and it had still been in use as recently as the nineteenth century, maybe even well into the twentieth century, until it was replaced by modern-day neurosurgery, performed while the patient was under anesthetic and using a power drill to open the skull instead of a sharp-toothed tool with a crank, similar to a can opener. She had no doubt Rhys would move heaven and earth to find a surviving example of the archaic tool to use in the episode and demonstrate how the procedure worked.

"Why so glum?" Gabe asked as he came into the bedroom to dress for work. He smiled at Alex, who'd just woken up and rolled onto his tummy to peer between the bars of his cot. Gabe lifted him out and handed him to Quinn, who cuddled him protectively.

"I just experienced a trepanning. It was awful, Gabe. Unspeakable. I'm reminded each and every day how lucky I am to live in this century, especially as a woman."

"It was no walk in the park for the men either, but I take your point," Gabe replied. "So, is that what killed her?"

"Colin believes Mary was alive when she went into labor, which would mean she survived the procedure."

"There are documented cases of coffin births where mother and child were both deceased at the time of the birth. The infant was expelled from the mother's body by a build-up of gasses," Gabe said as he buttoned his shirt. "Perhaps Mary was spared the horror of having to deliver her baby while entombed."

"I would tend to agree with you, except for one glaring flaw in your argument. Had Mary been dead at the time of delivery, her remains would lie flat in the coffin. Mary's skeleton was on its side, mouth wide open, head thrown back, hands crossed over the belly, and legs bent."

"I forgot about that," Gabe admitted. He selected a tie and held it up for Quinn's approval.

"Yes, that one will do nicely," she said absentmindedly. "Mary survived the trepanning, I'm sure of it. God, poor woman. What a way to go."

Quinn got out of bed, pulled on her dressing gown, and lifted Alex into her arms. He was already smacking his lips, reminding his parents that it was time for breakfast. Gabe kissed Alex's silky cheek, then gave Quinn a tender kiss. "Quinn, Mary's been gone for nearly four hundred years. Whatever she went through is long over. Don't let it affect you. You must remain emotionally detached if you plan to continue sharing these stories."

"Easy for you to say," Quinn muttered.

"Just trying to help," Gabe replied as he called out to Emma to get her shoes and coat on. Quinn saw them off and went into the kitchen to feed Alex and make herself something to eat. After breakfast, she'd stop by the bank before heading over to see Jo. She'd had an idea, and she hoped it would work.

. . .

Quinn bought a bunch of flowers to brighten Jo's flat and picked up a few essentials in case Seth hadn't had time to run out to the shops. She could make sandwiches for lunch, and Jo was bound to need tea and milk. She took the tube to Jo's flat, an experience Alex seemed to enjoy, and rang the bell.

Jo opened the door, a happy smile on her face, especially when she caught sight of Alex in his pram. She wore black tights and an oversized cream-colored wool jumper, and her hair was pulled back into a ponytail. She even wore a bit of makeup, which did wonders to hide her pallor.

"How're you feeling, sis?" Quinn asked as she handed her the flowers.

"Much better. It's nice to be home. It's also nice not to be alone," she added as she reached for a vase and filled it with water. "Seth arrived at seven, bearing pastries and freshly brewed coffee."

"Where's he now?" Quinn asked.

"He went out to do some shopping. I see you had the same idea."

"I thought I'd make some sandwiches," Quinn replied as she handed Jo the shopping bag and lifted Alex out of his pram. She removed his snowsuit and hat and ruffled his flattened hair.

"God, he's gorgeous," Jo gushed. "May I hold him?"

"Of course." Quinn handed Jo the baby, and Jo held him carefully, as if he were made of glass. She sat down on the sofa and settled Alex in her lap.

"My name is Jo," she said to him. "I'm your aunt. Aunt Jo. I like the sound of that," she added, giving Quinn a quivering smile. "I never imagined I'd have nieces and nephews. I can't wait to meet Emma. And Gabe."

"You have quite a few people to meet."

"I'm so looking forward to meeting Logan and Jude, but I must admit, I'm a little nervous. Do you think they'll resent me for not wanting to meet Sylvia?"

"Do what feels right to you, Jo. Logan and Jude will understand, given my own rocky relationship with our mother."

Jo had opened her mouth to reply when the doorbell buzzed. "That must be Seth." She pressed the buzzer and a minute later there was a knock on the door. Jo pulled it open to find a young man bearing a huge bouquet of flowers.

"Delivery," he announced unnecessarily.

"Well, those certainly put my flowers to shame. Who are they from?"

Jo's smile lit up the room. She smelled the flowers and slid the card into the pocket of her jumper. "They're from Rhys. To welcome me home. How sweet."

Quinn laughed. "I strongly suspect the man himself will be appearing very soon with a large tin of baked goods. He's good for that."

"I hope so," Jo replied, blushing furiously. "I like baked goods."

"And you like Rhys," Quinn replied with a silly grin. "I actually have something for you as well." She'd collected the jewelry from the bank before heading to Jo's flat.

Quinn opened her bag and took out a rectangular velvet box, which she held out to Jo. "These pearls belonged to our grandmother Rae. She left them to me, but I want you to have them. I got to meet her and talk to her; that's enough of a gift. I think she'd want you to have them."

Jo's eyes filled with tears as she accepted the box. Nestled on a bed of blue velvet was the pearl set Rae had left for Quinn. Quinn held her breath as Jo beheld the jewelry. Luminescent and perfectly matched in size, the pearls glowed in the light of the winter sun that streamed through the window, and the diamond flower that adorned the choker sparkled and dazzled with its delicate perfection. The matching earrings twinkled among the velvet folds.

"It's a gorgeous set, Quinn, but I can't accept it. She left it for you. I don't have much occasion to wear something this posh anyhow."

"Won't you at least try it on?" Quinn cajoled, watching Jo intently.

Jo shook her head. "I'd rather not." She shut the box and handed it back to Quinn. It was so fleeting, Quinn might not have noticed it had she not been looking for it, but there it was—the sliding away of the eyes, the sharp intake of breath, the sudden nervousness.

"Are you afraid to touch them?" Quinn asked, her heartrate increasing as she waited for Jo's answer. Jo looked like she was about to issue a flat-out denial, then shook her head, as if an internal argument was raging in her mind.

"Yes, I am. I get these flashes sometimes," she muttered. "They're disconcerting. I've had them since I was a child."

"You see the people the items belong to?" Quinn persisted.

"I suppose. The visions never last long, just a moment or two, but I hate them. They frighten me." Jo's eyes widened with dawning understanding. "You experience it too."

"Yes, and so does Brett. I see the lives of the people I investigate."

Jo's mouth opened in shock. "You mean, *Echoes from the Past?* Those episodes are not based solely on an educated guess and diligent research? You actually know what happened to those people?"

Quinn nodded. "I do."

"Does Rhys know?" Jo asked.

"Yes, Rhys knows. And Gabe, but no one else. In my line of work, it's best to keep this to myself, or my credibility will come into question and there will be those who will troll me on social media and accuse me of being a fraud."

Jo exhaled noisily. "You don't know how happy I am to hear you say that. I've always thought there was something wrong with me. I've learned to avoid touching anything that might have belonged to the dead. I haven't experienced a flashback in years. I am tempted to touch the pearls," Jo confessed. "It's the closest I can come to meeting Rae and learning something of that side of my family."

"Take them, then. Seth would be pleased."

"Does he possess the same ability?" Jo asked.

"No, he doesn't seem to. It must have skipped a generation."

"What about Rae? Was she psychic, do you think?" Jo asked, still clutching the box.

"Rae married into the family. She wasn't a Besson by birth. The gift is passed down the Besson line. I was able to trace it to our great-great-great-grandmother, who came to America from Trinidad on a slave ship. There's no way to know how many generations it goes back before her."

"Oh my God. Of course. I saw the episode about Madeline and Clara several times. I just never imagined it had anything to do with me personally. I wonder if Clara's sons were psychic as well."

"Very likely, but we'll never know for certain. Clara's sons and their families must have been freed after the Civil War, and without a surname, they were impossible to trace. They vanished into the mists of history, their stories with them."

Jo nodded. "That makes sense. I know you tried your best." The ringing of the doorbell put an end to their conversation.

"Seth is back," Jo said as she stowed the box in a drawer. "You know, I'd never believe it possible to be this happy, especially after being blown up and shot at, but I am," she said with an impish smile. "I don't need pearls or flowers, or even baked goods. I just need to know that you will always be in my life."

Quinn wrapped Jo in a warm hug. She was happy too, not because Jo shared her gift, but because they'd been able to talk about it openly and trust each other. Now there were no more secrets between them, and they could move forward without the sword of duplicity hanging over their necks. Finally, they broke apart, and Jo went to open the door. Seth stepped into the flat, bringing the smell of snow with him. He carried several shopping bags, and his cheeks were ruddy with cold.

"Quinny, nice to see you. And, Alex, what a treat!" Seth cried as he kissed the baby. "You want to say hello to Grandpa?" Seth crooned. "Tonight, I'm making dinner for my girl," he said as he bounced Alex on his knee and made him giggle. "I couldn't find half the ingredients I needed to make her a real Cajun gumbo, so I'll make fried chicken instead. Jo will taste the real thing when she comes to Louisiana this summer. Would be nice if you could join her, Quinn."

Quinn smiled. She hadn't thought she'd ever set foot in New Orleans again after what had happened to her there, but suddenly, returning didn't seem as traumatic. Perhaps she would visit Seth in Louisiana, and she'd even go and visit Madeline's grave. She wouldn't be ruled by her fears.

"How about I make you two some sandwiches for lunch?" Quinn asked.

"Sounds good to me," Seth replied. "Never met a sandwich I didn't like." Seth grinned and raised an eyebrow in a comical expression, as if something awful had just occurred to him. "Now, you wouldn't be making us fish paste, or cheese and pickle—a combination I just don't get. Or marmite?" he joked. "That stuff reminds me of shoe polish."

"Don't worry. I'm not out to assassinate your taste buds. I will make you a very American ham and cheese sandwich. Jo can have whatever she likes. And then I have to dash."

"Won't you stay for fried chicken?" Seth asked. "I love having you both here with me."

"I'd like to, but I have an appointment at two. You two enjoy."

"Oh, we will," Seth promised as he lifted Alex over his head and spun him around, making him squeal with delight.

SEVENTY-FIVE
JUNE 1621

St. Just, Cornwall

Mary came to with a hard jolt and gasped as uncontrollable coughing wracked her body. Her eyes streamed and she gulped for air, but it didn't seem to fill her burning lungs. She was shaking with cold, and her clothes were wet and smelled of seawater. Pressure was building in her head, which felt like it would split in two if the strain wasn't immediately relieved.

Mary carefully touched the top of her head and found a circular opening, the slimy surface of what must be her brain pulsating beneath. She yanked her hand away and tried to see if her head was bleeding, but although her eyes were wide open, she couldn't see anything, not even a chink of light. When she tried to move, her knees slammed into something hard and unyielding. Mary held her hands in front of her and tried to straighten them, but her palms met with solid wood.

Her chest heaved with panic as the reality of her situation began to sink in. She was trapped. "Help!" Mary screamed. "Please, help me!" Her voice echoed dully, but there were no other human sounds, just an eerie silence broken only by what she thought might be the crashing of waves or the flapping of wings.

She couldn't be sure what she heard since her head tolled like an iron bell.

Unbearable anxiety built inside her, rushing at her like an incoming tide, each wave coming harder and faster, and reaching further. Mary couldn't breathe, couldn't see, and couldn't make any sense of what was happening. Her jumbled thoughts scurried like mice, bumping into each other and scrambling in blind panic. And then the pains came, sharp and visceral, the pains of childbirth.

"No, please, no," Mary moaned as she wrapped her hands around her stomach and turned on her side, which helped marginally. The pain abated for a few minutes, but then returned, gripping her womb with cruel fingers and twisting it mercilessly. She clasped her hands and began to pray, begging God for help, but even as she mouthed the words, she knew there was no stopping what had already begun. The labor would continue until it culminated in a grim conclusion, for there could be no other outcome given her situation.

Mary tried to hold on to consciousness as contraction after contraction tore through her body, leaving her breathless and shaking. Her thighs were slick with blood, and her back felt as if it would snap. She was trapped in her awkward position, unable to open her legs wide enough to allow the child to vacate her body. As a terrible pressure built in her lower abdomen, she bore down, unable to stop even when stars exploded before her eyes as her brain strained against the opening in her skull. She pushed again and again, her body following the dictates of nature, indifferent to what she might be feeling.

Mary crossed her arms in front of her belly and rested her forehead against the rough wood of the coffin. She was so weak, and so tired. She knew, in that instinctive way people feel the approach of death, that she had only a short time left, and she was glad of it. She was ready. Whoever had interred her had condemned her to certain death, but perhaps the judgement had come down long before that. She'd tried to grab at happiness, going against the teachings of the Church and the laws of man. She'd attempted to thwart the natural order of things, and she was about to pay for her sins, not only with her own life, but with the life of her child, who'd spend eternity by her side.

They'd die alone and unloved, with no one to mourn them or even pay for a crude marker to identify their lonely grave. She'd never lie in consecrated ground, and her child would never know the glory of God, not having been baptized before it died. Death was frightening enough, but to know that she would forever remain in hell as punishment for her sins was terrifying. Mary opened her mouth in a silent scream as her body began to shut down. She felt the approach of death and knew with unwavering certainty that she was damned.

After a time, a wonderful peace stole over her, taking away the pain and the unspeakable terror of those final moments. Mary felt as if she were being cradled in loving arms. They wouldn't let her fall.

"I've got you," Walker's voice said softly. "You can let go now. I've got you both." Somewhere, in the deep recesses of her mind, she heard the haunting notes of his death song—but no, this was her own death song, her final act.

Mary was nearly gone by the time the infant slithered from her body, its nose pressing against the back of Mary's thighs and its hands balled into fists. Its tiny feet rested against Mary's bottom, but she couldn't feel the connection. The child whimpered once, and again, and then grew silent as the sodden wool of Mary's skirts smothered it as effectively as a feather pillow.

Waves crashed against the shore, and a hunter's moon rose slowly and majestically above the dusky expanse of the sea. A broken mast rose out of the water, its tattered sails hanging on by lengths of torn rigging, and chucks of broken wood floated toward the shore, along with an odd assortment of household items. A man's body lay face down in the sand, his dark hair plastered to his head. It had been the first to wash up, but it wouldn't be the last.

SEVENTY-SIX
MARCH 2015

London, England

Hazy spring sunshine shone through the plate glass windows, casting a golden glow on Rhys, who suddenly looked like a deity wearing a holy halo. Rhys, oblivious to his divine aura, looked across his desk at Quinn.

"Every time we wrap up one of these stories, I think there can't possibly be a worse way to die, and every time I'm proven wrong. Dear God, what that poor woman must have endured in her final hours," Rhys said, shaking his head in amazement. "I think she truly was damned to deserve such a gruesome end. People today complain nonstop about inequality, the incompetence of the government, and lack of services. They have no idea what life was like in centuries past when a person had no rights at all, especially a woman. Travesty lost her entire family because they'd been quarantined, Simon was sold into servitude for a crime he didn't commit, John was executed for being homosexual, and poor Mary was banished and essentially murdered by the well-intentioned Dr. Paulson. He must have arranged for Mary's coffin to be hidden in that cave, to avoid having to answer for her death. He got away scot-free."

"He didn't," Quinn replied, her tone grim.

"No?"

"No. Once I learned the name of the vessel Mary was on, I decided to trace its history. The *Constance* left Jamestown on March thirtieth and was due to arrive in Plymouth at the end of June. On June 28th, 1621, it ran aground near the coast of Cornwall, the ship smashing to bits on the rocks. Now, you might think this was spectacularly bad luck, given that they were due to reach Plymouth the next day, but the most likely explanation is that the ship was lured onto the rocks by wreckers, who were after the valuable cargo the ship was carrying from Virginia. The wreckers never allowed anyone to leave the shipwreck alive, for fear of being reported to the authorities and identified. They drowned anyone who came ashore. Per maritime records, all souls went down with the *Constance*, including Dr. Paulson.

"You see, whether you believe in fate or destiny, or some form of divine retribution, Mary wasn't meant to survive that voyage. She would have died regardless. My guess is that Mary slipped into a coma after the trepanning and was presumed dead. Rather than throw her body overboard, as the crew would have done had they been further out to sea, they laid her in a coffin, probably per Dr. Paulson's request, and would have had her properly buried once they reached Plymouth in a few days' time. The coffin must have been retrieved from the wreck with the rest of the cargo and taken ashore, where someone recognized it for what it was and shoved it in a cave just to get it out of the way and not confuse it with anything of value. The victims of the shipwreck, including Dr. Paulson, were buried at the parish cemetery in St. Just. They lie there still, and I think we should inter Mary and her baby's remains alongside them after we finish filming the episode."

"Yes, that seems fitting," Rhys agreed. "What I still don't understand is how Simon Faraday came to take legal possession of John Forrester's plantation," Rhys said, leaning back in his chair. "He had several years left on his indenture contract, and new colonists were coming over on every vessel. Surely that land would have been given to someone else, someone who wasn't a convicted criminal, and Faraday's contract would have been sold to someone else."

"There are some things we'll never know," Quinn replied as she gathered her belongings. "I can only see what Mary saw, so I have no way of knowing what occurred after she left the plantation."

"We'll have to come up with a plausible explanation," Rhys replied. "All loose ends need to be tied up before we begin filming."

"I'll leave that to you. I'm signing off for the next few days."

"Why is that?"

"We are moving," Quinn replied happily. "We closed on the house yesterday and Seth is in the process of buying our flat."

"Do you need any help?" Rhys asked with a smile that said, *I'm not carrying any boxes or getting my hands dirty, but if you need someone to bring you a cup of tea and a sandwich, I'm your man.*

"Thank you, but we have it under control."

"I'll walk you out." Rhys got to his feet and grabbed his coat as he followed Quinn out the door. "I have lunch plans."

"Are you blushing?" Quinn asked as they strolled toward the lift.

"Maybe." Rhys smiled sheepishly.

"I won't ask you who you're meeting, because I already know. Give my regards to Jo."

"I will. Quinn, did you ever ask her?"

"I have."

"And does she?"

"She does," Quinn replied, amused by the amazement on Rhys's face.

"What a fascinating family you are."

"Jealous?" Quinn joked.

"You bet."

They reached the lobby and walked out of the building into the mild spring afternoon. Quinn gave him a peck on the cheek and walked away, heading toward the tube station. The case of Mary Wilby was closed, the mystery solved, and now she had to turn her attention to her own life.

SEVENTY-SEVEN

Quinn kicked off her trainers and plopped down on the sofa, sinking deep into the cushions. "I'm never getting up again," she said as Gabe handed her a bottle of water. Every muscle in her body seemed to be moaning with fatigue.

"Twenty boxes unpacked, one hundred to go," he replied and sank down next to her. "Jill and Brian want to know when to drop off the children. Jill offered to keep them overnight, if we're not ready."

Quinn shook her head. "No need. Their bedrooms are set up, and everything else will get done in the next few days. Rome wasn't built in a day, you know."

"Tell me about it," Gabe replied wearily. "If I know you, this house will look as if we've lived here for years by the end of the week."

"I plan on it. Hey, want to have a party?" Quinn asked, draining the rest of the water.

"A housewarming do? Sure, why not? We have lots to celebrate. Maybe we can even combine it with Alex's christening. Have the after-party here. We can have it catered, so you don't have to lift a finger."

"If you think the hostess doesn't lift a finger on the day of her party, even if it's catered, you have much to learn about entertaining. But it's a good idea. Two birds with one stone and all that. I'd like to have Alex christened while Seth is still in London and before Jo accepts a new assignment and runs off to God-knows-where in pursuit of truth and justice."

Gabe considered that for a moment. "Will everyone play nicely, do you think?" He was referring to Jo and Sylvia, who had yet to meet in person, and Seth and Sylvia, who could barely stand the sight of each other given their history, and Quinn's mum and Sylvia, who were like the biblical mothers who appealed to King Solomon to decide which one got to keep the child they both claimed was theirs. Even Phoebe and Sylvia didn't get on. Phoebe's burgeoning dislike of Sylvia had turned into bitter resentment after Emma's dramatic birthday party last August, and although both women would do their best to remain civil for Quinn and Gabe's sake, there was no telling how long their civility would last.

"Are you suggesting I leave Sylvia off the guest list?" Gabe shrugged, implying he'd leave that up to her.

"I'll give it some thought," Quinn promised. "Even my brain is tired. Do we have anything to give the children for breakfast?"

Gabe sighed. "I'll run out to the shops and pick up the basics. You rest."

"If I were a good wife, I'd tell you to rest while I run out to the shops, but I won't." Quinn giggled. "I'll just sit here for a moment." Her eyes were already closing as she slid sideways to rest her head on a pillow. Gabe gave her a quick kiss and left her in peace.

Quinn was woken by the vibrating of her mobile in the pocket of her jeans. "Not a moment's peace," she grumbled as she reached for the phone and peered at the screen. There was a text from Rhys.

Need you in Ireland, the text read.

You've got to be kidding me, Quinn replied.

Trust me, darling, you'll want to see this, Rhys texted back. *The hotline was a stroke of genius.*

A photo popped up on the screen and Quinn peered at the

image, using her fingers to zoom in. She sucked in her breath as she stared at the find that had Rhys so excited. She lifted her eyes as Gabe walked into the room, several shopping bags in his hands.

"What is it?" he asked, clearly alarmed by her expression.

"I'm going to County Leitrim."

"Like hell you are," Gabe replied. Quinn silently handed him the phone and he stared at the image. "Is that a cross?" he asked.

"Yes, with someone's remains still attached to it."

"Right. You mean, *we* are going to County Leitrim," Gabe said, grinning happily.

"What about the kids?"

"I guess they're coming along for the ride," Gabe replied as he handed her back the phone. "Emma and I are off for Easter, remember?"

"And what better way to celebrate the Resurrection than excavating what appears to be a crucifixion?"

"An archeologist's dream," Gabe quipped as he pulled her to her feet and gave her a sound kiss. "Suddenly, I'm not tired anymore."

"Neither am I," Quinn replied, returning his grin. "Let's finish unpacking."

See you on Monday, boss, she texted and added a happy-face emoji.

EPILOGUE
APRIL 1621

Virginia Colony

A warm day gave way to a balmy night, the air heavy with the smell of new grass and wildflowers. A lazy moon floated in the sky, a perfect sphere that cast a silvery pall over the bed. Simon stretched out on the rumpled sheet, his naked body glistening with perspiration. The cabin was quiet, the silence of the night disturbed only by the chirping of crickets and the chorus of cicadas. Simon smiled to himself, pleased with his good fortune. Well, it wasn't good fortune exactly, it was the result of waiting, planning, and executing. He mentally cringed at the word but reminded himself that John's death wasn't really his fault. None of it was. He'd never forced anyone to do anything, and he'd never lied about his intentions. The people who had placed themselves at his mercy had done so willingly, and they had always known what the consequences of their actions would be should their activities come to light.

Simon rolled onto his side as his lover's eyes fluttered open. Oliver Hunt smiled lazily and blinked several times, still groggy with sleep. The lower half of his body was covered with a sheet, his hairless chest white in the moonlight. He was as soft as a woman, never having done a day's work, but despite his lack of physical beauty, he was surprisingly well endowed. Hunt pulled aside the sheet, exposing his stiffening shaft.

"Take it in your mouth this time," the secretary commanded, watching with hungry eyes as Simon slid down and wrapped his lips around the man's cock. Simon's eyes never left the secretary's face as he went to work, bringing Hunt to orgasm quickly and skillfully. Once he was done, he moved up, covered Hunt's body with his own, and looked deep into his eyes.

"I want this plantation," he said softly.

"What would you have me do?"

"I would have you sign it over to me."

"Simon, I have already purchased your indenture contract and given you your freedom. You may remain here until the new owner takes up residence, but then you will have to leave. I can't—"

"You can and you will, or you will greet the newcomers to this colony swinging off the crossbar of the gate. All I have to do is say the word."

"It'd be your word against mine," Secretary Hunt snapped, pushing Simon off and reaching for his breeches.

"No, it wouldn't be."

"What do you mean?"

"I mean that Travesty Brown would surely testify that Secretary Hunt visited me while John Forrester was still alive and demanded sexual favors in exchange for protection and eventual monetary compensation. And I'm sure at least one person would come forward once they heard her testimony, as I was seen leaving your house in the dead of night—more than once, I might add."

"Travesty knows about us?" Hunt gasped.

"Of course, she does, and she will do what I tell her to. Sign the plantation over to me and you will never have to fear exposure. I will settle down to a life of respectability. I might even marry."

Secretary Hunt stared at Simon, his eyes narrowed in anger. "Did you two plan this? Did you always intend to betray Forrester?"

Simon didn't reply, but the answer was there in his eyes. "You have until the end of the week. Have the deed signed over to me by Sunday morning, or we'll finally have a rousing church service. The choice is yours."

"You conniving son of a whore. You'll hang for this."

"If I do, you'll be hanging right alongside me."

The secretary hastily dressed and stormed out of the cabin, slamming the door behind him. Simon folded his arms behind his head and stared at the ceiling, smiling. All this would be his in a few days. Then he would marry Travesty, as he had promised, and they would begin their life together. Some men might not want a wife who knew all their transgressions, but Simon didn't mind. He needed a woman who was willing to do anything to survive, and who wouldn't be too squeamish to break a few rules, be those the rules of man or God. He'd done what he had to do to assure a desirable future for himself, and Travesty had played her part, accusing John and Mary and getting them out of the way so Simon would be free to apply pressure to Hunt. It had all worked out, and a lot quicker than either one of them had expected, thanks to the attack on Mary that had brought it all to a head. He did feel badly about Mary, but her banishment had worked in his favor, since there would be no offspring to lay claim to John's land and no widow to court had Mary inherited John's estate. Mary was beddable enough, but, for once in his life, he wanted to have a choice about his future.

Simon got out of bed and went to pour himself a cup of ale. His mouth still tasted of Hunt, and he needed to wash away all traces of him. Today was the last time he'd suck any man's cock. Today was the day he embraced his freedom.

A LETTER FROM THE AUTHOR

I hope you've enjoyed this installment of the *Echoes from the Past* series. If you want to join other readers in hearing all about my new releases and bonus content, you can sign up for my newsletter.

www.stormpublishing.co/irina-shapiro

If any of you have read the *Hands of Time* series, then you know I have an interest in Colonial America, and Jamestown in particular. It's not easy to envision what life must have been like in a time when there was nothing but wilderness all around, and survival was far from guaranteed. I'm also fascinated by the fate of the Roanoke colony and its inhabitants and have touched upon the fate of one family in this novel in the hope that those brave souls have left something of themselves behind.

My thanks to Mike and Susan Morelock for allowing me to use their names in this installment. If you're interested in appearing as characters in one of my books, please drop me a note.

The next book, *The Betrayed*, will address another one of my historical interests—the Spanish Inquisition. I hope you will join me on a quest to find out who Quinn found on that long-buried cross.

I love hearing your thoughts, so if you enjoyed this book and could spare a few moments to leave a review that would be hugely appreciated. Even a short review can make all the difference in encouraging a reader to discover my books for the first time. Thank you so much.

And, as always, thank you for your support. I hope you'll stay in touch—I have so many more stories and ideas to entertain you with!

Irina

irinashapiroauthor.com

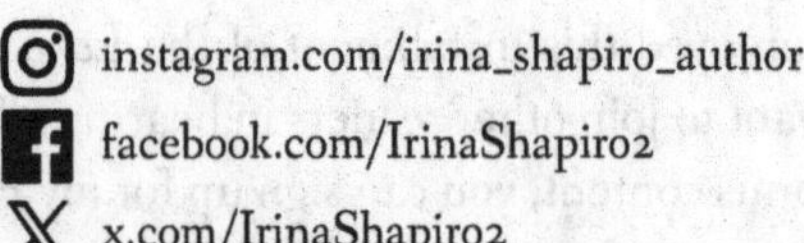

instagram.com/irina_shapiro_author
facebook.com/IrinaShapiro2
x.com/IrinaShapiro2